THE
PURPLE HEIGHTS

MARIE CONWAY OEMLER

1st WORLD
LIBRARY
Literary Society

The Purple Heights

Marie Conway Oemler

© 1st World Library, 2007
PO Box 2211
Fairfield, IA 52556
www.1stworldlibrary.com
First Edition

LCCN: 2007927841

Softcover ISBN: 978-1-4218-4557-9
Hardcover ISBN: 978-1-4218-4473-2
eBook ISBN: 978-1-4218-4641-5

Purchase *"The Purple Heights"*
as a traditional bound book at:
www.1stWorldLibrary.com/purchase.asp?ISBN=978-1-4218-4557-9

1st World Library Literary Society

Giving Back to the World

"If you want to work on the core problem, it's early school literacy."

- James Barksdale, former CEO of Netscape

"No skill is more crucial to the future of a child, or to a democratic and prosperous society, than literacy."

- Los Angeles Times

"Literacy... means far more than learning how to read and write... The aim is to transmit... knowledge and promote social participation."

- UNESCO

"Literacy is not a luxury, it is a right and a responsibility. If our world is to meet the challenges of the twenty-first century we must harness the energy and creativity of all our citizens."

- President Bill Clinton

"Parents should be encouraged to read to their children, and teachers should be equipped with all available techniques for teaching literacy, so the varying needs and capacities of individual kids can be taken into account."

- Hugh Mackay

To

JOHN NORTON OEMLER
FROM THE LADY
HIS SON USED TO CALL
"MRS. DADDY"

CONTENTS

CHARACTERS

PETER CHAMPNEYS: *Of Riverton, South Carolina, and Paris, France*

MARIA CHAMPNEYS: *His Mother*

CHADWICK CHAMPNEYS: *The God in the Machine*

EMMA CAMPBELL: *A Colored Woman*

ANNE CHAMPNEYS, NEE NANCY SIMMS: *Cinderella*

MRS. JOHN HEMINGWAY: *Peter's First Teacher*

JOHN HEMINGWAY: *An American*

JASON VANDERVELDE: *An Attorney at Law*

MRS. JASON VANDERVELDE: *Anne's Mentor*

MRS. MacGREGOR: *A Disciple of Hannah More*

GLENN MITCHELL: *A Bright Shadow*

BERKELEY HAYDEN: *The Other Man*

GRACIE: *A Gutter-Candle*

DENISE: *A Perfume*

THE QUARTIER LATIN.

RIVERTON, SOUTH CAROLINA.

THE CAROLINA COLORED FOLKS.

MARTIN LUTHER: *A Gray Cat*

SATAN: *A Black Cat*

THE RED ADMIRAL: *A Fairy*

CHAPTER I

THE RED ADMIRAL

The tiny brown house cuddling like a wren's nest on the edge of the longest and deepest of the tide-water coves that cut through Riverton had but four rooms in all,—the kitchen tacked to the back porch, after the fashion of South Carolina kitchens, the shed room in which Peter slept, the dining-room which was the general living-room as well, and his mother's room, which opened directly off the dining-room, and in which his mother sat all day and sometimes almost all night at her sewing-machine. When Peter tired of lying on his tummy on the dining-room floor, trying to draw things on a bit of slate or paper, he liked to turn his head and watch the cloth moving swiftly under the jigging needle, and the wheel turning so fast that it made an indistinct blur, and sang with a droning hum. He could see, too, a corner of his mother's bed with the patchwork quilt on it. The colors of the quilt were pleasantly subdued in their old age, and the calico star set in a square pleased Peter immensely. He thought it a most beautiful quilt. There was visible almost all of the bureau, an old-fashioned walnut affair with a small, dim, wavy glass, and drawers which you pulled out by sticking your fingers under the bunches of flowers that served as knobs. The fireplaces in both rooms were in a shocking state of disrepair, but one didn't mind that, as in winter a fire burned in them, and in summer they were boarded up with fireboards covered with cut-out pictures pasted on a background of black calico. Those gay cut-out pictures were a source of never-ending delight to Peter, who was intimately acquainted with every flower, bird, cat, puppy, and child of them. One little girl with a pink parasol and a purple dress, holding a posy in a lace-paper frill, he would have dearly loved to play with.

Over the mantelpiece in his mother's room hung his father's picture, in a large gilt frame with an inside border of bright red plush. His father seemed to have been a merry-faced fellow, with inquiring eyes, plenty of hair, and a very nice mustache. This picture, under which his mother always kept a few flowers or some bit of living green, was Peter's sole acquaintance with his father, except when he trudged with his mother to the cemetery on fine Sundays, and traced with his small forefinger the name painted in black letters on a white wooden cross:

PETER DEVEREAUX CHAMPNEYS
Aged 30 Years

It always gave small Peter an uncomfortable sensation to trace that name, which was also his own, on his father's headboard. It was as if something of himself stayed out there, very lonesomely, in the deserted burying-ground. The word "father" never conveyed to him any idea or image except a crayon portrait and a grave, he being a posthumous child. The really important figures filling the background of his early days were his mother and big black Emma Campbell.

Emma Campbell washed clothes in a large wooden tub set on a bench nailed between the two china-berry trees in the yard. Peter loved those china-berry trees, covered with masses of sweet-smelling lilac-colored blossoms in the spring, and with clusters of hard green berries in the summer. The beautiful feathery foliage made a pleasant shade for Emma Campbell's wash-tubs. Peter loved to watch her, she looked so important and so cheerful. While she worked she sang endless "speretuals," in a high, sweet voice that swooped bird-like up and down.

"I wants tuh climb up Ja-cob's la-ad-dah,
Ja-cob's la-ad-dah, Jacob's la-ad-dah,
I wants tuh climb up Ja-cob's la-ad-dah,
But I cain't—
Not un-tell I makes my peace wid de La-a-wd,
En I praise *Him*—de La-a-wd!
I'll praise Him—tell I di-e,
I'll praise Him—tell I die!
I'll si-ng, Je-ee-ru-suh-lem!"

Emma Campbell would sing, and keep time with thumps and clouts of sudsy clothes. She boiled the clothes in the same large black iron pot in which she boiled crabs and shrimp in the summer-time. Peter always raked the chips for her fire, and the leaves and pine-cones mixed with them gave off a pleasant smoky smell. Emma had a happy fashion of roasting sweet potatoes under the wash-pot, and you could smell those, too, mingled with the soapy odor of the boiling clothes, which she sloshed around with a sawed-off broom-handle. Other smells came from over the cove, of pine-trees, and sassafras, and bays, and that indescribable and clean odor which the winds bring out of the woods.

The whole place was full of pleasant noises, dear and familiar sounds of water running seaward or swinging back landward, always with odd gurglings and chucklings and small sucking noises, and runs and rushes; and of the myriad rustlings of the huge live-oaks hung with long gray moss;

and the sycamores frou-frouing like ladies' dresses; the palmettos rattled and clashed, with a sound like rain; the pines swayed one to another, and only in wild weather did they speak loudly, and then their voices were very high and airy. Peter liked the pines best of all. His earliest impression of beauty and of mystery was the moon walking "with silver-sandaled feet" over their tall heads. He loved it all—the little house, the trees, the tide-water, the smells, the sounds; in and out of which, keeping time to all, went the whi-r-rr of his mother's sewing-machine, and the scuff-scuffing of Emma Campbell's wash-board.

Sometimes his mother, pausing for a second, would turn to look at him, her tired, pale face lighting up with her tender mother-smile:

"What are you making now, Peter?" she would ask, as she watched his laborious efforts to put down on his slate his conception of the things he saw. She was always vitally interested in anything Peter said or did.

"Well, I started to make you—or maybe it was Emma. But I thought I'd better hang a tail on it and let it be the cat." He studied the result gravely. "I'll stick horns on it, and if they're *very* good horns I'll let it be the devil; if they're not, it can be Mis' Hughes's old cow."

After a while the things that Peter was always drawing began to bear what might be called a family resemblance to the things they were intended to represent. But as all children try to draw, nobody noticed that Peter Champneys tried harder than most, or that he couldn't put his fingers on a bit of paper and a stub of pencil without trying to draw something—a smear that vaguely resembled a tree, or a lopsided assort-ment of features that you presently made out to be a face.

But Peter Champneys, at a very early age, had to learn things less pleasant than drawing. That tiny house in Riverton represented all that was left of the once-great Champneys holdings, and the little widow was hard put to it to keep even that. Before he was seven Peter knew all those pitiful subterfuges wherewith genteel poverty tries to save its face; he had to watch his mother, who wasn't robust, fight that bitter and losing fight which women of her sort wage with evil circumstances. Peter wore shoes only from the middle of November to the first of March; his clothes were presentable only because his mother had a genius for making things over. He wasn't really hungry, for nobody can starve in a small town in South Carolina; folks are too kindly, too neighborly, too generous, for anything like that to happen. They have a tactful fashion of coming over with a plate of hot biscuit or a big bowl of steaming okra-and-tomato soup.

Often a bowl of that soup fetched in by a thoughtful neighbor, or an apronful of sweet potatoes Emma Campbell brought with her when she did the washing, kept Peter's backbone and wishbone from rubbing noses. But there were rainy days when neighbors didn't send in anything, Emma wasn't washing for them that week, sewing was scanty, or taxes on the small holding had to be paid; and then Peter Champneys learned what an insatiable Shylock the human stomach can be. He learned what it means not to have enough warm covers on cold nights, nor warm clothes enough on cold days. He accepted it all without protest, or even wonder. These things were so because they were so.

On such occasions his mother drew him closer to her and comforted him after the immemorial South Carolina fashion, with accounts of the former greatness, glory, and grandeur of the Champneys family; always finishing with the solemn admonition that, no matter what happened, Peter must never, never forget Who He Was. Peter, who was a literal child in his way, inferred from these accounts that when the South Carolina Champneyses used to light up their big house for a party, before the war, the folks in North Carolina could see to read print by the reflection in the sky, and the people over in Georgia thought they were witnessing the Aurora Borealis.

She was a gentle, timid, pleasant little body, Peter's mother, with the mild manners and the soft voice of the South Carolina woman; and although the proverbial church-mouse was no poorer, Riverton would tell you, sympathetically, that Maria Champneys had her pride. For one thing, she was perfectly convinced that everybody who had ever been anybody in South Carolina was, somehow, related to the Champneyses. If they weren't,—well, it wasn't to their credit, that's all! She preferred to give them the benefit of the doubt. Her own grandfather had been a Virginian, a descendant of Pocahontas, of course, Pocahontas having been created by Divine Providence for the specific purpose of ancestoring Virginians. Just as everybody in New England is ancestored by one of those inevitable two brothers who came over, like sardines in a tin, in that amazingly elastic *Mayflower*. In the American Genesis this is the Sarah and these be the Abrahams, the mother and fathers of multitudes. They begin our Begats.

Mrs. Champneys sniffed at *Mayflower* origins, but she was firm on Pocahontas for herself, and adamant on Francis Marion for the Champneyses. The fact that the Indian Maid had but one bantling to her back, and the Swamp Fox none at all, didn't in the least disconcert her. If he *had* had any children, they would have ancestored the Champneyses; so there you were!

Peter, who had a fashion of thinking his own thoughts and then keeping them to himself, presently hit upon the truth.

His was one of those Carolina coast families that, stripped by the war and irretrievably ruined by Reconstruction, have ever since been steadily decreasing in men, mentality, and money-power, each generation slipping a little farther down hill; until, in the case of the Champneyses, the family had just about reached rock-bottom in himself, the last of them. There had been, one understood, an uncle, his father's only brother, Chadwick Champneys. Peter's mother hadn't much to say about this Chadwick, who had been of a roving and restless nature, trying his hand at everything and succeeding in nothing. As poor as Job's turkey, what must he do on one of his prowls but marry some unknown girl from the Middle West, as poor as himself. After which he had slipped out of the lives of every one who knew him, and never been heard of again, except for the report that he had died somewhere out in Texas; or maybe it was Arizona or Idaho, or Mexico, or somewhere in South America. One didn't know.

Behold small Peter, then, the last of his name, "all the sisters of his father's house, and all the brothers, too." Little, thin, dark Peter, with his knock-knees, his large ears, his shock of black hair, and, fringed by thick black lashes, eyes of a hazel so clear and rare that they were golden like topazes, only more beautiful. Leonardo would have loved to paint Peter's quiet face, with its shy, secret smile, and eyes that were the color of genius. Riverton thought him a homely child, with legs like those of one's grandmother's Chippendale chair, and eyes like a cat's. He was so quiet and reticent that nearly everybody except his mother and Emma Campbell thought him deficient in promise, and some even considered him "wanting."

Peter's reputation for hopelessness began when he went to school, but it didn't end there. He really was somewhat of a trial to an average school-teacher, who very often knows less of the human nature of a child than any other created being.

Peter used the carelessly good-and-easy English one inherits in the South, but he couldn't understand the written rules of grammar to save his life; he was totally indifferent as to which states bounded and bordered which; and he had been known to spell "physician" with an f and two z's. But it was when confronted by a sum that Peter stood revealed in his true colors of a dunce!

"A boy buys chestnuts at one dollar and sixty cents the bushel and sells them at ten cents the quart, liquid measure. —Peter Champneys, what does he get?"

Peter Champneys stood up, and reflected.

"It all depends on the judge, and whether the boy's a white boy or a nigger," he decided. "It's against the law to use liquid measure, you know. But I should think he'd get about thirty days, if he's a nigger."

Whereupon Peter Champneys went to the principal with a note, and received what was coming to him. When he returned to his seat, which was decidedly not comfortable just then, the teacher smiled a real, sure-enough schoolma'am smile, and remarked that she hoped our brilliant scholar, Mister Champneys, knew now what the boy got for his chestnuts. The class laughed as good scholars are expected to laugh on such occasions. Peter came to the conclusion that Herod, Nero, Bluebeard, and The Cruel Stepmother all probably began their bright careers as school-teachers.

Peter was a friendly child who didn't have the useful art of making friends. He used to watch more gifted children wistfully. He would so much have liked to play familiarly with the pretty, impertinent, pigtailed little girls, the bright, noisy, cock-sure little boys; but he didn't know how to set about it, and they didn't in the least encourage him to try.

Children aren't by any means angels to one another. They are, as often as not, quite the reverse. Peter was loath to assert himself, and he was shoved aside as the gentle and the just usually are.

Being a loving child, he fell back upon the lesser creatures, and discovered that the Little Brothers do not judge one upon hearsay, or clothes, or personal appearance. Theirs is the infallible test: one must be kind if one wishes to gain and to hold their love.

Martin Luther helped teach Peter that. Peter discovered Martin Luther, a shivering gray midget, in the cold dusk of a November evening, on the Riverton Road. The little beast rubbed against his legs, stuck up a ridiculous tail, and mewed hopefully. Peter, who needed friendliness himself, was unable to resist that appeal. He buttoned the forlorn kitten inside his old jacket, and, feeling the grateful warmth of his body, it cuddled and purred. The wise little cat didn't care the tip of a mouse's tail whether or not Peter was the congenital dunce his teacher had declared him to be, only that morning. The kitten knew he was just the sort of boy to show compassion to lost kittens, and trusted and loved him at sight.

His mother was doubtful as to the wisdom of adopting a third member into a family which could barely feed two without one going half hungry. Also, she disliked cats intensely. She was most horribly afraid of cats. She was just about to say that he'd have to give the kitten to somebody better able to care for it, but seeing the resigned and hopeless expression that crept into Peter's face, she said, instead, that she reckoned they could manage to feed the little wretch, provided he kept it out of her room. Peter joyfully agreed, washed the cat in his own basin, fed it with a part of his own supper, and took it to bed with him, where it purred itself to sleep. Thus came Martin Luther to the house of Champneys.

When Peter had chores to do the cat scampered about him with, sidewise leapings and gambolings, and made his labor easier by seasoning it with harmless amusement. When he wrestled with his lessons Martin Luther sat sedately on the table and watched him, every now and then rubbing a sympathetic head against him. When he woke up at night in the shed room, he liked to put out his hand and touch the warm, soft, silky body near him. Peter adored his cat, which was to him a friend.

And then Martin Luther took to disappearing, mysteriously, for longer and longer intervals. Peter was filled with apprehensions, for Martin Luther wasn't a democratic soul; aside from his affection for Peter, the cat was as wild as a panther. The child was almost sick with anxiety. He wandered around Riverton hunting for the beast and calling it by name, a proceeding which further convinced Riverton folk that poor Maria Champneys's boy was not what one might call bright. Fancy carrying on like that about nothing but a cat! But Peter used to lie awake at night, lonesomely, and cry because he was afraid some evil had befallen the perverse creature of his affections. Then he prayed that God would look out for Martin Luther, if He hadn't already remembered to do so. The world of a sudden seemed a very big, sad, unfriendly place for a little boy to live in, when he couldn't even have a cat in it!

The disappearance of Martin Luther was Peter's first sorrow that his mother couldn't fully share, as he knew she didn't like cats. Martin Luther had known that, too, and had kept his distance. He hadn't even made friends with Emma Campbell, who loved cats to the extent of picking up other people's when their owners weren't looking. This cat had loved nobody but Peter, a fact that endeared it to him a

Marie Conway Oemler

thousandfold, and made its probable fate a darker grief.

One afternoon, when Martin Luther had been gone so long that Peter had about given up hopes of ever seeing him again, Emma Campbell, who had been washing in the yard, dashed into the house screeching that the woodshed was full of snakes.

Peter joyfully threw aside his grammar—snakes hadn't half the terror for him that substantives had—and rushed out to investigate, while his mother frantically besought him not to go near the woodshed, to get an ax, to run for the town marshal, to run and ring the fire-bell, to burn down that woodshed before they were all stung to death in their beds!

Cautiously Peter investigated. Perhaps a chicken-snake had crawled into the shed; perhaps a black-snake was hunting in there for rats; over there in that dark corner, behind sticks of pine, something was moving. And then he heard a sound he knew.

"Snakes nothin'!" shouted Peter, joyfully. "It's Martin Luther!" He got on his hands and knees and squirmed and wriggled himself behind the wood. There he remained, transfixed. His faith had received a shocking blow.

"Oh, Martin Luther!" cried Peter, with mingled joy and relief and reproach. "Oh, Martin Luther! How you've fooled me!" Martin Luther was a proud and purring mother.

Peter was bewildered and aggrieved. "If I'd called him Mary or Martha in the beginning, I'd be glad for him to have as many kittens as he wanted to," he told his mother. "But how can I ever trust him again? He—he ain't Martin Luther any more!" And of a sudden he began to cry.

Emma Campbell, with a bundle of clean wet clothes on her brawny arm, shook her head at him.

"Lawd, no, Peter! 'T ain't de cat whut's been foolin' you; it's you whut's been foolin' yo' own self. For, lo, fum de foundations ob dis worl', he was a she! Must n' blame de cat, chile. 'Cause ef you does," said Emma, waving an arm like a black mule's hind leg for strength, "ef you does, 'stead o' layin' de blame whah it natchelly b'longs—on yo' own ig'nance, Peter—you'll go thoo dis worl' wid every Gawd's tom-cat you comes by havin' kittens on you!"

"I feel like a father to those kittens," said Peter, gravely. But it was plain that Martin Luther's furry fourlegs had put Peter's nose out of joint!

Things were getting worse and worse at school, too, although Peter considerately concealed this from his mother. He didn't tell her that the promotions she was so proud of had come to him simply because his teachers were so desperately anxious to get rid of him! And only to-day an incident had happened that seared his soul. He had been forced to stand out on the floor for twenty cruel, grueling minutes, to be a Horrible Example to a tittering class. It had been a long, wearisome day, when one's head ached because one's stomach was empty. Peter's eyes stung and smarted, his lip was bruised because he had bitten it to keep it from trembling, and his heart was more like a boil in his breast than a little boy's heart. When he was finally released for the day he didn't linger, but got away as fast as his thin legs would carry him. Once he was sure he was out of sight of all unfriendly eyes he let himself go and cried as he trudged along the Riverton Road. And there, in the afternoon sunlight, he made the acquaintance of the Red Admiral.

Just at that spot the Riverton Road was tree-shaded and

bird-haunted. There were clumps of elder here and there, and cassena bushes, and tall fennel in the corners of the old worm-fence bordering the fields on each side. The worm-fence was of a polished, satiny, silvery gray, with trimmings of green vines clinging to it, wild-flowers peeping out of its crotches, and tall purple thistles swaying their heads toward it. On one especially tall thistle the Red Admiral had come to anchor.

He wore upon the skirts of his fine dark-colored frock-coat a red-orange border sewed with tiny round black buttons; across the middle of his fore-wings, like the sash of an order, was a broad red ribbon, and the spatter of white on the tips may have been his idea of epaulets; or maybe they were nature's Distinguished Service medals given him for conspicuous bravery, for there is no more gallant sailor of the skies than the Red Admiral.

When this gentleman comes to anchor on a flower he hoists his gay sails erect over his fat black back, in order that his under wings may be properly admired; for he knows very well that the cunningest craftsman that ever worked with mosaics and metals never turned out a better bit of jewel-work than those under wings.

It was this piece of painted perfection that caught Peter Champneys's unhappy eyes and brought him to a standstill. Peter forgot that he was the school dunce, that tears were still on his cheeks, that he had a headache and an empty stomach. His eyes began to shine unwontedly, brightening into a golden limpidity, and his lips puckered into a smile.

The Red Admiral, if one might judge by his unrubbed wings and the new and glossy vividness of his colorings, may have been some nine hours old. Peter, by the entry in his mother's Bible, was nine years old. Quite instinctively Peter's brown fingers groped for a pencil. At the feel of it he experienced a thrill of satisfaction. Down on his knees he went, and crept forward, nearer and nearer; for one must come as the wind comes who would approach the Red Admiral. Peter had no paper, so a fly-leaf of his geography would have to do. All athrill, he worked with his bit of pencil; and on the fly-leaf grew the worm-fence with the blackberry bramble climbing along its corners, and the fennel, and the elder bushes near by; and in the foreground the tall thistle, with the butterfly upon it. The Red Admiral is a gourmet; he lingers daintily over his meals; so Peter had time to make a careful sketch of him. This done, he sketched in the field beyond, and the buzzard hanging motionless in the sky.

It was crude and defective, of course, and a casual eye wouldn't have glanced twice at it, but a true teacher would instantly have recognized the value, not of what it performed, but of what it presaged. For all its faults it was bold and rapid, like the Admiral's flight, and it had the Admiral's airy grace and freedom. It seized the outlines of things with unerring precision.

The child kneeling in the dust of the Riverton Road, with an old geography open on his knee, felt in his thin breast a faint flutter, as of wings. He looked at the sketch; he watched the Red Admiral finish his meal and go scudding down the wind. And he knew he had found the one thing he could do, the one thing he wanted to do, that he must and would do. It was as if the butterfly had been a fairy, to open for Peter a tiny door of hope. He wrote under the sketch:

Jun. 2, 189- This day I notissed the red and blak buterfly on the thissel.

He stared at this for a while, and added:

Marie Conway Oemler

P.S. In futcher watch for this buterfly witch mite be a fary.

Then he went trudging homeward. He was smiling, his own shy, secret smile. He held his head erect and looked ahead of him as if in the far, far distance he had seen something, a beckoning something, toward which he was to strive. Barefooted Peter, poverty-stricken, lonely Peter for the first time glimpsed the purple heights.

CHAPTER II

THE PROMISE

It is written in the Live Green Book that one may not stumble upon one of its secrets without at the same discovering something about others quite as fascinating and worth exploring. This is a wise and blessed law, which the angels of the Little Peoples are always trying to have enforced. Peter Champneys suspected the Red Admiral of being a fairy; so when he ran fleet-footed over the fields and through the woods and alongside the worm-fences after the Admiral, the angels of the Little Peoples turned his boyish head aside and made him see birds' wings, and bees, and the shapes of leaves, and the colors of trees and clouds, and the faces of flowers. It is further written that one may not intimately know the Little Peoples without loving them. When one begins to love, one begins to grow. Peter, then, was growing.

Lying awake in the dark now wasn't a thing to be dreaded; the dark was no longer filled with shapes of fear, for Peter was beginning to discover in himself a power of whose unique and immense value he was not as yet aware. It was the great power of being able clearly to visualize things, of bringing before his mind's eye whatever he had seen, with every distinction of shape and size and color sharply present, and accurately to portray it in the absence of the original. If one should ask him, "What's the shape of the milkweed butterfly's wing, and the color of the spice-bush swallowtail, Peter Champneys? What does the humming-bird's nest look like? What's the color of the rainbow-snake and of the cotton-mouth moccasin? What's the difference between the ironweed and the aster?"—Ask Peter things like that, and lend him a bit of paper and a pencil, and he literally had the answers at his finger-tips.

But they never asked him what would, to him, have been natural questions; they wished him, instead, to tell them where the Onion River flows, and the latitude of the middle of Kamchatka, and to spell phthisis, and on what date the Battle of Somethingorother was fought, and if a man buys old iron at such a price, and makes it over into stoves weighing so much, and sells his stoves at such another price, what does it profit him, and other such-like illuminating and uplifting problems, warranted to make any school-child wiser than Solomon. It is a beautiful system; only, God, who is no respecter of systems, every now and then delights to flout it by making him a dunce like Peter Champneys, to be the torment of school-teachers—and the delight of the angels of the Little Peoples.

Those long, silent, solitary hours in the open gave Peter the power of concentration, and a serenity that sat oddly on his slight shoulders. Thoughts came to him, out there, that he couldn't put into words nor yet set down upon paper.

On warm nights, when his mother's sewing-machine was for a time still and the tired little woman slept, Peter slipped out of the shed room into a big, white, enchanted world, and saw things that are to be seen only by an imaginative and beauty-loving little boy in the light of the midsummer moon. Big hawk-moths, swift and sudden, darted by him with owl-like wings. Mocking-birds broke into silvery, irrepressible singing, and water-birds croaked and rustled in the cove, where the tide-water lipped the land. The slim, black pine-trees nodded and bent to one another, with the moon looking over their shoulders. Something wild and sweet and secret invaded the little boy's spirit, and stayed on in his heart. Maybe it was the heart-shaking call of the whippoorwill, or the song of the mocking-bird, truest voices of the summer night; or perhaps it was the spirit of the great green luna-moth, loveliest of all the daughters of the dark. Or perhaps the Red Admiral was indeed a fairy, as Peter said he was.

Peter was superstitious about the Red Admiral. He was a good-luck sign, a sort of flying four-leaf clover. Peter noticed that whenever the Red Admiral crossed his path now, something pleasant always impended; it meant that he wouldn't be *very* unhappy in school; or maybe he'd find a thrush's nest, or the pink orchid. Or the meeting might simply imply something nice and homey, such as a little treat his mother contrived to make for him when sewing had been somewhat better-paying than usual, and she could sit by the table and enjoy his enjoyment as only one's mother can. Decidedly, the Red Admiral was good luck!

So, all along, quietly, persistently, not exactly secretly but still all by himself, Peter had been learning to use his fingers, as he had been learning to use his eyes and ears. He was morbidly shy about it. It never occurred to him that anybody might admire anything he could do, as nobody had ever admired anything he had done.

On his mother's last birthday—though Peter didn't know then that it was to be her last—he made for her his first sketch in water-colors. By herculean efforts he had managed to get his materials; he had picked berries, weeded gardens until his head whirled and his back ached, chopped fire-wood, run errands, caught crabs. Presently he had his paper and colors.

It was a beautiful surprise for Peter's mother, that sketch, which was a larger copy of the one on the fly-leaf of his geography. There was the gray worm-fence, a bit of brown ditch, an elder in flower, a tall purple thistle, and on it the Red Admiral. Peter wished to make his mother personally acquainted with the Red Admiral, so he printed on the back of his picture:

My buterfly done for mother's burthday by her loveing son Peter Champneys the 11th Year of his Aige.

The little woman cried, and held him off the better to look at him, with love, and wonder, and pride, and drew his head to her breast and kissed his hair and eyes, and wished his dear, dear father had been there to see what her wonder-child could do.

"I can't to save my life see where you get such a lovely gift from, Peter. It must be just the grace of God that sends it to you. Your dear father couldn't so much as draw a straight line unless he had a ruler, I'm sure. And I'm not bright at all, except maybe about sewing. But you are different. I've always felt that, Peter, from the time you were a little baby. At the age of five months you cut two teeth without crying once! You were a *wonderful* baby. I *knew* it was in you to do something remarkable. Never you doubt your mother's word about *that*, Peter! You'll make your mark in the world yet! God couldn't fail to answer my prayers—and you the last Champneys."

Peter was too innately kind and considerate to dim her joy with any doubts. He knew how he was rated—berated is the better word for it. He knew acutely how bad his marks were: his shoulders too often bore witness to them. The words "dunce" and "sissy" buzzed about his ears like stinging gnats. So he wasn't made vainglorious by his mother's praise. He received it with cautious reservations. But her faith in him filled him with an immense tenderness for the little woman, and a passionate desire, a very agony of desire, to struggle toward her aspirations for him, to make good, to repay her for all the privations she had endured. A lump came in his throat when he saw her place the little sketch under his father's picture, where her eyes could open upon it the first thing in the morning, and close to it at night.

"Ah, my dear! God's will be done—I'm not complaining—but I wish, oh, how I wish you could be here to see what our dear child can do!" she told the smiling crayon portrait. "Some of these days the little son you've never seen is going to be a great man with a great name—*your* name, my dear, *your* name!"

Her face kindled into a sort of exaltation. Two large tears ran down her cheeks, and two larger ones rolled down Peter's. His heart swelled, and again he felt in his breast the flutter as of wings. Far, far away, on the dim and distant horizon, something glimmered, like sunlight upon airy peaks.

Peter's mother wasn't at all beautiful—just a little, thin, sallow woman with mild brown eyes and graying hair, and a sensitive mouth, and dressed in a worn black skirt and a plain white shirt-waist. Her fingers were needle-pricked, and she stooped from bending so constantly over her sewing-machine. She had been a pretty girl; now she was thirty-five years old and looked fifty. She wasn't in the least intellectual; she hadn't even the gift of humor, or she wouldn't have thought herself a sinner and besought Heaven to forgive sins she never committed. She used to weep over the Fifty-first Psalm, take courage from the Thirty-seventh, and when she hadn't enough food for her body feed her spirit on the

Twenty-third. She didn't know that it is women like her who manage to make and keep the earth worth while. This timid and modest soul had the courage of a soldier and the patience of a martyr under the daily scourgings inflicted upon the sensitive by biting poverty. Peter might very well have received far less from a brilliant and beautiful mother than he received from the woman whose only gifts and graces were such as spring from a loving, unselfish, and pure heart.

For Peter's sake she fought while she had strength to fight, enduring all things, hoping all things. She didn't even know she was sacrificing herself, because, as Emma Campbell said, "Miss Maria's jes' natchelly all mother." But of a sudden, the winter that Peter was turning twelve, the tide of battle went against her. The needle-pricked, patient fingers dropped their work. She said apologetically, "I'm sorry, but I'm afraid I'm too sick to stay up any longer." Nobody guessed how slight was her hold upon life. When the neighbors came in, after the kindly Carolina custom, she was cheerful enough, but quiet. But then, Maria Champneys was always quiet.

There came a day when she was unusually quiet, even for her. Toward dusk the neighbor who had watched with her went home. At the door she said hopefully:

"You'll be better in the morning."

"Yes, I'll be better in the morning," the sick woman repeated. After a while Emma Campbell, who had been looking after the house, went away to her cabin across the cove. Peter and his mother were alone.

It was a darkish, gusty night, and a small fire burned in the open fireplace. Shadows danced on the walls, and every now and then the wind came and tapped at the windows impatiently. On the closed sewing-machine an oil lamp burned, turned rather low. Peter sat in a rocking-chair drawn close to his mother's bedside and dozed fitfully, waking to watch the face on the pillow. It was very quiet there in the poor room, with the clock ticking, and the soft sound of the settling log.

Just before dawn Peter replenished the fire, moving carefully lest he disturb his mother. But when he turned toward the bed again she was wide awake and looking at him intently. Peter ran to her, kissed her cheek, and held her hand in his. Her fingers were cold, and he chafed them between his palms.

"Peter," said she, very gently, "I've got to go, my dear." There was no fear in her. The child looked at her piteously, his eyes big and frightened in his pale face.

"And now I'm at the end," said she bravely, "I'm not afraid to leave you, Peter. You are a brave child, and a good child. You couldn't be dishonorable, or a coward, or a liar, or unkind, to save your life. You will always be gentle, and generous, and just. When one is where I am to-night, that is all that really matters. Nothing but goodness counts."

Peter, with her hand against his cheek, tried not to weep. To conceal his terror and grief, and the shock of this thing come upon him in the middle of the night, to spare her the agony of witnessing his agony, was almost intuitive with him. He braced himself, and kept his self-control. She seemed to understand, for the hand he held against his cheek tried, feebly, to caress it. It didn't tire her to talk, apparently, for her voice was firm and clear.

"You're a gifted child, as well as a good child, Peter. But— our people here don't understand you yet, my dearest. Your sort of brightness is different from theirs—and better, because it's rarer and slower. Hold fast to yourself, Peter. You're going to be a great man."

Peter stroked her hand. The two looked at each other, a long, long, luminous look.

"My son,—your chance is coming. I know that to-night. And when it comes, oh, for God's sake, for my sake, for all the Champneyses' sake, take it, Peter, take it!" Her voice rose at that, her hand tightened upon his; she looked at him imploringly.

"Take it for my sake," she said with terrible earnestness and intensity. "Take it, darling, and prove that I was right about you. Remember how all my years, Peter, I toiled and prayed—all for you, my dearest, all for you! Remember me in that hour, Peter, and don't fail me, don't fail me!"

"Oh, Mother, I won't fail you! I won't fail you!" cried Peter, and at that the tears came.

His mother smiled, exquisitely; a smile of faith reassured and hope fulfilled, and love contented. That smile on a dying mouth stayed, with other beautiful and imperishable memories, in Peter's heart. Presently he ventured to ask her, timidly:

"Shall I go for somebody, Mother?"

"Are you afraid, dear?"

"No," said Peter.

"Then stay by me. Just you and me together. You—you are all I have—I don't need anybody else. Stay with me,

Son,—for a little while."

Outside you could hear the wind moving restlessly, and the trees complaining, and the tide-water whispering. The dark night was filled with a multitudinous murmuring. For a long while Peter and his mother clung to each other. From time to time she whispered to him—such pitiful comfortings as love may lend in its extremity.

The black night paled into a gray glimmer of dawn. Peter held fast to the hand he couldn't warm. Her face was sharp and pale and pinched. She looked very little and thin and helpless. The bed seemed too big for so small a woman.

More gray light stole through the windows. The lamp on the closed machine looked ghostly, the room filled with shifting shadows. Maria Champneys turned her head on her pillow, and stared at her son with eyes he didn't know for his mother's. They were full of a flickering light, as of a lamp going out.

"'Though I walk—through the valley—'" Here her voice, a mere thin trickle of sound, failed her. As if pressed by an invisible hand her head began to bend forward. A thin, gray shade, as of inconceivably fine ashes, settled upon her face, and her nostrils quivered. The eyes, with the light fading from them, fixed themselves on Peter in a last look.

"'—of the shadow of death, I will fear no evil; for thou art with me; thy rod and thy staff they comfort me.'" Peter finished it for her, his boyish voice a cry of agony.

A light, puffing breath, as of a candle blown out, exhaled from his mother's lips. Her eyes closed, the hand in Peter's fell limp and slack. The awful and mysterious smile of death fixed itself upon her pale mouth.

Marie Conway Oemler

So passed Maria Champneys from her tiny house in Riverton, in the dawn of a winter morning, when the tide was turning and the world was full of the sound of water running seaward.

CHAPTER III

AT GRIPS WITH LIFE

The best or the worst thing that can happen to a boy in this country is to be poor in it for a while, to be picked up neck and crop and flung upon his own resources; not always to remain poor, of course, for one may be damned quite as effectually and everlastingly upon the cross as off it; but to be poor long enough to acquire a sense of proportion by coming to close grips with life; to learn what things and people really are, the good and the bad of them together; to have to weigh and measure cant and sentimentality and Christian charity—which last is a fearsome thing—in the balance with truth and common sense and human kindness. It is an experience that makes or breaks.

Peter had always adored his mother; but it wasn't until now that he realized how really wonderful she had been. How she had kept the roof over his head, and his stomach somehow satisfied, and had sent him to church and to school decently enough clad, Peter couldn't imagine.

There was no possibility now of regular schooling. Nature hasn't provided as providently for the human grub as for the insect one. A human grub isn't born upon a food-plant that is a house as well, nor is nature his tailor and his shoemaker.

Marie Conway Oemler

Peter wasn't blood kin to anybody in Riverton, so there was no home open to him. He was deeply sensible of the genuine kindness extended to him in his dark hour, but he wouldn't, he couldn't, have gone permanently into any of their homes had he been asked to do so, which of course he wasn't. He clung to the little house on the big cove. His mother's presence lingered there and hallowed the place.

There was some talk of sending him to an orphanage—he was barely twelve, and penniless. But when Mrs. Cooke, the minister's wife, mentioned it to Peter, gently enough, the boy turned upon her with flaming eyes, and said he wouldn't stay in any asylum; he'd run away, and keep on running away until he died! Mrs. Cooke looked troubled, and said that Mr. McMasters, a vestryman in the church, was really the head and front of that project.

Peter went after Mr. McMasters, and found him in his grocery store—one of those long, dim country stores that sell everything from cradles to coffins. Mr. McMasters came from behind the counter, rubbing his hands.

"Well, Peter, what can I do for *you* this mawnin'?" he asked, jovially. He was that sort.

"You can let me alone, please," said Peter, succinctly.

"Eh? What's that?" The large man stared at the little man.

"I said you can let me alone, please," said Peter, patiently. "I hear it's you doing most of the talking about sending me to an orphanage."

"I try to do my duty as a man and a Christian," said the vestryman, piously. "You can't be allowed to run loose, Peter. 'T aint right. 'T ain't moral. 'T ain't Christian. You'll be better off in a good orphan-asylum, bein' taught what you'd ought to learn. That's the place for you, Peter!"

"I want to stay in my own house," said Peter.

"Shucks! You can't eat and wear a measly little house, can you? That's what I'm askin' the town right now. Sure you can't! The thing to do is to sell that place for what it'll fetch, sock the money in bank for you, and it'll be there—with *interest*—when you've grown up and aim to start in business for yourself. Yes, sir. That's my idea."

"Mr. McMasters," said Peter, evenly, "I want you to know one thing sure and certain. If you send me to any orphan-asylum, I'll send *you* to some place where you'll be better off, too, sir."

"Meanin'?"

Peter Champneys shot at the stout vestryman a glance like the thrust of a golden spear.

"The cemetery, Mr. McMasters," said he, with the deadly South Carolina gentleness.

The two stared at each other. It wasn't the boy's glance that fell first.

"Threatenin' me, hey? Threatenin' a father of a family, are you?" Mr. McMasters licked his lips.

"Oh, no, Mr. McMasters, I'm not threatening you, at all. I'm just telling you what'll happen."

The vestryman reflected. He knew the Champneyses. They had all been men of their word. And fine marksmanship ran in the family. He had seen this same Peter handle a shot-gun: you'd think the little devil had been born with a gun in his fist! He had a thumb-nail vision of Mrs. McMasters collecting his life-insurance—getting new clothes, and the piano she had been plaguing him for, too, and her mother always in the house with her. He turned purple.

"You—why, you beggarly whelp! You—you damned Champneys!" he roared. Peter met the angry eyes unflinchingly.

"I reckon you'd better understand I'm not going to any orphan-asylum, Mr. McMasters. I'm going to stay right here at home. And you are not going to get my cove lot," he added shrewdly.

"What do I care where you go? And who wants your old strip of sand and cockspurs? Get to hell out o' here!" yelled Mr. McMasters, violently.

Peter marched out. He knew that victory perched upon his banners. He wouldn't be sent away, willy-nilly, to a place the bare thought of which had made his mother turn pale. And she had wished him to keep the place on the cove, the last poor remnant of Champneys land. To this end had she pinched and slaved. When Peter thought of McMasters intriguing to take from him even this poor possession, his lips came together firmly. Somehow he would manage to keep the place. If his mother had been able to manage it, surely a man could do so, too! He hadn't the faintest doubt of his ability to take care of himself.

But the town was troubled and perplexed, until Peter solved his problem for himself with the aid of Emma Campbell. Emma had always been his friend, and she had been his mother's loyal and loving servitor. She and Peter had several long talks; then Emma called in Cassius, an ex-husband of hers who so long as he didn't live with her could get along with her, and had him widen the shed room, Peter taking in its stead his mother's bedroom. Cassius built a better wash-bench, with a shelter, under the china-berry trees in the yard, and strung some extra clothes-lines, and Emma Campbell moved in. Emma would take care of the house, and look after Peter. Riverton sighed, and shrugged its shoulders.

It was a sketchy sort of arrangement, but it worked very well. Sometimes Peter provided the meals which Emma cooked, for he was expert at snaring, crabbing, shrimping, and fishing. Sometimes the spirit moved Cassius to lay an offering of a side of bacon, a bushel of potatoes, a string of fish, or maybe a jug of syrup or a hen at his ex-spouse's feet. Cassius said Emma was so contrary he specked she must be 'flicted wid de moonness, which is one way of saying that one is a bit weak in the head. But he liked her, and she washed his shirts and sewed on a button or so for him occasionally, or occasionally cracked him over the sconce with the hominy-spoon, just to show that she considered her marital ties binding. Emma had been married twice since Cassius left her, but both these ventures had been, in her own words, "triflin' niggers any real lady'd jes' natchelly hab to throw out." When Cassius complained that his third wife was "diggin' roots" against him, Emma immediately set him to digging potatoes for herself, to offset the ill effects of possible conjure. She was a strategical person, and Peter didn't fare very badly, considering.

The boy fell heir to all those odd jobs that boys in his position are expected to tackle. When a task was too tiresome, too disagreeable, or too ill-paying for anybody else, Peter was sent for and graciously allowed to do it. It enabled people to feel charitable and at the same time get something done for about a fourth of what a man would have

Marie Conway Oemler

charged. Half the time he made his living out of the river, going partners with some negro boatman. They are daring watermen, the coast negroes. They took Peter on deep-sea fishing-trips, and at night he curled up on a furled sail and went to sleep to the sound of Atlantic waves, and of negro men singing as only negro men can sing. Sometimes they went seining at night in the river, and Peter never forgot the flaring torches, the lights dipping and glinting and sliding off brawny, half-naked figures and black faces, while the marshes were a black, long line against the sky, and the moon made a silver track upon the waters, and the salty smell of the sea filled one's nostrils.

Now that he could no longer attend school, Peter snatched at any book that came his way, getting all sorts and conditions of reading-matter from all sorts and conditions of people. His was the unappeasable hunger and thirst of those who long to know; and he wished to express what he learned, by making pictures and thus interpreting it for himself and others. It wasn't easy. Life turned a rather harsh face to him. He wasn't clothed like the birds of the air and the lilies of the field: he had to provide his own coverings as best he might. He wouldn't accept charity. He would wear his own old clothes but he wouldn't wear anybody else's.

"Peter," said Emma Campbell, anxiously, "yo' rind is comin' out o' doors. Dem britches o' yourn looks like peep-thoo-de-winduh; daylight's comin'." She added anxiously: "Don't you let a heavy rain ketch you in dem pants, Peter, or it'll baptize you plum nekked to yo' shirt-tail."

Peter looked alarmed. One may with decency run barefooted only to the knees. Upon reflection, he sold his mother's sewing-machine—it was an old machine and didn't bring much—and bought enough to cover himself with.

"I wish I'd been born with my clothes on me, like you were," he confided to the Red Admiral. "Gee, you're lucky!"

The Red Admiral flirted his fine coat vaingloriously. *He* didn't have to worry about trousers, nor yet shoes for his six feet! And all he had to do was to fly around a bit and he was sure to find his dinner waiting for him.

"Fairy," said Peter, soberly, "I'm not sniffling, but I'm not having what you'd call a good time. It's hard to be me, butterfly. Nothing nice has happened in such a long time. I wish you'd think up something pleasant and wish it to happen to me."

If you'll hold out your first and second fingers and wiggle them in the friendliest way you know how, you'll see how the Red Admiral moved his feelers just then.

When Peter Champneys went home that night, after a long afternoon of weeding an old lady's garden and whitewashing a long-suffering chicken house, Emma Campbell spread before him, on a hot platter, and of a crispness and brownness and odorousness to have made St. Simon Stylites slide down his pillar and grab for a piece of it, a fat chicken with an accompaniment of hot biscuit and good brown gravy. She didn't tell Peter how she had come by the chicken, nor did he wait to ask. He crammed his mouth, and Emma leaned against the door and watched him with profound satisfaction. When he had polished the last bone to an ivory whiteness, Emma reached behind her and handed Peter the book she had that morning wrested from a peddler whose shirt she had washed and ironed. Emma knew Peter liked books.

Now, Emma Campbell couldn't by any stretch of imagination be considered a beautiful person. She had pulled almost all of her hair out by the roots, from a fashion she had of twisting and winding it tightly around a tin spoon, or a match stem, to "pull her palate up." The colored people suffer from a mysterious ailment known as "having your palate down," for which the one specific is to take a wisp of your hair and wrap it as tightly around a tin spoon, or a match stem, as you can twist it; that pulls your palate up. It is, of course, absolutely necessary for you to have your palate up, even though you scalp yourself in the process of making it stay up. Emma generally had a couple of spoons and two or three matches in what was left of her wool. She could screw her mouth up until it looked like a nozzle, and she could shoot her eyes out like a crab's. She was so big that most folks were afraid of her. But as she stood there beaming at Peter with the book in his hand, the loveliest lady in the land couldn't have looked better or kinder.

Peter laid the Collection of Poetic Gems on the table, and blinked at Emma Campbell. Then, because he was only a boy, and because nothing so pleasant as this had happened to him for a long, long time—not since his mother died—he put his head down on the green-covered book and cried as only a boy can cry when he lets go.

Emma Campbell seemed to grow about nine feet tall. "Peter," said she, in a terrifying voice, "I axes you not to lemme see you cryin' like dat! When I sees Miss Maria's chile cryin', jes' 'cause a ole nigger woman gives 'im a book, I wants to go out an' bust dis town wide open wid a ax!"

When he had time to examine his Collection of Poetic Gems, Peter was overjoyed. The paper was poor, the cuts atrocious, the binding a poisonous green, but many of the Gems were of purest ray serene despite their wretched setting. Old-fashioned stuff, most of it, but woven on the loom of immortality. Peter, of course, had Simms's "War Poems of the South." He knew much of Father Ryan by heart. He, as well as another, could wave his brown stick of an arm and bid somebody "Take that banner down, 'tis tattered." He had been brought up on the story of the glory of the men who wore the gray, and for him the sword of Robert Lee would never dim nor tarnish. But these things were different. They talked to something deep down in him, that was neither Yankee nor Southerner, but larger and better than both. When Peter read these poems he felt the hair of his scalp prickle, and his heart almost burst with a rapture that was agony.

But one can't exist on a collection of gems in a vile binding. Shirts and shoes wear out, and trousers must be replaced when they're too far gone to stand another stitch. Peter was too small to do any responsible work, and he was getting too big to be paid in pennies and dimes. People didn't exactly know what to do with him. One can't be supercilious to a boy who is a Champneys born, but can one invite a boy who runs errands, is on very familiar footing with all the colored people in the county, and wears such clothes as Peter wore, to one's house, or to be one of the guests when a child of the family gives a birthday party? Not even in South Carolina!

For instance, when Mrs. Humphreys gave a birthday party for her little girl, she was troubled about Peter Champneys, who hadn't been invited. Peter had weeded her garden the day before, and mowed her lawn; and he had looked such a little fellow, running that lawn-mower out there in the sun! And now, while all the other children were playing and laughing, dressed in their party finery, Peter was splitting wood for old Miss Carruthers, a little farther down the street. Mrs. Humphreys could see him from her bedroom window. It was a little too much for the good-hearted woman, who had liked his mother. She compromised with herself by taking a plate if ice-cream and a thick slice of cake, slipping out of her back door, and hurrying down to Miss Carruthers's back yard.

Peter stood there, leaning on his ax. Seated on a larger woodpile was old Daddy Christmas, one of the town beggars. Daddy Christmas was incredibly old, wrinkled, ragged, and bent. His grizzled, partly bald head nodded while he tried to talk to Peter.

"Peter," said Mrs. Humphreys, hastily, "here's some ice-cream and cake for you." She blushed as she spoke. "It's a hot day—and you're working. I thought you'd like something cool and nice." She thrust the plate upon him.

Peter smiled at her charmingly.

"You're mighty kind, Mis' Humphreys," he told her.

"I'll come back for the plate and spoon, after a while," she said, hurrying off. But at the gate, beside the thick crape-myrtle bushes, she paused and looked back. Somehow she wanted to see Maria Champneys's boy eating that ice-cream and cake.

"Daddy Christmas," said a voice, gaily, "if there'd been two plates and two spoons, and if you'd had any sort of a dinner to-day, I'd be perfectly willing to share this treat with you. As it is, you'll have to eat it all by yourself." A second later the voice added: "Funny, you just saying the Lord would provide; but I bet you didn't think He'd provide ice-cream and cake!" Followed the brisk strokes of the ax, swung by a wiry, nervous little arm.

Mrs. Humphreys walked down the lane to her house, with a very thoughtful face.

CHAPTER IV

THE SOUL OF BLACK FOLKS

The negro to the white man, as the moon to the earth, shows one side only; the other is dark and unknown. It is an instinct with him to conceal the truth—any truth—from white men; who knows to what use they will put it and him? So deeply have ages of slavery and oppression ingrained this upon black men's subconsciousness, that only one white man in a thousand ever knows or suspects what his dark brethren think, or know, or feel. Peter Champneys happened to be the thousandth.

There wasn't a cabin in all that countrywide in which this barefooted last scion of a long line of slave-holding gentry wasn't known and welcome. There wasn't a negro in the county he didn't know by name: even "mean niggers" grinned amiably at Peter Champneys. They remembered what he had once said to a district judge whom he heard bitterly inveighing against their ingratitude, immorality, shiftlessness, and general worthlessness. Peter had lifted his quiet eyes.

"I've often thought, Judge, what a particularly mean nigger I'd have been, myself," he said, and studied the judge with disconcerting directness. "If you'd been born a colored man, and some folks talked and behaved to you like some folks talk and behave to colored men, don't you reckon you'd be in jail right this minute, Judge?"

The white men who heard Peter's remark smiled, and one of them said, spitting out a mouthful of tobacco juice, that it was just another piece of that boy's damfoolishness. But the negroes, who knew that judge as only negroes can know white men, chuckled grimly. They have an immense respect for intelligence, and they made no mistake where Peter's was concerned.

They knew him, too, a mild-eyed, brown-faced child reading out of a Book by the light of a kerosene lamp to groups of gray-headed, reverent listeners in lonely cabins. And Peter was always making pictures of them—Mindel at the wash-tub, Emma Campbell picking a chicken, old Maum' Chloe churning, Liza playing with her fat black baby, Joe Tuttle plowing, old Daddy Neptune Fennick leaning on his ax. Sometimes these sketches caught some fleeting moment of fun, and were so true and so amusing that they were received with shouts of delighted laughter, passed from hand to hand, and cherished by fortunate recipients.

Now, no simple and natural heart can even for a little while beat in unison with other hearts, encased in whatsoever colored skin may please God, without a quickening of that wisdom which is one of the keys of the Kingdom to come. To be able really to know, truly to understand and come human-close to the lowly, to men and women under the bondage of age-old prejudice, or outcast by the color of their skin, is a terrible and perilous gift. This is the much knowledge in which there is much grief.

Peter Champneys saw both sides. He saw and heard and knew things that would have made his mother turn in her grave had she known. He knew what depths of savagery and superstition, of brute sloth and ignorance, lay here to drive back many a would-be white helper in despair, and to render the labor of many a splendid negro reformer all but futile. But he knew, too, the terrible patience, the incredible resignation, with which poverty and neglect and hunger and oppression and injustice are borne, until at times, child as he was, his soul sickened with shame and rage. He relished the sweet earthy humor that brightens humble lives, the gaiety and charity under conditions which, when white men have to bear them, go to the making of red terrorists. Some of the things he saw and heard remained like scars upon Peter's memory. He will remember until he dies the June night he spent with Daddy Neptune Fennick in his cabin on the edge of the River Swamp.

That early June day had been cloudy from dawn; Peter was glad of that, for he meant to pick black-berries, and a sunless day for berry-picking is an unmixed blessing. The little negroes are such nimblefingered pickers, such locust-like strippers of all near-by patches, that Peter had bad luck at first, and was driven farther afield than he usually went; his search led him even to the edge of the River Swamp, a dismal place of evil repute, wherein cane as tall as a man grew thickly, and sluggish streamlets meandered in and out of gnarled cypress roots, and big water-snakes stretched themselves on branches overhanging the water. On the edges of the swamp the unmolested vines were thick with fruit. In the late afternoon Peter had filled his buckets to overflowing with extra-fine berries.

It had been a sultry day for all its sunlessness, and Peter was tired, so tired that his head and back ached. He looked at the heavy buckets doubtfully; it would be a man-size job to trudge the long sandy road home, so laden. While he sat there, hating to move, Daddy Neptune Fennick came in sight, hoe and rake and ax on his sturdy shoulder. The old man cast a shrewd, weather-wise eye at the darkening sky.

"Gwine to hab one spell o' wedder," he called. "Best come on home wid me, Peter, en wait w'ile."

Even as he spoke a blaze of lightning split the sky and lighted up the swamp. A loud clap of thunder followed on the heels of it. Daddy Neptune seized one bucket, Peter the other, and both ran for the shelter of the cabin, some eighth of a mile farther on. They reached it just as the rain came down in swirling, blinding sheets.

The old man built a fire in his mud fireplace, and prepared the evening meal of broiled bacon, johnny-cake, and coffee. He and his welcome guest ate from tin plates on their knees, drinking their coffee from tin cups. Between mouthfuls each gave the other what county news he possessed. Peter particularly liked that orderly one-roomed cabin, and the fine old man who was his host.

He was an old-timer, was Daddy Neptune, more than six feet tall, and massively proportioned. His bald head was fringed with a ring of curling gray wool, and a white beard covered the lower portion of an unusually handsome countenance. He had a shrewd and homely wit, an unbuyable honesty, and such a simple and unaffected dignity of manner and bearing as had won the respect of the county.

The old man lived by himself in the cabin by the River Swamp. His wife and son had long been dead, and though he had sheltered, fed, clothed, and taught to work several negro lads, these had gone their way. Peter was particularly attached to him, and the old man returned his affection with interest.

The dark fell rapidly. You could hear the trees in the River Swamp crying out as the wind tormented them. On a night like this, with lightning snaking through it and wild wind trying to tear the heart out of its thin cypresses, and the canebrake rustling ominously in its unchancy black stretches, one might believe that the place was haunted, as the negroes said it was. Daddy Neptune was moved to tell Peter some of his own experiences with the River Swamp. He spoke, between puffs of his corn-cob pipe, of the night Something had come out of it—*pitterpat! pitterpat!*—right at his heels. It had followed him to the very edge of his home clearing. Daddy Neptune wasn't exactly *afraid*, but he knew that Something hadn't any business to be pitterpattering at his heels, so he had turned around and said:

"Ef you-all come out o' hebben, you's wastin' good time 'yuh. Ef Dey-all lef' you come out o' hell, you bes' git right back whah you b'longs. One ways, *I* ain't got nothin' I kin tell you; t'other ways, *you* ain't got nothin' I's gwine to let you tell me. I's axin' you to *git*. En," finished Neptune, "dat t'ing done went right *out*—whish!—same lak I's tellin' you! Yessuh! hit went spang *out*!" He threw another chunk of fatwood on the fire, and watched the smoky flame go dancing up the chimney. In the red glow he had the aspect of a kindly Titan.

"It never bothered you again, Daddy Nep?" Peter was always curious about these experiences. He had a glimmer that negroes are nearer to certain Powers than other folks are, and although he wasn't superstitious, he wasn't skeptical, either.

"Never bothered me a-tall, less'n dat's whut's been meddlin' wid my fowls, whichin ef I catches it, I aims to blow its head plum off, ghostes or no ghostes," said the old man, stoutly.

"Ghosts don't steal chickens. I reckon it's a wild-cat gets yours. I heard one scream in the swamp not so long since."

"Well, I aims to git Mistuh Wildcat, den. I done got me a couple o' guinea-fowls for watch, en dey sho does set up a mighty potrackin' w'en anything strange comes a-snoopin' roun' de yahd."

After a while Daddy Neptune put away his pipe and took down from a shelf his big battered Bible, and Peter read the Twenty-first and Twenty-second chapters of Revelation, to which the old man listened with clasped hands and an uplifted face, his lips moving soundlessly as he repeated to himself certain of the words:

> And God shall wipe away all tears from their eyes; and there shall be no more death, neither sorrow, nor crying, neither shall there be any more pain; for the former things are passed away.... He that overcometh shall inherit all things; and I will be his God and he shall be my son ...

"I was born in slaveryment," said the old man, audibly.

Peter lay on his straw bed before the fire, sleepily watching Neptune finish his prayers. He still had a child's faith, but he was beginning to wonder how a laboring negro could retain it. One thing he was sure of; if there was such a thing as a Christian man, endowed with ideal Christian virtues, that old man kneeling in his cabin, pouring out his heart to his Maker, was a Christian. And remembering comfortable, complacent white Christians—well fed, well housed, well clothed; with education and all that it implies as their heritage; with all the high things of the world open to them by reason of their white skin; praying decorously every Sunday to a white man's God—Peter felt confused. How should the white man and the white man's God answer and account to the Daddy Neptunes, who had been "born in slaveryment," had lived and would die in slaveryment to poverty and prejudice? Where do they come in, these dispossessed dark sons of the Father? Surely, the Father has a very great deal to make up to them!—Then the firelighted cabin walls, the wavering figure of the kneeling old man, the soft sound of light rain on the roof, faded and went out. Peter fell asleep.

He slept a tired boy's dreamless slumber. The night deepened. The rain ceased, and a wan and sad moon climbed the sky, wearily, like a tired old woman. In the River Swamp frogs croaked, a whippoorwill at intervals gave its lonesome and lovely call, the shivering-owl's cry making it lovelier by comparison. The cypresses shook blackly in the blacker swamp water which licked their roots. From the drenched vegetation arose a fresh and penetrating odor, the smell of the clean June night. And presently, he didn't know why, Peter awoke with every sense instantly alert. It was as if his soul had sensed a sound, knew it for what it was, and was on guard.

A few red embers glowed in the big mud chimney. Save for these, the one-room cabin was in darkness. Somebody was moving about. Peter made out the figure of big Neptune standing with his head bent in a listening attitude at one of the shuttered windows. A bit of fatwood in the fireplace burst for a moment into an expiring flame, which flickered dully on the barrel of the gun in the negro's hands. Peter scrambled up, and stole noiselessly across the floor.

"Dem guineas potracked en waked me up, Son," whispered Neptune. "Now I aims to git whut's been sneakin' off wid my fowls."

At that moment a low knock sounded on the door. At such an hour, and in that lonely place, it gave the old man and the boy a distinct sensation of fear: who should come knocking so stealthily at the door of the cabin by the River Swamp at that eerie hour? Neptune, his gun gripped in his hands, twisted his head sidewise, listening. The knock came again, this time more insistent. Then a thick voice spoke, muffled by the intervening door:

"Daddy Nepshun, is you awake? For Gawd A'mighty's sake, Daddy Nepshun, lemme in!"

The old man stepped to the door and flung it wide. The figure that had been crouching against it tumbled in and lay panting on the floor.

"Light me dat lamp, please, Peter," said Neptune, peering down at his visitor.

Peter, who had recovered from his momentary fear, lighted the kerosene lamp. By its light they perceived a stained, muddy, disheveled wretch, in the last state of terror and exhaustion. Two wild eyes glared at them out of a gray, grimed face.

"Why, Jake! Lawd 'a' mussy, hit's Jake!" burst from Daddy Neptune. Peter recognized in the intruder a negro to whom the old man had been, as was his wont, fatherly kind. On a time he and his wife had sheltered and fed Jake.

Peter didn't know why, but something in the man's aspect, in his rolling eyes, his lips drawn back from his teeth, his torn clothes, his desperate look of a hunted beast, made him recoil. He had never before seen any one with just that look of brute cunning and terror. Daddy Neptune's steady eyes took in every detail. He stiffened in his tracks.

"Whut you been doin'?" he demanded. Jake turned his head from side to side; he refused to meet the direct old eyes. He mumbled:

"Is you got any w'isky, Da' Nepshun? For Gawd's sake, Da'Nepshun, gimme a drink en don't ast me no questions twell I's able to answer." His voice was hoarse and shaking; his whole body shook.

"I ain't got no w'isky, but I got coffee en bittles. Whichin you is welcome to," said Neptune. "You ain't say yit whut you been doin'. Whut you been up to, Jake?"

Jake writhed off the floor. Again Peter recoiled instinctively. As the negro got upon his feet his coat fell open, and the torn sleeve and cuff of a gingham shirt showed. On it was a dark stain which was not swamp water or mud. Peter's eyes fastened upon that dark red smear.

"Gimme a bite o' bittles so's I kin git on," implored Jake.

"I axes you once mo', Jake: whut you been doin'?" demanded Neptune. His voice was stern, and his face began to set.

"En I axes you to lemme git dem bittles fust, en I'll tell you, soon's I gits back mah wind," returned Jake, sullenly.

Still retaining his gun, Neptune went to the corner cupboard, from which he took a loaf of bread. Without cutting it he handed it to Jake, who began to tear it with his teeth. All the while he ate, he kept turning his head, listening, listening.

"Cain't wait for no coffee. Gimme drink o' water, please, suh." In silence Neptune handed him a gourd of water. When Jake had gulped this down, Neptune asked again, inexorably:

"Whut you been doin', Jake?"

Jake shifted from one foot to the other. He thrust his bullet head forward. His hands, hanging at his sides, opened and closed, the fingers twitching.

"Dem w'ite mens is atter—somebuddy—en dey say hit's me," he muttered hoarsely. His eyes rolled toward the door, which, not having been barred after his entrance, swung slightly ajar.

"Whut dey atter somebuddy *for*?" Neptune demanded. Outside, in the wet night, the screech-owl cried. The sweet wind danced on airy feet in and out of the cypresses and the gums, kissed them, stole their breath, and tossed it abroad odorously. Stars had come out to keep the pale moon company, and a faint light glinted on wet grass and bushes. Crickets and katydids and little green tree-frogs kept up a harsh concert. And then, above all the minor, murmuring noises of the night arose another sound, very faint and far off, but unmistakable and unforgetable—the deep, long, bell note of a hound upon the trail.

The three in the cabin stood like figures turned to stone in the attitude of listening. Jake's teeth chattered audibly. He edged toward the open door, but Neptune stepped in front of him, and flung up an arresting hand.

"*Whut for*?" His voice was like a whip-lash.

"Somebuddy—done meddled wid a w'ite gal—een de cawn-field. En dey 'low—hit wuz me."

A gasp, as if his heart had been squeezed, came from Neptune. Of a sudden he seemed to grow in height, to tower unhumanly tall above the cringing wretch he confronted. His eyes narrowed into red points that bored into the other's eyes, and plunged like daggers into his heart and mind. Before that glance, like a vivisectionist's knife, Jake wilted; he seemed to shrink, dwindle, collapse. And with a growing, cold, awful horror, a suspicion so hideous that his mind revolted from it, Peter Champneys stood staring from one black face to the other.

"You—you—" Neptune gulped, strangling. A long, slow shudder, as of one confronting unheard-of torture, went over his big frame. The fringe of hair on his bald head rose, his beard bristled. Sparks seemed to shoot from his eyes, burning with a terrible flame.

"Da' Nepshun—" Jake put out clawing, twitching hands. "Dey's—dey's—gwine to git me." His voice broke into a half-scream.

"Whut you do hit for?" This from Neptune, in a heart-shaken, anguished, rattling whisper. He asked no further questions. He had no doubt. Jake's rolling eyes had told him the unspeakable truth.

"I 'clah to Gawd, Da' Nepshun, I wuzn't meanin' no hahm—I never had no idea—She came down de cawn-field paff—wid de cow followin' 'er—en—en—I don't know *whut* mek me meddle wid dat gal. Seems lak hit wuz de debbil, 'stead o' me."

"Is de gal done daid?"

"Yas, suh, she done daid." Jake rocked himself to and fro, muttering her name.

Peter Champneys looked at the torn shirt-sleeve with the red stain upon it. The room shook and wavered, wind was in his ears. And the red of that girl's blood got into his eyes, and he saw things through a scarlet mist. The most horrible rage he had ever experienced shook him like a mortal sickness. Oh, God! oh, God! oh, God! That girl!

In the momentary silence that fell upon that tragic room, a sound shivered. Long, slow, bell-like. Nearer. It galvanized Jake into terror-stricken action. He started for the door.

"Dey'll git me, dey'll git me!" he croaked.

Peter would have flung himself upon the wretch, to reach for his throat with bare hands; but something in Neptune's face stopped him. Neptune's bigness seemed to fill the whole room. He drew a deep breath, and with one movement jerked the door wide.

"Run down de paff by de fowl-house," he said sharply. "Den—hit's de swamp for you."

Peter turned sick. Was Neptune like all other—niggers? Hadn't he the—proper sense of what this devil had done?

Jake leaped for the door, cleared the steps at a bound, and was flying down the path. Neptune took one forward step, filling the doorway. He lifted the shot-gun to his shoulder. Just as the fugitive neared the fowl-house, the gun spoke. The flying figure leaped high in the air, and then sprawled out and was suddenly still and inert. The guinea-hens set up a deafening potracking, and the cooped fowls squawked and flapped. Above all the noise they made rose the blood-hound's note.

It was done so quickly, it was so inevitable, that Peter could only stand and blink. He thought, sickly, that the very earth should shudder away from the soiling touch of that appalling carrion. But the earth was the one thing that would receive Jake unprotestingly. He lay on his face, his arms outflung, and from the gaping hole between his shoulders a dark stream welled. The indifferent earth, the uncaring grass, received it. The wind came out of the swamp on mincing feet and danced over him, and fluttered his torn shirt-sleeve.

Stonily, voicelessly, Neptune stood in the cabin door, staring at that which lay in the pathway. Then he lowered the smoking gun, and leaned on it. His bald head drooped until his gray beard swept his breast, and his throat rattled like a dying man's. Shudders went over him. And stonily young Peter Champneys stood beside him, his boyish eyes hard in a dead-white face, his boyish mouth a grim, pale line.

"Peter," said the old man presently, in a thin whisper, "I helped raise dat boy. Wuzn't sich a bad boy, neither. Used to sing en wissle roun' de house, en fetch water en fiah-wood. Chloe, she loved 'im. Used to say Ouah Fathuh right in dis same room 'fo' he went to sleep. Ef I'd 'a' knowed—

"En dat po' lil w'ite chile's daddy en mammy, *dey* done raise 'er—used to say 'er prayers—en laff en sing—en trus' de Almighty Gawd—"

He raised his sinewy arms and shook the gun aloft.

"Ah, Gawd Almighty! Gawd Almighty! Whah is You dis night? Whah is You?" cried the old man. And of a sudden he began to weep dreadfully; heart-broken cries of pain and of protest, the tortured cries of one suffering inhumanly.

"And all this while God said not a word."

Shaken to the soul, full of sick horror, and loathing, and rage, Peter Champneys yet had a swift, intuitive understanding of old Neptune; and as if through him he had caught a glimpse of the naked and suffering soul of the black people, the boy began to weep with him. With understanding merging into pity he crept nearer and put his slender, boyish arm around the big, shaking, agonized figure, and the old man turned his head and looked long and sorrowfully into the white child's face. He put out the big, seamed, work-hardened hand that had labored since it could hold an implement to labor with, and laid it on the child's shoulder.

Then, bareheaded and empty-handed, Neptune sat down on his cabin steps to wait for what should happen, and Peter Champneys sat beside him, the gun between his knees. Over there by the fowl-house lay Jake, a horrid blotch in the moonlight.

Presently, echoing through the River Swamp, the hunting hounds set up their thrilling, deep-mouthed belling. They were closing in on their quarry and the nearness of it excited them. A few minutes later, and here they were, a posse of some thirty or forty mounted men struggling pell-mell after them. One great hound leaped forward, stood rigid by that which lay in a heap in the cabin clearing, pointed his nose, and gave tongue. Other dogs bunched around him, sniffed, and joined in.

The mounted men came to an abrupt standstill, the horses, like the dogs, bunching together. Neptune had risen and Peter Champneys stood on the top step, his head about level with the old man's shoulder. He looked in vain for the sheriff; evidently, this was an independent posse. One of the men rode up to the door, shouting to make himself heard above the din of the dogs, and Peter recognized him, with a sinking of the heart—a tenant farmer named Mosely, of a violent and quarrelsome disposition.

"Shet up them damn dogs!" he yelled. And to Neptune, savagely: "Now then, nigger, talk! What's been doin' here?"

It was Peter Champneys who answered.

"Daddy Neptune's been worried by something or somebody stealing his fowls. He's been on the watch. So when he saw that—that nigger over there running by the chicken-house, he just blazed away. Got him between the shoulder-blades."

A yell so ferocious that Peter's marrow froze, burst from the posse, which had dismounted.

"It's him!" howled a farm-hand, and kicked the corpse in the face. "What in hell did that big nigger shoot him for, anyhow?" he roared. "He'd ought to be strung up himself, the old black—" And he cursed Neptune vilely. He felt swindled. There would be no burning, with interludes of unspeakable things. Nothing but senseless carrion to wreak vengeance upon. And all through a damned old meddling nigger's fault! A nigger taking the law into his own hands!

Somebody, discovering Daddy Neptune's woodpile, had kindled a fatwood torch. Others followed his example, and the red, smoky light flared over enraged faces and glaring eyes of maddened men; over the sweating horses, the baying dogs, and the black corpse with its bruised face. The guinea-hens, after their insane fashion, kept up a deafening potracking, flapping from limb to limb of the tree in which they roosted. The indifferent swamp chorus joined in, katydids and crickets shrilling all the while. And over it all the moon went about its business; the awful depths of the sky were silent. The wind from the swamp, the night, the earth, didn't care.

Somebody whipped out a knife and bent over Jake's body. A yell greeted this. Dogs and men moved confusedly around the thing on the ground, in a sort of demoniac circle upon which the hissing, flaring pitch-pine torches danced with infernal effect. Peter Champneys watched it, his soul revolting. He had no sympathy for Jake; he felt for him

Marie Conway Oemler

nothing but hatred. He couldn't think of that gay and innocent girl coming down the corn-field path, unafraid—to meet what she had met—without a suffocating sense of rage. She had been, Peter remembered, a very pretty girl, a girl who, as Neptune had said, used to sing, and laugh, and say her prayers, and trust Almighty God.

But Peter was seeing now the other side of that awful cloud which darkens the horizon of the South—the brute beast mob-vengeance that follows swiftly upon the heels of the unpardonable sin. There must be justice. But what was happening now wasn't justice. It was stark barbarism let loose.

Neptune, who had "helped raise" Jake, had meted out to him justice full and sure. He had avenged both the wronged white and the wronged black people. Peter looked at the men in the cabin clearing, and saw the thing nakedly, and from both angles. For instance, consider Mosely, who had done things —with a clasp-knife. And that other man, the farm-hand, shifty-eyed and mean, always half drunk, a bad citizen: *they* would be sure to be foremost in affairs like this. They had precious little respect for the law as law. And here they were, making the holy night indecent with bestial behavior. Again a sick qualm shook Peter: Mosely was calmly putting four severed black fingers into his coat pocket. Oh, where was the sheriff? Why didn't the sheriff come?

Peter caught a glimpse of a shapeless, battered, gory mass under trampling feet. Maddened by the little they were able to accomplish, and with the torture-lust that is as old as humanity itself roused to fury by frustration, the posse turned from that which had been Jake, to old Neptune, standing motionless by his doorway. Neptune had not moved or spoken since Peter had answered the posse's questions. He had not even appeared to hear the vile abuse heaped upon him. He was not in the least afraid for his life: He was beyond that. That which had happened, which was happening, had dealt the stern, simple-hearted old man so mighty a blow that his faculties were stunned. He couldn't think. He could only suffer a bewildered, baffled torment. He stood there, dumb as a sheep before the slaughterers, and the sight of his black face maddened the men who were out to avenge a black man's monstrous crime.

"Hang the damn nigger!" screamed Mosely, and the crowd surged forward ominously. You could see, by the shaking torch-light, faces in which the eyes glared wolf-like, brandished fists, glints of guns. Neptune, without a flicker of fear, regarded them with his sorrowful gaze. But Peter Champneys stepped in front of him, and thrust the cold muzzle of the shot-gun against Mosely's face. The man, a coward at heart, leaped back, trampling upon the toes of those behind him, who cursed him shrilly and vindictively.

Then spoke up small Peter Champneys, standing barefooted and bareheaded, clothed in a coarse blue blouse and a pair of patched and faded denim trousers, but for all that heir to a long line of dead-and-gone Champneyses who had been, whatever their faults, fearless and gallant gentlemen.

"Get back there, you, Mosely!" Peter Champneys spoke in the voice his grandfather had on a time used to a recalcitrant field-hand.

"Chuck that little nigger-lover in the swamp!"

"Knock him down an' git the nigger, Mosely!"

"Burn down the house!"

But the shot-gun in that steady young hand held them in

check for a breathing-space. They knew Peter Champneys.

"Mosely!" snapped Peter. "You, too, Nicolson! Stand back, you white-livered hounds! First one of you lays a hand on me or Daddy Nep gets his head blown off! Damn you, Mosely! don't make me tell you again to get back!"

And Mosely saw that in the boy's eyes that drove him back, swearing.

The huge farm-hand, who had shifted and squirmed his way to the back of the crowd, now lifted his arm. A rope with a noose at the end snaked over the tossing heads, and all but settled over black Neptune's. It slipped, writhing from the old man's shoulder and down his shirt. The mob set up a disappointed and yet hopeful howl.

"Try it again! Try it again!" they shrieked. Then a sort of waiting hush fell upon them. The farm-hand, to whom the rope had been tossed, was again making ready for a throw, measuring the distance with his eyes. Peter, his lips tightening, waited too. The farm-hand was a tall man, and the posse had shifted to allow him space. His arm shot up, the noosed rope whizzed forward. But even as it did so Peter Champneys's trigger-finger moved. The report sounded like a clap of thunder, and was followed by a roar of rage and pain. The rope-thrower, with the rope tripping his feet and impeding his movements, danced about wildly, shaking the hand from which three fingers had been cleanly clipped. At that instant another posse rode up, with a baying of hounds to herald it. One saw the sheriff on a large bay horse, a Winchester in the crook of his arm. With a merest glance at what had been Jake, he pushed his way through the throng, and was confronted by Peter Champneys standing in front of old Neptune Fennick, with a smoking shot-gun in his hands.

"You better do something, quick! If you let anything happen to Daddy Nep, you've got to kill me first," panted Peter.

"He'd ought to be shot for a nigger-lover, Sheriff!" shouted the farm-hand.

"All right. Do it. But you'll get your neck stretched for it! My name's *Champneys*," shouted Peter.

The sheriff moved restlessly on his bay. A Champneys had fed his parents. Chadwick Champneys had given him his first pair of shoes. The sheriff was stirred to the depths by the crime that had been committed, and he had no love for a nigger, but—

He turned to the menacing crowd. "Here, boys, enough o' this! The right nigger's dead, and that's all there is to it. No, you don't do no hangin'! I'm sheriff o' this county, an' I aim to keep the law. Let that old nigger alone, Mosely! If that young hell-cat puts a bullet in your chitlin's, it'll be your own funeral."

He straightened in the saddle, touched the rein, and in a second the big bay had been swung around to stand between Neptune and the white men. The muzzle of Peter's gun touched the sheriff's leg.

"Put that pop-gun up, Son," said he, turning his head to look down into the boy's face. Their eyes met, in a long look.

"I knew that girl since she was bawn," he said, and his hard face quivered. "Hell!" swore the sheriff, and the hand on his bridle shook. He knew old Neptune, too, and in his way liked him. But it was hard for the sheriff, who had seen the dead little girl, to look into any black face that night and retain any feeling of humanity.

"Yes, sir. I knew her, too," said Peter Champneys, gulping. "But—I know Neptune, too. And—what happened—wasn't his fault. It's got nothing to do with Neptune—and—and things that Mosely—" His voice broke.

"Hell!" swore the sheriff again. And he whispered, more gently, "All right, Peter. An' I reckon you better stay by the old nigger for a day or two until this thing dies down." After all, the sheriff thought relievedly, Neptune's swift action, actuated by whatsoever motive, had saved the county and himself from a rather frightful episode. Turning to the crowd, he yelled:

"Get them dogs started for home! They're goin' plum crazy! Get on your hawse, Mosely! You, over there, with your fist shot up, ride next to me. Mount, all o' you! Mount, I say! No, I'll come last.

"What's that you're sayin', Briggs? No, suh, not by a damn-sight you won't! Not while I'm sheriff o' this county an' upholdin' law an' order in it, you won't drag no dead nigger behind *my* hawse—nor yet in front of him, neither! Let the nigger lay where he is and rot—what's left of him."

"Do you want us to bury—it?" quavered Peter.

"Bury it or burn it. What the hell do I care what you do with it?" growled the sheriff. "He's dead, that's all I got to think about." He ran his shrewd eyes over the posse, saw that not one straggler remained to do further mischief, and drove them before him, willy-nilly. In five minutes the trampled yard was clear, and the sound of the horses' hoofs was already dying in the distance. In the sky all other stars had paled to make room for the morning star.

Peter and Neptune, left alone, looked at each other dumbly.

A thing remained to be done. The sun mustn't rise upon the horror that lay in the cabin yard. Neptune went to his small barn and trundled out a wheelbarrow, in which were several gunny-sacks, a piece of rope, and a spade.

Peter turned his head away while the old man covered the thing on the ground with sacking, rolled it over, floppily, and tied it as best he could. The sweat came out on them both as they saw the stains that spread on the clean sacking. Neptune heaped the bundle into his wheelbarrow. At a word from him Peter went into the house and returned with a lighted lantern, for the River Swamp was still very dark. The sun wouldn't be up for an hour or two yet. Peter held the lantern in one hand, and carried spade and shot-gun over the other shoulder. In the ghostly light they entered the swamp, every turn and twist of whose wide, watery acreage was known to Neptune, and was fairly familiar to Peter. They had to proceed warily, for the ground was treacherous, and at any moment a jutting tree-root might upset the clumsy barrow. Despite Neptune's utmost care it bumped and swayed, and the shapeless bundle in it shook hideously, as if it were trying to escape. And the stains on the coarse shroud grew, and spread.

In a small and fairly dry space among particularly large cypresses, Neptune stopped. At one side was a deep pool in whose depths the lantern was reflected. About it ferns, some of a great height, grew thickly. Neptune began to dig in the black earth. Sometimes he struck a cypress root, against which the spade rang with a hollow sound. It was slow enough work, but the hole in the swamp earth grew with every spade-thrust, like a blind mouth opening wider and wider. Peter held the lantern. The trees stood there like witnesses.

Presently Neptune straightened his shoulders, moved back to the barrow, and edged it to the hole. Swiftly and deftly he tipped it, and the shapeless bundle slid into the open mouth awaiting it. It was curiously still just then in the River Swamp.

When they emerged into the open, the sun was rising over a clean, fresh world. The dark tops of the trees were gilded by the first rays. Every bush was hung with diamonds, the young grass rippled like a child's hair, and birds were everywhere, voicing the glory of the morning.

The old negro dropped his wheelbarrow, and lifted a supplicating face and a pair of gnarled hands to the morning sky. His lips moved. One saw that he prayed, trustingly, with a childlike simplicity.

Peter Champneys watched him speculatively. He tried to reason the thing out, and the heart in his boyish breast ached with a new pain. Thoughts big, new, insistent, knocked at the door of his intellect and refused to be denied admittance.

He thought it better to take the sheriff's advice and stay with Neptune for a few days, but nobody troubled the good old man. The verdict of the whole county was in his favor. He went his harmless, fearless, laborious way unmolested. That autumn he died, and the cabin by the River Swamp was taken over by nature, who gave it to her winds and rains to play with. Her leaves drifted upon its floor, her birds built under its shallow eaves.

Nobody would live there any more. The negroes said the place was haunted: on wild nights one might hear there the sound of a shot, the baying of a hound; and see Jake running for the swamp.

CHAPTER V

THE PURPLE HEIGHTS

Emma Campbell had one of her contrary fits, and when Emma was contrary, the best thing to do was to keep out of her way. Her "palate was down," her temper was up; she'd had trouble with the Young Sons and Daughters of Zion, in her church, and hot words with a deacon who said that when he passed the cup Emma Campbell lapped up nearly all the communion wine, which was something no lady ought to do. And Cassius had taken unto himself a fourth spouse, and, without taking Emma into his confidence, had gotten her to wash and iron his wedding-shirt for him. So Emma's "palate was down," and not even three toothpicks and two spoons in her hair had been able to get it up. Peter, therefore, took a holiday. He filled his pockets with bread, and set out with no particular destination in mind.

At a turn in the Riverton Road he met the Red Admiral.

He stopped, reflectively. He hadn't seen the Admiral in some time, and it pleased him to be led by that gay adventurer now. The Admiral flitted down the Riverton Road, and Peter ran gaily after him. He led the boy a fine chase across fields, and out on the road again, and then down a lane, and along the river, and through the pines, and finally to the River

Swamp woods. Peter came fleet-footed to Neptune's old cabin, raced round it, and then stopped, in utter confusion and astonishment. On the back steps, with an umbrella beside her, and an easel in front of her, sat a young woman so busy getting a bit of the swamp upon her canvas that she didn't hear or see Peter until he was upon her. Then she looked up, with her paint-brush in her hand.

"Hello!" said she, in the friendliest fashion, "where did *you* come from?"

She was a big girl, blue as to eyes, brown as to hair, and with a fresh-colored, good-humored face. Her glance was singularly clear and direct, and her smile so comradely that Peter took an instantaneous liking to her. He wondered what on earth she meant by coming here, to this lonely place, all by herself. But she was making a picture, and his interest was more in that than in the painter.

"May I look at it, please?" he asked politely. He smiled at her, and Peter had a mighty taking smile of his own.

"Of course you may!" said the lady, genially. Hands behind his back, Peter stared at the canvas. Then he stepped back yet farther, lifted one hand, and squinted through the fingers. The young lady regarded him with growing interest.

"Well, what do you think of it?" she asked.

The young woman wasn't a quick worker, but she was a careful one, and very exact. Unfinished though it was, the picture showed that; and it showed, too, a lack of something vital; there was no spontaneity in it.

"I've never seen anybody paint before, though I've always wanted to," said Peter, and fetched an unconscious sigh of envy.

"You haven't said whether or not you like it," the girl reminded him.

"It isn't finished," said Peter. His eyes went to the familiar woods, the beloved woods, and came back to her canvas. "I think when it's finished it will be like a photograph," he added.

Claribel Spring—for that was the big girl's name—knew her own limitations; but to meet a criticism so exact and so just, from a barefooted child in the South Carolina wilds wasn't to be expected. She took a longer look at the boy and thought she had never before seen a pair of eyes so absolutely, clearly golden. Those eyes would create a distinct impression upon people: either you'd like them, or you'd find them so strange you'd think them ugly. She herself thought them beautiful.

"You seem to know something about pictures, even unfinished ones," she told him comradely. "And may I ask who you are, and why and how you come flying out of the nowhere into the here of these forsaken woods?"

"Oh, I'm only Peter Champneys," said the boy with the golden eyes, shyly. "I hope I didn't startle you? It's my butterfly's fault. You see, I never know where I've got to follow him, or what I'm going to find when I get there."

"Your butterfly? You mean that Red Admiral that just whizzed by? He skimmed over my easel," said the young lady.

"Is that his real name?" Peter was enchanted. "A black fellow with red on his coat-tails, and a sash like a general's? Then that's my butterfly!" said Peter, happily. He smiled at the girl again, and finished, naively: "I owe that butterfly a whole heap of good luck!"

She told him she was spending some time with the Northern people who had lately bought Lynwood Plantation, a few miles down the river. She liked to prowl around and paint things.

"And now," she asked, "would you mind telling me something more about that butterfly of yours? And where some more of the good luck comes in?" She was growing more and more interested in Peter.

Peter dropped down beside the easel, his hands clasped loosely between his knobby knees. It seemed the most natural thing in the world that he should find himself talking freely to this Yankee girl; it was the most natural thing in the world that she should understand. So Peter, who, as a rule, would have preferred to be beaten with rods rather than divulge his feelings, told her exactly what she wished to know. This must be blamed upon the Red Admiral!

She caught a sharp outline of the child's life, poor in material circumstances, but crowded to the brim with thought and feeling and emotion, and colorful as the coast country was colorful. He had kept himself, she thought, as sweet and limpid as a mountain spring. He was wistful, eager, and mad to know things. His eyes went back again and again, with a sort of desperate hunger in them, to the canvas on her easel, as if the secret of him lay there. The girl sat with her firm white chin in her firm white hands, and looked down at Peter with her bright blue Yankee eyes, and understood him as none of his own people had ever understood him. She even understood what his innate reticence and decency held back. Who shall say that the Admiral wasn't a fairy?

"I'd like to see that first little sketch," she said, when he had finished. Her eyes were very sweet.

For a second he hesitated. Then he rose, went into the deserted cabin, and took from the cupboard a dusty bundle of papers—pieces of white cardboard, sheets of letter-paper, any sort of paper he had been able to lay his hands on. Riverton and the surrounding country, as Peter Champneys saw it, unrolled before her astonished eyes. It was roughly done, and there were glaring faults; but there was something in the crude work that wasn't in the canvas on her easel, and she recognized it. She singled out several sketches of an old negro with a bald head and a white beard, and a stern, fine face innate with dignity. She said quietly:

"You are quite right, Peter: the Red Admiral is undoubtedly a fairy." And after a moment, studying the old man's face: "He's rather a remarkable old man, isn't he?"

Peter looked around him. On that terrible night Daddy Neptune had stood just where the easel was standing now; over there by the tumble-down chicken house, Jake had fallen; and the space that was now green with grass had been full of vengeful men, and howling dogs, and trampling horses. Peter took the sketch from her, looked at it for a long moment, and, as briefly as he could, and keeping himself very much in the background, he told her.

Claribel Spring looked around her, almost disbelieving that such a thing could happen in such a place. She looked at the quiet-faced boy, at the sketches, and shook her head.

When she was ready to go, Peter helped pack her traps, picked up her paint-box, and slung her folding-easel and camp-stool across his shoulder. Lynwood was some three miles from the River Swamp, and shall a gentleman allow a lady to lug her belongings that distance?

"Miss Spring," said Peter, anxiously, as they reached the porch of Lynwood, "Miss Spring, do you expect to go about these woods much—by yourself?"

"Why, yes! Nobody here has time to prowl with me, you see. And I can't stay indoors. I've got to make the most of these woods while I have the opportunity."

Peter looked troubled. His brows puckered. "I wonder if you'd mind if I just sort of stayed around so I could look after—I mean, so I could watch you painting? May I? *Please!*"

Claribel sensed something tense under that request. She longed to get at Peter's thought processes. She was immensely interested in this shabby little chap who made astonishing sketches and whose personality was so intriguing.

"Why, of course you may, Peter. But would you mind telling me just *why* you want to come with me—aside from the painting?"

Peter shifted from one bare foot to the other.

"Because somebody's *got* to go with you," he blurted flatly. "Don't the people here know you mustn't go off like that, by yourself? There—well, Miss Spring, there are bad folks everywhere, I reckon. Our niggers"—Peter's head went up— "are the best niggers, in the world. But—sometimes—And— and—" He looked at her, trying to make her understand.

Claribel Spring considered him. He might be about fourteen. His head just reached her shoulder. And he was offering to take care of her, to be her protector! That's what his anxiety meant. "Oh, you darling little gentleman!" she thought.

"I see. And I'll be perfectly delighted if you can manage to come with me, Peter," said she, sincerely. "And listen: I've been thinking about those sketches of yours, while we were walking home, and I've got the nicest little plan all worked out in my mind. You shall take me around these woods, which you know and I don't. You'll be my guide, philosopher, and friend. In return I'll teach you what I can. You needn't bother about materials: I have loads of stuff for the two of us. What do you say?"

It was so unexpected, so marvelous, that an electrified and transformed Peter looked at her with a face gone white from excess of astonished rapture, and a pair of eyes like pools in paradise when the stars of heaven tremble in their depths.

Claribel Spring was a better teacher than artist, as she discovered for herself. She had the divine faculty of imparting knowledge and at the same time arousing enthusiasm; and she had such a pupil now as real teachers dream of. It wasn't so much like learning, with Peter; it was as if he were being reminded of something he already knew. He had never had a lesson in his whole life, he didn't go about things in the right manner, and there were grave faults to be overcome; but he had the thing itself.

She taught him more than the rudiments of technique, more than the mere processes of mixing colors, more than shading and form, and perspective, and flat surfaces, and high lights, and foreshortening. She was the first person from the outside world with whom Peter had ever come into real contact, the first person not a Southerner with whom he had ever been intimately friendly. And oddly enough, Peter taught *her* a few things.

Marie Conway Oemler

Riverton learned that Peter Champneys had been engaged as a sort of fetch-and-carry boy by that big Vermont girl who was stopping at Lynwood. They thought Miss Spring charming, when they occasionally met her, but when it came to trapesing about the woods like a gipsy, quite as irresponsible as Peter Champneys himself—"Birds of a feather flock together," you know.

Claribel Spring was just at that time passing through a Gethsemane of her own, and she needed Peter quite as badly as he needed her. Peter was really a godsend to the girl. Her quiet self-control kept any one from discovering that she was cruelly unhappy, but Peter did at times perceive the shadow upon her face, and he knew that the silence that sometimes fell upon her was not always a happy one. At such times he managed to convey to her delicately, without words, his sympathy. He piloted her to lovely places, he made her pause to look at birds' nests, at corners of old fences, at Carolina wild-flowers. And when he had made her smile again, he was happy. To Peter that was the swiftest, happiest, most enchanted summer he had ever known.

It ended all too soon. He went up to Lynwood one morning to find Claribel packing for a hasty departure. It was a new Claribel that morning, a Claribel with a rosy face and shining eyes and smiling lips. She had gotten news, she told Peter joyously, that called her away at once—beautiful news. The most wonderful news in the world!

She turned over to Peter all the material she had on hand, and gave him painstaking directions as to how he was to proceed, what he was to strive for, what to avoid. And she said that when he had become a great man in the big world, one of these days, he wasn't to forget that she'd prophesied it, and had been allowed to play her little part in his career. Then she kissed Peter as nobody had ever kissed him except his mother. And so she left him.

He was turning fifteen then, and getting too big for the penny jobs Riverton had in pickle for him. Nothing better offering, he hired out that autumn to a farmer who fed his stock better than he did his men. Peter's mouth still twists wryly when he remembers that first month of heavy farm work. The mule was big and Peter wasn't, the plow and the soil were heavy, and Peter was light. Trammell, the farmer, held him to his task, insisting that "a boy who couldn't learn to plow straight couldn't learn to do nothin' else straight, and he'd better learn now while he had the chanst." Peter would have cheerfully forfeited his chance to learn to plow straight; but the thing was there to do, and he tried to do it.

Sunday, his one free day, was the only thing that made life at all endurable to Peter. It was a day to be looked forward to all through the heavy week. Early in the morning, with such lunch as he could come by, his worn Bible in his coat pocket and a package of paper under his arm, Peter disappeared, not to return until nightfall. The farmer's over-burdened wife was glad enough to see him go; that meant one less for whom to cook and to wash dishes.

All the week, after his own fashion, Peter had been observing things. On Sundays he tried to put them down on paper. He had the great, rare, sober gift of seeing things as they are, a gift given to the very few. A negro plowing in a flat brown field behind a horse as patient as himself; an old woman in a red jacket and a plaid bandana, feeding a flock of turkeys; a young girl milking; a boy driving an unruly cow—all the homely, common, ordinary things of everyday life among the plain people, Peter, who had been set down among the plain people, tried to crowd on his scanty supply of drawing-paper on Sunday in the woods.

Peter had learned to draw animals playing, and birds flying, and butterflies fluttering, and folks working. But he couldn't draw a decent living-wage for his daily labor. He was only a boy, and it seemed to be a part of the scheme of things that a boy should be asked to do a man's work for a dwarf's wages. And the food they gave him at the Trammell farm-house was beginning to tell on him. Peter asked for more money and was refused with contumely. He asked for a change of diet, and was informed violently that this country is undoubtedly going to the dogs when folks like himself "think theirselfs too dinged uppidy for good victuals. Eat 'em or leave 'em!"

Peter couldn't eat them any more, so he left them. He discharged himself out of hand, and went back to Riverton and Emma Campbell with forty dollars and a bundle of sketches.

The doctor in Riverton got most of the forty dollars. However, as he needed a boy in his drug store just then, he gave the place to Peter, who took it willingly enough, as he was still feeling the effects of bad food and heavy farm work. He learned to roll pills and weigh out lime-drops and mix soft drinks, and to keep his patience with women who wanted only a one-cent stamp, and expected him to lick it for them into the bargain.

Grown into a gawky chap of sixteen, Peter didn't impress people too favorably. They felt for him the instinctive distrust of the conservative and commercial mind for the free and artistic one. The Peter Champneyses of the world challenge the ideal of commercial success by their utter inability to see in it the real reason for being alive, and the chief end of man. They are inimical to smugness and to complacent satisfaction. Naturally, safe and sane citizens resent this.

There was one person in Riverton who didn't share the general opinion that Peter Champneys was trifling, and that was Mrs. Humphreys. Mrs. Humphrey still tasted that ice-cream and cake Peter had given to old Daddy Christmas on a hot afternoon. It was she who presently persuaded her husband to take Peter into his hardware store, at a better salary than the doctor paid him.

Everybody agreed that it was noble of Sam Humphreys to take Peter on. Of course, Peter was as honest as the sun, but he wasn't businesslike. Not to be businesslike is the American sin against the Holy Ghost. It is far less culpable to begin with the first of the deadly sins on Sunday morning and finish up the last of the seven on Saturday night, than to have your neighbors say you aren't businesslike. Had Peter taken to tatting, instead of to sketching niggers in ox-carts, and men plowing, and women washing clothes, Riverton couldn't have been more impatient with him. Artists, so far as the average American small town is concerned, are ineffectual persons, godless creatures long on hair and short on morals, men whom nobody respects until they are decently dead. It disgusted Riverton that Peter Champneys, who had had such a nice mother and come from a good family, should follow such examples.

But Peter meant to hold fast to his one power, though every hand in the world were against it, though every tongue shouted "Fool," though for it he should go hungry and naked and friendless to the end of his days. He wished to get away from Riverton, to study in some large city under good teachers. Claribel Spring had stressed the necessity of good teachers. Grimly he set himself to work to obtain at least a start toward the coveted end.

By incredible efforts he had managed to save one hundred and ten dollars, when Emma Campbell fell ill with a misery in her legs. Although she had a conjure bag around her neck, a rabbit foot in her pocket, and a horseshoe nailed above the door, she was helpless for a while, and Peter had to hire another colored woman to care for her.

Emma was just on her feet when Cassius took it into his head to die. There was a confusion of husbands and wives between Emma and Cassius, but she mourned for him shrilly. What deepened her distress was the fact that in repudiating him his last wife had carried off all his small possessions, and there was no money left to bury him. Now, not to be buried with due and fitting ceremonies and the displayed insignia of some churchly Buryin' Society, is a calamity and a disgrace. Emma felt that she could never hope to hold up her head again if Cassius had to be buried by town charity.

Peter Champneys hadn't lived among and liked the colored people all these years for nothing. He looked at big Emma Campbell sitting beside the kitchen table with her head buried in her arms, a prey to woe. Then he went to the bank and drew what remained of his savings. Cassius was gathered to his father's with all the accustomed trappings, and Emma's grief was turned to proud joy. But it was another proof of the unbusinesslike mind of Peter Champneys. His small savings were gone; he had to begin all over again.

Decidedly, the purple heights were a long, long way off!

CHAPTER VI

GOOD MORNING, GOOD LUCK!

On a particular Sunday Peter Champneys was making for his favorite haunt, the grass-grown clearing and the solitary and deserted cabin by the River Swamp. It was to him a place not of desolation but of solitude, and usually he fled to it as to a welcome refuge. But to-day his step lagged. The divine discontent of youth, the rebellion aginst the brute force of circumstance, seethed in him headily. Here he was, in the lusty April of his days, and yet life was bitter to his palate, and there was canker at the heart of the rose of Spring. Nothing was right.

The coast country, always beautiful, was at its best, the air sweet with the warm breath of summer. The elder was white with flowers, and in moist places, where the ditches dipped, huge cat-tails swayed to the light wind. Roses rioted in every garden; when one passed the little houses of the negroes every yard was gay with pink crape-myrtle and white and lilac Rose of Sharon trees. All along the worm-fences the vetches and the butterfly-pea trailed their purple; everywhere the horse-nettle showed its lovely milk-white stars, and the orange-red milkweed invited all the butterflies of South Carolina to come and dine at her table. There were swarms of butterflies, cohorts of butterflies, but among all the People of the Sky he missed the Red Admiral.

Peter particularly needed the gallant little sailor's heartening. It was a bad sign not to meet him this morning; it confirmed his own opinion that he was an unlucky fellow, a chap doomed to remain a nonentity, one fitted for nothing better than scooping out a nickel's worth of nails, or wrapping up fifty-cent frying-pans!

He walked more and more wearily, as if it tired him to carry so heavy a heart. Life was unkind, nature cruel, fate a trickster. One was caught, as a rat in a trap, "in the fell clutch of circumstance." What was the use of anything? Why any of us, anyhow?

And still not a glimmer of the Admiral! At this season of the year, when he should have been in evidence, it was ominously significant that he should be missing. Peter trudged another half-mile, and stopped to rest.

"Let's put this thing to the test," he said to himself, seriously. "That little chap has always been my Sign. Well, now, if I meet one, something good is going to happen. If I meet two, I'll get my little chance to climb out of this hole. If I meet three, it's me for the open and the big chance to make good. And if I don't meet any at all—why, I'll be nobody but Riverton Peter Champneys."

He didn't give himself the chance that on a time Jean Jacques gave himself when he threw a stone at a tree, and decided that if it struck the tree he'd get to heaven, and if it missed he'd go to hell—but so placed himself that there was nothing for that stone to do but hit the tree in front of it. Peter would run his risks.

And still no Admiral! It was silly; it was superstitious; it was childish; Peter was as well aware of that as anybody could be. But his heart went down like a plummet.

He had turned into the grassy road that led to the River Swamp. The pathway was bordered with sumac and sassafras and flowering elder, and clumps of fennel, and thickets of blackberry bramble. In clear spaces the tall candle of the mullein stood up straight, a flame of yellow flowers flickering over it. Near by was the thistle, shaking its purple paint-brush.

Peter stopped dead in his tracks and stared as if he weren't willing to believe his own eyesight. He went red and white, and his heavy heart turned a cart-wheel, and danced a jig, and began to sing as a young heart should. On the farthest thistle, as if waiting for him to come, as if they knew he must come, with their sails hoisted over their backs, were three Red Admirals!

Peter dropped in the grass, doubled his long legs under him, and watched them, his mouth turned right side up, his eyes golden in his dark face. Two of them presently flew away. The third walked over the thistle, tentatively, flattened his wings to show his sash and shoulder-straps.

"Good morning, good luck! You're still my Sign!" said Peter.

The Red Admiral fluttered his wings again, as if he quite understood. He allowed Peter to admire his under wings, the fore-wings so exquisitely jeweled and enameled, the lower like a miniature design for an oriental prayer-rug. He sent Peter a message with his delicate, sensitive antenna, a wireless message of hope. Then, with his quick, darting motion, he launched himself into his native element and was gone.

The day took on new loveliness, a happy, intimate, all-pervading beauty that flowed into one like light. Never had the trees been so comradely, the grass so friendly, the swamp water so clear, so cool.

For a happy forenoon he worked in Neptune's empty cabin, whose open windows framed blue sky and green woods, and wide, sunny spaces. He ate the lunch Emma Campbell had fixed for him. Then he went over to the edge of the River Swamp and lay under a great oak, and slipping his Bible from his pocket, read the Thirty-seventh Psalm that his mother had so loved. The large, brave, grave words splashed over him like cool water, and the little, hateful things, that had been like festering splinters in his flesh, vanished. There were flowering bay-trees somewhere near by, diffusing their unforgetable fragrance; the flowering bay is the breath of summer in South Carolina. He sniffed the familiar odor, and listened to a redbird's whistle, and to a mocking-bird echoing it; and to the fiddling of grasshoppers, the whispers of trees, the quiet, soft movement of the swamp water. The long thoughts that came to him in the open crossed his mind as clouds cross the sky, idly, moving slowly, breaking up and drifting with the wind. A bee buzzed about a spike of blue lobelia; ants moved up and down the trunk of the oak-tree; birds and butterflies came and went. With his hands under his head, Peter lay so motionless that a great brown water-snake glided upon a branch not ten feet distant, overhanging a brown pool whose depths a spear of sunlight pierced. The young man had a curious sense of personal detachment, such as comes upon one in isolated places. He felt himself a part of the one life of the universe, one with the whistling redbird, the toiling ants, the fluttering butterflies, the chirping grasshoppers, the great brown snake, the trees, the water. The earth breathed audibly against his ear. He sensed the awefulness and beauty of this oneness of all things, and the immortality of that oneness; and in comparison the littleness of his own personal existence. With piercing clarity he saw how brief a time he had to work and to experience the beauty and wonder of his universe. Then, healingly, dreamlessly, wholesomely, he fell asleep, to wake at sunset with a five-mile tramp ahead of him.

Long before he reached Riverton the dark had fallen. It was an evening of many stars. The wind carried with it the salty taste of the sea, and the smell of the warm country.

A light burned in his own dining-room, which was sitting-room as well, and a much pleasanter room than his mother had known, for books had accumulated in it, lending it that note books alone can give. He had added a reading-lamp and a comfortable arm-chair. Emma Campbell's flowers, planted in anything from a tomato-can to an old pot, filled the windows with gay blossoms.

Peter found his supper on a covered tray on the kitchen table. Emma herself had gone off to church. The Seventh Commandment had no meaning for Emma, she was hazy as to mine and thine, but she clung to church membership. She was a pious woman, given to strenuous spells of "wrastlin' wid de Speret."

Peter fetched his tray into the dining-room, and had just touched a match to the spirit kettle, when a motor-car honked outside his gate.

Peter's house was at some distance from the nearest neighbour's, and fancying this must be a complete stranger to have gotten so far off the beaten track as to come down this short street which was nothing but a road ending at the cove, he went to his door prepared to give such directions as might be required.

Somebody grunted, and climbed out of the car. In the glare of the lamps Peter made out a man as tall as himself, in a linen duster that came to his heels, and with an automobile cap and goggles concealing most of his face. The stranger jerked the gate open, and a moment later Peter was confronting the goggled eyes.

"Are you," said a pleasant voice, "by good fortune, Peter Champneys?"

"Well," said Peter, truthfully, "I can't say anything about the good fortune of it, but I'm Peter Champneys."

The stranger paused for a moment. He said in a changed tone: "I have come three thousand miles to have a look at and a talk with you."

"Come in," said Peter, profoundly astonished, "and do it." And he stepped aside.

His guest shook himself out of dust-coat and goggles and stood revealed an old man in a linen suit—a tall, thin, brown, very distinguished-looking old man, with a narrow face, a drooping white mustache, bushy eyebrows, a big nose, and a pair of fine, melancholy brown eyes. He stared at Peter devouringly, and Peter stared back at him quite as interestedly.

"Peter Champneys: Peter Devereaux Champneys, I have come across the continent to see you. Well! Here you are— and here I am. Have you the remotest idea *who* I am? what my name is?" Peter shook his head apologetically. He hadn't the remotest idea. Yet there was something vaguely familiar in the tanned old face, some haunting likeness to somebody, that puzzled him.

"My name," said the old gentleman, "is Champneys—Chadwick Champneys. Your father used to call me Chad, when we were boys together. I'm his brother—and your uncle, Nephew—and glad to make your acquaintance. I'll take it for granted you're as pleased to make mine. Now that I see you clearly, let me add that if I met your skin on a bush in the middle of the Sahara desert, I'd know it for a Champneys hide. Particularly the beak. You look like *me*." Peter stared. It was quite true: he did resemble Chadwick Champneys. The two shook hands.

"But, Uncle Chad—Why, we thought—Well, sir, you see, we heard you were dead."

"Yes. I heard so myself," said Uncle Chad, serenely. "In the meantime, may I ask you for a bite? I'm somewhat hungry."

Peter set another plate for his guest, and brewed tea, and the two drew up to the table. Emma Campbell had provided an excellent meal, and Mr. Chadwick Champneys plied an excellent knife and fork, remarking that when all was said and done one South Carolina nigger was worth six French chefs, and that he hadn't eaten anything so altogether satisfactory for ages.

The more the young man studied the elder man's face, the better he liked it. Figure to yourself a Don Quixote not born in Spain but in South Carolina, not clothed in absurd armor but in a linen suit, and who rode, not on Rosinante but in a motor-car, and you ll have a fair enough idea of the old gentleman who popped into Peter's house that Sunday night.

Peter asked no questions. He sat back, and waited for such information as his guest chose to convey. He felt bewildered, and at the same time happy. He who was so alone of a sudden found that he possessed this relative, and it seemed to

Marie Conway Oemler

him almost too good to be true. That the relative had never before noticed his existence, that he was supposed to be a trifler and a ne'er-do-weel, didn't cloud Peter's joy.

His relative put his feet on a chair, lighted and smoked a cutty, and presently unbosomed himself, jerkily, and with some reluctance. His wife Milly—and whenever he mentioned her name the melancholy in his brown eyes deepened—had been dead some twelve years now. They had had no children. He had wandered from south to west, from Mexico and California and Yucatan to Alaska, always going to strike it lucky and always missing it. To the day of her death Milly had stood by, loyally, lovingly, unselfishly, his one prop and solace, his perfect friend and comrade. There was never, he said, anybody like her. And Milly died. Died poor, in a shack in a mining-town.

He had done something of everything, from selling patent medicines to taking up oil and mining-claims. He couldn't stay put. He really didn't care what happened to him, and so of course nothing happened to him. That's the way things are.

Three years after Milly's death he had fallen in with Feilding, the Englishman. Feilding was almost on his last legs when the two met, and Champneys nursed him back to life. The silent, rather surly Englishman refused to be separated from the man who, he said, had saved his life, and the two struck up a partnership of mutual misfortune. They tramped and starved and worked together, until Feilding died, leaving to his partner his sole possessions—a mining-claim and a patent-medicine recipe. He had felt about down and out, the night Feilding died, for the Englishman was the one real friend he had made, the one person who loved him and whom he loved, after Milly.

But instead of his being down and out, the tide had even then turned for Chadwick Champneys. His friendless wanderings were about done. The mining-claim was worth a very great deal; and the patent medicine did at least some of the things claimed for it. He took it to a certain firm, offering them two thirds of the first and half of the second year's profits for handling the thing for him. They closed with the offer, and from the very first the medicine was a money-maker. It would always be a best-seller.

And then the irony of fate stepped in and took a hand in Chadwick Champneys's affairs. The man who had hitherto been a failure, the man whose touch had seemed able to wither the most promising business sprouts, found himself suddenly possessed of the Midas touch. He couldn't go into anything that didn't double in value. He wasn't able to fail. Let him buy a barren bit of land in Texas, say, and oil would presently be discovered in it; or a God-forsaken tract in the West Virginia mountains, and coal would crop out; or a huddle of mean houses in some unfashionable city district, and immediately commerce and improvement strode in that direction, and what he had bought by the block he sold by the foot.

Because he was alone, and growing old, Champneys's heart turned to his own people. He learned that his brother's orphaned son was still in the South Carolina town. And there was a girl, Milly's niece. These two were the only human beings with whom the rich and lonely man could claim any family ties.

Peter was so breathless with interest and sympathy, so moved by the wanderings of this old Ulysses, and so altogether swept off his feet by the irruption of an uncle into his uncleless existence, that he hadn't time for a thought as to the possible bearing it might have upon his own fortunes.

When, therefore, his uncle wound up with, "I'll tell you, Nephew, it's a mighty comforting thing for a man to have some one of his own blood and name close to his hand to carry on his work and fulfil his plans," Peter came to his senses with a shock as of ice-water poured down his backbone. He knew it wasn't in *him* to carry out any business schemes his uncle might have in mind.

"Uncle Chad," said he, honestly. "Don't be mistaken about me, and don't set your heart on trying to train me into any young Napoleon of Finance. It's not in me." And he added, gently, "I'm sorry I'm a dub. I'd like to please you, and I hate to disappoint you; but you might as well know the truth at once."

Uncle Chad looked him up and down with shrewd eyes.

"So?" said he, and fell to pulling his long mustache. "What's the whole truth, Nephew? If you don't feel equal to learning how to run a million-dollar patent-medicine plant, what *do* you feel you'd be good at, hey?"

"I'm good in my own line: I want to be an artist. I am going to be an artist, if I have to starve to death for it!" said Peter. He spread out his hands. "I have one life to live, and one thing to do!" he cried.

"Oh, an artist! I've never heard of any Champneys before you who had such a hankering, though I'm quite sure it's all right, if you like it, Nephew. There's no earthly reason why an artist shouldn't be a gentleman, though I could wish you'd have taken over the patent-medicine business, instead. Have you got anything I can see?"

Shyly and reluctantly, Peter began to show him. There were two or three oils by now; powerful sketches of country life, with its humor and pathos; heads of children and of negroes; bits of the River Swamp; all astonishingly well done.

"Paintings are curious things; some have got life and some haven't got anything I can see, except paint. There was one I saw in New York, now. I thought at first it was a mess of spinach. I stood off and looked, and I walked up close and looked, and still I couldn't see anything but the same green mess. But—will you believe it, Nephew?—that thing was The Woods in Spring! Thinks I, They evidently *boil* their Woods in Spring up here, before painting 'em! The things one paints nowadays don't look like the things they're painted from, I notice. I'm afraid these things of yours look too much like real things to satisfy folks it's real art.—You sure the Lord meant you to be an artist?"

Peter laughed. "I'm sure I mean myself to be an artist, Uncle Chad."

"Want to get away from Riverton, don't you? But that costs money? And you haven't got the money?"

"I want to get away from Riverton. But that costs money, and I haven't got the money," admitted Peter.

"I see. Now, Nephew, when it gets right down to the thing he really wants to do, every man has some horse sense, even if he happens to be a fool in everything else. I'll talk to your horse sense and save time."

Peter, in the midst of scattered drawings, and of the few oils backed up against the dining-room wall, paused.

"I could wish," said his uncle, slowly, "that you were— different. But you are what you are, and it would be a waste of time to try to make you different. You say you have one thing to do. All right, Peter Champneys, you shall have your chance to do it,—with a price-tag attached. Do you want to be what you say you want to be hard enough to be willing to pay the price for it?"

"You mean—to go away from here—to study? To see real pictures—and be a student under a real teacher?" Peter's voice all but failed him. His face went white, and his eyes glittered. He began to tremble. His uncle, watching him narrowly, nodded.

"Yes. Just that. Everything that can help you, you shall have—time, teachers, money, travel. But first you must pay me my price."

Peter could only lean forward and stare. He was afraid he was going to wake up in a minute.

"Let me see if I can make it quite clear to you, Peter. You never knew Milly—my wife Milly. You're not in love, Son, are you? No? Well, you won't be able to understand—yet."

"There was my mother, sir," said Peter, gently.

"I'm sorry," said the other, just as gently. "I wish it had come sooner, the luck. But it didn't, and I can't do anything for Milly,—or for your mother. They're gone." For a moment he hung his head.

"But, Peter, I can do considerable for you, and I mean to do it. Only I can't bear to think Milly shouldn't have her share in it. We never had a child of our own, but there's Milly's niece."

"Oh, but of course, Uncle Chad! Aunt Milly's niece ought to come in for all you can do for her, even before me," said

Peter, heartily, and with entire good faith.

"You are your father's son," said Uncle Chad, ambiguously. "But what I wish to impress upon you is, that neither of you comes before the other: you come together." He paused again, and from this time on never removed his eyes from his nephew's face, but watched him hawk-like. "You will understand there is a great deal of money—enough money to found a great American family. Why shouldn't that family be the Champneyses? Why shouldn't the Champneyses be restored to their old place, put where they rightfully belong? And who and what should bring this about, except you, and Milly's niece, and my money!"

"I'm afraid I don't quite understand," said Peter, and looked as bewildered as he felt. He wasn't a quick thinker. "What is it you wish me to do?"

Still holding his eyes, "I want you to marry Milly's niece," said Chadwick Champneys. "*That's my price.*"

"Marry? I? Oh, but, Uncle Chad! Why, I don't even know the girl, nor she me! I've never so much as heard of her until this minute!" cried Peter.

"What difference does that make? Men and women never know each other until after they're married anyhow," said his uncle, sententiously. "Peter, do you really wish to go abroad and study? Very well, then: marry Milly's niece. I'll attend to everything else."

"But *why*? My good God! why?" Peter's eyes popped.

"Nephew," said his uncle, patiently, "you are the last Champneys; she is Milly's niece—my Milly's niece. And Milly is dead, and I am practically under sentence of death myself. I have got to put my affairs in order. I'd hardly learned I was a very rich man before I also learned my time was limited. On high authority. Heart, Nephew. I may last for several years. Or go out like a puff of wind, before morning."

Peter was so genuinely shocked and distressed at this that his uncle smiled to himself. The boy was a true Champneys.

"There is no error in the diagnosis, so I accept what I can't help, and in the meantime arrange my affairs. Now, Nephew Peter, business man or artist the Champneys name is in your keeping. You are the head of the house, so to speak. I supply the funds to refurnish the house, we'll say, and I give you your opportunity to do what you want to do, to make your mark in your own way. In exchange you accept the wife I provide for you. When I meet Milly again, I want to tell her there's somebody of her own blood bearing our name, taking the place of the child we never had, enjoying all the good things we missed, and enjoying them with a Champneys, *as* a Champneys. If there are to be Champneys children, I want Milly's niece to bear them. I won't divide my money between two separate houses; it must all go to Peter Champneys and his wife, that wife being Milly's niece." His eyes began to glitter, his mouth hardened. "It is little enough to ask!" he cried, raising his voice. "I give you everything else. I do not ask you to change your profession. I make that profession possible by supplying the means to pursue it. In payment you marry Milly's niece."

His manner was so passionately earnest that the astonished boy took his head in his hands to consider this amazing proposition.

"But how in heaven's name can I study if I'm plagued with a wife?" he demanded. "I want to be foot-loose!"

"All right. You shall be foot-loose, for seven years, let's say," said his uncle, quietly. "I reason that if you are ever going to be anything, you'll at least have made a beginning within seven years! You're twenty now, are you not? When you marry my girl, you shall go abroad immediately. She'll stay with me until her education is completed. Your wife shall be trained to take her proper place in the world. On your twenty-seventh birthday you will return and claim her. I do not need anything more than the bare word of a Champneys that he'll be what a man should be. Milly's niece will be safe in your keeping.—Well?"

"Let me think a bit, Uncle."

"Take until morning. In the meanwhile, please help me get my car under shelter, and show me where I turn in for the night." Being in some things a very considerate old man, he did not add that he had found the day strenuous, and that his strength was ebbing.

Peter, lying on the lounge in the dining-room, was unable to sleep. Was this the chance his mother had said would come? Wasn't matrimony rather a small price to pay for it? Or was it? And—hadn't he promised his mother to take it when it came, for the sake of all the Champneyses dead and gone, and for her own sake who had loved him so tenderly and believed in him against all odds?

At dawn he stole out of the house, and walked the three miles to the country cemetery where his mother slept beside his father. He sat beside her last bed, and remembered the cold hand that had crept into his, the faltering whisper that prayed him to take his chance when it came, and to prove himself.

If he refused this miraculous opportunity, there would be

Riverton, and the hardware store, or other country stores similar to it, to the end of his days. No freedom, no glorious opportunities, no work of brain and hand together, no beauty wrought of thought and experience; the purple peaks fading into farther and farther distances until they faded out of his sky altogether; and himself a sorry plodder in a path whose dust choked him. Peter shuddered. Anything but that!

Mr. Chadwick Champneys was sitting by the dining-room table talking to astonished Emma Campbell, and stroking the cat, when Peter came swinging into the room.

"Well?" with a keen glance at his nephew's face.

"Yes," said Peter, deliberately.

The old man went on stroking the cat for a moment or so, while Emma Campbell, the hominy-spoon in her hand, watched them both. She understood that something momentous portended. Not for nothing had this shrewd, imperious old man whom she had known in his youth as wild Chad Champneys, led Emma on to tell him all she knew about the family history since his departure, years ago. When Emma had finished, Chadwick Champneys felt that he knew his nephew to the bone; and it was Champneys bone!

"Thank you, Nephew," said he, in a deep voice. "You're a good lad. You won't regret your bargain. I promise you that."

He turned to Emma Campbell:

"If my breakfast is ready, I'm ready too, Emma." And to Peter: "We were renewing our old acquaintance, Emma and I, while you were out, Nephew. She hasn't changed much: she's still the biggest nigger and the best cook and the faithfulest friend in all Carolina."

"Oh, go 'long, Mist' Chad! Who you 'speck ought to look after Miss Maria's chile, 'ceptin' ole Emma Campbell? Lawd 'a' mussy, ain't I wiped 'is nose en dusted 'is britches sense he bawn? Dat Peter, he belonged to Miss Maria en me. He's we chile," said Emma Campbell.

Over his coffee Mr. Champneys outlined his plans carefully and succinctly. Peter was to hold himself in readiness to proceed whither his uncle would direct him by wire. In the meantime he was to settle his affairs in Riverton.

"Uncle Chad," said Peter, to whom the thought had just occurred, "Uncle Chad, now that I have agreed to do what you wish me to do, what is the young lady's name? You didn't tell me."

"Her name? Why, God bless my soul, I forgot, I forgot! Well! Her name's Anne Simms. Called Nancy. Soon be Nancy Champneys, thank Heaven!" And he repeated: "Nancy Champneys! Anne Champneys!"

"Uncle," said Peter, deprecatingly, "you'll understand—I'm a little interested—excuse me for asking you—but what does the young lady look like?"

Mr. Chadwick Champneys blinked at his nephew.

"Look like? You want to know what Milly's niece looks like?"

"Yes, sir," said Peter, modestly. "I—er—that is, the thought occurred to me to ask you what she looks like."

Mr. Champneys scratched the end of his nose, pulled his mustache, and looked unhappy.

Marie Conway Oemler

"Nephew Peter," said he, "do what I do: take it for granted Milly's niece looks like any other girl—nose and mouth and hair and eyes, you know. But I can't describe her to you in detail."

"No? Why?" Peter wondered.

"Because I have never laid eyes on her," said his uncle.

"Oh!" Peter looked thunderstruck.

"I came to you first," explained his uncle. "I gave you first whack. Now I'm going to see her."

"Oh!" said Peter, still more thunderstruck.

"I'll wire you when you're to come," said his uncle, briskly, and got into dust-coat, cap, and goggles. A few minutes later, before the little town was well awake, he vanished in a cloud of dust down the Riverton Road.

CHAPTER VII

WHERE THE ROAD DIVIDED

Emma Campbell stood in the middle of the kitchen floor, lips pursed, eyes fixed on vacancy, a dish-cloth dangling from one hand, a carving-knife clutched in the other, and projecked. And the more she projecked about what was happening in Peter's house, the less she liked it. It had never occurred to Emma Campbell that Peter might go away from Riverton. Yet now he was going, and it had been taken for granted that she, Emma, who, as she said, had "raised 'im from a puppy up'ards," wouldn't mind staying on here after his departure. Fetching a cold sigh from the depths of an afflicted bosom, Emma moved snail-like toward the work in hand; and as she worked she howled dismally that nobody knew the trouble she saw, "nobody knew but you, Lawd."

When Peter came in to dinner, she addressed him with distant politeness as Mistuh Champneys, instead of the usual Mist' Peter. When he spoke to her she accordion-plaited her lips, and stuck her eyes out at him. Her head, adorned with more than the usual quota of toothpicks, brought the quills upon the fretful porcupine forcibly to one's mind.

Nobody but Peter Champneys could or would have borne with Emma Campbell's contrary fits, but as neither of them realized this they managed to get along beautifully. Peter was well aware that when the car that had suddenly appeared in the night had just as suddenly disappeared in the morning in a cloud of dust on the Riverton Road, Emma's peace of mind had vanished also. He understood, and was patient.

She clapped a platter of crisp fried chicken before him, and stood by, eyeing him and it grimly. And when hungry Peter thrust his fork into a tempting piece, "You know who you eatin'?" she demanded pleasantly.

Peter didn't know whom he was eating; fork suspended, he looked at Emma questioningly.

"You eatin' Lula, dat who you eatin'," Emma told him with grisly unction. "Dem's de same laigs use to scratch roun' we kitchen do'. Dat's de same lovin'-hearted hen I raise fum a baby. But, Lawd! Whut *you* care? *You's* de sort kin go trapesin' off by yo'se'f over de worl'. You dat uppidy dese days, whut *you* care 'bout eatin' up po' lil Lula? *She* ain't nobody but us-all's chicken, nohow!"

Peter looked doubtfully at "po' lil Lula's" remains, and laid down his fork. Somehow, one can't be keen about eating a loving-hearted hen.

"But, Emma, we eat our chickens all the time! You've fried me many a chicken without raising a row about it!" he protested.

"Who tol' you dey wuz ours?"

As Peter hadn't a fitting reply in return for this ambiguous query, Emma bounced out of the dining-room, to return in a moment with the tea-pot; when Peter held out his cup, she poured into it plain boiling water. At that she set the tea-pot hastily upon the table, threw her gingham apron over her head, and plumped upon the floor with a thud that made the house shake. It frightened the cat into going through the window at a leap, taking with him all the flowers planted in tomato-cans.

"Emma," said Peter, severely, "I'm ashamed of you! Take that silly apron off your head and listen to me. You know very well you aren't being left to shift for yourself. You'll be provided for better than you've ever been. Why, all you'll have to do—"

"All I'll hab to do is jes' crawl into my grave en stay dere. I done raised 'im fum de egg up, en now he's got comb en kin crow it's tail-feathers over de fence en fly off wid 'im! Ah, Lawd! You done made 'em en You knows whut roosters is like!"

"Emma! Look here, confound it!—"

"Who gwine look after 'im? I axes you fum my heart, who gwine do it?—Never did hab no mo' sense dan a rabbit widout I's by, en now dey aims to tun 'im loose! Ah, Lawd!"

"Emma, listen! Emma, what the—"

"Dem furrin women'll do 'im lak dem women done po' old Cassius. *Dey'll conjure 'im*! En widout I by, who gwine make 'im put one live frawg on 'is nekked stummick, so's to sweat de speret o' dat frawg een, en de speret o' dat conjure out? No-buddy. Den he'll up en die. Widout one Gawd's soul o' 'is own folkses to put de coppers on 'is eyes en' tie up de corpse's jaws.—Ah Lawd, ah Lawd!"

"Oh, shut up, you old idiot! I'm not coming home to my meals any more, if this is how you're going to behave!" This from Peter, disgustedly.

"Ain't you, suh? All right, suh, Mistuh Champneys, you's be boss. But I glad to my Gawd Miss Maria ain't 'yuh to see dis day!" And Emma began to sniffle.

Peter pushed his untouched dinner aside, and reached for his hat. He looked at Emma Campbell irefully.

"Damn!" exploded Peter.

Emma Campbell got to her feet with astounding quickness, ran into the kitchen, and returned in a moment with another platter of chicken, rice, and gravy.

"'Yuh, chile. Set down en eat yo' bittles. You ain't called on to hab no hard feelin's 'bout *dis* chicken. 'T ain't none o' ours, nohow." Peter resumed his chair and waived cross-examination.

Mr. Champneys having come, so to speak, between dark and daylight, Riverton knew nothing about his visit, for Peter hadn't thought to inform them. This affair seemed so unreal, so improbable, so up in the air, that he dared not mention it. Suppose it mightn't be true, after all. Suppose fate played a cruel joke. Suppose Mr. Champneys changed his mind. So Peter, who had a horror of talk, and writhed when asked personal questions by people who felt that they had a perfect right to know all about his business, kept strict silence, and enjoined the same silence upon Emma Campbell, who could be trusted to hold her tongue when bidden.

Now, one simply cannot remember the price of pots and pans and sheet-iron and plows and ax-handles, when one is living in the beginning of an astounding fairy story, when the most momentous change is impending, when one's whole way of life is about to be diverted into different channels. The things one hates, like being a hardware clerk, for instance, automatically slide into the background when the desire of the heart approaches.

But Mr. Humphreys, whose mind and fortune naturally enough centered in his hardware store, couldn't be expected to know that the impossible had happened for Peter Champneys. He would hardly be able to take Peter's bare word for it, even if Peter should tell him: he didn't know that his absent-minded clerk really liked him, and longed to tell him that he was leaving Riverton shortly—he hoped for years and years—and was only awaiting the message that should speed his departure. Mr. Humphreys, then, cannot be blamed for complaining with feeling and profanity that of all the damidjits he had ever seen in his life, Peter Champneys was about the worst. Loony was no name for him, and what was to become of such a chump he didn't know. "If this thing keeps up, he'll be drooling before he's forty, and we'll have to hire a nigger to feed him out of a papspoon," said Mr. Humphreys, forebodingly.

And in the meanwhile the days dragged and dragged—two whole weeks of suspense and expectancy. On the Monday of the third week the end of Peter's waiting and of Mr. Humphreys's patience came together. One, in fact, brought about the other. The postman who drove in with the daily mail brought for Peter Champneys the yellow envelope toward which he had been looking with such feverish impatience.

He was really to go! The young man experienced that reeling, ecstatic shock which shakes one when a long-delayed desire suddenly assumes reality. He stood with the telegram in his fingers, and stared about the dusty, dingy, uninteresting store, and saw as with new eyes how hopelessly hideous it really was; and wondered and wondered if he were really himself, Peter Champneys, who was going to get away from it.

At that moment stout old Mrs. Beach entered the store and waddled up to him. Mrs. Beach was a woman who never knew what she really wanted, or if, indeed, she really wanted anything in particular; but then again, as she said, she *might*. She didn't like to leave her house often; and when she did finally make up her mind to dress and go out, she popped into every store she happened to pass, on the chance that she *might* want something from it, and would thus save herself an extra trip to get it. She would say to a perspiring clerk:

"Now, let me see: there's something I wanted to get from this store. I know it, because on Tuesday last something happened to put me in mind of it—or was it Wednesday, maybe? I know it's something I need about the house—or maybe the yard. You'll have to help me out. I've got a poor memory, but you just sort of run over a list of things folks would be most likely to need and maybe you'll hit on the right thing, and if it's that I want, I'll get it right now. Don't stand there like a hitching-post, boy! Why can't you suggest something, and help out a woman old enough to be your mother?"

If by some fortuitous chance you happened to hit upon an article she thought she might happen to need, and it suited her, she would buy it. But it never occurred to her to thank you for your help, or to apologize for the nerve-racking strain to which she subjected you.

"Young man," said her testy voice in Peter's ear, "I've got to get something and I can't remember what it is. You've got to help me. I can't be wasting my time at my age o' life running around to hardware stores."

Peter thrust the miraculous telegram in his pocket, where he could feel it burn and tingle. Oh, it was true, it was true! He was going to get away from all this!

"For heaven's sake, boy, don't stand there gawping at me like a thunderstruck owl! You surely know about everything you've got in this store, don't you? Well, then, Peter Champneys, look about you and see if you can't light on what I'm most likely to need!"

Peter, mind on the telegram in his pocket, did indeed look at the old lady owlishly. Hazily he remembered certain grueling, sweating half-hours spent in trying to discover what Mrs. Beach thought she might want to buy. Hazily he looked from her to the littered shelves, and reached for the first object upon which his eyes happened to fall.

"Yes 'm, Mrs. Beach. I reckon this is what you'd most likely *need*," said Peter, gently, and placed in her hand a fine new muzzle. (Paris, maybe Rome; and Florence! Oh, names to conjure with! And he should see them all, walk their historic streets, view immortal work, stand before immortal canvases, and say with Correggio: "And I, too, am a painter!")

"Oh, my dear Lord, save me from bursting wide open! Why, you impudent young reprobate!" Mrs. Beach's outraged voice banished his dream. "For two pins, Peter Champneys, I'd take you across my knees and spank the seat off your breeches! I need a muzzle, do I? I'm to be insulted by a little squirt that's just learning to keep his ears clean! Well! Girl and woman I've been dealing with Sam Humphreys and his father before him, but from this day forth I put no foot of mine across this store door!" All the while she spoke she brandished the muzzle at Peter and kept backing him off into a corner.

Mr. Humphreys came hurriedly out of his office upon hearing the uproar, and sought with soothing speech to placate his irate old friend and customer. But Mrs. Beach wasn't to be placated. She went out of the door and down the street like a hat on a windy day.

Mr. Humphreys watched her go. Then he turned and looked at Peter Champneys, ominously:

"Peter,"—Mr. Humphreys, carefully restraining himself, spoke in low and dulcet tones—"Peter, I have tried to do my duty as a Christian man; now I have to do it as a hardware man, and right here is where you and I say good-by. I have passed over," said Mr. Humphreys, swallowing hard, "your sending gravel to the grocer and a bellows to the minister by mistake; but this is the limit. If there is anybody advertising for a gilt-edged failure as a salesman, you go apply for the job and say I recommend you enthusiastically. I hate like the devil to fire you, Peter, but it's a plain case of self-defense with me: I have to do it. You're fired. Now. Come on in the office," said Mr. Humphreys, eagerly, "and I'll pay you off."

Peter slid his hand into his pocket and pinched that precious slip of paper. Then he smiled into Mr. Humphreys's empurpled visage.

"Why, thank you, Mr. Humphreys," said he, gratefully. "I know just how you feel, and I don't blame you in the least. I've been wanting to tell you I had to quit, and you've saved me the trouble."

Sam Humphreys knew that Peter Champneys had no right to stand there and smile like that at such a solemn moment. He should have appeared ashamed, downcast, humanly perturbed; and he didn't in the least.

"I've been wondering ever since the first day I hired you how I was going to keep from firing you before nightfall. Now the end's come. Say—suppose you go on home, right now. Because," said Mr. Humphreys, softly, "I mightn't be able to refrain from committing justifiable homicide. I'll send you your salary to-night. Go on home. Please!"

To his horror, Peter Champneys of a sudden laughed aloud. It was genuine laughter, that rang true and gay and glad. His eyes sparkled, and a dash of good red jumped into his sallow cheeks.

"Good-by, then, Mr. Humphreys. And thank you for many kindnesses, and for real patience," said Peter. He waved his hand at the dusty store in a wide-flung gesture of glad farewell.

"Oh, my God! He's run plumb crazy!" cried Mr. Humphreys, mopping his brow. "I always said that boy wasn't natural!"

But Peter, walking home in the bright afternoon sunlight, for the first time in his life felt young and free and happy. He wanted to laugh, to sing, to shout, to skip. Emma Campbell was just bringing the washed-and-dried dinner dishes back into the dining-room when he bounced in.

"Emma," said he, sticking his thumbs into the armholes of his waistcoat, and beaming at her, "Emma, I'm out of a job. Kicked out neck and crop. Fired, thank God!"

Emma stacked her dishes on the old deal dresser.

"Is you?"

"I sure am. And, Emma, listen. I—I'm sort of waked up. Even if things shouldn't turn out as I hope they will, I'll manage to go ahead, somehow. I'd get out, now, under any circumstances. Pike's Peak or bust!" said Peter.

"When you 'speck to go?"

"Just as soon as I can get out. I'm expected in New York within ten days at the latest. And then, Emma, the wide world! No more little-town tittle-tattle! All I've got to do, in the big world, is to deliver the goods. And I'm going to deliver the goods!" said Peter.

But Emma Campbell put her grizzled head on the dining-room table and began to cry.

"I nussed you w'en you had de croup en de colic. I used to tromp up en down dis same no' wid you 'crost my shoulder. It was me dressed Miss Maria de day she married wid yo' pa, en it was me dressed 'er for de coffin. You en me been stannin' togedder ever sence. How I gwine stan' by my alonese 'f now? I ole now, Mist' Peter."

"Emma," said Peter, after a pause, "tell me exactly what you want me to do for you and if I can I'll do it."

"I wants to go wid you. I jes' natchelly ain't gwine stay 'yuh by my alonese 'f," wept Emma.

Peter looked at her with the sort of tenderness one must be born in the South to understand. Born in the last years of slavery, brought up in wild Reconstruction days, Emma couldn't read or write. She wasn't amenable to discipline. She was, as Cassius had complained, "so contrary she mus' be 'flicted wid de moonness." She wore a rabbit foot and a conjure bag and believed in ha'nts and hoodoos. But, as far back as he could remember, Emma Campbell had formed a large part of the background of his life. He wondered just what he would have done if it hadn't been for Emma, after his mother's death. There slid into his mind the picture of a shabby youngster weeping over a cheap green-and-gold Collection of Poetic Gems; and he reached over and laid a brown hand upon a black one.

"Well, and why not?" mused Peter. "You stood by me when I hadn't any money; why should you leave me the minute I get it? But are you sure you really want to go along, Emma? I'm going into a foreign country, remember. You won't be able to understand a word anybody says. You'll be a mighty lonesome old nigger over there."

"I can talk wid my cat, can't I?"

"Holy Moses! What, the cat, too?" Peter ran his hands through his hair, distractedly.

"Whah you goes, I goes. En whah I goes, dat cat goes. Dat cat 's we-all's folks."

"Oh, all right," said Peter, resignedly. After all, Emma Campbell and the cat *were* all the folks he had.

He went to Charleston the next morning, in accordance with the instructions his uncle had given him in their last talk, and the bank at which he presented himself treated him with distinguished consideration. Peter heard for the first time the dulcet accents of Money.

Like Mr. Wilfer in "Our Mutual Friend," Peter had never had everything all together all at once. When he had a suit his shoes were shabby, and when it got around to shoes his coat was shiny in the seams and his hat of last year's vintage. He was boyishly delighted to buy at one time all that he wanted, but as made-to-order clothes were altogether outside of his reckoning as yet, he bought ready-made. His taste was too simple to be essentially bad, but you knew he was a country boy in store clothes and a made tie.

He had never been in Charleston before, and he reveled in the ineluctable charm of the lovely old town. No South Carolinian is ever disappointed in Charleston. Peter thought the city resembled one of her own old ladies, a dear dignified gentlewoman in reduced circumstances, in a worn silk gown and a mended lace cap and a cameo brooch. It might be against the old gentlewoman's religious convictions to bestow undue care upon her personal appearance, but hers was a venerable, unforgetable, and most beautiful old face for all that, and perhaps because of it. She knew that the kingdom of God is within; and being sure of that, she was sure of herself, serene, unpainted, unpretentious.

Peter wandered by old walled gardens in which were set wrought-iron gates that allowed the passer-by a glimpse of greenery and flowers, but prevented encroachments upon family privacy. Every now and then a curving balustrade, a gable, a window, or an old doorway of surpassing charm made his fingers itch for pencil and paper. He reflected, without bitterness, that the doors of every one of these fine old houses had on a time opened almost automatically to a Champneys. Some of these folk were kith and kin, as his mother had remembered and they, perhaps, had forgotten. This didn't worry him in the least: the real interest the houses had for Peter was that this one had a picturesque garden gate, that one a door with a fan-light he'd like to sketch.

He climbed St. Michael's belfry stairway and looked over the city, and toward the sea; and later wandered through its historic churchyard. One very simple memorial held him longest, because it is the only one of its kind among all those records of state honor and family pride, and seems rather to belong to the antique Greek and Roman world which accepted death as the final fact, than to a Carolina churchyard.

> SARAH JOHNSTON
> born in this province
> 29th May 1690
> Died 26th April 1774
> In the 84th year of her age.

> How lovd how valu'd once avails Thee not
> To whom related or by whom begot
> A heap of dust alone remains of Thee.

That covered the Champneyses, too. To whom related or by whom begot, a heap of dust alone remained of them. So much for all human pride! Peter left St. Michael's dead to slumber in peace, and walked for an hour on the Battery, and in Legare Street, where life is brightest in the old city. All good Charlestonians think that after the final resurrection there may be a new heaven and a new earth for others, but for themselves a house in Legare Street or on the Battery.

Peter presently reappeared in Riverton, discreetly clad in his customary clothes, the habits of thrift being yet so firmly ingrained in him that he couldn't easily wear his best clothes on a week-day.

"Peter! You Peter Champneys! Look here a minute, will you?" Mrs. Beach called, as he was passing her house.

Peter stopped. His smiling countenance somewhat astonished Mrs. Beach.

"Peter, I've heard about Sam Humphreys firing you on account of me getting mad at you about that muzzle. Now, while I know in my heart you'd have been fired about something or other, sooner or later, I do wish to my Lord it hadn't been on account of me. Not that I don't think you're an impudent young rapscallion, that never sets his nose inside a church door, and insults old women with muzzles. But I knew your mother well, and I wish it wasn't on account of me Sam Humphreys discharged you." There was real feeling in the testy old lady's face and voice.

"Don't you bother your head about it one minute more, Mrs. Beach. All I'm sorry for is that I appeared to be impertinent to you, when I hadn't any such notion. I was thinking about something else at the time. So you'll just have to forgive me."

"I do," said the old lady, mollified. After all, Maria Champneys's boy couldn't be altogether trifling! "Is what I hear true, that you're going away from Riverton? Folks say you've got a job in the city."

"Yes 'm, I'm going away."

"I reckon it's just as well. You'll do better away from Riverton. You'll have to."

"Yes 'm, I'll have to," agreed Peter. He held out his hand, and the old lady found herself wringing it, and wishing him good luck.

At home he found Emma Campbell carefully packing up all the worthless plunder it had taken her many years to collect. When he had heartlessly rejected all she didn't need, she had one small trunk and a venerable carpet-bag. Everything else was nailed up. The house itself was to be looked after by the town marshal, who was also the town real-estate agent. Peter was very vague as to his return.

No railroad runs through Riverton, but the river steamers come and go daily, the town usually quitting work to foregather at the pier to welcome coming and speed departing travelers. All Riverton made it a point to be on hand the morning Peter Champneys left home to seek his fortune.

Peter never did anything like anybody else. There was always some diverting bit of individual lunacy to make his proceedings interesting. This morning Riverton discovered that Emma Campbell was going away, too. Emma appeared in a black cashmere dress, a blue-and-white checked gingham apron on which a basket of flowers was embroidered in red cross-stitch, and a white bandana handkerchief wound around her head under a respectable black sailor hat. She carried a large, square cage that had once housed a mocking-bird, and now held the Champneys big black cat. Laughter and delighted comments greeted the bird-cage, and her carpet-bag received almost as much attention and applause. Riverton hadn't seen a bag like that since Reconstruction, and it made the most of its opportunity.

"Emma! Aren't you afraid you'll let the cat out of the bag?"

Emma remained haughtily silent.

"Emma, where you-all goin'?"

"We-all gwine whah we gwine, dat's whah we gwine." This from Emma, succinctly.

"What you goin' to do when you get there?" persisted the wag.

"Who, us? We gwine do whut you-all ain't know how to do: we gwine min' our own business," said Emma, politely.

"Good-by, Peter! Don't set the world on fire, old scout!"

When the boat turned the bend in the river that hid the small town of his birth from his view, Peter felt shaken as he had never thought to be. Good-by, little home town, where the slings and arrows of outrageous fortune had rained upon him!

The boat swung into a side channel to escape a sand-bar. She was in deep water, but very close to the shore, so close that he could see the leaves on the trees quivering and shimmering in the river breeze and the late summer sunlight. Over there, as the crow flies, lay the River Swamp, and Neptune's gray, deserted cabin. They had been his refuge. No other place, no other woods in all the world could quite take their place, or be like them. And he knew there would be many a day when he must ache with homesick longing for the coast country, for the tide-water, and the jessamines, and the moon above the pines, and the scent of the bay in flower on summer nights. The world was opening her wide spaces. But the Carolina coast was *home*.

"I wish," said Peter, and his chin quivered, "I wish there were some one thing that typified you, something of you I could take with me wherever I go. I wish you had a spirit I could see, and know."

Out from the shore-line, where the earliest golden-rod was just beginning to show that it intended to blossom by and by, and the ironweed was purple, and the wild carrot was white and lacy, and the orange-red milkweed was about ready to close her house for the season, came fluttering with a quick, bold sureness the gallantest craft of all the fairy sail-boats of the sky, hovered for a bright second over the steamer's rail, and scudded for the other shore.

Peter Champneys straightened his shoulders. Youth and courage and hope flashed into his wistful face, and brightened his eyes that followed the Red Admiral.

CHAPTER VIII

CINDERELLA

It wasn't a pleasant house, being of a dingy, bilious-yellow complexion, with narrow window eyes, and a mean slit of a doorway for a mouth; not sinister, but common, stupid, and uninteresting. If one should happen to be a house-psychologist, one would know that behind the Nottingham lace curtains looped back with soiled red ribbons, was all the tawdry, horrible junk that clutters such houses, even as mental junk clutters the minds of the people who have to live in them. One knew that the people who dwelt in that house didn't know how to live, how to think, or how to cook; and that if by any chance a larger life, a real thought, or a bit of good cooking confronted them, they would probably reject it with suspicion.

The elderly gentleman in white linen who made acquaintance with this particular house on a very sultry noon in early August, hesitated before he rang the bell. He glanced over his shoulder at the hot, dusty street where a swarm of hot, dusty children were shrilling and shrieking, or staring at him round-eyed, dived into his pockets, fished up a handful of small change, whistled to insure their greater attention, and flung the coin among them. While they were snatching at the money like a flock of pigeons over a handful of grain, the elderly gentleman rang the bell. He could hear it jangling through the house, but it brought no immediate response. After a decent interval he rang again. This time the door was jerked open, and a girl in a bungalow apron, upon which she was wiping her hands, confronted him. She was a very young girl, a very hot, tired, perspiring, and sullen girl, fresh from a broiling kitchen and a red-hot stove.

She looked at the caller suspiciously, her glance racing over his linen suit, his white shoes, the Panama hat in his hand. She was puzzled, for plainly this wasn't the usual applicant for board and lodging. Perhaps, then, he was a successful house-to-house agent for some indispensable necessity—say an ice-pick that would pull nails, open a can, and peel potatoes. Or maybe a religious book agent. She rather suspected him of wanting to sell her Biblical Prophecies Elucidated by a Chicago Seer, or something like that. Or, stay: perhaps he was a church scout sent out to round up stray souls. Whatever he might be, she was bitterly resentful of having been taken from the thick of her work to answer his ring. She wasn't interested in her soul, her hot and tired body being a much more immediate concern. Heaven is far off, and hell has no terrors and less interest for a girl immured in a red-hot kitchen in a Middle Western town in the dog-days.

"If it's a Bible, we got one. If it's sewin'-machines, we ain't, but don't. If it's savin' our souls, we belong to church reg'lar an' ain't interested. If it's explainin' God, nothin' doin'! An' if it's tack-pullers with nail-files an' corkscrews on 'em, you can save your breath," said the girl rapidly, in a heated voice, and with a half-dry hand on the door-knob.

Mr. Chadwick Champneys's long, drooping mustache came up under his nose, and his bushy eyebrows twitched.

Marie Conway Oemler

"I am not trying to sell anything," he said hurriedly, in order to prevent her from shutting the door in his face, which was her evident intention.

She said impatiently: "If you're collectin', this ain't our day for payin', an' you got to call again. Come next week, on Tuesday. Or maybe Wednesday or Thursday or Friday or Sattiday." The door began to close.

He inserted a desperate foot.

"I wish to see Miss Simms—Miss Anne, or Nancy Simms. My information is that she lives in this house. I should have stated my errand at once, had I been allowed to do so." He looked at the girl reprovingly.

Before she could reply, a female voice from a back region rose stridently:

"Nancy! You Nancy! What in creation you mean, gassin' this hour o' day when them biscuits is burnin' up in the oven? Send that feller about his business, whatever it is, and you come tend to yours!"

The girl hesitated, and frowned.

"If you come to see Anne Simms, same as Nancy Simms, I'm her—I mean, she's me," said she, hurriedly. "I got no time to talk with you now, Mister, but you can wait in the parlor until I dish up dinner, and whilst they're eatin' I'll have time to run up and see what you want. Is it partic'ler?"

"Very."

"Come on in an' wait, then."

"Nancy! You want I should come up there after you? Oh, my stars, an' that girl *knows* how partic'ler Poppa is about his biscuits; they gotta be jest so or he won't look at 'em, an' her gassin' and him likely to raise the roof!" screamed the voice.

"Oh, shut up! I'm comin'," bawled the girl in reply. "You better sit over there by the winder, Mister," she told her visitor, hastily. "There's a breeze there, maybe. You'll find to-day's paper an' a fan on the table." She vanished, and he could hear her running kitchenward, and the shrieking voice subsiding into a whine.

Mr. Chadwick Champneys slumped limply into a chair. Everything he looked at added to his sense of astonishment and unease.

The outside of the house hadn't lied: the inside matched it. Mr. Champneys found himself staring and being stared at by the usual crayon portraits of defunct members of the family,—at least he hoped they were defunct,—the man with a long mule face and neck whiskers; and opposite him his spouse, with her hair worn like mustard-plasters on the skull. "Male and female created He them." Placed so that you had to see it the moment you entered the door, on a white-and-gold easel draped with a silkoline scarf trimmed with pink crocheted wheels, was a virulently colored landscape with a house of unknown architecture in the foreground, and mother-of-pearl puddles outside the gate. Mr. Champneys studied those mother-of-pearl puddles gravely. They hurt his feelings. So did the ornate golden-oak parlor set upholstered in red plush; and the rug on the floor, in which colors fought like Kilkenny cats; and a pink vase with large purple plums bunched on it; and the figured wall-paper, and the unclean lace curtains, and the mantel loaded with sorry plunder, and the clothespin butterflies, the tissue-paper parasols, and the cheap fans tacked to the walls. It was a hot and dusty room.

Marie Conway Oemler

The smell of bad cooking, of countless miserable meals eaten by men whose digestion they would ruin, clung to it and would not be gainsaid. Mr. Champneys thought the best thing that could happen to such houses would be a fire beginning in the cellar and ending at the roof.

His mind went back to another house—an old white house in South Carolina, set in spacious grounds, with high-ceilinged, cool, large rooms filled with fine old furniture, a few pictures, glimpses of brass and silver, large windows opening upon lawns and trees and shrubs and flowers, a flash of blue river, a vista of green marshes melting into the cobalt sky. A stately, lovely, leisurely old house, typifying the stately, leisurely life that had called it into being; both gone irrevocably into the past. He sighed.

He looked about this atrocious room, and his jaw hardened. This, for Milly's niece! Poor girl, poor friendless girl! He had known, of course, that the girl was poor. He and Milly had been poor, too. But, oh, never like this! This was being poor sordidly, vulgarly. He had seen and suffered enough in his time to realize how soul-murdering this environment might be to one who knew nothing better. He himself had had the memory of the old house in which he was born, and of low-voiced, gentle-mannered men and women; he had had his fine traditions to which to hold fast. He reflected that he would have a great deal to make up for to Nancy Simms!

The noon whistle had blown. People had begun to come in, men whose first movement on entering was to peel off collars and coats. They barely glanced at the quiet, white-clad figure as they passed the open parlor door, but stampeded for the basement dining-room. Mr. Champneys could hear the scraping of chairs, the rattling of dishes, the hum of loud conversation; then the steady clatter of knives and forks, and a dull, subdued murmur. Dinner was in full swing, a dinner of which boiled cabbage must have formed the *piece de resistance.*

Came a hurried footstep, and Nancy Simms entered the room. He was sitting with his back to the window; she sank into the chair fronting him, so that the light fell full upon her.

She was strong and well-muscled, as one could see under the enveloping apron. Her hands bore the marks of dish-washing and clothes-washing and floor-scrubbing and sweeping. They were shapely enough hands, even if red and calloused. The foot in the worn, down-at-the-heels shoe was a good foot, with a fine arch; and the throat rising from the checked gingham apron was full and strong; her face was prettily shaped, if one was observant enough to notice that detail.

She was not pretty; not even pleasant. Her discontented face was liberally peppered with the sort of freckles that accompany red and rebellious hair; her mouth was hard, the lips pressed tightly together. Under dark, uncared-for eyebrows were grayish-green eyes, their expression made unfriendly by her habit of narrowing them. She had good teeth and a round chin, and her nose would have passed muster anywhere, save for the fact that it, too, was freckled. Unfortunately, one didn't have time to admire her good points; one said at first sight of her, "Good heavens, what a disagreeable girl!" And then: "Bless me, I've *never* seen so many perfectly unnecessary freckles and so much fighting-red hair on one girl!"

"You'll hafta hurry," she admonished him, fanning herself vigorously with a folded newspaper. She wiped her perspiring face on her arm, tilted back her chair, revealing undarned stockings, and waited for him to explain himself.

He handed her his card, and at the name Champneys a faint

interest showed in her face.

"I had a aunt married a feller by that name," she volunteered. "Was you wishin' to find out somethin' about him or Aunt Milly? Because if so I don't know nothin' about him, nor yet her. I never set eyes on neither of 'em."

"I am your Aunt Milly's husband," he told her. "And I have come to find out something about *you*."

"It's took you a long time to find your way, ain't it?" Her manner was not cordial.

"We will waive that," said he, composedly. "I *am* here, and my visit concerns yourself. To begin with, do you like living with your mother's step-sister? That is her relationship to your mother and to my wife, I believe?"

"No: I don't like livin' with no step-aunt, though she ain't that, bein' further off: an' no real kin. If you want to know why I don't like it, it's all work an' no pay, that's why. First off, when I was too little to do anything else, I minded the children an' run errands an' washed doilies an' towels an' stockin's an' sich, an' set table an' cleared table an' washed dishes an' made beds an' emptied slops. Then I helped cook. Now I cook. Along with plenty other things. How'd you like it yourself?" Her tone was suddenly fierce. The fierceness of a strong and young creature in galling captivity.

His wandering life had given him an insight into such conditions and situations; and once or twice he had seen orphan children raised in homes where they "helped out." Chattel slavery is easier by comparison and pleasanter in reality.

Before he could answer, "Nan-cy! You Nan-cy! Come on

here an' set them pie-plates! My Gawd! that girl's goin' to run me ravin' crazy, tryin' to keep her on her job! Nancy!"

Nancy looked at Mr. Champneys speculatively.

"Is what you got to say worth me tellin' her to set them plates herself?" she asked.

"Well worth it," said Mr. Champneys, emphatically.

She jumped for the door with cat-like quickness. Also, she lifted her voice with cat-like ferocity.

"I'm busy! I can't co-ome. Set 'em yourself!"

"Can't come! What you doin'?" shrieked the other voice.

"I'm entertainin' comp'ny in the parler, that's what I'm doin'! It's somebody come to see *me*. An' I'm goin' to wait right here till I find out what they come *for*!"

On the heels of that, Nancy slammed the parlor door, and sat down.

"Now say what you got to say, an' don't waste no time askin' if I'm stuck on livin' here with somethin' like that!"

"You wish, then, to leave your aunt?"

"She ain't no aunt of mine, I tell you. She ain't nothin' but my mother's stepfather's daughter by his first wife. Sure I want to leave her. She took me because she needed a servant she didn't have to pay reg'lar wages to. I don't owe her nothin'. Nor him, neither. He's worse 'n her."

"They are not kind to you?"

"No, they ain't what you'd call kind to me. But you ain't come here to talk about them, I take it. What was you wantin' to see me about, Mister?"

"Suppose," said he, leaning forward, "that you should be offered, in exchange for *this*," his gesture damned the whole room, "a beautiful home, travel, culture, ease, all that makes life beautiful; would that offer appeal to you?" He looked at her earnestly.

"No housework, no cooking! Clothes made for me especial? Not hand-me-downs an' left-overs? No kids to mind, neither day nor night?"

"Housework? Old clothes? Minding children? Certainly not! I am not hiring a servant! What are you thinking of?"

"I'm thinkin' of *me*, that's what I'm thinkin' of! I'm wearin' her old clothes on Sundays now. I hate 'em. They look like her an' they smell like her and they feel like her—mean an' ugly an' tight. If I could ever get enough money o' my own together, an' enough clothes—" she stopped, and looked at him with the sudden ferocity that at times flashed out in her—"earned honest, though, and come by respectable," said she, grimly, "then I'd get out o' here an' try something else. I'm strong, an' if I had half a chanst I could earn my livin' easy enough."

His jaw hardened. He couldn't blind himself to the fact that he was disappointed in Milly's niece; so disappointed that he felt physically sick. Had he been less fanatical, less obstinate, less fixed upon his monomaniacal purpose, he would have settled a sufficient sum upon her, and gone his way. His disappointment, so far from turning him aside, hardened his determination to carry the thing through. He had so acutely felt the lack of money himself, that now, perhaps, he overestimated its power. Whatever money could accomplish for this girl, money should do. The zeal of the reformer gathered in him.

"I wish," he explained, "to adopt you—in a sense. I have no children, and it is my desire that you should bear the Champneys name—for your Aunt Milly's sake. I propose, then, to take you away from these surroundings, and to educate you as a lady bearing the name of Champneys should be educated. You will have to study, and to work hard. You will have to obey orders instantly and implicitly. Do you follow me?"

"As far as you go," said she, cautiously. "Go on: I'm waitin' to hear more."

"Aside from yourself, I have but one close relative, my brother's son. You two, then, are to be my children."

"How old is he?"

"About twenty."

"But if you got a real heir, where do I come in?" she wondered.

"Share and share alike. He's my nephew: you're Milly's niece."

She reflected, a puzzled frown coming to her forehead.

"You're aimin' to give us both a whole lot, ain't you? But I've found out nobody don't get somethin' for nothin' in this world. Where's the nigger in the woodpile? What do I do for what I get?"

"You make yourself worthy of the name you are to bear. You place yourself unreservedly in the hands of those appointed to instruct—and—ah—form you. Make no mistake on this head: it will be far from easy for you."

"Nothin' 's ever been easy for me, first nor yet last," said Nancy Simms. "So *that*'s nothin' new to me. I want you should speak out plain. What you really mean I'm to do?"

For a moment the iron-willed old man hesitated; he remembered young Peter, eager, hopeful, crystal-clear young Peter, back there in South Carolina. He looked challengingly and fiercely at the girl, as if his bold will meant to seize upon her as upon a piece of clay and mold it to his desire. Then, "I mean you're to marry," he said crisply.

"Me? Who to? You?" asked Nancy, blankly.

"*Me!*" gasped Mr. Champneys. "Are you demented?"

"Well, then, who?" she asked, not unnaturally. "And why?"

"The other heir. My nephew. Peter Champneys. Because such is my will and intention," said he, peremptorily and haughtily, bending his eagle-look upon her.

"What sort of a feller is he? He ain't got nothin' the matter with him, has he?"

A wild desire to slap Milly's niece came upon Chadwick Champneys at that.

"He is my nephew!" he said haughtily. "Why on earth should he have anything the matter with him?"

It occurred to him then that it mightn't be such an easy matter to get a high-spirited young fellow, with ideals, to take on trust this young female person with the red hair. He felt grateful that he had exacted a promise from Peter. The Champneyses always kept their promises.

"I'm wonderin'!" said Nancy, staring at him. "Why are you so bent on him an' me marryin'? You say it's just because you want it, but that ain't no explanation, nor yet no reason. After all, it's me. I got the right to ask why, then, ain't I? You can't expect to walk in unbeknownst an' tell a girl you want she should marry a feller she's never laid eyes on, without bein' asked a few questions, can you?"

He knew he must try to make it clear to her, as he had tried to make it clear to Peter. Peter, being Peter, had presently understood. Whether this girl would understand remained to be seen.

"I wish you to marry, because, as I have already told you, you are my wife's niece, and Peter is my brother's son. I have of late years become possessed of—well, let's say a great deal of money, and I propose that this money shall go to my own people—but on my own conditions. These conditions being that it shall all be kept in the Champneys name. It is an old name, a good name, it was once a wealthy and an honored name. It must be made so again. I say, it must be made so again! There are but you two to make it so. The boy is the last, on my side; and you're Milly's. Milly must have her share in the upbuilding—as if you were her child. Now, do you see?"

"Good Lord! ain't you got funny notions, though! Who ever heard the beat? One name's about as good as another, seems to me. But seein' you've got the money to pay for your notions, them that's willin' to take your money ought to be willin' to humor 'em." Nancy, in her way, had what might be called a sense of ethics.

"You agree?"

"Well, I just got to make a change, Mr. Champneys. I can't stand this place no more. If I was to say 'No' to you, an' stay here, an' have time to think it over, down in that sizzlin' kitchen, with her squallin' at me all day, I'd end up in a padded cell. If I was to leave just so, I'd maybe get me a job in a shop at less than I could live on honest. You see?"

He nodded, and she went on somberly:

"So I'm most at the end of my tether. It's real curious you should come just now, with me feelin' that desperate I been minded to walk out anyhow an' risk things. You sure that feller ain't got nothin' ails him? Not crazy, nor a dope, nor nothin'?"

"My nephew is perfectly normal in every respect," said Mr. Champneys, frigidly.

"What's he look like in the face?" she demanded. "Is he as ugly as me?"

"He is a gentleman," said Peter's uncle, even more frigidly. "As to his appearance, I believe he resembles me. At least, he looks like what I used to look like."

"Well—I've seen worse," said she, and fetched a sigh.

A sudden thought struck him. "Perhaps," he suggested, making allowance for the sentimentality of extreme youth, "perhaps you have some notion about—er—ah—marrying for love, or something like that? There may be some young fellow you think you fancy? Young people in your—ah—that is, in the circumstances to which you unfortunately have been subjected, often rush into ill-considered entanglements."

"In *love*? Who, me? Who with, for Gawdsake? One feller means just as much to me as another feller: they're all alike," said she, contemptuously. "I just asked about him for—for references. You know what you're gettin', an' I got a right to know what I'm gettin'."

"You have: so please remember that you are getting a considerable portion of the Champneys money for doing what you're told to do," said he.

"I never knew till you told me so that the Champneyses had any money. But if it's there, I'm willing to do what I'm told, for my share. Why not? There ain't nothin' better for me, nowheres, nohow."

"I am to understand, then, that you agree?"

"What else can I do but agree?" she asked, twisting a fold of her apron.

The parlor door opened with violence; a thick-set man with a bald head and a red face, followed by a shrewish, thin woman with pinched lips, appeared on the threshold.

"I s'pose," said the woman, with elaborate courtesy, "we kin come in our own parler, Miss Simms? Has you resigned your job that you gotta pick out the parler to set in whilst I'm doin' your work for you?"

Nancy's visitor rose, and at sight of the tall old gentleman an avid curiosity appeared in both vulgar faces.

"Mr. Champneys, this is the lady an' gentleman I live with and work for without wages, Mister an' Missis Baxter. Mister an' Missis Baxter, this gentleman is Aunt Milly's husband, an' he's come to see me; an' you ain't called to show off the manners you ain't got!"

"Well, why couldn't you say who he was at first, an' have done with it?" grumbled the man. "But no, you gotta upset the whole house! She's the provokin'est piece o' flesh on the created earth, when she starts," he explained to the visitor.

"To aggravate an' torment them that's raised her an' kept her out of the asylum an' fed an' clothed an' learned her like a daughter, is what Nancy Simms'd rather do than eat an' drink," supplemented Mrs. Baxter, acridly.

Nancy snorted. Mr. Champneys said nothing.

"Well! An' so you're poor Milly's husband!" said the woman, staring at him. "You wasn't so awful anxious to find out nothin' about her kith an' kin, was you? Not that I'm any kin," she added, hastily. "When all's said an' done, Nancy ain't no real kin, neither. You an' her's only connected by marriage, but bein' as you have come at last, I hope she'll have more gratefulness to you than she's got for *me*. As you ain't never done nothin' by her, an' I have, she's sure to."

"You make me so sick!" Nancy, with her hands on her hips, glared at the pair. "Anything you ever done for me you paid yourself for double. If you don't owe me nothin', like you said this mornin', I don't owe you nothin', neither, so it's quits. You'd oughta be glad I'm goin'."

"Goin'? Who's goin'? Goin' where?" Mrs. Baxter's voice rose shrilly. "Now, ain't it always so? You take a orphan child to your bosom an' after many days it'll grow up like a viper, an' the minute your back's turned it'll spit in your face!"

"Goin', hey? Where you goin' to when you go?" demanded Mr. Baxter, hoarsely.

"She is going with me," said Mr. Champneys. The whole situation nauseated him; he felt that if he didn't escape from that red-plush parlor very soon, he was going to be violently sick. "I am now in a position to look after my wife's niece, and I propose to do so. From what I have heard from you both, I should think you would be rather glad than sorry to part with her."

"You won't gain nothin' by raisin' a row," put in Nancy, in a hard voice. "I'm goin'. Make up your minds to *that*."

"Oh, you are, are you, Miss Simms? That's all the thanks I mighta expected from you, you red-headed freckle-face! I sure hope he'll get his fill of you before he's done! Walkin' off like a nigger without a minute's notice, an' me with my house full of men comin' to their meals they've paid for an' has to have!"

"Hire another nigger an' pay 'em somethin', so's they won't quit without notice, then," suggested the girl, unfeelingly.

"How you know this feller's Milly Champneys's husband?" asked Mr. Baxter. "Who's to prove it?"

Nancy looked at him and laughed. But Milly Champneys's husband said hastily: "Let us go, for God's sake! If there's a telephone here, ring for a cab or a taxi. How soon can you be ready?"

"I can walk out bag and baggage in ten minutes," she replied, and darted from the room.

The South Carolina Don Quixote looked at the sordid, angry pair before him. He felt like one in an evil dream, a dream that degraded him, and Milly's memory, and Milly's niece.

"If you wish to make any inquiries, I shall be at the Palace Hotel until this evening," he told them. "And—would a hundred dollars soothe your feelings?"

The woman's eyes slitted; the man's bulged.

"You musta come by money since Milly died," said Mrs. Baxter. "Yes, sure we'll take the hundred. We ain't refusin' money. It's little enough, too, considerin' all I done for that girl!"

Mr. Champneys counted out ten crisp bills into the greedy hand, and the three waited silently until Nancy appeared. Champneys almost screamed at sight of her. His heart sank like lead, and the task he had set for himself of a sudden assumed monumental proportions.

"I ain't took nothin' out of this house but the few things belongin' to my mother. You're welcome to the rest," she told the woman, briefly. The man she ignored altogether.

A cab rattled up to the door. In silence the aristocratic old man in white linen, and the red-headed girl in a cheap embroidered shirt-waist, a dark, shabby skirt, and a hat that was an outrage on millinery, climbed in. There were no farewells. The girl settled back, clutching her hand-satchel. "Giddap," said the driver, and cracked his whip. The cab rolled away from the dingy, smelly house, and turned a corner. So rode Nancy Simms out of her old life into her new one.

CHAPTER IX

PRICE-TAGS

When Mr. Chadwick Champneys had visualized to himself Milly's niece, it had always been in Milly's image and likeness—sweet, fair, brave, merry, gentle, and strong. Milly's niece, of course, would be companionable. He would only have to put upon her the finishing touches, so to speak, embellish her natural graces with a finer social polish. At the very worst, he hadn't dreamed that anybody belonging to Milly could be like this red-headed Nancy. Perhaps, though, she would be less objectionable when she was properly clad.

"Drive to the best department store in town," he told the driver, briefly.

Once in the store he summoned the manager and briefly stated his needs. The young lady must be furnished with everything she needed, and as quickly as possible. She needed, it appeared, about everything. The shrewd young Jew looked her over with his trained eyes.

"Should you prefer our Miss Smith to proffer aid and advice? Miss Smith is an expert."

Mr. Champneys reacted almost with terror against Nancy

Marie Conway Oemler

Simms's probable choice.

"See that the young lady gets the best you have; and make Miss Smith the final authority," he said, briefly.

At the end of two hours Nancy returned, the two clerks and the manager accompanying her. The store people were slightly flushed, Nancy herself sullenly acquiescent. For the first time in her life she had had the opportunity to buy enough clothes of her own, and yet she hadn't been allowed to choose what she really wanted. Gently but inexorably they had rejected the garments Nancy selected, smoothly insisting that these weren't "just the thing" for her. They slid her into quiet-colored, plainly cut things that she wouldn't have looked at if left to her own devices. It took their united tact, firmness, and diplomacy to steer Nancy over the reefs of what the manager called hired-girl taste.

Nancy was silent when she appeared before Mr. Champneys in her new clothes. She thought that if she had been allowed to pick them out for herself, instead of having been hypnotized—"bulldozed" is what she called it—into plain old dowdy duds by two shopwomen and a Jew manager, she'd have given him more for his money.

Mr. Champneys, looking her over critically, admitted that the girl was at least presentable. From hat to shoes she gave the impression of being well and carefully dressed. But her aspect breathed dissatisfaction, her bearing was ungracious-ness itself; nor did the two women clerks, trained to patience, tact, and politeness as they were, altogether manage to conceal their unfavorable opinion of her; even the clever, smiling young Jew, used to managing women shoppers, failed to hide the fact that he was more than glad to get this one off his hands.

Nancy hadn't taken time to eat her dinner before leaving the Baxter house, nor had Mr. Champneys had his lunch. They drove to his hotel, both hungry, and had their first meal together. Nancy hadn't been trained to linger over meals: one ate as much as one could get, in as short a space of time as possible. Mr. Champneys was grateful to a merciful Providence that he had ordered that repast served in his private sitting-room.

Her hunger quite satisfied, she shoved her plate aside, sighed, stretched luxuriously, and yawned widely, like the healthy animal she was.

"What we got to do now? Them women at the store said they'd get the rest of my things here, along with the travelin'-bags, in a coupla hours. I got a swell suit-case, didn't I? And oh, them toilet things! But between now and then, what you want I should do?"

It was then half-after four, and the train they were to take didn't leave until half-after seven.

"What would you like to do?" he asked.

"Can I go to the movies?"

He thought it an excellent idea. It would give him some idea of the girl's mental processes; the psychology of the proletariat, he thought, could be studied to advantage in their reaction to the movies.

He sat beside her for an unhappy hour while a famous screen comedian did the things with his feet and his backbone for which his managers paid him more in one year than the United States pays its Presidents in ten. At each impossible climax Nancy shrieked with laughter, the loud, delighted laughter of a pleased child. Her enthusiasm for the slapstick artist provoked him, but at the same time that gay laughter tickled his ears pleasantly. There's plenty of good in a girl who can laugh like that! After the grimacing genius there followed a short drama of stage mother-love, in which the angel-child dies strenuously in his little white bed. Nancy dabbled her eyes, and blew her nose with what her captious companion thought unnecessary vigor.

"Ain't it movin'?"

"Yes. Moving pictures," was the cold response. And to himself he was saying, defiantly: "Well, what else could I expect? She's not a whit worse than the vast majority! She's got the herd-taste. That's perfectly natural, under the circumstances. When I get her well in hand, she will be different."

"You don't like funny things, an' you got no feelin' for sad things," she ruminated, as they left the theater. In silence they walked back to their hotel.

The bulk of her purchases had been sent from the store, and a huge parcel awaited her in her room. It enchanted her to go over these new possessions, to gloat over her new toilet articles, to sniff at the leather of her traveling-kit. The smell of new leather was always to linger subconsciously in Nancy's memory; it was the smell of adventure and of change.

They dined together in Mr. Champney's sitting-room, although she would have preferred the public dining-room. Mr. Champneys was an abstemious man, but the girl was frankly greedy with the naive greed of one who had been heretofore stinted. She had seldom had what she really craved, and at best she had never had enough of it. To be allowed to order what and as much as she pleased, to be served first, to have her wishes consulted at all, was a new, amazing, and altogether delightful experience. Everything was brand-new to her.

She had never before traveled in a sleeping-car. It delighted her to watch the deft porter make up the berths; she decided that the peculiar etiquette of sleeping-cars required that all travelers, male and female, should be driven to bed by lordly colored men in white jackets, and there left in cramped misery with nothing but an uncertain, rustling curtain between them and the world; this, too, at an hour when nobody is sleepy. Nancy wondered to see free white citizens meekly obey their dusky tyrant. She got into her own lower berth, grateful that she hadn't to climb like a cat into an upper.

She lay there staring, while the train whizzed through the night. This had been the most momentous day of her life. That morning she had been the hopeless slavey in the Baxter kitchen, an unpaid drudge with her hand against every man and every man's hand against her. She had been bullied and beaten, she had eaten leavings, and worn cast-offs. Since her mother's death she had known the life of an uncared-for child, the minimum of care measured against the maximum of labor squeezed out of it. Until to-day her fate had been the fate of those who approach the table of Life with unshod feet and unwashen hands.

And to-night all that was changed. She was here, flying farther and farther away from all she had known. She wondered if she were not dreaming it. Panicky at that, she sat up in her berth, pressed the button that turned on the electric light, slipped her new kimono about her, and looked long and earnestly at the new clothes within reach of her hand. There they were, real to her touch; there was her fine new hand-bag; and most real of all was the feel of the money in it. Nancy fingered the money, thoughtfully smoothing out the bills. "As soon as we are settled, you will have your allowance, and I shall of course provide you with a check-book," Mr. Champneys had told her. "In the meanwhile you will naturally want money for such little things as you may need." And he had given her twenty five-dollar bills. She had received the money dumbly. This had been the crowning miracle—for she had never in the whole course of her life had so much as one five-dollar bill to do as she pleased with. She sat looking at the money, concrete proof of the reality of the change that had befallen her, and wondered, and wondered. With a sigh of content she thrust the hand-bag under her pillow, folded her kimono at the foot of her berth, switched out the light, and presently fell asleep.

In his berth opposite hers, Mr. Chadwick Champneys, more sleepless even than Nancy, was tabulating his estimate of the young woman he had acquired. It ran something like this:

Looks: bad; *may* improve.

Manners: worse; *must* improve. Particularly in speech.

Appetite: that of the seventeen-year locust. Must be restrained, to prevent an early death.

Character in general: suspend judgment until further study.

General summary of personal appearance: Nice teeth on which a little dentistry will work wonders. Not a bad figure, but doesn't know how to carry herself; has a villainous fashion of slouching, with her hands on her hips. Plenty of hair, but of terrifying redness; sullen expression of the eyes; fiendish profusion of freckles: may have to be skinned. Excellent nose. Speaks with appalling frankness at times but is not talkative.

What must be done for her? *Everything.*

He groaned, turned over, and after a while managed to sleep. Sufficient to the day was the red hair thereof; he couldn't afford to lie awake worrying about to-morrow.

He had long since decided upon New York as a residence until all his plans had matured. One had greater freedom to act, and far more privacy, in so large a city. They would stay at some quiet hotel until after the marriage; then he and Nancy would occupy the house he had recently purchased, in the West Seventies. It was a fine old house with a glimpse of near-by Central Park for an outlook, and what he had paid for it would have purchased half Riverton. He wanted its large, high-ceilinged rooms to be furnished as the old house in Carolina had been furnished, this being his standard of all that was desirable. He wished for Peter's wife such a background as Peter's forebears had known; and Peter's wife must be trained to appreciate and to fit into it, that's all!

The New York hotel, with its deft and deferential servants who seemed to anticipate her wishes, its luxury, its music, its shifting, splendidly dressed patrons, its light and glitter, filled Nancy with the same wonder that had fallen upon Aladdin when he found himself in the magic cave with all its treasures gleaming before his astounded, ignorant young eyes.

She hadn't thought the whole world contained so many people as she saw in New York in one day. Fifth Avenue amazed and absorbed more than it delighted her. The expressionless expressions of the women, their hand-made faces, their smart shoes, the way they wore their hair, the way they wore their clothes; the men's air of being well dressed, of having money to spend, of appearing importantly busy at any cost; a certain pretentiousness, as if everything were shown at once and there were no reserve of power, nothing held in disciplined abeyance, interested her profoundly. She had a native shrewdness.

"They're just like the same kind of folks back home, but there's more of 'em here," she decided.

The huge policemen she saw at every turn, lordly and massive monoliths rising superbly above lesser humanity, filled her with the deepest respect and admiration. The mere policemen in her home town were to these magnificent beings as daubs to Titians, as pigmies to Titans. If in those first days the girl had been called upon to do the seven bendings and the nine knockings before the one New York institution which impressed her most profoundly, she undoubtedly would have singled out one of those mastodons a-bossing everything and everybody, with a prize-ham paw.

She was cold to the Woolworth Building, as indifferent to the Sherman monument as Mr. Chadwick Champneys was acridly averse to it, and not at all interested in the Public Library. The Museum of Natural History failed to win any applause from her; the Metropolitan Museum bored her interminably, there was so much of it. Most of the antiquities she thought so much junk, and the Egyptian and Assyrian remains were so obviously the plunder of old graveyards that she couldn't for the life of her understand why anybody should wish to keep them above ground.

Mr. Champneys explained, patiently. He wished, by way of aiding and abetting the education he had in view for her, to arouse her interest in these remains of a lost and vanished world.

She stood by the glass case that contains the old brown mummied priest with his shaven skull, his long, narrow feet, his flattened nose and fleshless hands, and the mark of the embalmer's stone knife still visible upon his poor old empty stomach. And she didn't like him at all. There was something grisly and repellent to her in the idea that living people should make of this poor old dead man a spectacle for idle curiosity.

"There was a feller in our town used to keep stuffed snakes an' monkeys an' birds, an' dried grasshoppers an' bugs an' things like that in glass cases; but I never dreamed in all my born life that anybody'd want to keep dried people," she commented disgustedly. "I don't see no good in it: it's sickenin'." She turned her back upon mummied Egypt with a gesture of aversion. "For Gawdsake let's go see somethin' alive!"

He looked at her a bit helplessly. Plainly, this young person's education wasn't to be tackled off-hand! Agreeably to her wishes he took her to a certain famous shop filled at that hour with fashionable women wonderfully groomed and gowned. Here, seated at a small table, lingering over her ice-cream, Nancy was all observant eyes and ears. Not being a woman, however, Mr. Champneys was not aware that her proper education was distinctly under way.

A day or two later he took her to the Bronx Zoo. Here he caught a glimpse of Nancy Simms that made him prick up his ears and pull his mustache, thoughtfully. He had discovered how appallingly ignorant she was, how untrained, how undisciplined. To-day he saw how really young she was. She ran from cage to cage. Her laughter made the corners of his mouth turn up sympathetically.

There was something pathetic in her eager enjoyment, something so fresh and unspoiled in that laughter of hers that one felt drawn to her. When she forgot to narrow her eyes, or to furrow her forehead, or to screw up her mouth, she was almost attractive, despite her freckles! Her eyes, of an agaty gray-green, were transparently honest. She had brushed the untidy mop of red hair, parted it in the middle, and wore it in a thick bright plait, tied with a black ribbon. She wore a simple middy blouse and a well-made blue skirt. Altogether, she looked more like a normal young girl than he had yet seen her.

The Zoo enchanted her. She hurried from house to house. Once, she told him, when she was a little kid, a traveling-man had taken her to a circus, because he was sorry for her. That was the happiest day she had ever spent; it stood out bright and golden in her memory. There had been a steam-piano hoo-hooing "Wait till the clouds roll by, Jenny." Wasn't a steam-piano perfectly grand? She liked it better than anything she'd ever heard. She'd long ago made up her mind that if she was ever really rich and had a place of her own, she'd have a big circus steam-piano out in the barn, and she'd play it on Sundays and holidays—*hoo-hoo, hoo-hoo, hoo, hoo-hoo*—like that, you know.

And to-day reminded her of that long-ago circus day, with even more animals to look at! She had never seen as many different animals as she wanted to see, until now. She admitted that she sort of loved wild things—she even liked the wild smell of 'em. There was something in here—she touched her breast lightly—that felt kin to them.

There was not the usual horde of visitors, that day being a pay-day. A bearded man with a crutch was showing one or two visitors around, and at a word from him a keeper unlocked a cage door, to allow a young chimpanzee to leap into his arms. It hugged him, exhibiting extravagant affection; it thrust out its absurd muzzle to kiss his cheek, and patted him with its small, leathery, unpleasantly human hands.

"It's just like any other baby," said the keeper, petting it.

"I sure hope it ain't like any *I'll* ever have," said Nancy, so naively that the man with the crutch laughed. He looked at her keenly.

"Go over and see the baby lion," he suggested; and he added, smiling, "It's got red hair."

"It can afford to have red hair, so long as it's a lion," said Nancy, sturdily; and she added, reflectively: "I'd any day rather have me a lion-child with red hair, than a monkey-child with any kind of hair."

Somehow that blunt comment pleased Mr. Champneys. When he took his charge back to their hotel that evening, it was with something like a glimmering of real hope in his heart.

The next day, as he joined her at lunch, he said casually:

"I had a message from my nephew this morning. He will be here in a few days."

She turned pale; the hand that held her fork began to tremble.

"Is it—soon?" she asked, almost unaudibly.

"The sooner the better. I think we'd better have it here, in our sitting-room, say at noon on Wednesday. Don't be seared," he added, kindly. "All you have to do is just to stand still and say, 'I will,' at the right moment."

"An'—an' then?"

"My nephew's boat sails at about two. He drives to the pier. You and I go to our apartment, until our own house is ready for us. You see how nicely it's all arranged."

"I ain't—I mean, I don't have to see him nor talk to him before, do I?" She looked panic-stricken. "Because I won't! I can't! There's some things I just can't stummick, an' meetin' that feller before the very last minute I got to do it, is one of 'em."

"Of course, of course! You sha'n't meet him until the very last minute. Though he's a mighty nice chap, my nephew Peter is—a mighty nice chap."

"He must be! We're both of us a mighty nice pair, ain't we? Him goin' one way an' me goin', another way, all by our lonesomes!"

"The arrangement does not suit you?" he inquired politely.

"Oh, it suits me all right," she said, after a moment. "I said I'd do what I was told, an' I'll do it—I ain't the sort backs down. But I ain't none too anxious to get any better acquainted with this feller than what I am right now. I ain't stuck on men, noways."

"You are only sixteen, my dear," he reminded her.

"Women know as much about men when they're sixteen as they do when they're sixty," said she, coldly. "There ain't but one thing to believe about 'em—an' that is, you best not believe any of 'em."

"I hope," said he, stiffly, "that you have no just cause to disbelieve me, Nancy? Have I been unkind to you?"

"It ain't *me* you're either kind or yet unkind to," she told him. "It's Aunt Milly's niece: you're a little crazy on that head, I guess. It's Aunt Milly's niece you aim to marry to that nephew of yours. If I was just me myself without bein' any kin to her, you wouldn't wipe your old shoes on me." She gave him a clear, level look. "Let's don't have any lies about this thing," she begged. "I'm a poor hand for lies. I know, and I want you should know I know, and deal with me honest."

She surprised him. Her next question surprised him even more.

"What about my weddin'-dress?" she demanded. "I got nothin' fittin' to be married in."

"I should think a plain, tailored suit—" he began.

"Then you got another think comin' to you," she said, in a hard voice. "I got nothin' to do with pickin' out the groom: you fixed that to suit yourself. But I don't let no man alive pick out my dress. I want a weddin'-dress. I want one I want myself. I want it should be white satin' an' real bride-like. I've saw pictures of brides, an' I know what's due 'em. I ain't goin' to resemble just me myself, standin' up to be married in a coat-suit you get some floor-walker to pick out for me. White satin or nothin'. An' a veil and white satin slippers."

He looked at her helplessly. "White satin, my dear? And a veil?"

"Yes, sir. An' a shower bokay," said she, firmly. "I got to insist on the shower bokay. If I got to be a bride I'll be my kind of bride and not yours."

"My dear child, of course, of course. You shall choose your

own frock," said he, hastily. "Only—under the circumstances, I can't help thinking that something plain, something quite plain and simple, would be more in keeping."

"With me? 'T wouldn't, neither. It'd be something fierce, an' I won't stand for it. I don't mind bein' buried in somethin' plain, but I won't get married in it. Ain't it hard enough as it is, without me havin' to feel more horrid than what I do already? I want something to make me feel better about it, and there ain't anything can do that except it's a dress I want myself."

Mr. Champneys capitulated, horse and foot.

"We will go to some good shop immediately after lunch, and you shall choose your own wedding-dress," he promised, resignedly, marveling at the psychology of women.

It was a very fine forenoon, with a hint of coming autumn in the air. Even an imminent bridegroom couldn't altogether dampen the delight of whizzing through those marvelous streets in a taxi. Then came the even more marvelous world of the department store, which, "by reason of the multitude of all kind of riches, in all sorts of things, in blue clothes, and broidered work, and in chests of rich apparel," put one in mind of the great fairs of Tyre when Tyre was a prince of the sea, as set forth in the Twenty-seventh Chapter of Ezekiel.

Nancy would have been tempted to marry Bluebeard himself for the sake of some of the "rich apparel" that obliging saleswomen were setting forth for her inspection. Getting married began to assume a rosier aspect, due probably to the reflection of the filmy and lacy miracles that she might have for the mere choosing. She would almost have been willing to be hanged, let alone married, in a pink-silk combination.

The saleswomen scented mystery and romance here. The girl was no beauty, but then, she was astonishingly young; and the old gentleman was very distinguished-looking—quite a personage. They thought at first that he was the prospective bridegroom; learning that he wasn't deepened the mystery but didn't destroy the romance. Americans are all but hysterically sentimental. Sentimentality is a national disease, which rages nowhere more virulently than among women clerks. Would they rush through the necessary alterations, set an entire force to work overtime, if necessary, in order to have that girl's wedding-dress at her hotel on time? *Wouldn't* they, though! And they did. Gown, gloves, veil, shoes, fan, everything; all done up with the most exquisite care in reams of soft tissue paper.

She was to be married on the noon of Wednesday. On Tuesday night Nancy locked her door, opened her boxes, and spread her wedding finery on her bed. The dress was a magnificent one, as magnificent a dress as a great store can turn out; its lines had been designed by a justly famous designer. There was a slip, with as much lace as could be put upon one garment; such white satin slippers as she had never hoped to wear; and the texture of the silk stockings almost made her shout for joy. Achilles was vulnerable in the heel: fly, O man, from the woman who is indifferent to the lure of a silk stocking!

Nancy got into her kimono and turned on the hot water in her bath. At Baxters' there had never been enough hot water with which to wash the dishes, not to mention Nancy herself. Here there was enough to scald all the dishes—and the people—on earth, it seemed to her. She could hardly get used to the delight and the luxury of all the hot water and scented soap and clean towels she wanted, in a bath-room all to herself. Think of not having to wait one's turn, a very limited turn at that, in a spotted tin tub set in a five-by-seven hole in the wall, with an unshaded gas-jet sizzling about a foot above one's head! The shower-bath was to her an adventure—like running out in the rain, when one was a child. She couldn't get into the tub, and slide down into the warm, scented water, without a squeal of pleasure.

She skipped back to her bedroom, red as a boiled lobster, a rope of damp red hair hanging down her back, sat down on the floor, and drew on those silk stockings, and loved them from a full heart. She wiggled her toes ecstatically.

"O Lord!" sighed Nancy, fervently, "I wish You'd fix it so's folks could walk on their hands for a change! My feet are so much prettier than my face!"

Slipping on the satin slippers, she teetered over and reverently touched the satin frock. All these glories for her, Nancy Simms, who had worn Mrs. Baxter's wretched old clothes cut down for her!

She was afraid to refold the dress, almost afraid to touch it, lest she rumple it. It looked so shining, so lustrous, so fairy-like and glorious and almost impossible, glistening there on her bed! Carefully she smoothed a fold, slightly awry. Reverently she placed the thin tulle veil beside it, as well as the rest of her Cinderella finery, including the satin slippers and the fine silk stockings which her soul loved.

She took the two pillows off her bed, secured two huge bath-towels from her bath-room by way of a mattress and a coverlet; and with a last passionate glance at the splendors of her wedding-frock, and never a thought for the unknown groom because of whom she was to don it, the bride switched off her light, curled herself up like a cat, and in five minutes was sound asleep on the floor.

CHAPTER X

THE DEAR DAM-FOOL

"Dis place," said Emma Campbell, as the snaggle-toothed sky-line of New York unfolded before her staring eyes, "ain't never growed up natchel out o' de groun'; it done tumbled down out o' de sky en got busted uneven in de fall."

Clinging to the bird-cage in which her cat Satan crouched, she further remarked, as the taxi snaked its sinuous way toward the quarters which a friendly waiter on the steamship had warmly recommended to her:

"All I scared ob is, dat dis unforchunit cat's gwine to lose 'is min'. Seein' places like dis is 'nough to make any natchel cat run crazy."

Whereupon Emma relapsed into a colossal silence. She was fed up on surprises and they were palling upon her palate, which fortunately wasn't down. Things had been happening so fast that she couldn't keep step with them. To begin with, Peter had preferred to come north by sea, and although Emma had been raised on the coast, although she was used to the capricious tide-water rivers which this morning may be lamb-like and to-night raging lions, although she had crossed Caliboga Sound in rough weather and been rolled about like a ninepin, that had been, so to speak, near the shore-line. This was different: here was more water than Emma had thought was in the entire world; and she had been assured that this wasn't a bucketful to what she was yet to see! Emma fell back upon silent prayer.

Then had come this astounding city jutting jaggedly into the clouds, and through whose streets poured in a never-ceasing, turgid flow all the peoples of the earth. And, more astounding than waterful sea and peopleful city, was the last, crowning bit of news: *Peter was going to be married*! And he didn't know the young lady he was to marry, except that she was a Miss Anne Simms. He knew no more about his bride than she, Emma, knew.

That was all Emma needed to reduce her to absolute befuddlement. When food and drink were placed before her, she partook of both, mechanically. If one spoke to her, she stared like a large black owl. And when Peter had driven away in the taxi, leaving her for the time being in the care of a highly respectable colored family, whose children, born and raised in New York, looked upon the old South Carolina woman as they might have looked upon a visitor from Mars, Emma shut and locked her door, took the cat out of his cage, cuddled him in her arms, tried to projeck,—and couldn't. The feel of Satan's soft, warm body comforted her inexpressibly. He, at least, was real in a shifting universe. She began to rock herself, slowly, rhythmically, back and forth. Then the New York negroes heard a shrill, sweet, wailing voice upraised in one of those speretuals in which Africa concentrates her ages of anguish into a half-articulate cry. In it were the voices of their fathers long gone, come back from the rice-fields and the cane-brakes and the cotton-rows, voices so sweet and plaintive that they were haunted.

"I we-ent out een de wilderness,

En I fell upon—mah—knees,
En I called upon—mah—Savior,
Whut sh-all I do—for—save?
He replied:
Halleluian!
Sinnuh, sing!
Halleluian!
Ma-ry, Mar-tha, *halle—*
Hallelu—
Halleluian!"

"Good Lord!" breathed the oldest boy, who was a high-school scholar.

"How weird and primitive!" said the daughter, who was to be a teacher.

But the father's eyes narrowed, and the hair of his scalp prickled. 'Way back yonder his mother had sung like that, and his heart leaped to it. If he hadn't been afraid of his educated and modern children, he would have wept. Emma didn't know that, of course. She kissed the big cat, placed him carefully on the bed, and lay down beside him in the attitude of a corpse. She was resigning herself to whatever should happen.

Peter, upon telephoning his uncle, had been advised to prowl about until noon, when they were to lunch together. Wherefore he found himself upon the top of a bus, rolling about New York, seeing that of which he had read. He didn't see it as Nancy saw it; the city appeared to him as might some subtle, hard, and fascinatingly plain woman whose face had flashes of piercing and unforgetable beauty, beauty unexpected and unlike any other. Unlike the beauty of the Carolina coast, say, which was a part of his consciousness, there was here something sinister and splendid.

He got off at the Metropolitan Museum. He wished to see with his own eyes some of those pictures Claribel Spring had described to him, among them Fortuny's "Spanish Lady." He stood for a dazzled interval before her, so disdainful, passionate, provocative, and so profoundly human. When he moved away, he sighed. He wasn't wondering if he himself should ever meet and love such a lady; but rather when he should be able so to portray in a human face all the secrets of the body and of the soul.

At lunch his uncle, remarking his earnest face, said regretfully:

"Oh, Peter, why couldn't you be content to be a rich man and play the game according to Hoyle? Art? Of course! You could afford to buy the best any of 'em could do, instead of trying to sell something you do yourself. Art is a rich man's recreation. Artists exist in order that rich men may buy their wares."

"Rich men were invented for the use of poor artists: it's the only excuse they have for existing at all, that I can see," said Peter, composedly.

"But you'd have a so much better time buying, than selling— or rather, trying to sell," said one of the rich men, smiling good-humoredly.

"I'll have a better time working, than in either buying or selling," said Peter, and looked at his uncle with uncompromising eyes.

Mr. Chadwick Champneys sighed, face to face with Champneys obstinacy. Peter would keep his promise to the letter, but aside from that he would live his own life in his own way.

He had stared, and his jaw dropped, when he was calmly informed that Peter intended to take old Emma Campbell and a black cat along with him. Then he had laughed, almost hysterically, and incidentally discovered that being laughed at didn't move Peter in the least; he was too used to it. He allowed you to laugh at him, smiled a bit wryly himself, and went right ahead doing exactly what he had set out to do. This sobered Mr. Champneys.

"Peter," said he, after a pause, "allow me to ask you a single question: do you propose to go through life toting old niggers and black cats?"

"Uncle Chad," replied Peter, "do you remember how sweet potatoes roasted in the ashes of a colored person's fire used to taste, when you were a little boy?"

A reminiscent glow spread over Uncle Chad's face. He shaded his eyes with his hand, and stared under it at Peter. Something quizzical and tender was in that look.

"I see you do," said Peter, with the same look. "Well, Uncle Chad, Emma used to roast those potatoes—and provide them too. Sometimes they were all the dinner I had. Besides," mused Peter, "when all's said and done, nobody has more than a few friends from his cradle to his grave. If I've got two, and they don't want to part with me, why should they have to?"

Mr. Chadwick Champneys spread out his hands. "Put like that," he admitted, "why should they, indeed! Take 'em along if you like, Nephew." And of a sudden he laughed again. "Oh, Peter!" he gasped, "you dear dam-fool!"

Peter had a strenuous afternoon. Reservations had to be secured for Emma, for whom he also purchased a long coat and a steamer rug. He himself had to have another suit: his uncle protested vehemently against the nice new one he had bought in Charleston.

At dusk he watched New York's lights come out as suddenly and as goldenly as evening primroses. Riverton drowsing among its immemorial oaks beside the salty tide-water, the stars reflected in its many coves, the breath of the pines mingling with the wild breath of the sea sweeping through it, the little, deserted brown house left like a last year's nest close to the water—how far removed they were from this glittering giantess and her pulsating power! The electric lights winked and blinked, the roar of traffic arose in a multitudinous hum; and all this light and noise, the restless stir of an immense life, went to the head like wine.

The streets were fiercely alive. Among the throngs of well-dressed people one caught swift glimpses of furtive, hurrying figures, and faces that were danger signals. More than once a few words hissed into Peter's ears made him turn pale.

It was nearing midnight, and the street was virtually empty, when a girl who had looked at him sharply in passing turned and followed him, and after a glance about to see that no policeman was in sight, stepped to his side and touched him on the elbow. Peter paused, and his heart contracted. He had seen among the negroes the careless unmorality as of animals. There was nothing of the prude in him, but, perhaps because all his life there had been a Vision before his eyes, he had retained a singularly untroubled mental chastity. His mind was clean with the cleanliness of knowledge. He could not pretend to misunderstand the girl. She was nothing but a child in years. The immaturity of her body showed through her extreme clothes, and even her sharp, painted little face was immature, for all its bold nonchalance. She was smiling; but one sensed behind her deliberate smile a wolfish anxiety.

"Ain't you lonesome?" she asked, fluttering her eyelids, and giving the young man a sly, upward glance.

"No," said Peter, very gently.

"Aw, have a heart! Can't you stand a lady somethin' to eat an' maybe somethin' to drink?"

The boy looked at her gravely and compassionately. Although her particular type was quite new to him, he recognized her for what she was, a member of the oldest profession, the strange woman "whose mouth is smoother than oil, but whose feet go down to death. Her steps take hold on hell." Somehow he could not connect those terrible words with this sharp-featured, painted child. There was nothing really evil about her except the brutal waste of her.

"Will ten dollars be enough for you?" asked Peter. The wolfish look in her eyes hurt him. He felt ashamed and sad.

"Sure! Come on!" said she, and her face lighted.

"Thank you, I have had my dinner," said Peter. But she seized his arm and hurried him down a side street, willy-nilly. "Seen a cop out of the tail of my eye," she explained, hurriedly. "They're fierce, some of them cops. I can't afford to be took up."

When they had turned the corner, Peter stopped, and took out his pocket-book. With another searching glance at her, he handed her one five, and two ten-dollar bills. Perhaps that might save her—for a while at least. He lifted his hat, bowed, and had started to walk away, when she ran after him and clutched him by the arm.

"Take back that fiver," said she, "an' come and eat with me.

If you got a heart, come an' eat with me. I know a little place we can get somethin' decent: it's a dago caffay, but it's clean an' decent enough. Will you come?" Her voice was shaking; he could see her little body trembling.

"But why?" he asked, hesitatingly.

"Not for no reason, except I—I got to make myself believe you're real!" She said it with a gasp.

Peter fell in beside her and she led the way. The small restaurant to which she piloted him wasn't pretentious, but it was, as she had said, clean, and the food was excellent.

She said her name was Gracie Cantrell, and Peter took her word for it. While she was eating she discoursed about herself, pleased at the interest this odd, dark-faced young fellow with the soft, drawling voice seemed to take in her. She had begun in a box factory, she told him. And then she'd been a candy-dipper. Now, you work in a lowered atmosphere in order not to spoil your chocolate. For which reason candy-dippers, like all the good, are likely to die young. Seven of the girls in Gracie's department "got the T.B." That made Gracie pause to think, and the more she thought about it, the clearer it seemed to her that if one has to have a short life, one might at least make a bid for a merrier one than candy-dipping. So she made her choice. The short life and merry, rather than the T.B. and charity.

"And has it been so merry, Gracie?" asked Peter, looking at the hard young face wonderingly.

"Well, it's been heaps better than choc'late-dippin'," said Gracie, promptly. "I don't get no worse treated, when all's said an' done. I've got better clothes an' more time an' I don't work nothin' like so hard. An' I got chanst to see things. You don't see nothin' in the fact'ry. Say I feel like goin' to the movies, or treatin' myself to a ice-cream soda or a choc'late a-clair, why, I can do it without nobody's leave—when I'm lucky. You ain't ever lucky in the fact'ry: you never have nothin', see? So I'd rather be me like I am than be me back in the fact'ry."

"And do you always expect to be—lucky?" Peter winced at the word.

"I can't afford to think about that," she replied, squinting at the red ink in her glass. "You got to run your risks an' take your chances. All I know is, I'll have more and see more before I die. An' I won't die no sooner nor no painfuller than if I'd stayed on in the fact'ry."

Peter admitted to himself that she probably wouldn't. Also, that he had nothing to say, where Gracie was concerned. He felt helpless in the face of it—as helpless as he had felt one June morning long ago when he had seen old Daddy Neptune praying, after a night of horror, to a Something or a Somebody blind and indifferent. And it seemed to him that life pressed upon him menacingly, as if he and Neptune and this lost child of the New York streets had been caught like rats in a trap.

The girl, on her part, had been watching him with painful intensity.

"You're a new one on *me*," she told him frankly. "I feel like pinchin' you to see if you're real. Say, tell me: if you're real, are you the sort of guy that'd give twenty-five dollars, for nothin', to a girl he picked up in the street? Or, are you just a softy fool that a girl that picks him up in the streets can trim? There's more of *him* than the first sort," she finished.

"You must judge that for yourself," said Peter. "I may tell you, though, that I am quite used to being called a fool," he finished, tranquilly.

"So?" said she, after another long look. "Well, I—what I mean to say is, I wish to God there was more fools like you. If there was, there'd be less fools like me." After a pause she asked, in a subdued voice:

"You expect to stay in this town long?"

"I leave in the morning."

"I'm sorry," said she. "Not," she added hastily, "that I want to touch you for more money or anything like that, I don't. But I—well, I'd like to know you was livin' in the same town, see?"

Peter saw. But again he had nothing to say. Young as he was, he knew the absurdity of all talk of reform to such as Gracie. As things are they can't reform, they can't even be prevented. He looked at her, thoughtfully.

"I'm not only leaving New York, I'm leaving America to-morrow," he said at last. "I wish there was something I could do for you."

She shook her head. Her little painted face looked pinched. There were shadows under the eyes that should have been soft and dewy. "You can't do nothin'. I'll tell you why. Somehow—I—I'd like you to know."

And she sat there and told him.

"You see?" said she, when she had finished.

"I see," said Peter; and the hand that held his cigarette trembled. The thing that struck him most forcibly was the stupid waste of it all.

"Look here, Gracie," he said at last, "if you ever get—very unlucky—and things are too hard for you—sort of last ditch, you know,—I want you to go to a certain address. It's to my uncle," he explained, seeing her look blank. "You'll send in the card I'm going to give you, and you will say I sent you. He'll probably investigate you, you know. But you just tell him the truth, and say I told you he'd help. Will you do that!"

She in her turn reflected, watching Peter curiously. Then she fell to tracing patterns on the table-cloth with the point of her knife.

"All right," she said. "If ever I have to, an' I can find him, I will—an' say you sent me."

Peter took out his pocket memorandum, wrote his uncle's name and the address of the house in the Seventies which he was presently to occupy, added, "I wish you'd do what you can, for my sake," and signed it. He handed the girl the slip of paper, and she thrust it into her low-necked blouse.

"And now," he finished kindly, "you'd better go home, Gracie, go to bed, and sleep." He held out his brown hand, and she, rising from her chair, gripped his fingers as a child might have done, and looked at him with dog's eyes.

"Good-by!" said she, huskily. "You *are* real, ain't you?"

"Damnably so," admitted Peter. "Good-by, then, Gracie." And he left her standing by the table, the empty wine-glass before her. The streets stretched before him emptily.—That poor, done-for kid! What *is* one to do for these Gracies?

"Mister! For God's sake! I'm hungry!" a hoarse voice accosted him. A dirty hand was held out.

Mechanically Peter's hand went to his pocket, found a silver dollar, and held it out. The dirty hand snatched it, and without so much as a thank you the man rushed into a near-by bakery. Peter shuddered.

When he reached his room, he sat for a long time before his open window, and stared at the myriads and myriads of lights. From the streets far below came a subdued, ceaseless drone, as if the huge city stirred uneasily in her sleep— perhaps because she dreamed of the girls she prostituted and the men she starved. And it was like that everywhere. If the great cities gave, they also took, wastefully. Peter was tormented, confronted by the inexorable question:

"What am *I* going to do about it?"

He couldn't answer, any more than any other earnest and decent boy could answer, whose whole and sole weapon happened to be a paint-brush. One thing he resolved: he wouldn't add to the sum total; nobody should be the worse off because he had lived. So thinking, the bridegroom fell asleep.

When he awoke in the morning, he lay for a moment staring at the strange ceiling overhead; his mind had an uneasy consciousness that something impended. Then he sat up suddenly in his bed, and clutched his head in his hands.

"Lord have mercy on me!" cried Peter. "I've got to get up and get married!"

By ten o'clock his luggage was on its way to the steamer. Dressed in his new clothes, ring and license carefully tucked away in his pocket, Peter took an hour off and jumped on a bus. It delighted him to roll around the streets on top of a bus. He felt that he could never see enough of this wonderful, terrible, beautiful, ugly, cruel, and kind city. Everywhere he turned, something was being torn down or up, something was being demolished or replaced. New York was like an inefficient and yet hard-working housekeeper, forever housecleaning; her house was never in order, and probably never would be, hence this endless turmoil. Yet, somehow, Peter liked it. She wasn't satisfied with things as they were.

He stopped at Grant's Tomb, looked at the bronze tablet commemorating the visit of Li Hung Chang, then went inside and stared reflectively at the torn and dusty flags.

"It was worth the price," he decided. "But," he added, with a certain deep satisfaction, "I'm glad we gave them a run for their money while we were at it!" The Champneyses, one remembers, were on the other side.

When he got back to his hotel the car that his uncle had sent for him had just arrived. Deferential help brought out his remaining belongings, were tipped, and stood back while the door was slammed upon the departing one. The car was held up for seven minutes on Forty-second Street, while Peter leaned forward to get his first view of congested traffic. He had once seen two Ford cars and an ox-cart tie up the Riverton Road.

Arrived at Emma Campbell's quarters, he found her sitting stiffly erect, her foot upon her new suit-case, her new cloak over her arm, and the bird-cage under her hand. The expressman who had called for her trunk early that morning had good-naturedly offered to carry the bird-cage along with it, but Emma had flatly refused to let the cat get out of her sight. Even when she climbed into the car she held fast to the cage.

"I don't say nothin' 'bout *me*. All I scared ob is, dat dis unforchnate cat's gwine to lose 'is min' before we-all finishes up."

It was with difficulty that Peter persuaded her to leave the cage in the car when they reached his uncle's hotel.

"Mistuh," said Emma to the chauffeur, "is you-all got any fambly dependin' on you?"

"One wife. Three kids," said the chauffeur, briefly.

"I ain't de kin' ob lady whut makes threats agin' a gent'man," said Emma, looking him unblinklngly in the eye. "All I says is, dat I started whah I come fum wid dat cat an' I 'specks to lan' up whah I 's gwine to wid dat same cat in dat same cage. Bein' as you's got dem chillun en dat wife, I calls yo' 'tenshun to dat fac', suh."

The chauffeur, a case-hardened pirate, laughed. "All right, lady," said he, genially. "It ain't in my line to granny cats, but that one will be the apple of me good eye until you git back. I wouldn't like the missus to be a widder: she's too darn good-lookin'."

With her mind at ease on this point, Emma consented to leave Satan in the car and follow Peter. Emma looked resplendently respectable, and she knew it. She was dressed as well as if she had expected to be buried. By innate wisdom she had retained the snowy head-handkerchief under her sailor hat, and she wore her big gold hoop-earrings. Smart colored servants were common enough at that hotel, but one did not often see such as this tall and erect old woman in her severe black-and-white. Emma belonged almost to another day and generation, although her face, like the faces of many old colored women, was unwrinkled. She had a dignity that the newer generation lacks, and a pride unknown to them.

Peter and Emma went up in an elevator and were ushered into a private sitting-room, where were awaiting them Mr. Chadwick Champneys, a gentleman who was obviously a clergyman, another who was as obviously a member of the Bar, and the latter's wife, a very handsome lady handsomely and expensively panoplied. There was the usual hand-shaking, as Peter was introduced, and the handsome lady stared openly at Emma; one doesn't often see a bridegroom come in accompanied by an old colored woman. Emma courtesied, with the inimitable South Carolina bending of the knees, and then took a modest seat in the background and faded into it. She had good manners, had Emma.

Mr. Champneys glanced at his watch, and presently left the room. The clergyman, book in hand, stepped into the middle of the floor, and looked importantly religious. The lawyer smilingly invited Peter to take his place beside him. Everybody assumed a solemn look.

And then the door opened and the bride appeared, leaning on her uncle's arm. Emma Campbell, leaning forward, got one glimpse of the face but slightly concealed by the thin, floating tulle veil pinned on with a wreath of orange-blossoms, caught one gleam from the narrowed eyes; and her own eyes bulged in her head, her mouth fell open. Emma wished to protest, to cry, to pray aloud.

The bride was magnificently dressed, in a gown that was much too elaborate for her angular and undeveloped young figure. It made her look over-dressed and absurd to a pitiful degree, as if she were masquerading. The hair-dresser whom she had called to her aid had done her worst. Nancy had an unusual quantity of hair, and it had been curled and frizzed, and puffed and pulled, until the girl's head appeared twice its natural size. Through the fine lace of her sleeves were visible her thin, sunburned arms. Her naturally dark eyebrows had been accentuated, and there was a bright red patch on each cheek, her lips being equally crimson. Out of the rouged and powdered face crowned by towering red hair, the multitude of freckles showed defiantly, two fierce eyes lowered.

As Peter met the stare of those narrowed eyes, to save his life he couldn't keep from showing his downright consternation. His aversion and distaste were so manifest, that a deeper red than rouge stained the girl's cheek and mottled her countenance. Her impulse was to raise her hand and strike him across his wincing mouth.

What Nancy saw was a tall, thin, shambling young fellow whose face was pale with an emotion not at all complimentary to herself. He didn't like her! He thought her hideous! He despised her! So she read Peter's expressive eyes. She thought him a fool, to stand there staring at her like that, and she hated him. She detested him. Puppy!

She saw his glance of piteous entreaty, and Mr. Chadwick Champneys's bland, blind ignoring of its silent reproach and appeal. And then the long-legged young fellow pulled himself together. His head went up, his mouth hardened, and his voice didn't shake when he promised to cherish and protect her, until death did them part.

All the while Peter felt that he was struggling in a hideous dream. That bride in white satin wasn't real; his uncle wouldn't play him such a trick! Peter cringed when the defiant voice of the girl snapped her "I do" and "I will."

The clergyman's voice had trailed off. He was calling her "Mrs. Champneys." And Mr. Vandervelde and his handsome wife were shaking hands with her and Peter, and saying pleasant, polite, conventional things to them both. She signed a paper. And that old nigger-woman kept staring at her; but Peter avoided meeting her eyes. And her uncle was saying that she must change her frock now, my dear: Peter's boat sailed within the hour, remember. And then she was back in her room, tearing off the dress that only last night she had so fondly fingered.

It lay on the floor in a shimmering heap, and she trampled on it. She had torn the tulle veil and orange-blossoms from her hair, and she stamped on those, too. The maid who had been engaged to help her stood aghast when the bride kicked her wedding-gown across the room. She folded it with shaking hands and smoothed the torn veil as best she could. The beautiful lace-and-ivory fan was snapped and torn beyond hope of salvage. Nancy tossed it from her. With round eyes the maid watched her tear hair-pins out of her hair, rush into the bath-room, and with furious haste belabor her head with a wet brush to remove the fatal frizzings; but the work had been too thoroughly done to hope to remove all traces of it so easily. Nancy brushed it as best she could, and then rolled it into a stout coil on the top of her head. Her satin slippers came hurtling across the room as she kicked them off, and the maid caught them on the fly.

Back into the bath-room again, and the maid could hear her splashing around, as she scrubbed her face. When she came out, it was brick-red, but powderless and paintless. She got into her blue tailored suit without assistance, and, sitting on the floor, buttoned her shoes with her own fingers, to the maid's disgust. Then she jerked on her hat, stuck a hat-pin through it carelessly, snatched up gloves and hand-bag, and was ready for departure. The expression of her face at that

Marie Conway Oemler

moment sent the maid cowering against the wall, and tied her tongue; the bride looked as if she were quite capable of pitching an officious helper out of a ten-story window.

"My God!" said the girl to herself, as Nancy, without so much as a word or a look in her direction, slammed the door behind her. "My God, if that poor fellow that's just been married to *her* was any kin to me, I'd have a High Mass said for his soul!"

The brick-red apparition that swept into the room put the final touch upon Peter's dismay. He thought her the most unpleasant human being he had ever encountered, and almost the ugliest. The Vanderveldes had taken the clergyman off in their car, and only Peter, his uncle, and Emma remained.

"I'm ready!" snapped the bride. She didn't glance at the bridegroom, but the look she bestowed upon Emma made that doughty warrior quail. Emma conceived a mortal terror of Peter's wife. She took the place of the Boogerman and of ha'nts.

Chadwick Champneys had his hand on his nephew's shoulder, and was talking to him in a low and very earnest voice—rather like a clergyman consoling a condemned man with promises of heaven after hanging. Peter received his uncle's assurances in resigned silence.

Two cars were waiting outside the hotel for the wedding-party. As Emma Campbell stepped into the one that was to convey her and Peter to the boat, Nancy saw her stoop and lift a large bird-cage containing, of all things, an immense black cat, which mewed plaintively at sight of her. It was the final touch of grotesqueness upon her impossible wedding. The two Champneyses wrung hands silently. The older man said a few words to the colored woman, and shook hands with her, too.

Then the two cars were rolling away, Nancy sitting silent beside her uncle. At the corner Peter's vanished. The bride hoped from the bottom of her heart that she would never lay eyes upon her bridegroom again. She didn't exactly wish him any harm, greatly as she disliked him, but she felt that if he would go away and die he would be doing her a personal favor.

Peter and Emma made their boat ten minutes before the gang-plank was pulled in. A steward took Emma in charge, and carried off the bird-cage containing Satan. Emma, who had been silent during the drive to the pier, opened her mouth now:

"Mist' Peter," said she, "ef yo' uncle's wuth a million dollars, he ought to tun it over to you dis mawnin'. 'T ain't for me," said Emma, beginning to tremble, "to talk 'bout Mis' Champneys whut you done got married to. But I used to know Miss Maria. And dat's how-come," finished Emma, irrelevantly, "dat's how-come I mighty glad we's gwine to furrin folkses' countries, whichin I hopes to Gawd dey's a mighty long way off fum dat gal." And Peter's heart echoed Emma's sentiments so fully that he couldn't find it in him to reprove her for giving utterance to them.

With a sense of relief, he watched New York receding from his sight. Hadn't he paid too high a price, after all? Remembering his bride's eyes, pure terror assailed him. No woman had ever looked at Peter like that before. He tried to keep from feeling bitter toward his uncle. Well! He was in for it! He would make his work his bride, by way of compensation. For all that he was a bridegroom of an hour or so, and a seeker bound upon the quest of his heart's desire, Peter turned away from the steamer's railing with a very heavy heart.

A tall, fair-faced woman turned away from the railing at the same instant, and their eyes met. Hers were brightly, bravely blue, and they widened with astonishment at sight of Peter Champneys. She stared, and gasped. Peter stared, and gasped, too.

"Miss Claribel!" cried Peter.

"Mrs. Hemingway," she corrected, smiling. "It isn't—Yes, it is, too! Peter! Oh, that Red Admiral *is* a fairy!"

CHAPTER XI

HIS GRANDMOTHER'S HOUSE

"It is rather wonderful to turn around and find *you* here, Peter,—and to find you so unchanged. Because you haven't changed, really; you've just grown up," said Mrs. Hemingway, holding his hand. Her face was excited and glad. "I should have known you instantly, anywhere."

"I am told my legs are quite unmistakable. Some have said I appear to be walking on fishing-poles," said Peter.

Mrs. Hemingway laughed. "They seem to be good, long, serviceable legs," she said, gaily. "But it is your eyes I recognized, Peter. One couldn't mistake your eyes."

Peter smiled at her gratefully. "The really wonderful thing is that you should remember me at all," he told her happily, and his face glowed. That her reappearance should be timed to the outset of his great adventure into life seemed highly significant. One might almost consider it an omen.

As if they had parted but yesterday, they were able to resume their old sympathetic friendship, with its satisfying sense of comradely understanding. Her heart warmed to him now as it had warmed to the shabby boy she had first seen running

Marie Conway Oemler

after the Red Admiral in the fields beyond the river swamp. No, she reflected appraisingly, he had not changed. He had somehow managed to retain a certain quality of childlikeness that made her feel as if she were looking through crystal. She was grateful that no contact had been able to blunt it, that it remained undimmed and serene.

Briefly and rather baldly Peter outlined his years of struggle, dismissing their bleak hardships with a tolerant smile. What he seemed chiefly to remember was the underlying kindness and good humor of the folk back there in Riverton; if they had ever failed to be kind, it was because they hadn't understood, he thought. There was no resentment in him. Why, they were his own folks! His mother's grave was one of their graves, his name one of their names, their traditions and heritages were part and parcel of himself. The tide-water was in his blood; his flesh was dust of the South Carolina coast.

She saw that, while he was speaking. And against the vivid, colorful coast background she caught haunting glimpses of a tireless small figure toiling, sweating, always moving toward a far-off goal as with the inevitable directness of a fixed law. She marveled at the patience of his strength, and she loved his gentleness, his sweetness that had a flavor of other-worldliness in it.

He was telling her now of Chadwick Champneys and how his coming had changed things. But of the price he had had to pay he said nothing. He tried not to think of the bride his uncle had forced upon him, though her narrowed eyes, her red hair, her mouth set in a hard red line haunted him like a nightmare. His soul revolted against such a mockery of marriage. He could imagine his mother's horror, and he was glad Maria Champneys slept beside the husband of her youth in the cemetery beside the Riverton Road. She wouldn't have asked him to pay such a price, not for all the Champneyses dead and gone! But Chadwick Champneys had held him to his bargain, had forced him to give his name, his father's name, of which his mother had been so proud.

Peter smarted with humiliation. It was as if he had been bought and sold, and he writhed under the disgrace of such bondage. He felt the helpless anger of one who realizes he has been shamefully swindled, yet is powerless to redress his injury; and what added insult to injury was that a Champneys, his father's brother, had inflicted it.

Yet he had no faintest notion of breaking or even evading his pledged word; such a thought never once occurred to him. He meant to live up to the letter of his bargain; his honor would compel him to fulfil his obligation scrupulously and exactly.

"And so my uncle and I came to terms," he told Mrs. Hemingway. And he added conscientiously: "He is very liberal. He insisted upon placing to my credit what he says I'll need, but what seems to me too much. And so here I am," he finished.

"Yes, here you are. It had to be," said she, thoughtfully. "It's your fate, Peter."

"It had to be. It's my fate," agreed Peter.

"And that nice, amusing old colored woman who kept house for you—what became of her?"

"Emma? Oh, she wouldn't stay behind, so she came along with me. And she couldn't leave the cat, so he came along, too," said Peter, casually.

Mrs. Hemingway laughed as his uncle had laughed.

"There's an odd turn to your processes, Peter," she commented. "One sees that *you'll* never be molded into a human bread pill! I'm glad we've met again. I think you're going to need me. So I'm going to look after you."

"I have needed you every day since you left," he told her.

He didn't as yet know what deep cause he had to feel grateful for Mrs. John Hemingway's promise to look after him; he didn't as yet know what an important person she was in the American colony in Paris, as well as in certain very high circles of French society itself. And what was true of her in Paris was also true of her in London. Mrs. John Hemingway's promise to look after a young man hall-marked him. She was more beautiful and no less kind than of old, and absence had not had the power to change his feelings for her. As simply and whole-heartedly as he had loved her then, he loved her now. So he looked at her with shining eyes. Reticence was ingrained in Peter, but the knowledge that she liked and understood him had the effect of sunlight upon him.

"He's as simple as the Four Gospels," she thought, "and as elemental as the coast country itself. One couldn't spoil him any more than one could spoil the tide-water.

"Yes, indeed! I'm going to look after you," she repeated.

He discovered, from what she herself chose to tell him, that there had been some unpleasant years for her too. But that had all ended when she married John Hemingway, then with a New York firm and later sent abroad to represent the interests of the company of which he was now a member. His chief office was in Paris, though he had to spend considerable time in London. When she spoke of John Hemingway his wife's face glowed with quiet radiance. The one drop of bitterness in her cup was that there were no children.

"I hope you marry young, Peter, and that there'll be a houseful of little Champneys," she said, and sighed a bit enviously.

At that the face of Mrs. Peter Champneys rose before her bridegroom and the very soul of him winced and cringed. He averted his face, staring seaward.

"I know so many charming young girls," said Mrs. Hemingway, musingly, as if she were speaking to herself.

"They don't come any prettier than they come in Riverton," Peter parried. "And you're to remember I'm coming over here to *work*."

"I'll remember," said she, smiling. "But all the same, I mean you to go about it the right way. I'm going to introduce you to some very delightful people, Peter."

Then Peter took her to see Emma Campbell and the cat.

Emma would have crawled into her berth and stayed there until the ship docked if it hadn't been for the cat. Satan had to be given a daily airing; he had to be looked after by some one she could trust, and Emma rose to the occasion. She crawled out of her berth and on deck, where, steamer rug over her knees, her head tightly bound in a spotless white head-handkerchief, she sat with her hand on the big bird-cage set upon a camp-stool next her chair.

"I don' say one Gawd's word about *me*, dough I does feel lak

I done swallahed my own stummick. All I scared of is dat dis po' unforch'nate cat's gwine to lose 'is min' befo' we-all lan's," she told Mrs. Hemingway, and cast a glance of deep distaste at the tumbling world of waters around her. Emma didn't like the sea at all. There was much too much of it.

"I got a feelin' heart for ole man Noah," she concluded pensively.

When they sighted the Irish coast, Emma discovered a deep sense of gratitude to the Irish: no matter what they didn't have, they did have *land*; and land and plenty of it, land that you could walk on, was what Emma craved most in this world. When they presently reached England, she was so glad to feel solid earth under her feet once more that she was jubilant.

"Cat, we-all is saved!" she told Satan. "You en me is chillun o' Israel come thoo de Red Sea. We-all got a mighty good Gawd, cat!"

They went up to London with Mrs. Hemingway, and were met by Hemingway himself, who gave Peter Champneys an entirely new conception of the term "business man." Peter knew rice- and cotton- and stock-men, even a provincial banker or two—all successful men, within their limits. But this big, quiet, vital man hadn't any limits, except those of the globe itself. A tall, fair man with a large head, decided features, chilly gray eyes, and an uncompromising mouth adorned with a short, stiff mustache, his square chin was cleft by an incomprehensible dimple. His wife declared she had married him because of that cleft; it gave her an object in life to find out what it meant.

Hemingway studied Peter curiously. He had a great respect for his wife's nice and discriminating judgment, and it was plain that this long-legged, unpretentious young man was deeply in her good graces. Evidently, then, this chap must be more than a bit unusual. Going to be an artist, was he? Well, thank God, he didn't *look* as if he were afflicted with the artistic temperament; he looked as if he were capable of hard work, and plenty of it.

People liked to say that John Hemingway was a fine example of the American become a cosmopolitan. As a matter of fact, Hemingway wasn't. He liked Europe, but in his heart he wearied of its over-sophistication, its bland diplomacy. His young countryman's unspoiled truthfulness delighted him. He was proud of it. A man trained to judge men, he perceived this cub's potential strength. That he should so instantly like his wife's protege raised that charming lady's fine judgment even higher in his estimation. A man always respects his wife's judgment more when it tallies with his own convictions.

The Hemingways insisted that Peter should spend some time in England. Mrs. Hemingway was going over to Paris presently, and he could accompany her. In the meantime she wanted him to meet certain English friends of hers. Peter was perfectly willing to wait. He was enchanted with London, and although he would have preferred to be turned foot-loose to prowl indefinitely, his affection for Mrs. Hemingway made him amenable to her discipline. At her command he went with Hemingway to the latter's tailor. To please her he duteously obeyed Hemingway's fastidious instructions as to habiliments. He overcame his rooted aversion to meeting strangers, and when bidden appeared in her drawing-room, and there met smart, clever, and noted London.

Hemingway thereafter marked his progress with amusement not unmixed with amazement. It came to him that there was a greater difference, a deeper divergence between himself and Peter than between Peter and these Britishers. The earmark of your coast-born South Carolinian is the selfsame, absolute sureness of himself, his place, his people, in the essential scheme of things. Wasn't he born in South Carolina? Hasn't he relatives in Charleston? Very well, then!

In Peter's case this essential sureness had developed into a courtesy so instinctive, a democracy so unaffectedly sincere, that it flavored his whole personality with a pleasing distinctiveness. The British do not expect their very young men to be too knowing or too fatally bright; they mark the promise rather than the performance of youth, and spaciously allow time for the process of development. And so Peter Champneys found himself curiously at home in democratically oligarchic England.

"I feel as if I were visiting my grandmother's house," he confided to a certain lady next whom he was seated at one of Mrs. Hemingway's small dinners.

"And where is your mother's house?" wondered the lady, who found herself attracted to him.

"Over home in Riverton," said Peter Champneys. And his face went wistful, remembering the little town with the tidewater gurgling in its coves, and its great oaks hung with long gray swaying moss, and the sinuous lines of the marshes against sky and water, and the smell of the sea—all the mellow magic of the coast that was Home. It didn't occur to him that an English lady mightn't know just where "over home in Riverton" might be. She was so great a lady that she didn't ask. She looked at him and said thoughtfully:

"I wonder if you wouldn't like to see an old place of ours. I'm having the Hemingways down for a week, and I should like you to come with them." And she added, with a charming smile: "As you are an artist, you'll like our gallery. There's a Rembrandt you should see."

Peter's eyes of a sudden went deep and golden, and their dazzling depths had so instant and so sweet a recognition that her heart leaped in answer. It was as if a young archangel had secretly signaled her in passing.

When the formal invitation arrived, Mrs. Hemingway was delighted with what she termed Peter's good fortune. The invitations to that house were coveted and prized she explained. Really, Peter Champneys was unusually lucky! She felt deeply gratified.

Peter hadn't known that there existed anywhere on earth anything quite so perfect as the life in a great English country house. He thought that perhaps the vanished plantation life of the old South might have approximated it. His delight in the fine old Tudor pile, in its ordered stateliness, its mellowed beauty, pleased his hostess and won the regard of the rather grumpy gentleman who happened to be her husband and its owner. To her surprise, he took Peter under his wing, and showed himself as much interested in this modest guest as he was ordinarily indifferent to many more important ones. It was his custom to take what he called a stroll before breakfast—a matter of a mere eight or ten miles, maybe—and he found to his hand a young man with walking legs, seeing eyes, and but a modicum of tongue. He showed Peter that country-side with the thoroughness of a boy birds'-nesting, as Peter had once showed the Carolina country-side to Claribel Spring. They went over the venerable house with the same thoroughness, and Peter sensed the owner's impersonally personal delight in the stewardship of a priceless possession. He held it in trust, and he loved it with a quiet passion that was as much a part of himself as was his English speech. Every now and then he would pause before some rusty sword, or maybe a tattered and dusty banner; and although he was of a very florid complexion, and his nose was even bigger than Peter's, in such moments there was that in the eye and brow, in the expression of the firm lips, that made him more than handsome in the young man's sight. Through him he glimpsed that something silent and large and fine that is England.

"And we're going," said the nobleman, pausing before the portrait of a gentleman who had fallen at Marston Moor. "Oh, yes, we are vanishing. After a while the great breed of English gentlemen will be as extinct as the dodo. And this house will be turned into a Dispensary for Dyspeptic Proletarians, or more probably an American named Cohen will buy it and explain to his guests at dinner just how much it cost him."

Peter remembered broken and vine-grown chimneys where stately homes had stood, the extinction of a romantic plantation life, the vanishing of the gentlemen of the old South, as the Champneys had vanished. They had taken with them something never to be replaced in American life, perhaps; but hadn't that vanished something made room for a something else intrinsically better and sounder, because based on a larger conception of freedom and justice? The American looked at the cavalier's haughty, handsome face; he looked at the Englishman thoughtfully.

"Yes. You will go," he agreed presently. "All things pass. That is the law. In the end it is a good law."

"I should think it would altogether depend on what replaces us," said the other, dryly.

"And that," said Peter, "altogether depends upon you, doesn't it? It's in your power to shape it, you know. However, if you'll notice, things somehow manage to right themselves in spite of us. Now, over home in Carolina we haven't come out so very badly, all things considered."

"Got jolly well licked, didn't you?" asked the Englishman, whose outstanding idea of American military history centered upon Stonewall Jackson.

"Just about wiped off the slate. Had to begin all over, in a world turned upside down. Yet, you see, here I am! And I assure you I shouldn't be willing to change places with my grandfather." With a shy friendliness he laid his fingers for a moment on his host's arm. "Your grandson won't be willing to change, either, because he'll be the right sort. *That's* what your kind hands down." He spoke diffidently, but with a certain authority. Each man is a sieve through which life sifts experiences, leaving the garnering of grain and the blowing away of chaff to the man himself. Peter had garnered courage to face with a quiet heart things as they are. He had never accepted the general view of things as final, therefore he escaped disillusionment.

"They thought the end of the world had come—my people. So it had—for them. But not for us. There's always a new heaven and a new earth for those who come after," he finished.

The Englishman smiled twistedly. After a while he said unexpectedly:

"I wish you'd have a try at my portrait, Mr. Champneys. I think I'd like that tentative grandson of mine to see the sort of grandfather he really possessed."

"Why, I haven't had any training! But if you'll sit for me I'll do some sketches of you, gladly."

Marie Conway Oemler

"Why not now?" asked the other, coolly. "I have a fancy to see what you'll make of me." He added casually: "Whistler used the north room over the stables when he stayed here. You've seen his pastels, and the painting of my father."

"Yes," said Peter, reverently. And he stared at his host, round-eyed.

"We've never changed the room since his time. Should you like to look over it now? You'll find all the materials you are likely to need,—my sister has a pretty little talent of her own, and it pleases her to use the place."

"Why, yes, if you like," murmured Peter, dazedly. And like one in a dream he followed his stocky host to the room over the stables. One saw why the artist had selected it; it made an ideal studio. A small canvas, untouched, was already in place on an easel near a window. One or two ladylike landscapes leaned against the wall.

"She has the talent of a painstaking copyist," said her brother, nodding at his sister's work. "Shall you use oils, or do you prefer chalks, or water-colors?"

"Oils," decided Peter, examining the canvas. "It will be rough work, remember." He made his preparations, turned upon his sitter the painter's knife-like stare, and plunged into work. It was swift work, and perhaps roughly done, as he had said, but by the miracle of genius he managed to catch and fix upon his canvas the tenacious and indomitable soul of the Englishman. You saw it looking out at you from the steady, light blue eyes in the plain face with its craggy nose and obstinate chin; and you saw the kindness and delicacy of the firm mouth. There he stood, flat-footed, easy in his well-worn clothes, one hand in his pocket, the other holding the blackthorn walking-stick he always carried, and looked at you with the quiet sureness of integrity and of power. Peter added a few last touches; and then, instead of signing his name, he painted in a small Red Admiral, this with such exquisite fidelity that you might think that gay small rover had for a moment alighted upon the canvas and would in another moment fly away again.

His lordship studied his painted semblance critically.

"I rather thought you could do it," he said quietly. "I usually manage, as you Americans say, to pick a winner. You'll be a great painter if you really want to be one, Mr. Champneys. Should you say sixty guineas would be a fair price for this?"

"That's something like three hundred dollars, isn't it?" asked Peter, interestedly. "Suppose we call this a preliminary sketch for a portrait I'm to paint later—say when I've had a few years of training."

"You will charge me very much more than sixty guineas for a portrait, two or three years from now," said the other, smiling. He looked at the swiftly done, vivid bit of work. "*This* is what I want for my grandson; it is his grandfather as nature made him. It is as true and as homely as life itself." And he looked at Peter respectfully, so that that young man blushed to his ears. And that is how and when Peter Champneys painted his first ordered picture, signed with the Red Admiral; and how he won the faithful friendship of a crusty Englishman. It was a very real friendship. His lordship had what he himself called a country heart, and as Peter Champneys had the same sort, and neither man outraged the other by too much talk, they got along astonishingly well.

"He's deucedly intelligent," his lordship explained, with quiet enthusiasm. "We'll tramp for miles, and I give you my word that for an hour on end he won't say three words!"

Hemingway, to whom this confidence was given, chuckled. It amused him to watch his wife's wild goose putting on native swan feathers. Yet it pleased him, for he knew the boy appealed to her romantic as well as to her maternal instinct. She handled him skilfully, and it was she who passed upon his invitations. She wished him to meet clever and brilliant men and women; and at times she left him in the hands of young girls, pink-and-white visions who troubled as well as interested him. He felt that he was really meeting them under false pretenses. Their youth called to his, but he might not answer. Between him and youth stood that unloved and unlovely girl in America.

Mrs. Hemingway watched him with the eyes of the woman who has a young man upon her hands. His reactions to his contacts interested her immensely. His worldly education was progressing with entire satisfaction to her.

"I want him to marry an English wife," she confided to her husband. They were to leave for Paris that night, and she was summing up the results of his stay in London, the balance being altogether in his favor. "A well-bred, normal English girl with good connections, a girl entirely untroubled by temperament, who will love him tenderly, look out for his physical well-being, and fill his house with healthy children, is exactly what Peter Champneys needs. And the sooner it happens to him the better. Peter has a lonely soul. It shouldn't be allowed to become chronic."

Hemingway looked at her apprehensively. "Sounds to me as if you were trying to make Peter pick a peck of pickled peppers," he commented. And Peter coming in at this opportune moment, he grinned at the boy cheerfully.

"Peter," he smiled, "the sweet chime of merry wedding-bells in the distance falls softly on mine ear; my wife thinks you should be altar-broke. Charming domestic interior, happy fireside clime, flag of our union fluttering from the patent clothes-line! Futurist painting of Young Artist Pushing a Pram! Don't look at me with such an agonized expression of the ears, Peter!"

But Peter had no answering smile. His face had changed, and there was that in his eyes which gave Hemingway pause.

"Why, old chap, I was merely joking!" he began, with real concern.

"Peter!" said the woman, softly. "You have had—a disappointment? But, my dear boy, you are so *very* young. Don't take it too much to heart, Peter. At your age nothing is final, really." And she smiled at him.

A flush suffused the young man's forehead. He felt shamed and miserable. He *couldn't* flaunt his price-tag before these unbuyable souls whose beautiful and true marriage was based upon love, and sympathy, and mutual ideals! He *couldn't* rattle his chains, or explain Anne Champneys. He couldn't, indeed, force himself to speak of her at all. The thing was bad enough, but to talk about it—No! He lifted troubled eyes.

"I am afraid—in my case—it is final," he said, in a low voice. And after a pause, in a louder tone: "Yes—please understand—it is final."

"Oh, Peter dear, I'm sorry! But—"

"You're talking nonsense. Why, you're barely twenty-one!" protested Hemingway. "Much water must flow under the bridge, Peter, before you can say of anything: it is final. You've got a long life ahead of you to—"

"Work in," finished Peter. "Yes, I know that. I have my chance to work. That is enough." At that his head went up.

Mrs. Hemingway puckered her brows. She leaned toward him, her eyes lighting up.

"Peter!" said she, mischievously, her cheek dimpling. "Peter, aren't you rather leaving the Red Admiral out of your calculations?"

CHAPTER XII

"NOT BY BREAD ALONE"

Mrs. Peter Champneys drove away from the scene of her wedding, feeling as if boiling water had been poured over her. No man of all the men she had ever met had looked at her with just such an expression as she had encountered in Peter Champneys's eyes, and the memory of it filled her with a rankling sense of injustice. He had married her for the same reason she had married him, hadn't he? Then why should he think himself a whit better than she was? It seemed to her that all the unkindness, all the slights she had ever endured, had come to a head in Peter's distressed and astonished glance.

Nancy had no illusions as to her own personal appearance, but it occurred to her that her bridegroom left considerable to be desired in that respect, himself. With his hatchet face and his outstanding ears and his big nose—why, he was as homely as that dried old priest in the glass case in the museum!—and him looking down on people every mite as good as he was! That was really the crux of the thing: Nancy had her own pride, and Peter had managed to trample upon it roughshod. She felt she could never forgive him, and her sense of injury included Chadwick Champneys as well. She hadn't asked him to make his nephew marry her, had she?

The suggestion had come from the Champneys, not from her. Yet it was plain to her that both these men considered her a very inferior person. She couldn't understand them.

She liked the furnished apartment she and Mr. Champneys were to occupy until their house was ready, better than she had liked the hotel, though the Japanese butler, Hoichi, overawed her. She wasn't used to Japanese butlers and she didn't know exactly how to treat this suave, deft, silent yellow man who was so efficient and so ubiquitous. It was different where the maids were concerned; she who had been so lately an unpaid drudge was afraid these trained, clever servants might suspect her former state of servitude and she covered her fear with a manner so insupportable that Mr. Chadwick Champneys, who looked upon arrogant rudeness to social inferiors as a sort of eighth deadly sin, was presently forced to remonstrate.

"Nancy," he ventured one morning, "I have been observing your manner to the servants with—er—disapproval. A habitual lack of consideration is a serious deficiency. It is really a lack of breeding—and of heart. A lady"—he fixed his large dark eyes upon her—"is never impolite."

He touched her on the quick. She *knew* these Champneys didn't think she was a lady, but for this old man to come right out and say so to her face—"Say, I guess I know how to be a lady without you havin' to tell me!"

"I am more than willing to be convinced," said the South Carolinian, pointedly.

At that, of a sudden, Nancy flared. She lifted a pair of sullen and mutinous eyes, and her lips quivered. He saw with surprise that she was trembling.

"Say, you look here—I done what you told me to do, didn't I? I ain't no more nor no less a lady than I was before I done it, am I? What you pickin' on me for, then? What more you want?"

He sighed. Milly's niece was distinctly difficult, to say the least. How, he asked himself desperately, was one to make a dent in her appalling ignorance? She irritated him. And as is usual with people who do not understand, he took exactly the wrong course with her.

"I want you at least to try to live up to your position," he said with cold directness, beetling his brows at her. "I want you to do what you're told—and to keep on doing it! Do you understand that?" He felt that he was allowing himself to be more wrought up than was good for him, and this added to his annoyance.

She considered this, sullenly. "I'm not exackly straight in my mind what I understand and what I don't understand, yet," she replied. "But I got this much straight: If I done what I done to please you, I done it to please me, too!"

This was logical enough; it had even a note of common sense and justice. But her crude method of expressing it filled him with cold fury. The Champneys temper strained at the leash.

"Ah!" said he, a dark flush staining his face, "ah! Then get this straight, too: you'll please me only *if* you carry out your part of our contract. What! do you dream I would ruin my nephew's life for a self-willed, undisciplined minx? Nothing could be farther from my thoughts! Nancy, *I* made you Mrs. Peter Champneys: you will qualify for the position—or lose it!" He tapped his foot on the floor, and glared at her.

Nancy gave him glare for glare. "Yeah, you said it! You

made me Mrs. Peter Champneys, and all I got to do is to do what I don't want to do, to hold down the job! What you askin' *him* to do to please *me*? How's *he* qualifyin'? Is he so much I'm nothin'? Because that's what he thinks! Oh, you needn't talk! I guess I got eyes, at least!"

"I suggest that you use them to your own advantage, then," said he, disgustedly. "Let us have done with such squabbling! You agreed to obey. Very well, then, you will do so, or I shall take steps to put you outside of my calculations. In other words, I will wash my hands of you. Is that perfectly clear to you?" How else, he asked himself, was he to make her understand?

She saw that he was in a towering rage, and she reflected that if she had made Baxter that mad he'd have banged her with his fists. For a long minute the two stared at each other. She was about to make a defiant reply and let come what might, when a sort of spasm distorted his face. His mouth opened gaspingly, his eyes rolled back in his head like a dying man's. He seemed to crumple up, and she caught him as he fell. Her terrified shriek brought Hoichi, who took instant charge of the situation. He made the unconscious man comfortable on a divan, applied such restoratives as were at hand, and directed a frightened maid to telephone for physicians.

Nancy fled to her own room, and sat on the edge of her bed, frightened and subdued. That quarrel and its serious effect made a turning-point in her life, though she attached no blame to herself for the man's illness. She had no love for him, but her heart was not callous to suffering, and his distorted and agonized face had terrified and shocked her.

The suddenness of the seizure made his words more impressive. Suppose he died: what of her? She was not sure that any definite provision had as yet been made for her. What, then, should she do?

Suppose he recovered: what then? She had cause for serious thought. All this luxury and ease, this pleasant life of plenty, in which she reveled with the deep delight of one quite unused to it, hung upon a contingency—the contingency of absolute obedience. She was not naturally supine, and her spirit rose against an unconditional self-surrender to a hot-tempered, imperious old man, who would mold her to his will, make her over to his own notions, quite as high-handedly as if she'd been a lump of putty and not a human being. Nancy tasted the bitterness of having no voice in the making of her own destiny.

Well, but suppose she defied him? He was quite capable of washing his hands of her, just as he had threatened. And then? Before that possibility Nancy recoiled. No. She couldn't, she wouldn't go back to that old life of squalid slavery—eating bad food, wearing wretched clothes, suffering all the sodden and sordid misery of the ignorant, abjectly poor, a suffering twice as poignant now that she knew better things. She knew poverty too well to have any illusions about it. The Baxter kitchen rose before her. Why! while she was sitting here now, in this luxurious room, back there they'd be getting ready for the noonday dinner. The close kitchen would be reeking with the odor of boiling potatoes and cabbage, from which a greasy steam would be arising, so that one saw things as through a hot mist. One of the children would be screaming, somewhere about the house, and Mrs. Baxter, in an unsavory wrapper, her face streaming with perspiration, her hair in sticky strands on her hot forehead, would be shrilly threatening personal chastisement: "You shut up, out there! Just you wait till I get this batch o' biscuits off my hands an' I bet I fix *you*! didn't I say shut up?" The hateful voice seemed so close to Nancy's ear that the girl shrank back, shivering with distaste.

She fingered the soft, fine stuff of the frock she was wearing. She stared about the room,—*her* room, which she didn't have to share with one of the Baxter children, who squirmed and kicked all night in summer, and pulled the bed-coverings off her in winter. She went over to her dressing-table and fingered its pretty accessories, sniffing with childish pleasure the delicately scented powder and cologne. She looked at her reflection in the mirror, and scowled. Then she began to walk restlessly up and down the room. She had to think this thing out.

Why should she go, and leave the road clear for Peter Champneys? It occurred to her that, seen from his point of view, her elimination from the scene might be regarded somewhat in the light of providential interference in his behalf. She flushed. It wasn't fair! The thought of Peter Champneys was gall and wormwood to her.

Nancy wasn't a fool. Her honesty had a blunt directness, a sort of cave-woman frankness. In her, truthfulness was not so much a virtue as an energy. The hardness of her unloved life had bred a like hardness in her sense of values; she was distrustful and suspicious because she had never had occasion to be anything else. In that suspicion and distrustfulness had lain her safety. She had no sense of spiritual values as yet. Religion had meant going to church on Sundays when you had clean clothes in which to appear. Morals had meant being good, and to Nancy being good simply meant not being bad—and you couldn't be bad, go wrong, if you never trusted any man. A girl that trusted none of 'em could keep respectable. Nancy had seen girls who trusted men, in her time. Nothing like that for *her*! But she knew, also, the price the woman pays whether she trusts or distrusts, and the matrimony which at times rewarded the distrustful didn't appear much more alluring than the potter's field which waited for the credulous. Anyway you looked at it, what happened wasn't pleasant. And it was worse yet when you knew there was something better and different. You had to pay a price to get that something better and different, of course. The fact that one pays for everything one gets was coming home to Nancy with increasing force; the problem, then, was to get your money's worth.

She took her head in her hands, and tried to concentrate all her faculties. She wasn't a shirker, and she realized that she must decide upon her course of conduct now and stick to it. If she didn't look out for herself, who would? And presently she had reached the conclusion that when Mr. Peter Champneys reappeared upon the scene, he must find Mrs. Peter Champneys occupying the foreground, and occupying it creditably, too. She'd do it! When Mr. Chadwick Champneys recovered, she'd come to terms with him. She'd keep faith.

She spent three or four anxious days, while specialists came and went, and white-capped, starched, authoritative personages relieved each other in the sick-room, their answers to all queries being that the patient was doing quite as well as could be expected. At the end of the fifth day they admitted that the patient was recovering,—was, in fact, out of danger, though he wouldn't leave his room for another week or ten days; and he wasn't to be worried or disturbed about anything.

Satisfied, then, that he was on the highroad to recovery, and having made up her mind as to her own course of procedure, Nancy rather enjoyed these few days of comparative freedom. She supplied herself with a huge box of bonbons, "Junie's Love Test" and "The Widowed Bride,"—books begun long ago, but wrested from her untimely by the ruthless Mrs. Baxter, on the score of takin' her time off: her rightful work for them that'd took her in, and fillin' her red head with the foolishest sort o' notions. She had had so much to do that to have nothing to do but lie around in a red silk kimona and nibble chocolates and read love stories, seemed to her the supreme height of felicity.

She reveled in these novels. They represented that something different toward which her untutored and stinted heart groped blindly. Otherwise her mind, by no means a poor one, lay fallow and untilled. The beauty and wonder of the world, the pity and terror of fate, the divine agony of love which sacrifices and endures, did not as yet exist for her. She merely sensed that there was something different, somewhere—maybe on the road ahead. And so she wept over the woes of star-crost lovers, and sentimentalized over husky heroes utterly unlike any male beings known to nature, and believed she didn't believe that disinterested and unselfish love existed in the world. As she hadn't the faintest gleam of self-knowledge, in all this she was perfectly sincere.

She did not see Mr. Champneys for two weeks or so. In his nervous condition he evinced a singular reluctance to have her come near him, although others saw him daily. For instance, Mr. Jason Vandervelde appeared at half after ten o'clock every morning during his client's convalescence, was immediately admitted to Mr. Champney's room, and left it upon the stroke of eleven.

Nancy watched this man curiously. When he met her in the hall, he spoke to her in a nice, full-toned, modulated voice, exceedingly pleasing to the ear. His eyes were small but of a deep and bright blue, and although he was heavily built he wore his clothes so well that he gave the effect of strength rather than of clumsiness. He was clean-shaven and ruddy, and his large, well-shaped mouth was deeply curled at the corners. His hands were not fat and white, as one might expect, but tanned and muscular, and slightly hairy. His glasses gave him a certain precision, and his curled lips suggested irony. Nancy liked to look at him. He discomfited her understanding of men, for, she couldn't tell why, she both liked and trusted him. There was nothing romantic about him,—a well-fed, well-groomed lawyer-man in his late thirties, with a handsome wife in a handsome house,—yet he had the faculty of making her wonder about him, and wonder with kindness at that. She wished she knew just how much he knew about her, her early upbringing, her sad lack of education. What had Mr. Champneys told him? Or had he really told him anything?

When her uncle finally overcame his reluctance and sent for her, she entered his room quietly and stood looking at him with an honest concern that was in her favor. She was always honest, he reflected. There was nothing of the hypocrite or the coward in those wary gray-green eyes that always met one's glance without flinching.

The change in his appearance shocked her. His eyes were hollow, his tall form looked meager and shrunken. He was growing to be an *old* man. She said awkwardly:

"I'm real sorry you been so sick." And she made no attempt to apologize for her share in the quarrel that had led to his seizure. She ignored it altogether, and for this he was grateful.

"Thank you. I am getting along nicely," he said civilly. And with a slightly impatient gesture he dismissed all further mention of illness. He leaned back in his chair and closed his eyes, the better to collect his thoughts. He wished to make his wishes perfectly clear to her. But she surprised him by saying quietly:

Marie Conway Oemler

"I been thinking things over while you was sick, and I come to the conclusion you was right. I got to have more education. There's things I just got to know—how to talk nice, and what to wear, and what fork you'd ought to eat with. Forks and things drive me real wild."

"I had thought, at first, of sending you to some particularly fine boarding-school—" he began, but Nancy interrupted him.

"If I was six instead o' sixteen, you might do it. As 't is, I wouldn't learn nothin' except to hate the girls that'd be turnin' up their noses at me. No. I don't want to go to boardin'-school. I've saw music-teachers that come to folks' houses to give lessons, and I been thinkin', why can't you get me a school-teacher that'll teach me right at home!"

"As I was saying when interrupted,"—he looked at her reprovingly—"I had at first thought of sending you to some finishing school. I gave up that idea almost at once. I agree with you that it is best you should be taught at home. In fact, I have already engaged the lady who will be your companion as well as your teacher."

"I don't know as I'm crazy about a lady companion as a steady job," said Nancy, doubtfully. She feared to lose her new liberty, to forego the amazing delight of living by herself, so to speak. "But now you've done it, I sure hope you've picked out somebody *young*. If I got to have a lady companion, I want she should be young."

"Mr. Vandervelde attended to the matter for me," said Mr. Champneys, in a tone of finality. "He is sure that the lady in question is exactly the person I wish. Mrs. MacGregor is an Englishwoman, the widow of a naval officer. She is in reduced circumstances, but of irreproachable connections.

She has the accomplishments of a lady of her class, and her companionship should be an inestimable blessing to you. You will be governed by her authority. She will be here tomorrow."

"A ole widder woman! Good Lord! I—" here she stopped, and gulped. An expression of resignation came over her countenance. "Oh, all right. You've done it an' I'll make the best of it," she finished, not too graciously.

"It is not proper to refer to a lady as 'a ole widder woman'."

"Well, but ain't she?" And she asked: "What else you know about her?"

"Mr. Vandervelde attended to the matter," he repeated. "He is thoroughly satisfied, and that is enough for me—and for you. I sent for you to inform you that she is to be here tomorrow. See that you receive her pleasantly. Your hours of study and recreation will be arranged by her. She will also overlook your wardrobe. And, I do not wish to hear any complaints."

"I can't even pick out my own clothes?"

"You lack even the rudiments of good taste."

"What's wrong with my clothes?" she demanded.

"Everything," said he, succinctly, and with visible irritation. He remembered the wedding-gown, and his face twitched. She watched him intently.

"Oh, all right. I said I'd obey, an' I will. I ain't forgettin'," said she, wearily.

"Very well. I am glad you understand." He closed his eyes, and understanding that the interview was at an end, Nancy withdrew.

Mrs. MacGregor arrived on the morrow. The attorney had been given explicit orders and instructions by his exacting client, who had his own notions of what a teacher for his niece should and shouldn't be. Vandervelde congratulated himself on having been able to meet them so completely in the person of the estimable Mrs. MacGregor.

Mr. Champneys demanded a lady middle-aged but not too middle-aged, not overly handsome, but not overly otherwise; an excellent disciplinarian, of a good family, and with impeccable references.

For the rest, Mrs. MacGregor was a tall, spare, high-nosed lady, with a thin-lipped mouth full of large, sound teeth of a yellowish tinge, and high cheek-bones with a permanent splash of red on them. Her eyes were frosty, and her light hair was frizzled in front, and worn high on her narrow head. She dressed in plain black silk of good quality, wore her watch at her waist, and on her wrist a large, old-fashioned bracelet in which was set a glass-covered, lozenge-shaped receptable holding what looked like a wisp of bristles, but which was a bit of the late Captain MacGregor's hair.

Mr. Champneys had wanted a lady who was a church member. He had a vague idea that if a lady happened to be a church member you were somehow or other protected against her. Mrs. MacGregor was orthodox enough to satisfy the most rigid religionist. Mr. Champneys gathered that she believed in God the father, God the son, and God the Holy Ghost, three in One, and that One a dependable gentleman beautifully British, who dutifully protected the king, fraternally respected the Archbishop of Canterbury and the

Prime Minister, and was heartily in favor of the British Constitution. Naturally, being a devout woman, she agreed with Deity.

An American family domiciled for a while in England had secured her services as companion to an elderly aunt of theirs, fetching her along with them, on their return to America. The aunt had been a family torment until the advent of Mrs. MacGregor, but in the hands of that disciplinarian she had become a mild-mannered old body. On her demise the grateful family settled a small annuity upon her whom they couldn't help recognizing as their benefactor. Finding Americans so grateful, Mrs. MacGregor decided to remain among them and with her recommend-dations secure another position of trust in some wealthy family. This, then, was the teacher selected by Mr. Jason Vandervelde, who thought her just what Mr. Champneys wanted and his ward probably needed.

Mrs. MacGregor never really liked anybody, but she could respect certain persons highly; she respected Mr. Chadwick Champneys at sight. His name, his appearance, the fact that Jason Vandervelde was acting for him, convinced her that he was "quite the right sort"—for an American. She was as gracious to him as nature permitted her to be to anybody. And the salary was very good indeed.

It was only when Nancy put in her appearance that Mrs. MacGregor's satisfaction withered around the edges. The red on her high cheeks deepened, and she fixed upon her new pupil a cold, appraising stare. She made no slightest attempt to ingratiate herself; that wasn't her way; what she demanded, she often said, was Respect. The impossible young person who was staring back at her with hostile curiosity wasn't overcome with Respect. The two did not love each other.

Strict disciplinarian though she might be where others were concerned, Mrs. MacGregor treated herself with lenient consideration. She was selfish with a fine, Christian zeal that moved Nancy to admiring wonder. Nancy's own selfishness had been superimposed upon her by untoward circumstances. This woman's selfishness was a part of her nature, carefully cultivated. She believed her body to be the temple of the Holy Ghost, and she made herself exceedingly comfortable in the building, quite as if the Holy Ghost were an obliging absentee landlord. Nancy observed, too, that although the servants did not like her, they obeyed her without question. She got without noise what she wanted.

But she really could teach. Almost from the first lesson, Nancy began to learn, the pure hatred she felt for her instructress adding rather than detracting from her progress. Had the woman been broader, of a finer nature, she might have failed here; but being what she was, immovable, hard as nails, narrow and prejudiced, sticking relentlessly to the obviously essential, she goaded and stung the girl into habits of study.

Her reaction to Mrs. MacGregor really pushed her forward. She knew that the woman could never overcome a secret sense of amaze that such a person as herself should be a member of Chadwick Champneys's family—the man was a *gentleman*, you see. And she called Nancy "Anne." Her lifted eyebrows at Nancy's English, her shocked, patient, parrot-like, "Not 'seen him when he done it,' *please*. You *saw* him when he *did* it!—No, 'I come in the house' isn't correct. Try to remember that *well-bred* persons use the past tense of the verb; thus: 'I *came* into the house.'—What *do* I hear, Anne? You '*taken*' it? No! You TOOK it!" And she would look at Nancy like a scandalized martyr, ready to die for the noble cause of English grammar! Rather than endure that look, rather than face those uplifted eyebrows, Nancy, gritting her teeth, set herself seriously to the task of making over her method of speech.

It was Mrs. MacGregor who, discovering the girl's unstinted allowance of candy, cut off the supply. She didn't care much for candies herself, but she did like fruit, and fruit was substituted for the forbidden sweets. She had the healthy, wholesome English habit of walking, and unless the weather was impossible she forced her unwilling charge to take long tramps with her, generally immediately after breakfast. They would set out, Nancy dressed in a plain blue serge, her pretty, high-heeled pumps discarded for flat-heeled walking-shoes, Mrs. MacGregor flat-footed also, tall, bony, in a singular bonnet, but nevertheless retaining an inherent stateliness which won respect. Sometimes they tramped up Riverside Drive, their objective being Grant's tomb. Mrs. MacGregor respected Grant; and the stands of dusty flags brought certain old British shrines to her mind. On stated mornings they visited the Library, while Mrs. MacGregor selected the books Nancy was to read, books that Nancy looked at askance. They had their mornings for the museums, too. Mrs. MacGregor knew nothing of art, except that, as she said to Nancy, well-bred persons simply *had* to know something about it. After their walk came lessons, grueling, dry-as-dust, nose-to-the-grindstone lessons, during which Nancy's speech was vivisected. At two o'clock they lunched, and Nancy had further critical instructions. The dishes she had once been allowed to order were changed, greatly to her annoyance; Mrs. MacGregor liked such honest stuff as mutton chops and potatoes, just as she insisted upon oatmeal for breakfast. Porridge, she called it. In the afternoon they motored; Mrs. MacGregor, who detested speed, became the bane of the hard-faced chauffeur's life.

They dined at seven, and for an hour thereafter Mrs. MacGregor either read aloud from some book intended to edify the young person, or forced Nancy to do so. She was possibly the only person alive who delighted in Hannah More. She said, modestly, that at an early age she had been taught to revere this paragon, and whatever happy knowledge of the virtues proper to the female state she possessed, she owed in a large measure to that model writer. Nancy conceived for Hannah More a hatred equaled in intensity only by that cherished for Mrs. MacGregor herself.

Mrs. MacGregor's notions of dress and her own were asunder, even as the poles. But here again that rigid duenna did her invaluable service, for if she didn't look handsome in the clothes selected for her, she didn't, as that lady said frankly, look vulgar in them. No longer would you be liable to mistake her for somebody's second-rate housemaid on her day out. The simple diet and the inexorable regularity of her hours also told in her favor, although she herself wasn't as yet aware of the change taking place. Already you could tell that hers was a supple and shapely young body, with promise of a magnificent maturity; you glimpsed behind the fading freckles a skin like a water-lily for creamy whiteness; and that red hair of hers, worn without frizzings, began to take on a glossy, coppery luster.

That spring they moved into the new house. It was so different from the average newly-rich American home that it moved even Mrs. MacGregor to praise. Nancy thought it rather bare. It hadn't color enough, and there were but few pictures. Yet the old rosewood and mahogany furniture pleased her. She remembered that golden-oak, red-plush parlor at Baxter's with a sort of wonder. Why! she had thought that parlor handsome! And now she was beginning to understand how hideous it had been.

She saw little of Mr. Champneys, who seemed to be plunged to the eyes in business. Occasionally he appeared, looked at her searchingly, said a few words to her and Mrs. MacGregor, and vanished for another indefinite period. Mr. Jason Vandervelde was almost a daily visitor when Mr. Champneys happened to be in the city. At times Mr. Champneys went away, presumably to look after business interests, and Nancy thought that at such times the lawyer accompanied him. She had no friends of her own age, and Mrs. MacGregor wasn't, to say the least, companionable. And the books she was compelled to read bored her to distraction. She took it for granted they must be frightfully good, they were so frightfully dull! The deadliest, dullest of all seemed to be reserved for Sunday. She didn't mind going to church; in church you could watch other people, even though Mrs. MacGregor sat rigidly erect by your side, and expected you to be able to find your place in a Book of Common Prayer entirely unfamiliar to you. While she sat rapt during what you thought an unnecessarily long sermon, you could look about you slyly, and take note of the people within your immediate radius.

Nancy liked to observe the younger people. Sometimes a bitter envy would almost choke her when she regarded some girl who was both pretty and prettily dressed, and, apparently, care-free and happy. She watched the younger men stealthily. Some of them pleased her; she would have liked to be admired by at least one of them, and she felt jealous of the fortunate young women singled out for their attentions. Think of being pretty, and having beautiful clothes, and swell fellows like that in love with you! That any one of these fine young men should cast a glance in her own direction never entered her mind. No. Loveliness and the affection and gaiety of youth were for others; for her— Peter Champneys. At that she fetched a deep sigh. She always went home from church silent and subdued. Mrs. MacGregor thought this a proper attitude of mind for the Sabbath.

The girl was vaguely disturbed and uneasy without knowing why. The newness and glamour of the possession of creature comforts, the absence of want, was wearing thin in spots. She was conscious of a lack. She was beginning to think and to question, and as there was no one in whom she might confide, she turned inward. Naturally, she couldn't answer her own questions, and all her thoughts were as yet chaotic and confused. She wanted—well, what did she want, anyhow? She repeated to herself, "I want something different!" That something different should not include a dreary round of Mrs. MacGregor, a cold inspection by Mr. Chadwick Champneys; nor the thought of Peter Champneys. It *would* include laughter and—and people who were neither teachers nor guardians, but who were gay, and young, and kind. She began to be conscious of her own isolation. She had always been isolated. Once poverty had done it; and now money was doing it. Those girls she saw at church—she'd bet they went to parties, had loads of friends, had a good time, were loved; plenty of people wanted their love. For herself, as far back as she could look, she had never had a friend. Who cared for her love? Sometimes she watched the new maid, a distractingly pretty little Irish girl, black-haired, blue-eyed, rosy-faced. The girl tried to be demure, to restrain the laughter that was always near the surface; but her eyes danced, her cheek dimpled, she had what one might call a smiling voice. And the handsome young policeman on the corner was acutely aware of her. Nancy remembered one afternoon when she and Mrs. MacGregor happened to be coming in at the same time with Molly. It was Molly's afternoon off and she was dressed trimly, and with taste. Under her little close-fitting hat her hair was like black satin, her face like a rose. The young policeman managed to pass the house at that moment, and lifted his cap to her; Nancy saw the look in the young man's eyes. She followed Mrs. MacGregor into the house, rebelliously. Nobody had ever looked at *her* like that. Nobody was ever going to look at her like that. She remembered Peter Champneys's eyes when they had first met hers. A dull flush stained her face, and bitterness overwhelmed her.

Mr. Champneys was busy; Mrs. MacGregor was satisfied— she had a position of authority; her creature comforts were exquisitely attended to; her salary was ample. The man saw his plans being carried forward, if not brilliantly at least creditably; the woman saw that her tasks were fulfilled. It never occurred to either that the girl might or should ask for more than she received, or that she might find her days dull. But Nancy was discovering that the body is more than raiment, and that one does not live by bread alone.

CHAPTER XIII

THE BRIGHT SHADOW

The Champneys chauffeur, greatly to Mrs. MacGregor's terror and disapproval, seemed to live for speed alone; in consequence, one afternoon Mrs. MacGregor and Nancy very narrowly escaped dying for it. Whereupon Mr. Champneys summarily dismissed the chauffeur and engaged in his place young Glenn Mitchell, accidentally brought to his notice. Mr. Champneys congratulated himself upon the discovery of Glenn Mitchell. To begin with, he was a South Carolinian, one of those well-born, penniless, ambitious young Southerners who come to New York to make their fortune. One of his forebears had married a Champneys. That was in ante bellum days, but South Carolina has a long memory, and this far-off tie immediately established the young fellow upon a footing of family relationship and of cousinly friendliness. He was a personable youth of twenty, who had worked his way through high school and meant presently to go through the College of Physicians and Surgeons,—his grandfather had been a distinguished physician, Mr. Champneys remembered. The boy proposed to use his skill in handling a motor-car as a means toward that end.

Mr. Chadwick Champneys would gladly have paid Glenn's

college expenses out of his own pocket, but the young man, delicately sounded, politely but sturdily declined. The next best thing the kindly old Carolinian could do, then, was to make the boy a member of his own household. Hoichi had orders to prepare a room for Mr. Mitchell, and Mrs. MacGregor was advised that he would take his meals with the family. She was at first inclined to be scandalized: to bring your chauffeur to your own table was Americanism with a vengeance! But when she met the young man, she was mollified. This chauffeur was a gentleman, and in Mrs. MacGregor's estimation a gentleman may do many things without losing caste. She remembered that the perfectly decent younger son of a certain poverty-stricken nobleman had driven a car. This young Mitchell was exceptionally good-looking in a nice, boyish, fresh-faced way, and she saw in his manner a youthful reflection of the courtliness which distinguished Mr. Chadwick Champneys. He had a great deal of that indefinable something we call charm, and before she knew it Mrs. MacGregor was won over to him, and looked upon his presence as a distinct addition to the Champneys menage.

When he had been introduced to Nancy, she was mentioned as "My niece, Mrs. Champneys." Mrs. MacGregor called her "Anne." Mr. Champneys spoke to her as "Nancy," and Glenn thought he must have been mistaken as to that "Mrs." There was no sign of a husband anywhere; neither was there any indication of widowhood. Nobody mentioned Peter—Mr. Champneys because he was more interested in talking about Glenn's business than his own, on the occasions when he had time to talk about anything; Mrs. MacGregor, because she had never seen Peter, knew nothing at all about him, except that there was a nephew somewhere in the background of things, and wasn't in the least interested in anything but her own immediate affairs; besides, it never would have occurred to her to talk about her employer's affairs, even if she had known anything about them. An employer who was a gentleman, and very wealthy, belonged to the Established Order, and Mrs. MacGregor had the thorough-going British respect for Established Order. Nancy, for her part, wished to forget that Peter existed. She never by any chance mentioned him, or even thought of him if she could help it. So when young Glenn Mitchell, after the pleasant South Carolina fashion, addressed her as "Miss Nancy" it seemed perfectly all right to everybody.

Nancy was a little over eighteen then. She had grown taller, but she retained the pleasant angularity of extreme youth. Because she didn't know how to arrange her hair, Mrs. MacGregor sternly forbidding frizzing and curling, and insisting upon a "modest simplicity becoming to a young girl" she wore her red mane in a huge plait. She had been so teased and badgered about her red hair, had hated it so heartily, been so ashamed of it, that she didn't realize how magnificent it was now, after two years of care and cleanliness. It wasn't auburn; it wasn't Titian; it was a bright, rich, glittering, unbuyable, undeniable red, and Nancy wore her plait as a boy wears a chip on his shoulder. Young Glenn Mitchell was seized with a wild desire to catch hold of that braid that was like a cable of gleaming copper, and wind it around his wrists. For the first time, he thought, he was seeing the true splendor and beauty of red hair; and the girl had the wonderfully white skin that accompanies it. He suspected that she must have been pretty badly freckled when she was a child, for the freckles were still fairly visible, though one saw that they would presently vanish altogether. The curve of her throat and chin, the "salt-cellars" at the base of the neck, left nothing to be desired. Altogether there was that about this girl that caught and held his boyish attention. It wasn't that she was pretty,—he had at first thought her plain. It was rather that here lay a tantalizing promise of unfoldment by and by, a sheathed hint of something rare and perilous.

He didn't quite know what to make of Mr. Champneys's niece. She was abnormally silent, unbelievably unobtrusive, singularly still. Watching her, he found himself wishing she would smile, at least occasionally: he longed to see what her mouth would look like if it should curve into laughter. She had exquisite teeth, and her eyes, when one was allowed to get a glimpse of them, were of a curious, agaty, gray green, with one or two little spots or flecks in the iris. Hers was an impassive, emotionless face; yet she gave a distinct impression of feeling, emotion, passion held in check; it was as if her feelings had been frozen. But suppose a spring thaw should set in—what then? Would there be just a calm brook flowing underneath placid willows, or a tempestuous torrent sweeping all before it? He wondered!

She sat opposite him at table three times a day, and never addressed a word to him, or to Mrs. MacGregor, who carried on whatever conversation there might be. Mrs. MacGregor liked to give details of entertainments "at home," at which she herself had been present, or of events in which A Member of My Family had participated. "I said to the dear Bishop,"—"His Lordship remarked to My Cousin." Sometimes during these recitals the thin, fine edge of a smile touched Nancy's lips. It was gone so quickly one wasn't quite sure it had been there at all; yet its brief passage gave her a strange expression of mockery and of weariness. She offered no opinions of her own about anything; she made no slightest attempt to keep the conversation alive; you could talk, or you could remain silent—it was all one to her. Yet dumb and indifferent though she appeared to be, you felt her presence as something very vital, listening, and immensely honest and natural.

He wished she would speak to him, say something more than

a mere "Yes" or "No." Girls had always been more than willing to talk to Glenn Mitchell—very much prettier and more fascinating girls than this silent, stubborn, red-headed Anne Champneys. He began to feel piqued, as well as puzzled.

And then, one day, he happened to glance up suddenly and in that instant encountered a full, straight, intense look from her—a look that weighed, and wondered, and searched, and was piercingly, almost unbearably eager and wistful. He felt himself engulfed, as it were, in the bottomless depths of that long, clear gaze, that went over him like the surge of great waters, and drenched his consciousness to the core. Brand-new Eve might have looked thus at brand-new Adam, sinlessly, virginally, yet with an avid and fearful questioning and curiosity. For the second his heart shook and reeled in his breast. Then the dark lashes fell and veiled the shining glance. Her face was once more indifferent and mask-like.

As a matter of fact, Nancy was avidly interested in Glenn, in whom for the first time she encountered youth. He came like a fresh breeze into an existence in which she stifled. From his first appearance in the house she had watched him stealthily, looking at him openly only when she thought herself unobserved. Conscious of her own defects, she was timid where this good-looking young man was concerned. It never occurred to her that she might interest him, but she did not wish him to think ill of her. She kept herself in the background as much as possible.

She had none of the joyousness natural to a girl of her age. She had no young companions. Was there some reason? Wasn't she happy? He felt vaguely troubled for her. She aroused his sympathy, as well as his curiosity. He couldn't forget that look he had surprised. It stayed in his memory, perilously. At night in his room, when he should have been studying, that astonishing glance came before him on his book, and cast a luminous spell upon him.

He surprised no more such glances. She still relegated to Mrs. MacGregor the full task of talking to him; a task that lady performed nobly. Just as she walked every morning with Mrs. MacGregor, she took her place in the car every afternoon, apparently obeying orders. Sometimes, twisting his head around, he could glimpse her profile turned toward the moving panorama of the crowded streets through which he was skilfully manoeuvering his way. But if she were interested in what she gazed at so fixedly, she made no comment. One never knew what she thought about anything.

One memorable evening she appeared at dinner in a yellow frock, instead of the usual serge or plain blue silk. It wasn't an elaborate dress, but its prettily low neck allowed one to admire her full throat, with a string of amber beads around it. Her hair hung in two thick braids across her shoulders, and the straight lines of the yellow satin accentuated the youthfulness of her figure. Glenn's heart behaved unmannerly.

She appeared not to see his quick, pleased glance, but turned instead to Mrs. MacGregor, who was regarding her critically. Mrs. MacGregor hadn't been consulted about the yellow frock, and she viewed it with distinct disapproval. Glenn found himself solidly aligned against Mrs. MacGregor, and siding with the girl. He liked that yellow frock; somehow it suited her coloring, enabled one to see how unusual she really was. He wondered that he had thought her so plain, at first. She agitated him. He wished intensely that she would look at him; and just then she did, and for the first time saw admiration in a young man's eyes, not for another girl, but for herself! She held his glance, doubtfully, timidly; but she couldn't doubt the evidence of her senses. Glenn was pleased with her, he admired her! His ingenuous face beamed the fact, from frank eyes and smiling lips. There was somewhat more than admiration in his look, but Nancy was more than content with what appeared on the surface. Her eyes widened, a flush rose to her cheek, a naive and pleased smile transformed her dissatisfied young mouth. When he ventured to speak to her presently, she ventured to reply, shyly, but with new friendliness. Once, when Mrs. MacGregor said something sententious, and Glenn laughed, Nancy laughed with him.

That frank and boyish admiration restored to her, as it were, some rightful and precious heritage long withheld, an indispensable birthright the lack of which had beggared and stripped her. She had a sense of profound gratitude to this likable and handsome young man, a moved and touching interest in him. He made her feel glad to be alive; through him the world seemed of a sudden a kindlier place, full of charming surprises. And when she accompanied Mrs. MacGregor to church on the following Sunday, she looked with a secret sisterliness at the girls she had envied and disliked. It was as if she had been elected to their ranks, been made one of them; she wasn't on the outside of things any more; somebody—a very desirable and handsome some-body—admired her, too. She didn't analyze her feelings. Youth never thinks or analyzes, it feels and realizes; that is why it is divine, why it is lord of the earth. Her growing liking for him was so shy, so naive, so touchingly sincere, that Glenn was profoundly moved when he became aware of it. He had the old South Carolina chivalry; to him women were still invested with a halo, and one approached them with a manly reverence. He had liked girls, many girls; he would have told you, himself, that he never met a pretty girl without loving her some! But this was the first time Glenn had ever really fallen in love, and he fell headlong, with an impetuous ardor that all but swept him off his feet, and that was like strong wine to Nancy, whose drink heretofore had been lukewarm water.

He didn't know whether or not she was Mr. Champney's sole heir, and he didn't care: what difference could that make? He was as well born as any Champneys, wasn't he? And if he wasn't blessed with much of this world's goods just now, he took it for granted he was going to be, after a while. As for that, hadn't Chadwick Champneys himself once been as poor as Job's turkeys? And hadn't Mr. Champneys acknowledged the relationship existing between them, slight and distant though it was? Who'd have the effrontery to look down on one of the Mitchells of Mitchellsville, South Carolina? He'd like to know! Glenn began to dream the rosy dreams of twenty.

It took Nancy somewhat longer to discover the amazing truth. She was more suspicious and at the same time very much more humble-minded than Glenn. But suspicion faded and failed before his honest passion. His agitation, his eagerness, his face that altered so swiftly, so glowingly, whenever she appeared, would have told the truth to one duller than Nancy. If Mrs. MacGregor could have suspected that anybody could fall in love with Anne Champneys, she must have seen the truth, too. But she didn't. She was serenely blind to what was happening under her eyes.

Nancy never forgot the day she discovered that Glenn loved her. Mrs. MacGregor had one of her rare headaches. She was a woman who hated to upset the fixed routine of life, and as their afternoon outing was one of the established laws, she insisted that Nancy should go, though she herself must remain at home. Half fearful, half delighted, Nancy went. Glenn had looked at her, mutely entreating; in response to that entreaty she took the seat beside him. For some time neither spoke—Glenn because he was too wildly happy, Nancy because she hadn't anything to say. She was curious;

she waited for him to speak.

"I wonder," gulped Glenn, presently, "if you know just how happy I am."

Nancy said demurely that she didn't know; but if he was happy she was glad: it must be very nice to be happy!

"Aren't *you* happy?" he ventured.

Nancy turned pink by way of answer. As a matter of fact, she was nearer being happy then than she had ever been. They fell into an intimate conversation—that is, Glenn talked, and the girl listened. He explained his hopes, ambitions, prospects. He talked eagerly and impetuously. He wished her to understand him, to know all about him,—what he was, what he hoped to be. A boy in love is like that.

In return for this confidence Nancy explained that she hated oatmeal, and Hannah More; some of these days she meant to buy every copy of Hannah More she could lay her hands on, and burn them. Of herself, her past, she said nothing.

"And so you're going to be a doctor!" she turned the conversation back to him, as being much more interesting.

"Yes. Or rather, I'm going to be a great surgeon." And then he asked, smilingly:

"And you—what do *you* want to be?"

"I want to be happy," said Nancy, half fiercely.

"There isn't any reason why you shouldn't be—a girl like you."

Nancy looked a bit doubtful. But no, he wasn't poking fun. And after a pause, he asked, as one putting himself to the test:

"Miss Anne—Nancy—do you think you could be happy—with *me*?"

"*You*?" breathed Nancy, all a-tremble. She thought she could be happier with Glenn than with anybody else. Why! there *wasn't* anybody else! That is, nobody that cared. She was afraid to say so. But her moved and changed face said it for her.

"Because, if you could be happy with me, why shouldn't you be?" asked Glenn, brilliantly. But Nancy understood, and her heart crowded into her throat with delight, and terror, and a sort of agony. She felt that she loved and adored this boy to distraction. She would have adored anybody who loved and desired her, who found her fair. But she didn't understand that; neither did Glenn.

"You care?" said the boy, leaning toward her. They were running slowly, along a road high above the river. "Nancy, you care?"

Care? Of course she cared! She considered him the most beautiful and desirable of mortals; she was so enraptured, so thrilled with the astounding fact that he cared for her, that she couldn't speak, but looked at him with swimming eyes. He brought the car to a stop, slipped an arm around her shoulder, and drew her close. She knew that something momentous was going to happen to her, and looked at him, full of a sweet terror. "I love you!" said Glenn, and kissed her on the mouth.

His beard was the ghost of down on his cheek; her hair hung

Marie Conway Oemler

in a braid to her waist; their kiss was the kiss of youth,—tender, passionately pure. Everything but that morning face, pale with young emotion, looking at her with enamored eyes, vanished from her mind; everything else counted for nothing, went like chaff upon the wind. The one fact alone remained: *Glenn loved her*! Her senses were in a delicious tumult from the power and the glory of it: *Glenn loved her*! It was as if a skylark sang in her breast, as if she walked in a rosy and new-born world. Had Nancy been called upon to die for him then, she would have gone to her death shining-eyed, fleet-footed, joyous.

"I love you, I love you!" Glenn repeated it like a litany. "Nancy! Does it make you as happy because I love you as it makes me because you love me?"

"Oh, ten thousand times ten thousand times more!" she said fervently.

"I think it was your hair I fell in love with, first off," he told her presently. "I have never seen a girl with such hair, and such a lot of it. I'm crazy about your hair, Nancy."

"I think you must be," she agreed whole-heartedly. She wasn't vain, his girl!

They had no more plans than birds or flowers have. Plenty of time for sober planning by and by, when one grew accustomed to the sweet miracle of being beloved as much as one loved! Glenn simply took it for granted he was going to marry her. He had known her all of three months—a lifetime, really!—and she had allowed him to kiss her, had admitted she cared. He supposed they would have to wait until he had been through his training and won that coveted degree. Until then, they would keep their beautiful secret to themselves; they didn't wish to share it with anybody, yet.

It was only when she was alone in her room that night that Nancy realized the true situation that confronted her. On the one side was Glenn, dear, wonderful Glenn, who loved her. On the other was Peter Champneys, who had married her as she had married him, for the Champneys money. Peter Champneys! who despised her, and whom she must consider a barrier between herself and whatever happiness life might offer her! She could understand how Glenn had made his mistake. Nobody had explained Peter to him. To tell him the truth now meant to lose him. She was like a person dying of thirst, yet forbidden to drink the cup of cold water extended to her.

Wasn't it wiser to take what life offered, drain the cup, and let come what might? Why not snatch her chance of happiness, even though it should be brief? Suppose one waited? Deep in her heart was the hope that something would happen that would save her; youth always hopes something is going to happen that will save it. Wasn't it possible Peter might fall in love with somebody, and divorce her? One saw how very possible indeed such a thing was! For the present, let Glenn love her. It was the most important and necessary thing in the world that Glenn should love her. What harm was she doing in letting Glenn love her? Particularly when Peter Champneys didn't, never would, any more than she ever could or would love Peter Champneys.

Even Mrs. MacGregor noticed the change taking place in Anne Champneys. The girl had more color and animation, and at times she even ventured to express her own opinions, which were strikingly shrewd and fresh and original. Her eyes had grown sweeter and clearer, now that she no longer slitted them, and her mouth was learning to curve smilingly. Decidedly, Anne was vastly improved! And her manner had subtly changed, too; she was beginning to show an individuality that wasn't without a nascent fascination.

Marie Conway Oemler

Mrs. MacGregor plumed herself upon the improvement in her pupil, which she ascribed to her own civilizing and potent influence, for she was a God-fearing woman. She didn't understand that the greatest Power in heaven and earth was at work with Nancy.

But although Glenn became daily more enamored of the girl, he wasn't so satisfied with things as they were. He couldn't say that Nancy really avoided him, of course. He drove her and Mrs. MacGregor, whom at times he wished in Jericho, out in the car every afternoon. He sat opposite her at table thrice daily. Sometimes in the evening he spent an hour or two with her and Mrs. MacGregor, before going to his own room to study. But it so happened that he never was able to see her alone any more; and Nancy certainly made no effort to bring about that desirable situation. This made him restive and at the same time increased his passion for her.

For her part, she was perfectly content just to look at him, to know that he was near. But Glenn was more impatient. He wanted the fragrance of her hair against his shoulder; he wanted the straight, strong young body in his arms; he wished to kiss her. And she held aloof. Although she no longer veiled her eyes from him, although he was quite sure she loved him, she was always tantalizingly out of his reach. She didn't seem to understand the lover's desire to be alone with the beloved, he thought. He grew moody. The weeks seemed years to his ardent and impetuous spirit. One night, happening to need a book he had noticed in the library, he went after it. And there, oh blessed vision, sat Nancy! She had been sleepless and restless, and had stolen out of her room for something to read that hadn't been selected by Mrs. MacGregor. It was rather late, but finding the quiet library pleasanter to her mood than her own room, she curled up in a comfortable chair and began to read. The book was Hardy's "Tess," and its strong and somber passion and tragedy filled her with pity and terror. Something in her was roused by the story; she felt that she understood and suffered with that simple and passionate soul.

She looked up, startled, as Glenn entered the room. He came to her swiftly, his arms outstretched, his face alight.

"You!" he cried, radiant and elate. "You!"

Nancy rose, torn between the desire to retreat, and to fling herself into those waiting arms. Glenn left her no choice. He seized her, roughly and masterfully, and held her close, pressing her against his body. His lips fastened upon hers. Nancy closed her eyes and shivered. She felt small and helpless, a leaf before the wind, and she was afraid.

"Nancy!" he whispered. "Nancy! You've got to marry me. We'll just have to risk it, degree or no degree! What's the use of waiting all our lives, maybe, when we love each other? When will you marry me, Nancy?"

She knew then that she had to tell him the truth, and she trembled.

"Glenn, I—I—" she stammered. Her tongue seemed to cleave to the roof of her mouth.

"Soon? Say yes, Nancy! I'm crazy about you, don't you know that? Why don't you say when, Nancy?"

She felt desperate, as if some force were closing in upon her, relentlessly. She had to speak, and yet she couldn't. She tried to escape from the arms that held her, but they clasped her all the closer. His eager lips closed on hers.

"Nancy! Ah, darling, why not let everything go and marry

me at once?"

Ah, why not, indeed? As if Peter Champneys had reached across the sea to divide her and Glenn, a stern voice answered Glenn's question.

"Because she has a husband already," it said harshly. Chalky white, with blazing eyes, Chadwick Champneys confronted Peter's wife in another man's arms. "She is married to my nephew, Peter Champneys. Is it possible you do not know?"

Glenn's arms dropped. Intuitively he moved away from her. His visage blanched, and he stared at her strangely.

"Nancy, is this thing true?"

Nancy nodded. She said in a lifeless voice: "Oh yes, it's true. I was trying to tell you, but—" And then she broke into a cry: "Glenn, you don't understand! Glenn, listen, please listen! I did love you, I do love you, Glenn! You—you don't know—you don't understand—"

The boy staggered. He was an honorable, clean-souled boy, heir to old heritages of pride, and faith, and chivalry. A dull, shamed red crept from cheek to brow, replacing his pallor. His gesture, as he turned away from her, made her feel as if she had been struck across the face. She winced. She saw herself judged and condemned.

"Mr. Champneys," stammered Glenn, painfully, "surely you know I didn't understand—don't you? I—we—fell in love, sir. We'd meant to wait—that's why I didn't come to you at once—but I—that is, I was very much in love with her, and I was going to make a clean breast of it and ask you what we'd better do. And you're not to think I'm—dishonorable—" he choked over the word.

Knowing the boy's breed, Champneys laid a not unkindly hand on his shoulder.

"I see how it was," he said. "And—I guess you're punished enough, without any reproaches from me."

Glenn turned to Nancy. "Why did you do it?" he cried. "I loved you, I trusted you. Nancy, why did you do such a thing—to *me*?"

She twisted her fingers. Well, this was the end. She was to be thrust out of the new brightness, back into the drab dreariness, the emptiness that was her fate. She lifted tragic eyes.

"I never expected you to love me. But when you did—I just *had* to let you! Nobody else cared—ever. And I loved you for loving me—I couldn't help it, Glenn; I couldn't help it!" Her voice broke. She stood there, twisting her fingers.

An old, wise, kind woman, or an old priest who had seen and forgiven much, or men who knew and pitied youth, would have understood. Neither of the men to whom she spoke realized the significance of that childishly pitiful confession. Champneys felt that she had shamed his name, belittled the sacred Family which was his fetish; Glenn thought she had made a fool of him for her own amusement. Never again would he trust a woman, he told himself. And in his pain and shame, his smarting sense of having been duped, his hideous revulsion of feeling, he spoke out brutally. Nancy was left in no doubt as to the estimation in which he now held her. And she understood that it was his pride, even more than his love, that suffered.

She made no further attempt to explain or to exculpate herself; what was the use? She knew that had they changed places, had Glenn been in her shoes and she in his, her judgment had not been thus swift and merciless. Her larger love would have understood, and pitied, and forgiven. Pride! They talked of Pride, and they talked of Name. But she could only feel that the one love she had ever known, or perhaps ever was to know, was going from her, must go from her, unforgiving, as if she had done it some irreparable wrong. She looked from one wrathful, accusing face to the other, like a child that has been beaten. How could Glenn, who had seemed to love her so greatly, turn against her so instantly? Not even—Peter Champneys—had looked at her as Glenn was looking at her now! And of a sudden she felt cold, and old, and sad, and inexpressibly tired. So this was what men were like, then! They always blamed. And they never, never understood. She would not forget.

She checked the impulse to cry aloud to Glenn, to try once more to make him understand. Her eyes darkened, and two bright spots burnt in her cheeks. Without a further word or glance she walked out of the room and left the two standing close together. So stepped Anne Champneys into her womanhood.

She locked her door upon herself. Then she went over, after her fashion, and stared at herself in her mirror. The herself staring back at her startled her—the flushed cheeks, the mouth like coral, the eyes glowing like jewels under straight black brows. The ropes of red hair seemed alive, too; the whole figure radiated a personality that could be dynamic, once its powers should be fully aroused.

She viewed the woman in the glass impersonally, as if it had been a stranger's face looking at her. That vivid creature couldn't be Nancy Simms, not quite three years ago the Baxter slavey, the same Nancy that Peter Champneys had shrunk from with aversion, and that Glenn had repudiated to-night!

"Yes,—it's me," she murmured. "But I ain't—I mean I am not really ugly any more. I'm—I don't know just *what* I am— or whether I ought to like or hate me—" But even while she shook her head, the face in the glass changed; the mouth drooped, the color faded, the light in the eyes went out. "But whatever I am, I'm not enough to make anybody keep on loving me." Then, because she was just a girl, and a very bewildered, sad, and undisciplined girl, she put her red head down on her dressing-table and wept despairingly.

The next morning Mr. Champneys explained to the concerned and regretful Mrs. MacGregor that Mr. Mitchell had been called away suddenly, last night, and didn't think he would be able to return. The ladies were to accept Mr. Mitchell's regrets that he hadn't been able to bid them good-by in person. Mr. Champneys bowed for Mr. Mitchell, in a very stately manner. He went on with his breakfast, while Nancy made a pretense of eating hers, hating life and wishing with youthful intensity that she was dead, and Glenn with her. His empty place mocked and tortured her. He had gone, and he didn't, wouldn't, couldn't understand. She could never, never hope to make Glenn understand! She rather expected Mr. Champneys to sit in judgment upon her that morning, but a whole week passed before Hoichi brought the message that Mr. Champneys wished to see her in the library. Her uncle was standing by the window when she entered, and he turned and bowed to her politely. He was thinner, gaunter, more Don Quixotish than usual. If only he had been kind! But his face was set, and hers instinctively hardened to match it.

"Nancy," he began directly, "I have not sent for you to load you with reproaches for your inexplicable conduct. But I must say this: deliberately to deceive and befool an honest gentleman, to trifle with his affections out of mere greedy vanity, is so base that I have no words strong enough to condemn it."

"I didn't mean to fool him. He fooled himself, and I let him do it," said she, dully. He thought her listlessness indifference, and any bluntness in moral tone in a woman, scandalized him. He could understand a Mrs. MacGregor, who was without subtleties; or soft, loving, courageous women like Milly and his sister-in-law, Peter's mother. But this girl he couldn't fathom. He beat his hands together, helplessly.

"I—you—" he groaned. And then: "Oh, Peter, what have I done to you!"

"I can't see you've done anything to him, except pay him to go away and learn how to make something out of himself," returned Nancy, practically. It brought him up short. "Uncle Chadwick, please keep quiet for a few minutes: I want you to listen to me." She met his eyes fully. "I didn't do Glenn Mitchell any real harm: he'll fall in love with somebody else pretty soon. I suppose it's easy for Glenn to love people because it's easier for people to love Glenn. And he's done me this much good: I won't be so ready to believe it's easy for folks to love *me*, Uncle Chadwick. I guess I'm the sort they mostly—*don't*. I'll not forget." She spoke without bitterness, even with dignity. "One thing more, please. If ever Peter Champneys finds out he loves somebody, and he'll let me know, I'll give him his freedom. Fortune or no fortune, I won't hold him. I know now—a little—what loving somebody means," she finished.

Her voice was so steady, her eyes so clear and direct, her manner so contained, that he was uncomfortably impressed. He felt put upon the defensive. As a matter of fact, in his first anger and surprise at what he still considered her shameless behavior, he had seriously considered the advisability of having Peter's marriage annulled. As soon as he had become calmer, his pride and obstinacy rejected such a course. After all, no harm had been done. She was very young. And he hoped Glenn's outspoken condemnation had taught her a needed and salutary lesson. Looking at her this morning, he realized that she had been punished. But that she should so calmly speak of divorcing Peter, of making way for some other woman, horrified him.

"You are talking immoral nonsense!" he said, angrily. "Let him go, indeed! Divorce your husband! What are we coming to? In my day marriage was binding. No respectable husband or wife ever dreamed of divorce!"

"But they were real husbands and wives, weren't they?" asked Nancy.

"All husbands and wives are real husbands and wives!" he thundered.

She considered this—and him—carefully. "Then you don't want Mr. Peter Champneys and me ever to be divorced? I thought maybe you might."

"I forbid you even to *think* such wickedness," cried he, alarmed. "A girl of your age talking in such a manner! It's scandalous, that's what it is,—scandalous! Shows the dry-rot of our national moral sense, when the very children"—he glared at Nancy—"gabble about divorce!"

"Then I—I mean, things are just to go along, the same as they have been?" She looked at him pleadingly.

For a few minutes he drummed on the library table with his thin brown fingers. His bushy brows contracted. He asked unexpectedly:

Marie Conway Oemler

"Would you like to go away for a while? To travel?"

"Where?"

"Where? Why, anywhere! There's a whole world to travel in, isn't there? Well, take Mrs. MacGregor and travel around in it, then."

She shook her head.

"What's the use? Anywhere I went I'd have to go with *me*, wouldn't I? And I can't seem to like the idea of traveling around with Mrs. MacGregor, either."

"What *do* you want, then?"

"I don't know," said she, in a low voice. And she added: "So I think I might just as well stay right on here at home, if it's all the same to you."

"Well, if it pleases you, of course—" he began doubtfully.

"If I do stay, you needn't be afraid I'll fall in love with anybody else you hire," said she, with a faint flush. "I'm only a fool the same way once." Her bomb-shell directness all but stunned him. He stammered, confusedly:

"Why—very well then, very well then! Quite so! I see exactly what you mean! I—ah—am very glad we understand each other." But as the door closed behind her, he mumbled to himself:

"Now, that was a devil of an interview, wasn't it! What's come over the girl? And what's the matter with *me*?" After a while he telephoned Mr. Jason Vandervelde.

Everything went on as usual in the orderly, luxurious house, for some ten quiet months or so. And then one memorable morning at the breakfast-table Mr. Champneys suddenly gasped and slid down in his chair. Nancy and Hoichi carried him into the library and placed him on a lounge. He opened his eyes once, and stared into hers with something of his old imperiousness. She took his hand, pitifully, and bent down to him.

"Yes, Uncle Chadwick?"

But he didn't speak—to her. His eyes wandered past her. His lips trembled, into a whisper of "*Milly*!" With that he went out to the wife of his youth.

CHAPTER XIV

SWAN FEATHERS

While Mr. Chadwick Champneys was alive, Nancy had been able to feel that there was some one to whom she, in a way, belonged. Now that he was gone, she felt as if she had been detached from all human ties, for she couldn't consider Peter as belonging. Peter wasn't coming home, of course. He was content to leave his business interests in the safe hands of Mr. Jason Vandervelde, and the trust company that had the Champneys estate in charge. A last addition to Mr. Champneys's will had made the lawyer the guardian of Mrs. Peter Champneys until she was twenty-five.

While he was putting certain of his late client's personal affairs in order, Mr. Vandervelde necessarily came in contact with young Mrs. Peter. The oftener he met her, the more interested the shrewd and kindly man became in Anne Champneys. When he first saw her in the black she had donned for her uncle, the unusual quality of her personal appearance struck him with some astonishment.

"Why, she's grown handsome!" he thought with surprise. "Or maybe she's going to be handsome. Or maybe she's not, either. Whatever she is, she certainly can catch the human eye!"

He remembered her as she had appeared on her wedding-day, and his respect for Chadwick Champneys's far-sighted perspicacity grew: the old man certainly had had an unerring sense of values. The girl had a mind of her own, too. At times her judgment surprised him with its elemental clarity, its penetrating soundness. The power of thinking for herself hadn't been educated out of her; she had not been stodged with other people's—mostly dead people's—thoughts, therefore she had room for her own. He reflected that a little wholesome neglect might be added to the modern curriculum with great advantage to the youthful mind.

Her isolation, the deadly monotony of her daily life, horrified him. He realized that she should have other companionship than Mrs. MacGregor's, shrewdly suspecting that as a teacher that lady had passed the limit of usefulness some time since. Somehow, the impermeable perfection of Mrs. MacGregor exasperated Mr. Vandervelde almost to the point of throwing things at her. She made him understand why there is more joy in heaven over one sinner saved, than over ninety and nine just persons. He could understand just how welcome to a bored heaven that sinner must be! And think of that poor girl living with this human work of supererogation!

"Why, she might just as well be in heaven at once!" he thought, and shuddered. "I've got to do something about it."

"Marcia," he said to his wife, "I want you to help me out with Mrs. Peter Champneys. Call on her. Talk to her. Then tell me what to do for her. She's changed—heaps—in three years. She's—well, I think she's an unusual person, Marcia."

A few days later Mrs. Jason Vandervelde called on Mrs. Peter Champneys, and at sight of Nancy in her black frock experienced something of the emotion that had moved her husband. She felt inclined to rub her eyes. And then she wished to smile, remembering how unnecessarily sorry she and Jason had been for young Peter Champneys.

Marcia Vandervelde was an immensely clever and capable woman; perhaps that partly explained her husband's great success. She looked at the girl before her, and realized her possibilities. Mrs. Peter was for the time being virtually a young widow, she had no relatives, and she was co-heir to the Champneys millions. Properly trained, she should have a brilliant social career ahead of her. And here she was shut up—in a really beautiful house, of course—with nobody but an insufferable frump of an unimportant Mrs. MacGregor! The situation stirred Mrs. Vandervelde's imagination and appealed to her executive ability.

Mrs. Vandervelde liked the way she wore her hair, in thick red plaits wound around the head and pinned flat. It had a medieval effect, which suited her coloring. Her black dress was soft and lusterless. She wore no jewelry, not even a ring. There were shadows under her grave, gray-green eyes. Altogether, she looked individual, astonishingly young, and pathetically alone. Mrs. Vandervelde's interest was aroused. Skilfully she tried to draw the girl out, and was relieved to discover that she wasn't talkative; nor was she awkward. She sat with her hands on the arms of her chair, restfully; and while you spoke, you could see that she weighed what you were saying, and you.

"I am going to like this girl, I think," Marcia Vandervelde told herself. And she looked at Nancy with the affectionate eyes of the creative artist who sees his material to his hand.

"Jason," she said to her husband, some time later, "what would you think if I should tell you I wished to take Anne Champneys abroad with me?"

"I'd say it was the finest idea ever—if you meant it."

"I do mean it. My dear man, with proper handling one might make something that approaches a classic out of that girl. There's something elemental in her: she's like a birch tree in spring, and like the earth it grows in, too, if you see what I mean. I want to try my hand on her. I hate to see her spoiled."

"It's mighty decent of you, Marcia!" said he, gratefully.

"Oh, you know how bored I get at times, Jason. I need something real to engage my energies. I fancy Anne Champneys will supply the needed stimulus. I shall love to watch her reactions: she's not a fool, and I shall be amused. If she managed to do so well with nobody but poor old Mr. Champneys and that dreary MacGregor woman, think what she'll be when *I* get through with her!"

Vandervelde said respectfully: "You're a brick, Marcia! If she patterns herself on you—"

"If she patterns herself on anybody but herself, I'll wash my hands of her! It's because I think she won't that I'm willing to help her," said his wife, crisply.

Some six weeks later the Champneys house had been closed indefinitely, the premises put in charge of the efficient Hoichi, and Mrs. MacGregor bonused and another excellent position secured for her, and Mrs. Peter Champneys was making her home with her guardian and his wife.

She might have moved into another world, so different was everything,—as different, say, as was the acrid countenance of Mrs. MacGregor from the fresh-skinned, clear-eyed, clever, handsome face of Marcia Vandervelde. Everything interested Nancy. Her senses were acutely alert. Just to watch Mrs. Vandervelde, so calm, so poised and efficient, gave her a sense of physical well-being. She had never really liked, or deeply admired, or trusted any other woman, and the real depths of her feeling for this one surprised her. Mrs. Vandervelde possessed the supreme gift of putting others at their ease; she had tact, and was at the same time sincere and kind. Nancy found herself at home in this fine house in which life moved largely and colorfully.

A maid had been secured for her, whom Mrs. Vandervelde pronounced a treasure. Then came skilful and polite persons who did things to her skin and hair, with astounding results. After that came the selection of her wardrobe, under Mrs. Vandervelde's critical supervision. Although the frocks were black, with only a white evening gown or two for relief, Nancy felt as if she were clothed in a rosy and delightful dream. She had never even imagined such things as these black frocks were. When she saw herself in them she was silent, though the super-saleswomen exclaimed, and Mrs. Vandervelde smiled a gratified smile.

"I am going to keep her strictly in the background for the time being, Jason," she explained to her husband. "As she's already married, she can afford to wait a year—or even two. I mean her to be perfect. I mean her to be absolutely *sure*. She's going to be a sensation. Jason, have you ever seen anything to equal her team-work? When I tell her what I want her to do, she looks at me for a moment—and then does it. One thing I must say for old Mr. Champneys and that MacGregor woman: they certainly knew how to lay a firm foundation!"

Nancy was perfectly willing to remain in the background. She was interested in people only as an on-looker. She responded instantly to Mrs. Vandervelde's suggestions and instructions, and carried them out with an intelligent thoroughness that at times made her mentor gasp. It gave her a definite object to work for, and kept her from thinking too much about Glenn Mitchell. And she didn't want to think about Glenn Mitchell. It hurt. She watched with a quiet wonder—quite as if it had been a stranger to whom all this was happening—the change being wrought in herself; the immense difference intelligent care, perfectly selected clothes, and the background of a beautiful house can make not only in one's appearance but in one's thoughts. Sometimes she would stare at the perfectly appointed dinner-table, with its softly shaded lights; she would look, reflectively, from Marcia Vandervelde's smartly coiffured head to her husband's fine, aristocratic face; the reflective glance would trail around the beautiful room, rest appreciatively upon the impressive butler, come back to the food set before her, and a fugitive smile would touch her lips and linger in her eyes. There were times when she felt that she herself was the only real thing among shadows; as if all these pleasant things must vanish, and only her lonesome self remain. She watched with a certain wistfulness the few people she knew. Marcia, now—so admired, so sure, with so many interests, so many friends, and with Jason Vandervelde's quiet love always hers—did *she* ever have that haunting sense of the impermanence of all possessions; of having, in the end, nothing but herself?

"What are you thinking, when you look at me like that?" Marcia asked her one evening, smilingly. She was as curious about Nancy as Nancy was about her.

"I was just—wondering."

"About what?"

"I was wondering if you were ever lonely?" said Nancy,

truthfully. "I mean, as if all this,"—they were in the drawing-room then, and she made a gesture that included everything in it,—"just *things*, you know, all the things you have—and—and the people you know—weren't *real*. They go. And nothing stays but just *you*. *You*, all by yourself." She leaned forward, her eyes big and earnest.

Marcia Vandervelde stared at her. After a moment she said, tentatively: "There are always things; things one has, things one does. There are always other people."

"Yes, or there wouldn't be you, either. But what I mean is, they go. And you stay, don't you?" She paused, a pucker between her brows, "All by yourself," she finished, in a low voice.

"Does that make you afraid?" asked Mrs. Vandervelde.

"Oh, no! Why should it? It just makes me—wonder."

Mrs. Vandervelde said quietly: "I understand." Nancy felt grateful to her.

A few days later Mrs. Vandervelde said to her casually: "An old friend of ours dines with us to-night, Anne,—Mr. Berkeley Hayden, one of the most charming men in the world. I think you will like him."

Mrs. Vandervelde always said that Berkeley Hayden was the most critical man of her acquaintance, and that his taste was infallible. He had an unerring sense of proportion, and that miracle of judgment which is good taste. He was one of those fortunate people who, as the saying goes, are born with a gold spoon in the mouth. Unlike most inheritors of great wealth, he not only spent freely but added even more freely to the ancestral holdings. He was moneyed enough to do as he pleased without being considered eccentric; he could even afford to be esthetic, and to prefer Epicurus to St. Paul. He had a highly important collection of modern paintings, and an even more valuable one of Tanagra figurines, old Greek coins, and medieval church plate. He had, too, the reputation of being the most gun-shy and bullet-proof of social lions. At thirty he was a handsome, well-groomed, rather bored personage, with sleekly-brushed blond hair and a short mustache. He looked important, and one suspected that he must have been at some pains to keep his waist line so inconspicuous. For the rest, he was as really cultivated and pleasing a pagan as one may find, and so wittily ironical he might have been mistaken for a Frenchman.

Mrs. Vandervelde had planned that he should be the only guest. She knew this would please him, as well as suit her own purpose, which was that he should see young Mrs. Peter Champneys. She was curious to learn what impression Anne would create, and if Berkeley Hayden's judgment would coincide with her own. She had informed him that Jason's ward was stopping with them; would, in fact, go abroad with her shortly. Mr. Hayden was not interested. He thought a ward rather a bore for the Vanderveldes.

He was standing with his back to the mantel, facing the door, when Nancy entered the room. In the filmy black Mrs. Vandervelde had selected for her, tall and slim, she paused for the fraction of a second and lifted her cool, shining, inscrutable green eyes to his lazy blue ones. Mrs. Vandervelde had prevailed upon her to retain her own fashion of wearing her hair in plaits wound around her head, and the new maid had managed to soften the severity of the style and so heightened its effectiveness. A small string of black pearls was around her throat, and pendants of the same beautiful jewels hung from her ears. Berkeley Hayden started, and his eyes widened. Mrs. Vandervelde, who had been watching him intently, sighed imperceptibly.

"I wasn't mistaken, then," she thought, and smiled to herself.

She could have hugged Anne Champneys for her beautifully unconscious manner. Of course the girl didn't understand she was being signally honored and favored by Hayden's openly interested notice, but Marcia reflected amusedly that it wouldn't have made much difference if Anne had known. He didn't interest her, except casually and impersonally. She thought him a very good-looking man, in his way, but rather old: say all of thirty:—and Glenn Mitchell had been handsome, and romantic, and twenty. Young Mrs. Champneys, then, didn't respond to Mr. Berkeley Hayden's notice gratefully, pleasedly, flutteringly, as other young women—and many older ones—did. This one paid a more flattering attention to Mr. Jason Vandervelde than to him. But he had seen other women play that game; he wondered for a moment if this one were designing. But he was himself too clever not to understand that this was real indifference. Then he wondered if she might be—horrible thought!— stupid. He was forced to dismiss that suspicion, too. She wasn't stupid. The truth didn't occur to him—that he himself was spoiled. It provoked him, too, that he couldn't make her talk.

Mrs. Vandervelde smiled to herself again. Berkeley was deliberately trying to make himself agreeable, something he did not often have to trouble himself to do. He was at his best only when he was really interested or amused, and he was at his best to-night. He aroused her admiration, drew the fire of her own wit and raillery, stung even quiet Jason into unwonted animation. Anne Champneys looked from one to the other, concealing the fact that at times their conversation was over her head. She didn't always understand them. The sense of their unreality in relation to herself came upon her.

She turned to watch this strange man who was saying things that puzzled her, and he met her eyes, as Glenn Mitchell had once met them. She wasn't looking at him as she had looked at Glenn, but Berkeley Hayden's sophisticated, well-trained, wary heart gave an unprecedented, unmannerly jump when those green eyes sought to fathom him.

Marcia spoke of their proposed stay abroad. She had gone to school in Florence, and she retained a passionate affection for the old city, and showed her delight at the prospect of revisiting it.

"This will be your first visit to Italy, Mrs. Champneys?" asked Hayden.

"Yes."

"I envy you. But you mustn't allow yourself to be weaned away from your own country. You must come back to New York." He smiled into her eyes—Berkeley Hayden's famous smile.

"Yes, I suppose I must," said Nancy, without enthusiasm.

He felt puzzled. Was she unthinkably simple and natural, or was she immeasurably deep? Was her apparent utter unconsciousness of the effect she produced a superfine art? He couldn't decide.

He usually knew exactly why any certain woman pleased him. He had usually demanded beauty; he had worshiped beauty all his life. But beauty must go hand in hand with intellectual qualities; he hated a fool. To-night he found himself puzzled. He couldn't tell exactly why Anne Champneys pleased him. Studying her critically, he decided that she was not beautiful. He could not even call her pretty.

Perhaps it was her unusualness. But wherein was she so unusual? He had met women with red hair and white skin and gray-green eyes before—women far, far more seductive than Jason's ward. Yet not one of them all had so potently gripped his imagination.

Mrs. Vandervelde was a brilliant pianist, and after dinner Hayden begged her to play. Under cover of the music, he watched Mrs. Champneys. She was sitting almost opposite him, and he could observe her changing countenance. Nancy was beginning to love and understand good music. Men create music; women receive and carry it as they receive and carry life. It is quite as much a part of themselves.

Nancy's eyes shadowed. She leaned back in her chair, and the man watched the curve of her white cheek and throat, and the thick braids of her red hair. She had forgotten his presence. He was saying to himself, with something of wonder, "No, she's not beautiful: but, my God! how *real* she is!" when, subtly drawn by the intensity of his gaze, she turned, looked at him with her clouded eyes, and smiled vaguely. Still smiling, she turned her head again and gave herself up to listening, unconscious that destiny had clapped her upon the shoulder.

The man sat quite still. It had come to him with, the suddenness of a lightning stroke, and his first feeling was one of stunned amazement, and an almost incredulous resentment. He had gone to and fro in the earth and walked up and down in it, comfortably immune, an amused and ironic looker-on. And now, at thirty, without rhyme or reason he had fallen in love with a red-haired young woman of whom he knew absolutely nothing, beyond the bare fact that she was Jason Vandervelde's ward. A woman who didn't conform to any standard he had ever set for himself, whose mind was a closed book to him, of whose very existence he had been ignorant until to-night. Old Dame Destiny must have sniggered when she thrust Mrs. Peter Champneys, nee Nancy Simms, into the exquisitely ordered life of Mr. Berkeley Hayden!

He presently discovered from Jason all that the trustee of the Champneys estate knew of Mrs. Peter, which really wasn't very much, as the lawyer and his wife had never seen Nancy until the morning of her marriage. And he didn't have much to say about her as she was then. Hayden gathered that it was a marriage of convenience, for family reasons—to keep the money in the family. He asked a few questions about Peter, whom Vandervelde thought a likely young fellow enough, but whom Hayden fancied must be a poor sort—probably a freak with a pseudo-artistic temperament. There couldn't have been very much love lost between a husband and wife who had consented to so singular a separation. Hayden had a *very* poor opinion of Mr. Peter Champneys! But he was fiercely glad it hadn't been a love-match, glad that that other man's claim upon Anne was at the best nominal, that theirs was a marriage in name only.

He saw her several times before her departure, and came no nearer to understanding her. The night before they sailed, he gave a dinner in his apartment, an old aunt of his, more enchanting at sixty than at sixteen, being the only other guest. That apartment with its brocaded walls and its marvelous furniture was a revelation to Nancy. It was like an opened door to her.

She looked at her host with a new interest. He appeared to greater advantage seen, as it were, against his proper and natural background. And that background had the glamour of things strange, exciting, and alluring, smacking somewhat of, say, an Arabian Night's entertainment. Over the dining-room mantel hung a curious and colorful landscape, in which two brown girls, naked to the waist and from thence to the knees wrapped in straight, bright-colored stuff, raised their angular arms to pluck queer fruit from exotic trees.

He knew all that, she thought; he had seen that strange landscape and those brown women, and tasted the fruit they reached to pluck. Just as he knew those tiny terra-cotta figurines over there, and that pottery which must have been made out of ruby-dust. Just as he knew everything. All this had been in his world, always. A world full of things beautiful and strange. He had had everything that she had missed. It seemed to her that he incarnated in his proper and handsome person all the difference and the change that had come into her life.

And quite suddenly she saw Nancy Simms dusting the Baxter parlor, pausing to stand admiringly before a picture on a white-and-gold easel, that cherished picture of a house with mother-of-pearl puddles in front of it. A derisive and impish amusement flickered like summer lightning across her face, and with an inscrutable smile she mocked the mother-of-pearl puddles and her old admiration of them. She lifted her eyes to the painting over Berkeley Hayden's mantel, and the smile deepened.

"Perhaps it is her smile," thought he, watching her. "Yes, I am sure it must be her smile. I am rather glad Marcia is taking her abroad. I do not wish to make a fool of myself, and there'd be that danger if she remained." Yet the idea of her absence gave him an unaccustomed pang.

He filled her quarters aboard ship with exquisite flowers. She was not yet used to graceful attentions, they had been for other women, not for her. She had no idea at all that she was of the slightest importance, if only because of the Champneys money; her comparative freedom was still too recent for her to have changed her estimate of herself. She thought it touchingly kind and thoughtful of this handsome, important man to have remembered just *her*, particularly when there wasn't anybody else to do so, and she looked at him with a pleased and appreciative friendliness for which he felt absurdly grateful. While Marcia was busied with the other friends who had come to see her off, he stood beside Mrs. Champneys, who seemed to know no one but himself, and this established a measure of intimacy between them.

"It occurs to me," said he, tentatively, "that it has been some time since I saw Florence. All of two or three years."

They stood together by the railing, and she leaned forward the better to watch a leggy little girl with a brickdust-red pigtail in a group on the pier.

"Yes?" said she, absently. The leggy girl had just thrust out her tongue at an expostulating nurse. She seemed to be a highly unpleasant child; one of those children of whom aunts speak as "poor Mary" or whatever their name may be. Anne Champneys, watching her, put her hand up and touched her own hair, that gleamed under her close-fitting black hat. Her eyes darkened; she smiled, secretly, mysteriously, rememberingly.

In that instant Berkeley Hayden made his decision. There was no longer any doubt in his mind. When she turned away from the railing, he said pleasantly:

"You and Marcia have put me in the humor to see Florence again. If I come strolling in upon you some fine day, I hope you'll be glad to see me, Mrs. Champneys?"

"Oh, yes!" said she, politely. And then Marcia and Vandervelde came up, and a few minutes later the two men went ashore. Hayden's face was the last thing Nancy saw as the steamer moved slowly outward. There were hails, laughter, waving of hand-kerchiefs. He alone looked at *her*. And so he remained in her memory, standing a little apart from all others.

CHAPTER XV

"I, TOO, IN ARCADIA"

If Riverton was his mother's house and England his grandmother's, France was peculiarly his own. Peter Champneys felt that he had come home, and even the fact that he couldn't speak understandable French didn't spoil the illusion. Nobody laughed at his barbarous jargon; people were patient, polite, helpful. He thought the French the pleasantest people in the world, and this opinion he never changed. Later, when he learned to know them better, he concluded that they were very deliberately and very gallantly gay in order to conceal from themselves and from the world how mortally sad they were at heart. They eschewed those virtues which made one disagreeable, and they indulged only in such vices as really amused them, and in consequence they made being alive a fine art.

The Hemingways knew Paris as they knew London, and they smoothed his path. In their drawing-room Peter met that dazzling inner circle of Parisian society which includes talent and genius as well as rank, beauty, and wealth. Then, Mrs. Hemingway having first seen to it that he met those whom she wished him to meet, Peter was permitted to meet those whom he himself wished to meet. He was introduced to two deceptively mild-mannered young Englishmen, first cousins

Marie Conway Oemler

named Checkleigh, students in one of the great ateliers, who were by way of being painters; and to a shock-headed young man from California, a sculptor, named Stocks. The Englishmen were closely related to a large-toothed, very important Lady Somethingorother, high up in the diplomatic sphere, and the Californian possessed a truly formidable aunt. Hence the three young men appeared in fashionable circles at decent intervals. Later, Peter learned to know their redoubtable relatives as "Rabbits" and "The Grampus," and he once saw a terrifyingly truthful portrait of "Rabbits" sketched on a skittish model's bare back, and a movingly realistic little figure of "The Grampus" modeled by her dutiful nephew in a moment of diabolical inspiration. It was explained to him that God, for some inscrutable purpose of his own, generally pleases himself by bestowing only the most limited human intelligence upon the wealthy relatives of poor but gifted artists; but that if properly approached, and at not too frequent intervals, they may be induced to loosen their tight purse-strings. Wherefore one must somehow manage to keep on good terms with them. Witness, Stocks said, his forgiving—nay, kindly—attitude toward The Grampus; see how he went to her house and drank her loathly tea and ate her beastly little cakes, even though she regarded a promising sculptor as a sort of unpromising stone-cutter who couldn't hold down a steady job, and had vehemently urged him to go in for building and contracting in Sacramento, California. "And yet that woman has got about all the money there is in our family!" finished Stocks, bitterly.

"Rabbits takes you aside and talks to you heart to heart," said the younger Checkleigh, gloomily. The elder Checkleigh's face took on a look of martyrdom.

"We have Immortal Souls," said he, in a tone of anguish and affliction. "I ask you, as man to man: Is it our fault?"

It was these three Indians, then, who took Peter Champneys under their wing, helped him find the pleasantest rooms in the Quartier, helped him furnish them at about a third of what he would have paid if left to his own devices, and also helped him to shed his skin of a timid provincial by plunging him to the scalp in that bubbling cauldron in which seethes the creative brain of France. Serious and sad young men who were going to be poets; intense fellows who were going to rehabilitate the Drama, or write the Greatest Novel; illustrators, journalists, critics, painters, types in velvet coats, flowing ties, flowing locks, and astonishing hats, sculptors, makers of exquisite bits of craftsmanship, models, masters, singers of sorts, actors and actresses, sewing-girls, frightful old concierges; students from the four corners of the earth driven hither by the four winds of heaven, came and went in the devil-may-care wake of Stocks and the Checkleighs and disported themselves before the reflective and appreciative eyes of Peter Champneys. These gay Bohemians laughed at him for what Stocks called his spinterishness, but ended by loving him as only youth can love a comrade.

In six months he knew the Quartier to the core. He met men who were utter blackguards, whose selfish, cold-blooded brutality filled him with loathing; he met women with the soul of the cat. But the Quartier as a whole was sound-hearted; Peter himself was too sound-hearted not to know. He met Youth at work, his own kind of work. They were all going to do something great presently,—and presently many of them did. The very air he breathed stimulated him. Here were comrades, to whom, as to himself, art was the one supremely important thing in the universe. They, too, were climbers toward the purple heights.

Shy young men who work like mules are as thick as hops in any art center; but shy young men who are immensely talented, who have a genius for steady labor, and who at the same time have not only the inclination but the opportunity to be generous, are not numerous anywhere.

Peter Champneys never talked about himself, made no parade, was so simple in his tastes that he spent very little upon himself, and while he could say "No" to impudence, he had ever a quick, warm "Yes" for need. That he should be able to become an artist had been the top of his dream; that by a very little self-denial he could help others to remain artists, left him large-eyed at his own good fortune. He experienced the glowing happiness that only the generous can know.

On Sundays he went to see Emma Campbell, for whom he had found a little house on the summit of Montmartre, on the very top of the Butte. It had a hillside garden, with a dove-cote in it, and a little kiosk in which Emma liked to sit, with the cat Satan on her lap, and projeck at the strange world in which she found herself. She shared the house with a scene-painter and his wife, and as the scene-painter was an Englishman, Emma could talk to somebody and be under-stood. Emma's idea of happiness was leisure to sew squares of patchwork together for quilts. She had brought her cut-out quilt scraps with her, and she sat in the kiosk and sewed little pieces of colored calico together, while the big cat scampered about the garden, or lay and blinked at her, and all Paris lay spread out far below, the spires of Notre Dame showing as through a mist.

On Sundays she cooked for Peter,—old homely Riverton dishes,—and waited on him while he ate. Because she couldn't read, she looked forward to Peter's reading what she reverently called "de Book." Peter had been reading the Bible to old darkies all his life, and he accepted it as a matter of course that he should take the long climb, and give up a part of his Sundays, to save Emma Campbell from being disappointed now. Afterward, Emma spoke of his mother, and of old, familiar things they both remembered. Then he went back to the Quartier feeling as refreshed and rested as if he'd had a swim in the river "over home."

At regular intervals he appeared at Mrs. Hemingway's, and kept up his acquaintance with her friends. When she told him to accept an invitation, he resignedly obeyed, looking, the elder of the Checkleigh boys told him, as if he were doing it for God's sake. He was beginning to speak French less villainously, and this made things easier for him. He could carry on a simple conversation, by going slowly; and he *almost* understood about half of what strangers said to him. He interested one or two fine ladies greatly, and they were extremely gracious to him. Artists—that is, young and unknown artists in the Quartier—are more or less pleasant to read about in the pages of Muerger and others, but they are too often beggarly and quite impossible persons in real life. But this young American who lived in the Quartier was at the same time on a footing of intimacy in the exclusive home of those so charming Hemingways, who were, one knew, of the *grand monde*. Was it true that the American painter was very wealthy? Yes? Ah, *ciel*! That droll young man was then amusing himself by living in the Quartier? But what an original! His family approved? He was an *orphan*? With no relations save that old uncle whose heir he was? Ah, *mon Dieu*! That touched one's heart! One must try to be very pleasant to that so lonely young man! And that so lonely young man was extended mead and balm in the shape of invitations to very smart affairs. To some of which he found, at the last minute, he couldn't go, for the simple and cogent reason that Checkleigh or Stocks had appropriated his dress suit.

"It's infernally unlucky, Rabbits having an affair on to-night. But you know how it is, Champ—she'd never forgive me if I didn't show up. Big-wigs from home, and all that, and she feels it's her duty to make me show 'em I haven't become an Apache. And my togs are out at interest—one has to pay one's rent *sometimes*, you understand," explained Checkleigh, who was dressing before Peter's mirror. "*You* don't have to care: *you* aren't compelled to keep in her good graces!"

"Oh, all right. I don't mind. I only accepted to please Mrs. Hemingway."

"Mrs. Hemingway is my very good friend. At the first opportunity I shall explain to her. She can readily understand that

"One may go without relatives, cousins, and aunts—
But civilized man can*not* go without pants.

I wish you hadn't such deucedly long legs, Champ. Regular hop-poles!" grumbled Checkleigh, ungratefully.

"They are poor things, but mine own," said Peter, mildly. "You will find a five-franc piece in the waistcoat pocket, Checkleigh, if you happen to want it. I keep it there for cab fare."

"If I happen to want it!" shrieked Checkleigh. "Oh, bloated plutocrat, purse-proud millionaire, I always happen to want it!" He waved an eloquent hand to the circumambient air. "He has five-franc pieces in his waistcoat pocket—and no Rabbits in his family!" cried Checkleigh. "Now, have you a presentable pair of gloves, Croesus?—Oh, damn your legs, Champneys! Look at these beastly breeches of yours, will you? I've had to turn 'em up until you'd fancy I was wearing cuffs on the ankles, and still they're too long!"

"You should have cut 'em off a bit—then you wouldn't look as though you were poulticing your shins. And they'd fit me, too," commented Stocks, who had sauntered in.

Checkleigh looked at Peter's watch—his own was "out at interest" along with his dress suit—and shook his head dolefully.

"If you'd just suggested it sooner, I could have done it—now it's too late." he lamented. "Your progeny will probably resemble herons, Champneys, and serve 'em right!—Are those *new* gloves? I *am* a credit to Rabbits!" And he rushed off.

> "What a friend we have in Champ-neys,
> All his gloves and pa-ants to wear!"

Stocks sang in a voice like the scraping of a mattock over flint; one saw that he had been piously raised. Then he hooked his arm in Peter's and the two went forth to join the joyous hordes surging up the Boul' Miche, and to dine in their favorite restaurant, where the waiters were one's good friends, and Madame the proprietress addressed her Bohemians as "mes enfants." Having dined, one joined one's brother workers who waged the battle of Art with jaws and gestures. Bawling out the slang of the studios, they grimaced, sneered, shrugged, praised, demolished. Nothing was sacred to these young savages but the joy of the present. They had no past, and the future hadn't arrived. They lived in the moment, worked, laughed, loved, and, when they could, dined. When one had a handful of silver, how gay the world was! How one wished to pat it on the back and invite it to come and be merry with one!

In the full stream of this turbulent tide, behold Peter Champneys; with a lock of his black hair falling across his forehead; his head cocked sidewise; and his big nose and clear golden eyes giving him the aspect of a benevolent hawk, like, say, Horus, Hawk of the Sun. Those golden eyes of his saw tolerantly as well as clearly. This quiet American worked like a fiend, yet had time to look on and laugh with you while you played. He was gravely gay at his best, but he didn't neglect the good things of his youth. And he had a genius for playing impromptu Providence when you were down on your luck and about all in. Maybe you hadn't dined for a couple of days, or maybe you were pretty nearly frozen in your room, as you had no fire; and you were wondering whether, after all, you weren't a fool to starve and freeze for art's sake, and whether, all things considered, life was worth living; and there'd be a gentle tap at your door, and Peter Champneys would stick his thin dark face in, smilingly. He'd tell you he'd been lonely all day, and would you, if you hadn't done so already, kindly come and dine with him? He spoke French with a South Carolina accent, in those days, but an archangel's voice could not then have sounded more dulcet in your ears than his. Presently, over your cigarettes, you found yourself telling him just how things were with you. Maybe you slept on a lounge in his studio that night, because it was warmer there. And next morning you could face life and work feeling that God's in his heaven, all's right with the world. That's what Peter Champneys meant to many a hard-pressed youngster.

With his immense capacity for work, at the end of a year Peter Champneys had made great strides. But he was troubled. Like Millet, he couldn't take the ordered direction. He felt that he was merely marking time, that he wasn't on the right track. His robust and original talent demanded heartier food than was offered it. Reluctantly enough, Peter withdrew from the official studio to which he was attached, and went on his own. It was a momentous step.

One Sunday afternoon he said to Emma Campbell, seriously:

"You've never laid eyes on a goddess, Emma, have you? Or a nymph? Well, neither have I. And I can't paint what I don't know." He walked up and down the little graveled garden path. And he burst out: "That is not life. It is not truth. I don't want gods. I only see *men*! I don't want goddesses. I want *women*!"

Emma Campbell said in a scandalized voice:

"Dat ain't no kind o' way to talk! Leastwise," she compromised, "not on Sundays."

Peter burst out laughing. Emma wore her usual Sunday cashmere, with a snowy apron and head-handkerchief. Satan lay upon the small table beside her, in the attitude of a sphinx, his black, velvety paws stretched in front of him, his inscrutable eyes watching the restless young man. Peter paused, and his eyes narrowed. Then he snapped his fingers, as he had done when he was a little boy back in Riverton and something had pleased him.

"I've got it!" he shouted. "Emma, you're It!"

No one ever had a more patient model. She couldn't exackly understan' why Mist' Peter should want to paint a ole nigger like her, but if Peter Champneys had wanted to bury her alive in the ground, with only her head sticking out, Emma would have known it had to be all right, somehow. So she sat for weary hours, while Peter made rough sketches, and tried out many theories, before he settled down to work in dead earnest.

And presently Emma saw herself as it were alive on a square of canvas, so alive that she was more than a bit afraid. She said it looked like her own ha'nt, and Emma wasn't partial to ha'nts. There she sat in her plain black dress and her plain white apron and head-handkerchief, and her gold hoop earrings. On the table beside her were the vegetables she was to prepare. She had forgotten work for the time being. Emma projecked, one hand resting idly on the table, the other on the great black cat in her lap. She looked at you, with the wistfully animal look of a negro woman, who is loving, patient, kind, long-suffering, imbued with a terrible patience, and of a sound, sly, earthy humor; and who at the same time is childishly credulous, full of dark passions, and with the fires of savagery banked in her heart. There she sat, that sphinx that is Africa, who has seen the white races come, and who will probably see them go; you could almost sense the half-slumbrous brain of her throbbing under her head-handkerchief. She wasn't a mere colored woman; she was a symbol and a challenge. And her eyes that had seen so much and wept so much were as inscrutable as fate, as sphinx-like as the cat's who watched you from her knee. The whole picture breathed an amazingly bold and original power, and was so arrestingly vital that it gripped and held one. Down in one corner, painted with exquisite care and delicacy, was a Red Admiral.

The Quartier came, squinted through the fingers, and praised and dispraised, after its wont. The Symbolists sneered and told Peter to his teeth he was a Philistine; they said you can't boot-lick Nature: you've got to bully her, demand her soul, *make* her give you her Sign! Quieter men came and studied Emma Campbell and her cat, and clapped Peter on the back; the more exuberant Latins kissed him, noisy, hearty, hairy kisses on both cheeks. Undoubtedly, it would be accepted, they said!

It was, and hung conspicuously. There were always small groups before it, for it created something like the uproar that

Manet's "Olympia" had raised in its time. Peter learned from one critic that his technique was magnificent, his picture a masterpiece of psychology and of portraiture, and that if he kept on he'd soon be one of the Immortals. He learned from another that while he undoubtedly had technique, his posing was commonplace, his subject banal, his imagination hopelessly bourgeois; that he was a painter of the ugly and the ordinary, without inspiration or imagination; that the one pretty and delicate note in the whole canvas was the butterfly in the lower left-hand corner, and that *that* was obviously reminiscent of Whistler, who on a time had used a butterfly signature! But on the whole the criticisms were highly favorable; it was admitted that a young painter of promise had arisen.

Peter Champneys went about his business, indifferent to praise or blame. *He* knew he was a way-faring man whose business it was to follow his own road, a road he had to hack out for himself; and somewhere on the horizon were the purple heights.

The unbounded delight, the disinterested pride of the Hemingways, couldn't have been greater had he been their son. Mrs. Hemingway gave a brilliant entertainment in his honor, and he was feted and made much of. Young ladies who danced divinely found his stork-like hopping pleasing, and his stammering French delightful. This charming Monsieur Champneys, you see, was not only invested with the glamour of art; he was the heir of an American millionaire! Ah, the dear young man!

The picture was sold to a Spanish nobleman, who said it reminded him of Velasquez's "AEsop"; he was so delighted with the painter's power that he commissioned Peter to portray his own long, pale, melancholy visage. Whereupon the two Checkleighs and Stocks called loudly for a proper celebration, and Peter honored their clamorous demand. It was a memorable affair, graced by the Quartier's darlingest models, who had long since voted M'sieu Champnees a *bon garcon*. A Spanish student, in a velvet coat and with long black hair, insisted upon charcoaling mustachios and imperial upon his host's countenance, in honor of his countryman who had distinguished himself as a patron of art. Later, a laughing girl whose blue-black hair was banded Madonna-wise around a head considerably otherwise, washed it off with a table napkin dipped in wine. She sat on his knee to perform the operation, scanned his clean face with satisfaction, and taking him by the ears as by handles, kissed him gaily. Then she went back to her own *cher ami*, who wasn't in the least disturbed.

"It is like kissing thy maiden aunt, Jacques," she told him. "Now, with thee—" They looked at each other eloquently, and Peter Champneys, whose eyes had followed the girl, smiled crookedly. An unaccountable gloom descended upon him. All these lusty young men shouting and laughing around him, all these handsome, ardent young women, snatched what joy from life they could; they lived their hour, knowing how brief that hour must be. They ate to-day, starved to-morrow; but they were rich because they loved, because they laughed, because theirs was the passionate unforced comradeship, the intoxicating joy of youth. Peter Champneys, whose good luck was being celebrated, looked at his penniless, hilarious comrades, and twisted a smile of desperate gaiety to his lips. He had never in his life felt more utterly alone.

The affair ended at six o'clock the next morning, in a last glad, mad romp up the Boul' Miche. Peter and Stocks waved good-by to the last revelers, looking somewhat jaded in the fresh morning air. The two young men, both rather tired, walked slowly. Venders in clacking sabots pushed their carts ahead of them, shouting their wares. Crowds of working-people poured through the streets. At a little restaurant they knew, they had coffee and rolls. While they were drinking, a girl came in. Peter looked up and saw Denise.

His first thought was that she would have been lovely if she hadn't been so thin. Then he saw how shabby she was, and how neat. Nothing could have been more charming than her chestnut hair, or her blue eyes that had a look of innocence, or her fair and transparent complexion, though one could have wished she were rosier. She did not look around with the quick, alert, bright glance of the Parisienne whom everything interests and amuses; she had the abstracted and sad air of a child who suffers, and whom suffering bewilders.

Stocks said, in a low voice, tinged with pity:

"*L'amie de Dangeau.*"

Peter received that announcement with a shock of surprise and distaste. Dangeau was such an utter brute! Handsome in his way, without conscience or pity, Dangeau would have eaten his mother's heart to satisfy his own hunger, or wiped his feet upon his father's beard. The gifted, intellectual, and rapacious savage seized whatever came near him that pleased his fancy or aroused his curiosity, extracted the pith, and tossed aside what no longer amused or served him. There was no generosity in him, only an insatiable and ferocious demand that life should give him more, always more! Peter, who both admired and detested him, was sorry for this gentle creature fallen into his remorseless claws. And he wondered, as decent men must, at the fatal fascination animals like Dangeau seem to possess for women.

He saw her occasionally after that, always alone. Plainly, things were not well with her. Her pale face grew paler and thinner; her dress shabbier. The look of bewilderment was now a look of pain. Her eyes were heavy, as if they wept too much. Peter watched her with a troubled heart. One day Henri, the garcon, murmured confidentially, as she left the cafe after a particularly slim meal:

"These thin little blondes, they do not last long. That one was like a rose when I first saw her. *Pauvre enfant!*" And he looked after her with a compassionate glance.

"She seems—different," said Peter. "It is not well with her?"

"Alas, no! She is from the provinces, Monsieur, come to Paris to earn more. And so she wearied her *ami*. You know him, Monsieur; he is a restless man, quickly tiring—that sculptor! Also, he feared she would fall sick upon his hands—you see how frail she is, and he abhors all that is not robust." And Henri made an expressive gesture. He added: "*She* is of the sort that love, Monsieur; and, you understand, that is fatal!"

"And how does she manage now?" asked Peter.

Henri shrugged significantly. Peter drummed on the table and scowled. A little girl, from the provinces! One understood now how she had fallen into Dangeau's hands, and how, inevitably, he had tired, and tossed her aside like a wilted flower. And now she was facing slow starvation—Oh, damn!

Peter slipped some change into Henri's palm. "You are a man of sense, Henri. Also, I see that you have a good heart," said he. "Now we must see what we can do for this poor little Mademoiselle, you and I. You will place before her the best the house affords—I leave that to you. And when she protests you will say to her: 'Your venerable godfather has arranged for it, Mademoiselle. His orders are, that you come here, seat yourself, tap once with your forefinger upon the table,—and your orders will be obeyed."'

"And if she questions further, Monsieur?"

"Explain that you obey orders, but do not know her godfather," said Peter, gravely.

"Trust me, Monsieur!" cried the delighted Henri. And from that moment the kindly fellow adored Peter Champneys.

The little game began the next day. Denise gave her tiny order; Henri came back with a loaded tray, whose savory contents he placed before her. Out of the corner of his eye Peter could see the girl's astonished face when Henri politely insisted that the meal was hers—that her venerable godfather had ordered it for her! She looked timidly and fearfully around; but nobody was paying the slightest attention to her, and after deftly arranging the dishes, Henri had whisked himself off. She waited for a few minutes; but Henri hadn't come back. And then, because she was almost famished, she ate what had been given her. Peter felt his eyes blur.

Henri came back to her presently with wine. He dusted the bottle lovingly, and filled her glass with a flourish. She looked up with a tremulous smile:

"My godfather's order, Henri?"

"Your venerable godfather's order, Mademoiselle," he replied sedately. When she had finished her dinner, he glibly, and with an expressionless countenance repeated Peter's instructions: she was to come in, seat herself, tap with her forefinger, and give her orders, which would be instantly obeyed! No, he did not know her godfather. Nor did

Monsieur le patron. No, he might not even take the sous she offered him: all, all, had been arranged, Mademoiselle!

She hesitated. Then she called for pen and paper, and scribbled in violet ink:

MONSIEUR MY GODFATHER,
I see that the good God still permits miracles. You are one. Accept, then, a poor girl's thanks and prayers!
Thy godchild,
DENISE.

She gave this to Henri, who received it respectfully. Then she went out, feeling very much better and brighter because of a sadly needed dinner. She was bewildered, and excited; but she wasn't afraid. She accepted her miracle, which had come just in the nick of time, gratefully, with a childlike simplicity. But she used her blue eyes, and one day they met Peter Champneys's, regarding her with a good and kind satisfaction; for indeed she looked much better and brighter, now that she was no longer half starved. Denise had encountered other eyes, men's eyes; but none had ever met hers with just such a look as she saw in these clear and golden ones. A flash of intuition came to her. Only one person in the world could have eyes like that—it must be, it was, he! And she watched him with an absorbed and breathless interest.

In these small restaurants of the Quartier one sits so close to one's neighbors, in a busy hour, that conversation isn't difficult; it is, rather, inevitable.

"Monsieur," said the young girl, bravely and yet timidly, on an occasion when they almost touched elbows, "Monsieur,— is it you who have a god-daughter?"

"Mademoiselle," stammered Peter, who hadn't expected the question. "I do not know your godfather!" And then he turned red to his ears.

Her face broke into a swift and flashing smile. She looked so like a happy child that Peter had to smile back at her, and presently they were chatting like old acquaintances. After that they always managed to dine together.

They found each other delightful. That gloomy sense of loneliness which had oppressed Peter vanished in the girl's presence. As for Denise, no one had ever been so kind, so gentle, so generous to her as this wonderful Monsieur Champneys. She grew quite beautiful; her eyes were a child's eyes, her face like one of those little sweet pinkish-white roses one sees in old-fashioned gardens.

She had no relations; neither had Peter. And so he took Denise into his life, just as he had once taken a lost kitten out of the dusk on the Riverton Road: there really was nothing else for him to do! He had for her something of the same whimsical and compassionate affection that had made him share his glass of milk with the little cat. She belonged to him; there was nobody else.

She was rather a silent creature, Denise. She had none of that Latin vivacity which wearies the listener, but her love for him showed itself in a thousand gracious ways, in innumerable small services, in loving looks. Just to touch him was a never-failing joy to her. She delighted to stroke his face, to trace with her small fingers the outline of his features. "That is the pattern on the inside of my heart," she told him. She had a quick, light tread, pleasant to listen to, and her rare and lovely laughter was always a delicious surprise, as if one heard an unexpected chime of little bells.

Her housewifely ways, her pretty anxiety about spending money, amused him tenderly. When she could perform some small service for him, she hummed little hymns to the Virgin. Her ministrations extended to Stocks and the Checkleighs, whose shirts she mended so expertly that they didn't have to borrow so many of Peter's. She was so happy that Peter Champneys grew happy watching her. It hadn't seemed possible to Denise that anybody like him could exist; yet here he was, and she belonged to him!

Nobody had ever loved Peter Champneys in quite the same way. She had so real and true a genius for loving that she exhaled affection as a flower exhales perfume. Loving was an instinct with Denise. She would steal to his side, slip her arm around his neck, kiss him on the eyes—"thy beautiful eyes, Pierre!"—and cuddle her cheek against his, with so exquisite a tenderness in touch and look that the young man's kind heart melted in his breast. He couldn't speak. He could only gather her close, pressing his black head against her soft young bosom.

Her cruel experience with Dangeau was not forgotten; but that had been capture by force, and she remembered it as a black background against which the bright colors of this present happiness showed with a heavenlier radiance. Peter himself didn't guess how wholly his little comrade loved him, though he did realize her utter selflessness. She never asked him troublesome questions, never annoyed him with irritating jealousy, made no demands upon him. Was he not himself? Very well, then: did not that suffice? Denise didn't think: she felt. She had the exquisite wisdom of the heart, and in her small hands the flower of Peter Champneys's youth opened and blossomed. He was young, he was loved, he was busy. Oh, but it was a good world to be alive in! He whistled while he worked. And how he worked! To this period belong those angelic heads, chestnut-haired, wistfully smiling, with blue eyes that look deep into one's heart. The airy butterfly that signs these canvases is not so much a symbol as a prescience.

When was it he first noticed that for all his love and care he wasn't going to be able to keep Denise? How did he learn that the great last lover was wooing her away? She was not less happy. A deep and still joy radiated from her, her eyes had the clear and cloudless happiness of a child's. But he observed that on their pleasant excursions into the country she tired quickly. Her little light feet didn't run any more. She preferred to sit cuddled against his side, holding his hand in both hers, her head pressed against his shoulder. She didn't talk, but then, he was used to her silence; that was one of her sweetest charms. Her cheek grew thinner, but the rose in it deepened. Then the pretty dresses he loved to lavish upon her began to hang loosely upon her little body.

It was a frightened young man who called in doctors and specialists. But, as Henri had once told him, they do not last long, these frail blondes. Also, she was of the sort that loves—and that, you understand, is fatal!

Stocks, who had made a great pet of Peter's pretty sweetheart, blubbered when he learned the truth, and the younger Checkleigh, who delighted to sketch her, left off because his hand shook so, and he couldn't see clearly. The Spanish student in the velvet coat, who could sing lustily to a guitar, came and sang for her, not the ribald songs the Quartier heard from him, but the beautiful and soft love songs he had heard as a child in Andalusia—how love is an immortal rose one carries through the gates of the grave into the gates of paradise. And the Quartier, which knows so much sorrow as well as so much joy, came with its gayest gossip to make her smile. Peter himself lived in a sort of tormented daze.—It was Denise, his little Denise, who

Marie Conway Oemler

was going!

Denise herself was the calmest and cheerfulest of them all. Her high destiny had been to love Peter Champneys, and she had fulfilled it. The good, the kind God had given her that which in her estimation outweighed everything else. She had lived, she had loved. Now she could go, and go content.

"It is better so," she told him, with that piercing good sense of the French which is like a spiritual insight. "Very dear one, suppose *I* had been called upon to let *thee* go: how could I have endured that?" And she added, pressing his fingers, "Do not grieve, my adored Pierre. Observe that I am but a poor little one to whom in thy goodness of heart thou hast been kind: but thou art all my life—all of me, Pierre."

He put his head against her side, and she stroked it, whispering,

"I had but a little while to stay, beloved. Because of thee, that stay has been happy—oh, very, very happy!"

"You have given me all I ever had of youth and love," said Peter.

"Ah, but I am glad!" she said naively. "Because of *that*, I think you must remember!" She looked at him with her blue eyes suddenly full of tears. "It is only when I think you may forget that I am afraid, it is then as if the dark pressed upon me," she said in a whisper sharp with pain. "I lie still and dream how great you will become, how much beloved—for who could fail to love you, Pierre? And I am glad. It rests my heart, which is all yours. But when I begin to remember how I have been but a little, little part of your life, who have been all of mine, when I think you may forget, then I am afraid, I am afraid!" And she looked at him like a frightened child who is being left alone to go to sleep in the dark.

Peter picked her up, wrapped in the bedquilt, and held her in his arms. She was very light. It was as if he held a little ghost. She shook her bright hair over his shoulders and breast, and he hid his quivering face in it, as in a veil. Presently, in a soft voice:

"Godfather!"

"Yes, my little sweetheart."

"Very dear and precious godfather,—a long, long time from now, when *She* comes, She whom you will love as I love you, tell her about me."

"Denise, Denise!" cried poor Peter, straining her to him.

"Tell her I had blue eyes, and a fair face, and bright, bright hair, Godfather. She will like to know. Say, 'Her whole wisdom lay in loving me with all her heart—that poor Denise!' Then tell her that she cannot love you more, my Pierre,—but that in my grave I shall despise her if she dares to love you less."

"I—Oh, my God!" strangled Peter, and he felt as if his heart were being wrenched out of his breast. He was in his twenties, and the girl in his arms was all he knew of love.

Some six weeks later Denise died as quietly as she had lived, her small cold hands clinging to Peter Champneys's, her blue eyes with their untroubled, loving gaze fixed upon his face. When that beloved face faded from her the world itself had faded from Denise.

He hadn't dreamed one could suffer as he was called upon to

suffer then. The going of little Denise seemed to have torn away a living and quivering part of his spirit. She had loved him absolutely, and Peter couldn't forget that. His gratitude was an anguish. It is not the duration but the depths of an experience which makes its ineffaceable impression upon the heart.

Mrs. Hemingway saw his changed looks with concern. If she and her husband suspected anything, they did not torment him with questions; they didn't even appear to notice that he was silent and abstracted.

"What on earth is the matter with the boy?" worried Mrs. Hemingway. "John, do you think it's a—"

"Petticoat? What else should it be?"

"I can't bear to think of Peter getting himself into some sort of scrape with possibly some miserable woman—who will prey upon him," murmured Mrs. Hemingway.

"Peter's not the sort that falls for adventuresses. He might fall in love with some girl, and be cut up if she didn't reciprocate. That's what's the matter with him now, if I'm not mistaken."

Hemingway took Peter fishing with him. It is a pleasant place, the Seine near Poissy. Hemingway let Peter sit in a boat all day, and didn't seem to observe that the line wasn't once drawn in. The river was rippling, the sky bright blue, the wind sweet. All around them were other boats, full of people who appeared to be happy. And Hemingway's silent companionship was strong and kind and serene. Insensibly Peter reacted to his surroundings, to the influence of the shining day. When they were returning to Paris that evening, he looked at his big compatriot gratefully. Then he told him. Hemingway listened in silence. Then:

"I'm damned glad she had you," said he, and polished his eyeglasses, and put his hand on Peter's shoulder with a consoling and sympathetic touch. Hemingway understood. He was that sort.

Youth departs, love perishes, faith faints; but that we may never be left hopeless, work remains and saves us. Peter's work came to his succor. Just at this crucial time his Eminence the Austrian Cardinal appeared, and Peter hadn't time to mope.

The cardinal had seen the picture of Emma Campbell and her cat. He had seen an enchanting sketch of the Spanish student in the velvet coat, recently purchased by a friend of his. And now his own portrait must be painted. He was so great a cardinal, of so striking a personality, that his own noble family had an immense pride in him, and the Vatican, along with certain great temporal powers, took him very seriously. So the painting of the cardinal's portrait wouldn't be a light undertaking, to be given at random. This and that great painter was urged upon him. But the astonishing portrait of that old colored woman and her cat decided his Eminence, who had a will of his own. Here was his artist! Also, he insisted upon the cat.

The anticlerical press of Paris was insisting that the cardinal's stay in the French capital was of sinister import. The cardinal smiled, and Peter Champneys besought his gods to let him get that smile on canvas. His Eminence was an ideal sitter. He spoke English beautifully, and it pleased him to converse with the lanky young American painter in his mother tongue. He felt drawn to the young man, and when the cardinal liked one, he was irresistible. Peter was so fascinated by this brilliant and versatile aristocrat, so deeply interested in the psychology of a great Roman prelate, a prince of the Church, that he forgot everything except that he was a creative artist—and a great sitter, a man worthy of his best, was to be portrayed.

He gave his whole heart to his task, and he brought to it a new sense of values, born of suffering. When he had finished, you could see the cardinal's soul looking at you from the canvas. The smile Peter prayed to catch curves his lips, a smile that baffles and enchants. He wears his red robes, and one fine, aristocratic hand with the churchly ring on it rests upon the magnificent cat lying on the table beside him. That superb "Cardinal with the Cat" put the seal upon Peter Champneys's reputation as a great artist.

He knew what he had achieved. Yet his lips quivered and his eyes were smileless when, down in the left-hand corner, he painted in the Red Admiral.

CHAPTER XVI

THE OTHER MAN

In Florence the nascent swan-feathers of Anne Champneys grew into perfect plumage. She was like a spirit new-born to another world, with all the dun-colored ties of a darker existence swept away, and only a residue of thought and feeling left of its former experience. This bright and rosy world, enriched by nature and art, was so new, its values were so different, that at first she was dazed into dumbness by it.

She came face to face with beauty and art made a part of daily life. She thought she had never seen color, or flowers, or even a real sky, until now. An existence unimaginably rich, vistas that receded into an almost fabled past, opened and spread before her glamourously. The vividness of her impressions, her reaction to this new phase of experience, the whole-souled ardor with which she flung herself into the study of Italian, her eagerness to know more, her delight in the fine old house in which they had set up their household gods, amused and charmed Mrs. Vandervelde. She felt as if she were teaching and training an unspoiled, delighted, and delightful child, and contact with this fresh and eager spirit stimulated her own.

Marie Conway Oemler

Many of her former school friends, girls belonging to fine Florentine families, some now noble matrons, mothers of families, one or two great conventual superioresses, still resided in the city, and these welcomed their beloved Marcia delightedly. There were, too, the American and English colonies, and a coterie of well-known artists. Marcia Vandervelde was a born hostess, a center around which the brightest and cleverest naturally revolved. She changed the large, drafty rooms of the old palace into charming reflections of her own personality. A woman of wide sympathies and cultivated tastes, she delighted in the clever cosmopolitan society that gathered in her drawing-room; and it was in this opalescent social sea that she launched young Mrs. Champneys.

Mrs. Champneys was at first but a mild success, a sort of pale luminosity reflected from the more dominant Mrs. Vandervelde. But it so happened, that a gifted young Italian lost his heart at sight to her red hair and green eyes, and discovering that she had no heart of her own—at least, none for him—he wrote, in a sort of frenzy of inspiration, a very fine sonnet sequence narrating his hapless passion. The poet had been as extravagantly assertive as poets in love usually are, and the sonnets were really notable; so the young man was swept into a gust of fame; all Italy read his verse and sympathized with him. The object of a popular poet's romantic and unfortunate love is always the object of curiosity and interest, as Anne Champneys discovered to her surprise and annoyance.

"He was such a little idiot!" she told Marcia Vandervelde, disgustedly. "Always sighing and rolling his eyes, and looking at one like a sick calf,—more than once I was tempted to catch him by the shoulders and shake him!"

"He's a poet, my child," said Mrs. Vandervelde,

mischievously, "and you're the lady in the case. It's been the making of him, and it hasn't done you any harm: you'll be a legend in your own lifetime."

Marcia was quite right. The poet's love clung to Anne like an intangible perfume, and a halo of romance encircled her red head. The Florentines discovered that she was beautiful; the English and Americans, cooler in judgment, found her charming. And a noted German artist came along and declared that he had found in her his ideal Undine.

Mrs. Peter remained unchanged and unimpressed. She shrugged indifferent shoulders; she wasn't particularly interested in herself as the object of poetic adoration.

She was, however, immensely interested in the beauty and romance of Florence. The street crowds, so vivacious, so good-humored, the vivid Florentine faces, enchanted her. More astonishing than storied buildings, or even imperishable art, were the figures that moved across the red-and-gold background of the city's history,—figures like Dante, Lorenzo the Magnificent, and that great prior of San Marco whose "soul went out in fire." Curiously enough, it was Savonarola who made the most profound impression upon her. It seemed to her that the immortal monk still dominated Florence, and when she saw his old worn crucifix in his cell at San Marco, something awoke in her spirit,—a sense of religious values. Religion, then, was not a mere fixed convention, subscribed to as a sort of proof of conservatism and respectability; religion was really a fixed reality, an eternal power. She read everything that she could lay her hands on covering the history of Fra Girolamo. Then she bought a picture of his red Indian-like visage, and hung it up in her room. The titanic reformer remained, a shadowy but very deep power, in the background of her consciousness, and it was this long-dead preacher who taught her to pray.

He won her profoundest reverence and faith, because he had been true, he had sealed his faith with his life; she felt that she could trust him. His honesty appealed to her own.

It was such curious phases as this of the girl's unfolding character, that made her a never-failing source of interest to Marcia Vandervelde. Under her superimposed, surface indifference, Marcia reflected, Anne had a deep strain of pure unworldliness, vast possibilities. Give Anne an ideal, once arouse her enthusiasm, and she was capable of tossing aside the world for it. Marcia was vastly interested, too, in the serene detachment of the girl's attitude toward all those with whom she came in contact. One might evoke interest, sympathy, compassion, even a quiet friendliness, but her heart remained quiet, aloof, secure from invasion. Handsome young men who fell in love with her—and there were several such—seemed unable to stir any emotion in her, except perhaps, an impatient resentment. Marcia, of course, knew nothing of Glenn Mitchell. But Anne Champneys remembered him poignantly. She had learned her lesson.

They had been some six or eight months in Florence when Mr. Berkeley Hayden put in his appearance, somewhat to Mrs. Vandervelde's surprise. She had not expected this! She studied her old friend speculatively. H'm! She remembered the pale face of the young Italian poet whose sad sonnets all Italy was reading with delight. Then she looked at the red-headed source of those sonnets,—and she had no doubt as to the cause of Mr. Hayden's appearance in Florence at this time,—and wondered a bit. The situation gave a fillip to her imagination; it was piquant. One wondered how it would end.

Peter Champneys? Marcia scented disruption, where that impalpable relationship was concerned. She was ignorant as to Anne's real feelings and intentions in regard to her absentee husband. Anne never mentioned him. She bore his name, she held herself rigidly aloof from all lovers; herein one saw her sole concessions to the tie binding her. Marcia didn't see how it was possible that the two should avoid hating each other; the mere fact that they had been arbitrarily forced upon each other by the imperious will of old Chadwick, would inevitably militate against any hope of future affection between them. And now here was Berkeley Hayden, quite as imperious as Chadwick Champneys had ever been, and who was quite as successful in getting what he wanted.

Anne had welcomed Mr. Hayden gladly. She was honestly delighted to see him. Florence had taught her, signally, the depths of her own lack of culture, and this biting knowledge increased her respect for Mr. Berkeley Hayden. Marcia was immensely clever, charmingly cultivated, a woman of the world in the best sense, but Anne's native shrewdness told her that Marcia's knowledge was not equal to Hayden's. His culture was surer and deeper. He was more than a mere amateur; he *knew*. He stood apart, in her mind, and just a little higher than anybody else. She turned to him eagerly, and there was established between them, almost unconsciously, the most potent, perfect, and dangerous of all relationships, because it is the most beautiful and natural,—that, in which the man is the teacher and the woman the pupil.

Hayden saw her, too, to greater advantage, here under this Florentine sky, against the background of perhaps the most beautiful city in the world. She glowed, splendidly young and vivid. She did not laugh often, but when she did, it was like a peal of music; it came straight from her heart and went direct to yours. It was as catching as fire, as exhilarating as the chime of sleigh-bells on a frosty Thanksgiving morning, as clear and true as a redbird's whistle; and it had tucked away in it a funny, throaty chuckle so irresistibly infectious that suspicious old St. Anthony himself, would have joined in accord with it, had he heard its silver echo in his wilderness. Berkeley Hayden's immortal soul stood on the tiptoe of ecstasy when Anne Champneys laughed.

She no longer thought of herself as Nancy Simms; she knew herself now as Anne Champneys, a newer and better personality dominating that old, unhappy, ignorant self. If at times the man glimpsed that other shadowy self of hers, it was part of her mysterious appeal, her enthralling, baffling charm. It invested her with a shade of inscrutable, prescient sorrow, as of old unhappy far-off things. He hadn't the faintest idea of Nancy Simms, a creature utterly foreign to his experience. And because she did not love him, Anne Champneys never spoke of that old self, never confided in him. He did not know her as she had been, he only knew her as she was now. That, however, fully satisfied his critical taste. The marvel of her alabaster skin, fleckless and flawless, the glory of her glittering red hair, the sea-depths of her cool, gray-green eyes, the reserve of her expression, the virginal curve of her lip, enchanted him. He liked the tall, slender strength of her, the lightness of her step, her grace when she danced, her spirited pose when she rode. Here was the woman, the one woman, to bear his name, to be the mistress of his house. She was the only woman he had ever really wished to marry. And she was nominally married to Peter Champneys.

Hayden was honorable. Had hers been a real marriage, had she been a happy wife, he would have respected the tie that bound her, and gone his way. But the situation was exceptional. She wasn't really a wife at all, and like Mrs. Vandervelde, he could see in such a marriage nothing but a cause for mutual disgust and dislike. Well, then, if he loved her, and Peter Champneys didn't, he certainly was not working Peter Champneys any harm in winning away from him a wife he didn't want. Why should he stand aside and let her go, for such a shadow as that ceremony had been? The Champneys money? That meant nothing weighed in the balance with his desire. He could give her as much, and more, than she would forego. Mrs. Berkeley Hayden would eclipse Mrs. Peter Champneys.

Deliberately, then, but delicately, after his fashion, Hayden set himself to win Anne Champneys. He felt that his passion for her gave him the right. He meant to make her happy. She could have her marriage annulled. Then she would become Mrs. Berkeley Hayden. Even the fact that he really knew very little about her did not trouble him. He coveted her, and he meant to have her.

He read the young Italian's sonnets, which she had inspired, and they made him thoughtful. He could readily understand the depths of feeling such a woman could arouse. Had she no heart, as the Italian lamented? He wondered. It came to him that she was, in truth, detached, sufficient to herself, an ungregarious creature moving solitarily in a mysterious world all her own. What did she think? What did she feel? He didn't know. He was allowed to see certain aspects of her intelligence, and her quickness of perception, the delicacy of her fancy, her childlike and morning freshness, and a pungently shrewd Americanism that flashed out at odd and unexpected moments, never failed to delight him. But her deeper thoughts, her real feelings, her heart, remained sealed and closed to him.

He saw half-pleasedly, half-jealously the interest she aroused in other men. Nothing but her almost unbelievable indifference held his jealousy in check. He reflected with satisfaction that she was on a friendlier footing with him than with any other man of her acquaintance, that she had a more instant welcome for him than for any other, and for which cause he was cordially hated by several otherwise amiable gentlemen. And then he waxed gloomy, remembering how emotionless, how impersonal, that friendship really was. At times he laughed at himself wryly, recalling the passionate friendship other women had lavished upon him, and how wearisome it had been to him, how he had wished to escape it. If but a modicum of that passion had been bestowed upon him by this girl, how changed the world would be for him!

And in the meantime Anne Champneys liked him serenely, was grateful to him, aware that his intellect was as a key that was unlocking her own; welcomed him openly and was maddeningly respectful to him. This made him rage. What did she think he was, anyhow? An old professor, an antiquarian, an archaeologist? She might as well consider him an antediluvian at once!

"Marcia," he said to Mrs. Vandervelde one evening, "I want you to tell me all you know about this Champneys business. Just exactly how does the affair stand?" Anne had been carried off by some American friends, the smart throng that had filled Mrs. Vandervelde's rooms had gone, and Hayden and his hostess had the big, softly lighted drawing-room to themselves. At his query Mrs. Vandervelde turned in her chair, shading her eyes with her hand the better to observe him.

"Why, you know as much as I do, Berkeley! You know how and why the marriage was contracted, and what hinges upon it," said she, cautiously.

He made an impatient gesture. "I want to know what she's going to do. Surely she isn't going to allow herself to be bound by that old lunatic's will, is she?"

"He wasn't an old lunatic; he was an old genius. Jason had an almost superstitious reverence for his judgment. Somehow, his plans always managed to come out all right,—in the end. Even when they seemed wild, they came out all right. They're still coming out all right."

"And you think this insane marriage is likely to come out all right in the end, too?" he asked sharply.

"I don't know. Stranger things have happened. Why shouldn't this?"

"Why should it? That fellow Champneys—"

"Is said to be a great painter. At least, he is certainly a very successful one. Whether or not he can make good as Anne Champneys's husband remains to be seen." Mrs. Vandervelde was not above the innate feminine cattiness. Hayden rose abruptly and began to pace the room. He was vaguely aware that he had been astrally scratched across the nose.

"And you think a girl like Anne will be willing to play patient Griselda?" he asked, scornfully.

"I don't know. You think she shouldn't?"

"I think she shouldn't. I tell you frankly he doesn't deserve it."

"Oh, as for that!" said Mrs. Vandervelde, airily.

Hayden paused in his restless walk, and looked at her earnestly.

"Berkeley," said she, changing her light tone, "am I to

understand that you are—really in earnest?"

"I am so much in earnest," he replied, deliberately, "that I do not mind telling you, Marcia, that I want this girl. More, I mean to have her, if I can make her care for me."

She considered this carefully. He had never known what it meant to have his wishes thwarted, and now he would move heaven and earth to win Anne Champneys. Well, but!—She liked Hayden, and she didn't think, all things considered, that Anne Champneys could do better, if she wished to have her marriage to Peter annulled, than to marry Berkeley. But how would Jason consider such a move? Jason had been greatly attached to old Mr. Champneys. Indeed, his connection with that astute old wizard had just about doubled their income. Jason wouldn't be likely to look with friendly eyes upon this bringing to naught, what he knew had been Champneys's fondest scheme. She said, after a pause:

"Does Anne know?"

"Who knows what Anne knows? But on the face of it, I should say she doesn't. At least, she doesn't appear to. I have been very—circumspect," said he, moodily. And he added angrily: "She seems to regard me as a sort of cicerone, a perambulating, vocal Baedeker!"

Mrs. Vandervelde smiled openly. "It is your surest hold upon her. I shouldn't cavil at it, if I were you. To Anne you are the sum total of human knowledge. Your dictum is the last word to be said about anything."

But Berkeley still looked sulky. The idea of being what Sydney Smith said Macaulay was—*a book in breeches*— didn't appeal to him at all.

"What would you advise me to do?" he asked, after a pause.

She said reflectively: "Let her alone for a while, Berkeley. If her liking for you grows naturally into affection,—and it may, you know,—that would be best. If you try to force it, you may drive her from you altogether. I tell you frankly, she is not in the least interested in any man as a lover, so far as I can judge."

He was forced to admit the truth of this. She wasn't. She seemed to dislike any faintest sign of loverliness from any man toward her. Hayden had observed her icy attitude toward the painter who had fancied he found in her his ideal Undine, and who showed too openly his desire to help her gain a soul for herself. The idea that she might look at him as she had looked at the painter was highly unpleasant to him. He asked again:

"But what am I to do?"

"Nothing," said Mrs. Vandervelde, succinctly.

"But suppose she falls in love with somebody else."

"She is more likely to fall in love with you, I should imagine, if you keep quiet for a while and allow her to do so. Just remain her guide, philosopher, and friend, can't you?"

The clever, cosmopolitan Mr. Berkeley Hayden tugged at his short mustache and looked astonishingly like a sulky school-boy.

"Well, if you think that's the best thing I can do—" he began.

"I know it is," said she. And she reflected that even the cleverest man, when he is really in love, is something of a fool.

Here Anne herself came in and the three dined together, a statuesque maid in a yellow bodice and a purple skirt waiting on them. Agata's "Si?" was like a flute-note, and the two women loved to see her moving about their rooms. It was like having Hebe wait on them.

Anne turned to Hayden eagerly. She wished his opinion of a piece of tapestry an antiquarian in the Via Ricasoli wished to sell her. Would he go and look at it with her? And there was an old lamp she fancied but of the genuineness of which she wasn't sure. And she added, dropping her voice, that she'd gotten a copy of one of Fra Girolamo Savonarola's sermons, beautifully done on vellum, evidently by some loving monkish follower of his. Didn't he want to see it? She looked at him eagerly. Mrs. Vandervelde, catching his eye, smiled.

Hayden played his part beautifully, concealing the tumult of his feelings under the polished surface of the serene manner that Anne so greatly admired. He made himself indispensable; he gave her his best, unstintedly, and Hayden at his best was inimitable. Marcia Vandervelde regarded him with new respect and admiration. Berkeley was really wonderful!

When he took his departure, Anne Champneys felt that the glamour of Florence had departed with him. It was as if the sunshine had been withdrawn, along with that polished presence, that gem-like mind. She missed him to an extent that astonished her. She thought that even Giotto's Campanile looked bleak, the day Berkeley Hayden left.

"I'm going to miss you hideously," she told him truthfully.

"I hope so," he said guardedly. He did not wish to show too plainly how overjoyed he was at that admission. "And I'm going to hope you'll find me necessary in New York. I'm looking forward to seeing you in New York, you know. I have two new pictures I want you to see."

Her face brightened. "Your being there will make me glad to go back to New York," she said happily. And Hayden had to resist a wild impulse to shout, to catch her in his arms. He went away with hope in his heart.

But Mrs. Vandervelde, watching her closely, thought she was too open in her regret. N-no, Anne wasn't in love with Hayden—yet. She picked up her studies, to which he had given impetus, with too hearty a zest. And when he wrote her amusing, witty, delightful letters, she was too willing to have Marcia read them.

They remained in Italy six months or so more; and then one day Anne returned from a picnic, and said to Marcia abruptly:

"Would you mind if I asked you to leave Florence,—if I should want to go home?"

Marcia said quietly: "No. If you wish to go, we will go. Are you tired of Italy?"

Anne Champneys looked at her with wide eyes. For a moment she hesitated, then ran to Marcia, and clung to her with her head against her friend's shoulder.

"You're so good to me—and I care so much for you,—I'll tell you the truth," she said in a whisper. "I—I heard something to-day, Marcia,—*he's* coming to Rome—soon. And of course he'll come here, too."

"He?—Who?"

"Peter Champneys," said Peter's wife, and literally shook in her shoes. Her clasp tightened. Marcia put her arms around her, and felt, to her surprise, that Anne was frightened.

"You are sure?"

"Yes. I heard it accidentally, but I am sure. You know how pretty the Arno is at the spot where we picnicked. We strolled about, and I—didn't want to talk to anybody, so I slipped away by myself. There were a couple of English artists painting near by, and just as I came up I overheard what they were saying. Marcia,—they were talking about—*him*. They said he'd been called to Rome to paint somebody's picture,—the pope's, maybe,—and they'd probably see him here, later. They seemed to be—friends of his, from the way they spoke." She shivered. "Italy isn't big enough to hold us two!" she said, desperately. "Marcia, I can't—run the risk of meeting Peter Champneys. Not until I have to. I—I've got to get away!" Her voice broke.

"All right, dear. We'll go," said Marcia, soothingly. "Jason's about finished his work in Brazil, and he'll be back in New York by this. Do you want to go directly home?"

"Yes," said Anne Champneys. "Italy's a very little place compared with America. Let's go back to America, Marcia."

Mrs. Vandervelde stroked the red head. It seemed to her that fate was playing into Mr. Berkeley Hayden's hands.

CHAPTER XVII

THE GUTTER-CANDLE

Although the Champneys house was tightly closed, with the upper door and windows boarded up, the blonde person in shoddy fineries rang the area bell on the chance that there must be a caretaker somewhere about the premises. She felt that when one has come upon such an errand as hers, one mustn't leave any stone unturned; and she couldn't trust to a haphazard letter. An impassive and immaculate Japanese opened the door, and stood looking at her without any expression at all. Had the blonde person baldly stated her errand, the Japanese would probably have closed the door and that would have been the end of it. But she didn't speak; after a sharp glance at him she opened her gay hand-bag, extracted a slip of paper, handed it to him, and stood waiting.

The Japanese read: "I wish you'd do what you can, for my sake," and saw that it was addressed to Mr. Chadwick Champneys and signed by Mr. Peter Champneys. It had evidently been carefully kept, and for a long time, as the creases showed. The Japanese stood reflecting for a few moments, then beckoned the blonde person inside the house, ushering her into a very neat basement sitting-room.

"For you?" he asked, glancing at the slip of paper.

"Me? No. I come for a lady friend o' mine. You might tell 'em she's awful sick an' scared,—just about all in, she is,—or she wouldn't of sent. But he said she was to come here an' hand in that slip I've just gave you. That's how I come to bring it."

"All right. You wait," said the Japanese, and glided from the room. It was the first time Hoichi had received any message from the new master, as he knew Mr. Peter Champneys to be; if the message was genuine, he was sure that Mr. Chadwick Champneys, had he been alive, would have investigated it. Hoichi couldn't imagine how the blonde person had gotten hold of such a slip of paper, signed by Mr. Peter Champneys. If there was some trick behind it, some ulterior motive underlying it, then Hoichi proposed to have the trickster taught a needed lesson. He was a suspicious man and visions of clever robbers planning a raid on the premises rose before him. He would run no risks, take no chances. He rang up Mr. Jason Vandervelde, fortunately caught the lawyer at home, and faithfully repeated the blonde person's message. He insisted that the signature was genuine; he had seen many letters addressed to the late Mr. Champneys by his nephew, and he would recognize that writing anywhere. He asked to be instructed.

"Tell her to wait half an hour and I'll be there," said the lawyer upon reflection.

The blonde person was leaning back in a Morris chair, tiredly, when Vandervelde was ushered into the basement sitting-room. He recognized her type with something of a shock. She was what might be called—charitably—a peripatetic person, and she reeked of very strong perfume. The lawyer's eyes narrowed, while he explained briefly that he represented the Champneys interests. Would she explain as concisely as possible just why and for whom she had come?

She explained ramblingly. Mr. Vandervelde gathered that a certain "lady friend" of hers, one Gracie Cantrell, now in the hospital, said her prayers to Mr. Peter Champneys, whom she had met on a time, and who had advised her if ever she needed help to apply to his uncle, and to tell him that he had sent her. Feeling herself *down and out* now, she had done so.

"Honest to Gawd, the poor little simp thinks this feller's a angel. Why,—when she gets out o' her head, she don't rave about nothin' but him, beggin' him to help her. Ain't it somethin' fierce, though?" The blonde person dabbed at her eyes with a scented handkerchief.

Mr. Vandervelde rubbed his nose thoughtfully. A girl down and out, a waif in a city ward, in her delirium calling upon Peter Champneys for help, didn't sound at all good to him. In connection with that penciled slip which seemed to imply that she had a right to expect help, it smacked of possible heart-interest—sob-stuff—so dear to enterprising special writers for a yellow press. He couldn't understand how or where Peter had met the girl; possibly some youthful foolishness back there in Carolina. Maybe she'd followed him north, to become what her friendship with such as the blonde person indicated. Vandervelde was a cautious man and he thought he had better investigate that message, written before Chadwick Champneys's death.

"My car's outside," he told the blonde person briefly. "We'll see this Gracie at once and find out just what's to be done."

It was past the hour for visitors, but Vandervelde's card procured them admittance to the ward where Gracie lay. At sight of the big-eyed, white-faced, wasted little creature who looked at him with such a frightened and beseeching stare, Vandervelde's suspicions of her died. No matter what she had been,—and the house-physician's brief comment on her case left him in no doubt,—this poor wrecked bit of humanity beached upon the bleak shore of a charity ward was harmless. He absolved her of all evil intent, of any desire to obtain anything under false pretenses. He even absolved the blonde person, who despite her brassy hair, her hectic face, had of a sudden become a kind, gentle, and soothing presence. "Well, dearie, you got a straight tip from that feller. All I had to do was to show that piece o' paper he give you, and this kind gent'man come right off to see you," said the blonde cheerfully. "An' now maybe he'll be wantin' to talk with you, so I'll leave you be. Good night, dearie," and she stepped away quietly, a trail of perfume in her wake, so that Vandervelde's nose involuntarily wrinkled.

Gracie lay and looked at her visitor.

"You ain't his uncle. You don't look nothin' at all like him," said she, disappointedly.

"No. His uncle is dead. I'm the lawyer who has the estate in charge. So you can tell me just exactly what you know about Mr. Peter Champneys, and then tell me what I can do for you."

He spoke so kindly that Gracie's spirits revived. She told him just exactly what she knew about Mr. Peter Champneys, which of course was very, very little. Yet this much was luminously clear: of all the men Gracie had ever encountered, of all her experiences, Peter Champneys and the hour he had sat and talked with her stood out clearest, clean, touched with a soft and pure light, a solitary sweet remembrance in a sodden and sordid existence.

"Like a angel, he was. I never seen nobody with such a way o' lookin' at you. Never pretended he didn't understand, but treated me like a lady. I couldn't never forget him. I kep' the piece o' paper he give me, mostly because it was somethin' belongin' to him an' it sort o' proved I hadn't dreamed him. I never meant to ask for no help—but when I come here—an' there wasn't nothin' else to do, I kep' rememberin' he said I was to go to his uncle an' say he'd sent me. I—I'm scared! My Gawd!—I'm scared!"

He remembered once seeing a trapped rabbit die of sheer terror. This girl, trapped by the inevitable, reminded him unpleasantly of the rabbit. His kind heart contracted. He asked gently:

"What is it you are so afraid of, Gracie? Try to tell me just what you want me to do for you." Perspiration appeared upon her forehead. She clutched him with a skeleton hand.

"I'm scared o' bein' cut up!" she whispered fearfully. "Oh, for Gawdsake, save me from bein' cut up!" Her eyes widened; in her thin breast you could see her laboring heart thumping. "I want you keep 'em from cuttin' me up!" she repeated feverishly.

"Cutting you up!" Vandervelde looked at her wonderingly.

"Yes. I heard 'em say I didn't have no chanst. They put you in the morgue—afterward—when you're folks like me, and then the doctors come and get you and cut you up. I don't want to be cut up! For Christ's sake, don't you let 'em cut me up!"

Vandervelde felt a sort of sick horror. He couldn't quite understand Gracie's psychology; her unreasoning, ignorant terror.

"Why, my poor girl, what a notion! You—" he stammered.

"I been treated bad enough alive without bein' cut up when I'm dead," said she, interrupting him. "I get to thinkin' about it, wakin' up here in the night. He said his folks'd help me if I asked 'em."

"Of course, of course! Certainly we'll help!" said Vandervelde hastily.

"If I had any money saved up, 't wouldn't be so bad. But I ain't. We never do. I—I been sick a long time. What clothes I had they kep' against the rent I was owin', when they told me to get out. An' I walked an' walked,—an' then one o' them cops in Central Park, he seen me, an' next thing I knew I was here."

She was getting hysterical, and he saw that it was quite useless to try to reason with her; the one way to allay her terror was to make the promise she implored.

"Well, now that your message has reached us, Gracie, you need not be afraid any more, because what you fear won't happen; it can't happen. There!—Put it out of your mind."

She stared at him intently, and decided that this large, fair man was one to be implicitly trusted.

"You bein' one o' his people, if you say it won't happen, then it won't happen," she told him, and fetched a great sight of relief. "Oh! I was that scared I 'most died! I—I just naturally can't bear the idea o' bein' turned over to them doctors." And she shuddered.

"Well, now that you're satisfied you won't be, suppose you tell me something more immediate that I can do for you. Isn't there something you'd like?"

"I'd like it most of anything if you'd tell me somethin' about *him*," she said timidly. "I know I got no right to ast, me bein' what I am," she added, apologetically. "You see, nobody ever behaved to me like he did, an' I can't forget him."

She looked so pathetically eager, her look was so humble, that Vandervelde couldn't find it in his heart to deny the request. He found himself telling her that Peter Champneys had become a great painter, that he had never returned to America, and that his wife also was abroad.

"Is the lady he's married to as nice as him? I sure hope she's good enough for him," was Gracie's comment.

Seeing how mortally weak she was, Vandervelde took his departure, promising to see her again. He had a further interview with the house-physician and the head nurse. Whatever could be done for her would be done, but they had handled too many Gracies to be optimistic about this particular one. They knew how quickly these gutter-candles flicker out.

Commonplace as the girl was, she managed to win Vandervelde's interest and sympathy. That she had won young Peter Champneys's didn't surprise him. He was glad that she had had that one disinterested and kindly deed to look back to. The boy's quixotic behavior brought a smile to the lawyer's lips. Fancy his wishing to send such a girl to his uncle and being sure that old Chadwick wouldn't misunderstand! Gracie cast a new light upon Peter Champneys, and a very likable one. Vandervelde had seen in the uncle something of that same unworldliness that the nephew displayed, and it had established the human equation between Peter and the shrewd old man.

Busy as he was, he managed to see Gracie again. She had

refused to be put into a private room; she preferred the ward.

"It's not fittin'," she said. "Anyhow, I don't want to stay by myself. When I wake up at night I want to feel people around me,—even sick people's better than nobody. It's sort o' comfortin' to have comp'ny," and she stayed in the ward, sharing with less fortunate ones the fruit and flowers Vandervelde had sent to her. Once the gripping fear that had obsessed her had been dispelled, once she was sure of a protecting kindness that might be relied upon, she proved a gay little body. As the blonde person said, Gracie wasn't a bad sort at all. As a matter of fact, neither was the blonde person. Vandervelde saw that, and it troubled his complacent satisfaction with things. He saw in the waste of these women an effect of that fatally unmoral energy ironically called modern civilization. He wondered how Marcia, or Peter's wife, would react to Gracie. Should he tell them about her? N-no, he rather thought not.

Marcia had cabled that she and Anne were leaving Italy— were, in fact, on their way home. During his wife's absence he had had to make two or three South American trips, to safeguard certain valuable Champneys interests. The trips had been highly successful and interesting, and he hadn't disliked them, but Vandervelde was incurably domestic; he liked Marcia at the household helm.

"I wanted to hire half a dozen brass-bands to meet you," he told his wife the morning of her arrival, and kissed her brazenly. "Marcia, you are prettier than ever! As for Anne—" At sight of Anne Champneys his eyes widened.

"Why, Anne!—Why Anne!" He took off his glasses, polished them, and stared at his ward. Marcia smiled the pleased smile of the artist whose work is being appreciated by a competent critic. She was immensely proud of the tall fair girl, so poised, so serene, so decorative.

"As a target for the human eye," said Vandervelde, fervently, "you're more than a success: you're a riot!"

Anne slipped her hand into the crook of his arm. "I'm glad you like me," said she, frankly. "It's so nice when the right people like one."

Hayden was not in town. He didn't, as a matter of fact, know that they had left Italy, for Anne's last letter had said nothing of any intention to return to America shortly. Anne felt curiously disappointed that he wasn't at the pier with Jason to meet them. She was surprised at her own eagerness to see him. He pleased her more than any man she had ever met, and her impatience grew with his absence.

Marcia, a born general, was already planning with masterly attention to details the social career of Mrs. Peter Champneys. With the forces that she could command, the immense power that Berkeley Hayden would swing in her favor, and the Champneys money, that career promised to be unusually brilliant, when one considered Anne herself.

The Champneys house was to be reopened. In the main, as Chadwick Champneys had planned it, it pleased Marcia's critical taste. Anne herself appreciated as she had been unable to do when she first came to it. She liked its fine Aubusson carpets, its lovely old rosewood and mahogany furniture, its uncluttered stateliness. But there were certain changes and improvements she wished made, and she took a businesslike pleasure in supervising the carrying out of her orders. The portrait of Mr. Chadwick Champneys, painted the year before his death hung over the library mantel and seemed to watch her thoughtfully, critically, with its fine brown eyes. The girl he had snatched from obscure slavery liked to study the visage of the old monomaniac who had been the god in the machine of her existence. Her judgment of him now was clear-eyed but cold. He had been liberal because it fell in with his plans. He had never been loving.

She was sitting in the library one morning, looking up at him rather somberly. Workmen came and went, and somewhere in the back regions a hammer kept up a steady tapping.

"Mr. Hayden," said Hoichi, as he ushered that gentleman into the room.

She turned her head and looked at him for a full moment, before rising to greet him: one of Anne Champneys's long, still, mysterious looks, that made his heart feel as if it were a candle, blown and shaken by the wind. Then she smiled and held out her hand. It was good to see him again! She was prouder of his friendship than of anything that had yet come to her. It gave her a sense of security, raised her in her own estimation.

She explained, eagerly, the changes and improvements she was planning, and he went over the house with her. He liked it as Marcia liked it; once or twice he offered suggestions; the relationship of pupil and master was at once resumed,— but this time the pupil was more advanced.

Then he took her out to lunch. It was with difficulty that he restrained the exuberant delight he felt; just to have her with him went to his head. "Marcia's advice was wise, but my behavior's going to be otherwise, if I don't keep a tight hold upon myself," he told himself.

He jealously watched her social progress, and he contributed not a little toward it. He had a sense of proprietorship in her, and he did not mean that she should be just one among many; he wished her to be a great luminary around which lesser lights revolved. Under Marcia Vandervelde's wing, then, Mrs. Peter Champneys was launched, and from the very first she was a success. She played her part beautifully, though she was curiously apathetic about her triumphs. The incense of adulation did not make as sweet an odor in her nostrils as one might have supposed. Anne Champneys was oddly lacking in personal vanity, and she retained her sense of values, she was able to see things in their just proportions. That she had created a sensation didn't turn her red head. But she had a feeling that she had, in a sense, kept her word to Chadwick Champneys, discharged part of her debt. This was what he had wished her to accomplish. Very well, she had accomplished it. She was glad. But she sensed a certain hollowness under it all. Sometimes, alone in her room, she would stand and look long and earnestly at the red Indian face of Fra Girolamo Savonarola, brought from Florence and now hanging on her wall. That room had changed. It was plain and simple, almost austere; the "honest monk" who had died in the fire, and the wooden crucifix under him, seemed to dominate it. That treasure of a maid whom Marcia had secured for her, secretly sniffed at Mrs. Champneys's bed-chamber. She couldn't understand it. It wasn't in keeping with the rest of the house. For, it was a brilliant house, as the home of an exceedingly fashionable, wealthy, and handsome woman should be.

Anne bore the name of Champneys like a conquering banner. What had happened on a smaller scale in Florence, happened on a large scale here at home. Something of the Champneys story had crept out,—the early marriage, which had kept all the wealth in the family; the departure of the bridegroom to become an artist, and the fact that he had really become a noted one. The halo of romance encircled her head. She was considered beautiful and clever, and the glamour of much money added to the impression she created; but she was also considered cold, inaccessible, and perhaps, as the Italian had said, without a heart. She became, as Marcia had laughingly predicted, a legend in her own lifetime.

Jason Vandervelde watched her speculatively. He adored Anne, and he hoped she wasn't going to be spoiled by all the pother made over her. And he watched with a growing concern Berkeley Hayden's quiet, persistent, deliberate pursuit of her. Jason wasn't under any illusions about the Champneys marriage, but he had, as his wife said, an almost superstitious respect for Chadwick Champneys, and that marriage had been the old man's darling plan. It was upon that he had builded, and Vandervelde hated to see that plan brought to naught. Anne wouldn't really lose, of course,— Hayden could give her as much as she might forego,—but Vandervelde somehow didn't relish the idea. That girl Gracie, lingering on in the hospital ward, had brought the real Peter Champneys poignantly close to his trustee. He couldn't help thinking that if Anne could know that real Peter, there might be a hope that old Chadwick's judgment would be once more vindicated. At the same time, he cared a great deal for Berkeley Hayden, and the latter wanted Anne. And when Hayden wanted anything, he generally got it. What Anne herself thought, or what she might know, he couldn't determine. And Marcia, when he ventured to speak to her about the matter, said cryptically:

"Why worry? What is to be, will be. Kismet, Jason, kismet!"

* * * * *

On a certain afternoon the house-physician telephoned Mr. Vandervelde that the girl Gracie was very low, and that she had asked for him. Vandervelde finished the letter he was dictating to his secretary, gave a few further instructions to that faithful animal, and had himself driven to the hospital.

He couldn't explain his feelings where Gracie was concerned. There was something to blame, somewhere, for these Gracies. It made him feel a bit remorseful, as if he and his sort had left something undone.

The house-physician said that Gracie's hold upon life was a mystery and a miracle; by all the laws she should have been gone some months since. She had certainly taken her time about dying! Her little, sharp, immature face had lost all earthliness; only the eyes were alive. They looked at Vandervelde gratefully. He had been very kind, and Gracie was trying to thank him.

"Good-by," said Gracie. "You been white. Tell *him*—I couldn't never forget him." She put out a claw of a hand, and the big man took it.

"Is there—anything else I can do for you, Gracie? Isn't there something you'd like?" The business of seeing Gracie go wasn't at all pleasant.

Her eyes of a sudden sparkled. She smiled.

"There's one thing I been wanting awful bad. But I ain't sure I ought to ask."

"Tell me, my child, tell me."

"I want to see *her*," said Gracie, unexpectedly.

"Her?"

"His wife. I got no right to ast, but I want somethin' awful to see his wife. Just once before I—I go, I want to see her."

Vandervelde felt bewildered. He had never spoken of Gracie

Marie Conway Oemler

to Marcia, or to Anne. They were so far removed from this poor little derelict that he was not sure they would understand. He said after a moment's painful reflection:

"My poor child, I will see what I can do. But if I—that is, if she—" He paused, not knowing exactly how to put his dilemma into words without wounding her. But Gracie understood.

"You mean if she won't come? That's what I want to know," said she, enigmatically. So weak was she that with the words on her lips she dropped into sudden slumber. He stood looking down upon her irresolutely. Then he tiptoed away, meeting at the door the house-physician.

"How long?" asked the lawyer, jerkily.

"Probably until morning. Or at any minute," said the doctor, indifferently. He thought it the best thing Gracie could do.

Vandervelde nodded. Then, moved by one of those impulses under the influence of which the most conservative and careful people do things that astonish nobody more than themselves, he got into his car and went after Anne Champneys.

* * * * *

Anne was for the moment alone. The spring dusk had just fallen, and she was glad to sit for a breathing-space in the shadowy room. Berkeley Hayden had just left. His visit had been momentous, and as a result she was shaken to the depths. She had come face to face with destiny, and she was called upon to make a decision.

For the first time Hayden had broken the rigid rule of

conduct he had set for himself. He felt that he could endure no more. He had to know. They had chatted pleasantly, idly. But of a sudden Berkeley had risen from his chair, gone to the window, looked out, turned and faced her.

"Anne," said he, directly, "what are you going to do about Peter Champneys?"

She started as if she had received an electric shock. After a moment, looking at him with a confused and startled stare, she stammered:

"W-why do you ask!"

"I have to know," said Hayden, and his voice trembled. "You must be aware, Anne, that I love you. I have loved you from the first moment of our meeting. You are the only woman I have ever really wished to marry. That is why I must ask you: What are you going to do about Peter Champneys?"

"I—I don't know," said she, twisting her fingers.

"Do you fancy you might be able to love him,—later?"

"No," said she, violently. "No!"

"Why, then, do you not have this abominable marriage annulled?" he demanded. "I know nothing of Champneys, except that he's an artist,—and, truth forces me to say, a great one. But if he doesn't love you, if you do not love him, do you think anything but misery is ahead for you both, if you decide to carry out the terms of that promise extorted from you?"

She shrank back in her chair. She made no reply, and Hayden came and stood directly before her, looking down at her.

"And I—am I nothing to you Anne? I love you. What of me, Anne?"

"What can I say?" said she, falteringly. "I am not free."

"If you were free, would you marry me? For that is what I am asking you to do,—free yourself, and marry me."

She lifted her troubled eyes. "If I were free," she said, "if I were free—Berkeley, give me time to consider this. It isn't only the annulling of my marriage to a man I had never seen until the day I married him, and have never seen since,—it's the breaking of my promise to Uncle Chadwick—" They were in the library, and she looked up at the portrait above the mantel. Hayden's glance followed hers.

"He had no right to extort any such promise from you!" he cried. "Anne, think it over! Weigh Peter Champneys and me in the balance. And,—let the best man win, Anne. Will you?"

She regarded him steadfastly. "Yes," she said.

"And when you have decided, you will let me know?"

"I will let you know," said she, smiling faintly.

Berkeley took her hand and kissed it. He looked deep into her eyes. Then he left her. He had been very quiet, but his passion for her glowed in his eyes, rang in his voice, and was in the lips that kissed her palm.

She had not been in the least thrilled by it, but she was not displeased. She liked him. As for loving him, she didn't think it was really in her to love anybody. Looking back upon her youthful infatuation for Glenn Mitchell, she smiled at herself twistedly. She knew now that she had been in love with the bright shadow of love.

But, she reflected, if she did not love Hayden, she respected him, she was proud of him; he represented all that was best and most desirable in her present life. Life with Berkeley Hayden wouldn't be empty. And life as she faced it now was as empty as a shell that has lost even the faintest echo of the sea. Despite its outward glitter, its mother-of-pearl sheen, she was beginning to be more and more aware of its innate hollowness. Her young and healthy nature cried out against its futility. She was in the May morning of her existence, and yet the joy of youth eluded her.

She had, perhaps, one more year of freedom. Then,—Peter Champneys. Berkeley might well ask what she was going to do about it! Was she to accept as final that contract which would make her the unloved wife of an unloved husband? Now that she had grown somewhat older and considerably wiser, now that her horizon had widened, her sense of values broadened, she perceived that she owed to herself, to her sacredest instincts, the highest duty. She did not like to break her pledged word; but that pledge wronged Berkeley, wronged her, wronged Peter.

Her feeling toward that unknown husband was one of stark terror, a sick dislike that had grown stronger with the years. In her mind he remained unchanged. She saw him as the gawky, shrinking boy, his lips apart, his eyes looking at her with uncontrollable aversion. Oh, no! Life with Peter Champneys was unthinkable! There remained, then, Berkeley Hayden. It wasn't unpleasant to think of Berkeley Hayden. It made one feel safe, and assured; there was a glamour of gratified pride about it,—Nancy Simms,—Mrs.

Marie Conway Oemler

Peter Champneys,—Mrs. Berkeley Hayden. A little smile touched her lips.

Into these not unpleasant musings Mr. Jason Vandervelde irrupted himself, with the astounding request that she come with him now, immediately, to a hospital where a girl unknown to her prayed to see her. Hoichi had turned the lights on upon Mr. Vandervelde's entrance, and Anne looked at her visitor wonderingly.

"I do sound wild," admitted Jason, "but if you could have seen the poor thing's face when she asked to see you—Anne, she'll be dead before morning." The big man's glance was full of entreaty.

"But if she doesn't know me, why on earth should she wish to see me,—at such a time?" asked Anne, still more astonished.

Flounderingly Vandervelde tried to tell her. A questionable girl, to whom Peter Champneys had been kind,—she couldn't exactly gather how. Dying in a hospital, and before she went wishing to see Peter Champneys's wife.

Peter Champneys's wife, fortunately for herself, was still too near and close to the plain people to consider such a request an outrageous impertinence, to be refused as a matter of course. The terrible power of money had not come to her soon enough to make her consider herself of different and better clay than her fellow mortals. She wasn't haughty. The heart she was not supposed to possess stirred uncomfortably. She looked at Vandervelde questioningly.

"You wish me to go?"

"I leave that to you entirely," said he, uncomfortably. "But," he blurted, "I think it would be mighty decent of you."

"I will go," she said.

When they reached the hospital, the blonde person was with Gracie. The blonde person had been crying, and it had not improved her appearance. Her nose looked like a pink wedge driven into the white triangle of her face. Screens had been placed around the bed. A priest with a rosy, good-humored face was just leaving.

Gracie turned her too-large eyes upon Peter Champneys's wife with a sort of unearthly intensity, and Anne Champneys looked down at her with a certain compassion. Anne had a bourgeois sense of respectability, and she had involuntarily stiffened at sight of the blonde drab sitting by the bedside, staring at her with sodden eyes. She hadn't expected the blonde. She ignored her and looked, instead, at Gracie. One could be decently sorry for Gracie.

A faint frown puckered Gracie's brows. Her hand in the blonde person's tightened its grasp. After a moment she said gravely:

"You came?"

"Yes," said Anne, mechanically. "I came. You wished to see me?" Her tone was inquiring.

"I wanted to see if you was good enough—for *him*," said the gutter-candle, as if she were throwing a light into the secret places of Anne Champneys's soul. "You ain't. But you could be."

Vandervelde had the horrid sensation as of walking in a nightmare. He wished somebody in mercy would wake him up.

Anne's brows came together. She bent upon Gracie one of her long, straight, searching looks.

"Thank you—for comin'," murmured Gracie. "You got a heart." Her eyelids flickered.

"I am glad I came, if it pleases you to see me," said Anne. "Is that all you wished to say to me!"

"I wanted to see—if you was good enough for *him*," murmured Gracie again. "You ain't. But remember what I'm tellin' you: you could be." Her eyes closed. She fell into a light slumber, holding the blonde person's hand. Vandervelde touched Anne on the arm, and they went out.

As they drove home Vandervelde told her, as well as he could, all that the little wrecked vessel which was now nearing its last harbor had told him. He was deeply moved. He said, patting her hand.

"It was decent of you to come. You're a little sport, Anne."

For a while she was silent. Peter Champneys, then, was capable of kindness. He could do a gentle and generous deed. And perhaps he also was finding the heavy chain of his promise to his uncle, of his marriage to herself, galling and wearisome. She reached a woman's swift decision.

"I'm going to be a better sport," said she. "I'm going to reward Peter Champneys by setting him free. I shall have our marriage annulled."

CHAPTER XVIII

KISMET!

Peter Champneys was packing up for a summer's work on the coast when he received Vandervelde's letter, advising him that Mrs. Champneys had instituted proceedings to have her marriage annulled. The attorney added that by this action on Anne's part the entire Champneys estate reverted to him, Peter Champneys, with the exception of fifty thousand dollars especially allotted to Anne by Chadwick Champneys's will. Vandervelde took it for granted there would be no opposition from Peter. He hoped his client would find it possible to visit America shortly, there being certain details he should see to in person.

Opposition? Peter's sensation was one of overwhelming relief. This was lifting from his spirit the weight of an intolerable burden: he felt profoundly grateful to that red-haired woman who had had the courage to take her fate in her own hands, forego great wealth, and sever a bond that threatened to become an iron yoke. He couldn't but respect her for that; he determined that she shouldn't be too great a loser. He thought she should have half the estate, at the very least.

He had never had the commercial mind. He had never asked

Marie Conway Oemler

that the allowance settled upon him by his uncle should be increased. As his own earnings far outstripped his modest needs, that allowance had been used to allay those desperate cases of want always confronting the kindly in a great city. The Champneys estate back there in America had bulked rather negligently in his mind, obscured and darkened by the formidable figure of the wife who went with it. She had loomed so hugely in the foreground that other considerations had been eclipsed. And now this ogress, moved thereto God knew why, had of a sudden opened her hand and set him free!

That strenuous and struggling childhood of his, whose inner life and aspirations had been so secret and so isolated, had taken the edge off his gregariousness. He did not continuously feel the herd-necessity to rub shoulders with others. The creative mind is essentially isolated. Peter loved his fellows with a quiet, tolerant affection, but he remained as it were to himself, standing a little apart. His heart was like a deep, still, hidden pool, in which a few stars only have room to shine.

A successful man, he had been romantically adored by many idle women and angled for by many an interested one. At times he had lightly lent himself to those amiable French arrangements of good comradeship which end naturally and without bitterness, leaving both parties with a satisfied sense of having received very good measure. He had never been able to deceive himself that he loved. He had loved Denise, but there had been in his affection for her more of compassion than passion, as Denise herself had known. She remained in his memory like a perfume. That had been his one serious liaison. But the woman he could really love with his fullest powers, and to whom he could give his best, had not yet appeared.

Mrs. Hemingway had been troubled by his celibacy. She had persisted in her desire to have him marry young, his wife being some one of her girl friends. She wished to see Peter set up an establishment, which would presently center around a nursery full of adorable babies who would bring with them that tender and innocent happiness young children alone are able to confer. To dispel these pleasant day-dreams of hers, Peter had found it necessary to tell her of his American marriage.

Mrs. Hemingway was astonished, a little chagrined, but not hopeless. He should bring his young wife to Paris. To make her understand *that* marriage as it really was, to explain his own attitude toward it, Peter made a swift and frightfully accurate little sketch of Nancy Simms as she had appeared to him that memorable morning.

His friend was appalled. It took Peter some time to explain his uncle to Mrs. Hemingway. At the best, she thought, he had been insane. Not even the fact that Peter was co-heir to the Champneys fortune consoled her for what she considered a block to his happiness, a blight upon his life. The more she thought about that marriage, the more she disliked it; and as the time approached for Peter literally to sacrifice himself upon the altar, Mrs. Hemingway grew more and more perturbed, though she wasn't so troubled about it as Emma Campbell was. Emma's terror of "dat gal" had grown with the years. Neither of them ventured to question Peter, but Emma Campbell began to have frequent spells of "wrastlin' wid de sperit," and her long, lugubrious "speretuals" were dismal enough to set one's teeth on edge. She would howl piercingly:

"Befo' dis time anothuh yeah,
I ma-ay be gone,
Een some ole lone-some graveyahd,

O Lawd, ho-ow long?"

She had left the high Montmartre cottage and had come down to keep house for Peter, his being a very simple menage. Oddly, the denizens of the Quartier didn't faze her in the least. She chuckled over them, an old negro woman's sinful chuckle. She made no slightest attempt to conquer the French language, which she didn't in the least admire. She learned the equivalents for a few phrases of her own,—"I hongry," "How much?" "Gimme dat," and "Mistuh Peter gone out," and on this slight foundation she managed to keep a fairly firm footing. The frequenters of Peter's studio were delighted with Emma Campbell; they recognized her artistic availability, and she and her black cat were borrowed liberally.

As a rule, she was willing to lend herself to art, and was a patient model, until one rash young man took it into his head, that he must have Emma Campbell as a favorite old attendant upon the *Queen of Sheba* he proposed to paint. He was a very earnest young German, that painter, speaking fairly good English. Emma had liked him more than most; but her faith received a blow from which it never recovered. That young man wished to paint her *au naturel*—her, Emma Campbell, who had been a member in good standing of the Young Sons and Daughters of Zion, the Children of Mary Magdalen, and the Burying Society of the Sons and Daughters of the Rising Star in the Bonds of Love! In the altogether! Emma Campbell gasped like a hooked fish. She made a nozzle of her mouth and protruded her eyes. She said ominously:

"I bawn nekked, but I ain't had nuttin' to do wid dat. Dat de fust en de last time I show up wid mah rind out o' doors. I been livin' in clo'es evuh sence, en I 'speck to die in clo'es."

The artist, who wanted Emma in his picture, tried to make her understand. He reasoned with her manfully:

"Ach, silly nigger-woman! Clothes, clothes! What are clothes! See, now: you are the Queen of Sheba's old slave. Your large black feet and legs are bare, a glittering amulet swings between your withered breasts of an old African, you wear heavy bracelets and anklets, around your lean flanks is a little, thin striped apron, and you hold in your hand the great fan of peacock feathers! Magnificent! You are the queen's old slave, imbecile!"

"Is I? Boy, is you evuh hear tell o' Mistuh Abe Linkum? Aftuh Gin'ral Sherman bun down de big house smack en smoove, en tote off all de cow en mule en hawg en t'ing, en dem Yankees tief all de fowl, en we-all run lak rabbit, Mistuh Linkum done sen' word we's free. En jus' lak Mistuh Linkum say, hit's so; aftuh us git shet o' Gin'ral Sherman, we 's free. All dat time I been a-wearin' clo'es, en now you come en tarrygate me, sayin' I got to stan' up in de nekked rind en wave fedders 'cause I in slaveryment? You bes' ain't let Mistuh Peter Champneys hear you talkin' lak dat!"

The bewildered and baffled young man raved in three languages, but Emma Campbell flatly refused either to be in "slaveryment" or in the "nekked rind." Visions of herself being caught and painted bare-legged, with a trifling little dab of an apron tied around her waist even as one ties a bit of ribbon around the cat's neck, and of this scandal being ferreted out by the deacons, sisters, and brethren, of the Mount Zion Baptist Church in Riverton, South Carolina, haunted her and made her projeck darkly. When she ventured to voice her opinion to Mist' Peter, he clapped her on the back and grinned. Emma Campbell began to look with a jaundiced eye upon art and the votaries of art.

Marie Conway Oemler

She was relieved when Peter decided to spend the summer on the coast; she was a coast woman herself, and she longed for the smell of the sea. And then, to add to her joy, had come this last, astonishing news: "dat gal" was going to divorce Mist' Peter! That incomprehensible marriage would be done away with, that grim, red-headed dragoness would go out of their lives! Emma's speretuals took a more hopeful trend; and Peter whistled while he worked.

He had written Vandervelde that he couldn't forego his summer's work, but would probably be in New York that autumn. In the meantime, let Vandervelde look after his interests as usual and see to it that Mrs. Champneys was more adequately and liberally provided for. He forgot to inquire as to the real value of his possessions. He did say to himself soberly:

"Jingo! This thing sounds like money—as if I were a mighty rich man! I'll have to do something about this!"

But he wasn't overly upset, or even very greatly interested. His real concern had never been money; it had been, like Rousseau's and Millet's, to make the manifestation of life his first thought, to make a man really breathe, a tree really vegitate.

And so he went to the coast, as happy as a school-boy on a holiday. The sea fascinated him, and the faces of the men who go down to the sea in ships. It was going to be the happiest and most fruitful summer he had known for years. He bade the Hemingways a gay farewell. Mrs. Hemingway, he noted, looked at him speculatively. Her matrimonial plans for him had revived.

He worked gloriously. He ate like a school-boy, and slept like one, dreamlessly. What was happening in the outside world didn't interest him; what he had to do was to catch a little of the immortal and yet shifting loveliness of the world and imprison it on a piece of canvas. He didn't get any of the newspapers. When he smoked at night with his friend the cure, a gentle, philosophic old priest who had known a generation of painter-folk and loved this painter with a fatherly affection, he heard passing bits of world gossip. The priest took several papers, and liked to talk over with his artist friend what he had read. It was the priest, pale and perturbed, who told him that war was upon the world. Peter didn't believe it. In his heart he thought that the fear of war with her great neighbor had become a monomania with the French.

"It will be a bad war, the worst war the world has ever known. We shall suffer frightfully: but in the end we shall win," said the cure, walking up and down before his cottage. He fingered his beads as he spoke.

France began to mobilize. And then Peter Champneys realized that the French fear hadn't been so much a mono-mania as a foreknowledge. The thing stunned him. He wished to protest, to cry out against the monstrousness of what was happening. But his voice was a reed in a hurricane; he was a straw in a gigantic whirlpool. He felt his helplessness acutely.

He couldn't work any more; he couldn't sleep; he couldn't eat. There is a France that artists love more than they may ever love any woman. Peter Champneys knew that France. Nobody hated and loathed war more than he, born and raised in a land, and among a people, stripped and darkened by it. And that had been but a drop in the bucket, compared with what was now threatening France. He couldn't idly stand by and see that happen! He thought of all that France had given him, all that France meant to him. The faces of all those comrades of the Quartier rose before him; and gently, wistfully appealing, the sweet face of little lost Denise. He packed his paintings finished and unfinished, and went to tell his friend the cure farewell, bending his pagan knees to receive the old man's blessing. The cure, too, was part of that which is the spirit of France.

They were enlisting in the Quartier. Peter was one of very many. When the preliminaries were passed and he had put on the uniform of a private soldier of the republic, he felt rather a fool. He wasn't in the least enthusiastic. There was a thing to be done, and he meant to help in its accomplishment; but he wasn't going to shout over it or pretend that he liked doing it.

When he went to tell Mrs. Hemingway good-by, just before his regiment left, she put her arms around him and kissed him. She was going to stay in Paris, and Emma Campbell would stay in her house. Emma Campbell had been very silent. She had acute and very unpleasant recollections of one war. She didn't understand what this one was about, but she didn't like it. And when she saw Peter in uniform, saying good-by, going away to get himself killed, maybe, she broke into a whimper:

"Oh, Miss Maria! Oh, Miss Maria! Look at we-all chile! Oh, my Gawd, Miss Maria, we-all's chile's gwine to de war!"

Peter put his arm around her shoulder. His face twitched. Emma said in a low voice: "I help Miss Maria wean 'im, en he bit me on de knuckles wid 'is fust toofs. Nevuh had no trouble wid 'im, 'cept to dust 'is britches wunst in a w'ile. Ah, Lawd! I sho did love dat chile! Use to rake chips for de wash-pot fire, en sit roun' en wait for ole Emma Campbell to fix 'is sweet 'taters for 'im. Me en Miss Maria's chile. En now he soldier en gwine to de war! Me en 'im far fum home, en he gwine to de war!" She threw her white apron over her head. Emma hated to have anybody see her cry.

So Peter Champneys went to the war, along with the other artists of France, and was made use of in many curious ways. Presently he was taken out of his squad, and set at other work where the quick and sure eye, and deft, trained hand, of the painter were needed.

He saw unbelievable, unimaginable things, things so unspeakable that his soul seemed to die within him. The word *glory* made him shudder. There was a duty to do, and he did it to the best of his ability, without noise, without fear. Wherever he looked around him, other men were doing the same thing. Every now and then, after some particularly nightmarish experiences, he would be called out—he himself questioned why—and kissed on both cheeks, and a medal or so would be pinned upon him. He accepted it all politiely, apathetically; it was all a part of the game. And the game itself seemed never-ending. It went on and on, and on.

It seemed to him that he wasn't Peter Champneys the artist any more, the lover of beauty, the man who was to rebuild the house of his forebears, and for whom a great fortune was waiting over there in America. He was just a soul in torment, living his bit of hell, hating it with a cold impatience, an incurable anger. One thing only kept him from losing all hope for mankind: at times he had piercing, blinding glimpses of the soul of plain men laid bare. With torment, a humanity larger even than his art was born in him.

At the end of the third year a sniper got him. He was wounded so badly that at first it was thought a leg would have to be amputated. But even in that hideous welter of the nations, Peter Champneys wasn't unknown. Overburdened and busy as they were, doctors and nurses fought for the life of the American artist. He came to to hear a poilu in his ward praising the saints that it was *his* hand and not the painter's that had gone, and another say philosophically that if one of two *had* to be blinded, he was glad M. Champneys's eyes had been saved.

"You will see for us, Monsieur," said he cheerfully. And in his heart Peter swore to himself that he would. He would see for the plain people, the common people of God.

As soon as he was able to be moved, the Hemingways and Emma Campbell came and took him home. Now, a spirit like his cannot see and hear and know such things as Peter had been experiencing for three years, without showing signs of the conflict. Peter had changed physically as well as spiritually. His face had paled to an ivory tone, the features had a cameo sharpness and purity of outline; cheeks and chin were covered with a heavy, jet-black beard,—as if his countenance were in morning for its lost boyishness. And out of this thin, quiet, black-haired, black-bearded face looked a pair of golden eyes of an almost intolerable clarity. *Don Pedro* Mrs. Hemingway called him laughingly, and *El Conquistador*. Secretly, she was immensely proud of him.

Peter didn't recuperate as quickly and completely as had been hoped. He was weary with an almost hopeless weariness, and Mrs. Hemingway, who watched him with the affection of an older sister, was worried about his condition. She didn't like his apathy. He was as gentle, as considerate, and even more exquisitely sympathetic than of old. But in all things that concerned himself, he was quietly disinterested. She and Hemingway had several long talks. Then Hemingway began to get busy. Presently he suggested, that it might be a very good idea if Peter should go over to America for a while, and look after those interests to which he hadn't given a thought since he had put on a uniform. After all, Hemingway reminded him, his uncle had placed considerable trust in him. It was only fair now that Chadwick Champneys's wishes should come in for at least a little attention, wasn't it?

Peter pondered this idea, and found it just. Besides, he wasn't unwilling to go back to America now that he didn't have to face that girl. He wondered, vaguely, what had become of her. Had she found happiness for herself? He hoped so. Yes, he'd rather like to see New York again. He couldn't be of any further use here now, and he couldn't do his own work, for all inspiration seemed to have left him. He felt empty, arid, useless.

He might just as well act upon Hemingway's suggestion, and find out how things were over there. And after he'd seen Vandervelde, he'd go down south and visit that tiny brown house on the cove, and the River Swamp, and Neptune's old cabin, and the cemetery alongside the Riverton Road. It seemed to him that he smelled the warm, salt-water odors of the coast country again, saw the gray moss swaying in the river breeze, heard a mocking-bird break into sudden song. A homesick longing for Carolina came upon him. Oh, for the flat coast country, the marsh between blue water and blue sky, the swamp bays in flower, a Red Admiral fluttering above a thistle in a corner of an old worm-fence!

Emma Campbell discovered this homesick longing in herself, too. Emma was hideously afraid of the passage across, but she was willing to risk it, just to get "over home" once more. She thought of herself sitting in her place in Mount Zion Church, with ole Br'er Shadrach Timmons liftin' up de tune, fat Sist' Mindy Sawyer fanning herself with a palm-leaf fan and swaying back and forth in time to the speretual, and busybody Deacon Williams rolling his eye to see that nobody took too long a swallow out of the communion cup he passed around. She thought of possum parties, with accompaniments of sweet 'taters and possum gravy. Her lip trembled, tears rolled down her black cheeks. She had been living in the midst of air raids, her ears had been stunned with the roar of *Big Bertha*. Now she nevuh wanted to hear nuttin' louder dan bull-frawg in de river so long as she lived. She was sorry to leave Mrs. Hemingway, for whom she had acquired a great affection. And she had one real grief: Satan had gone to the heaven of black cats, so she couldn't take him back to Carolina. She wouldn't replace the dear, funny, cuddly beastie with a French cat. French cats were amiable animals, very nice in their way, but they weren't, they couldn't be, "we-all's folks" as the Carolina cat had been.

Hemingway arranged everything. And so one morning, Peter Champneys walking with a stick, and old Emma Campbell, stiffly erect and rustling in a black silk frock that Mrs. Hemingway had bought for her, turned their faces to America once more.

Vandervelde, who met them in response to Hemingway's cable, knew Emma Campbell at sight, but failed to recognize in the tall, distinguished, very foreign-looking gentleman, the gangling Peter Champneys he had seen married to Nancy Simms. He kept staring at Peter, and the corners of his mouth curled more than usual. And he liked him, with the instantaneous liking of one large-natured man for another. Vandervelde had never approved of the annulment of the Champneys marriage, although Marcia did. Not even the fact that Anne was going to marry Berkeley Hayden, had been able to convince Vandervelde that the bringing to naught of Chadwick Champneys's plans could be right. And looking at Peter Champneys now, he was more than ever convinced that a mistake had been made. That little gutter-girl, Gracie, had been right about Peter Champneys; and Anne had been wrong.

Vandervelde asked, presently, if Peter wished to see the reporters. Once they scented him, they would be clamoring at his heels. And then Peter learned to his surprise and annoyance that he was something of a hero and very much of a celebrity. His expression made Vandervelde chuckle. But, the attorney demanded, could a famous artist, a man who for distinguished and unusual service had been decorated by two governments, the heir to the Champneys millions, and one of the figures of a social romance, hope to hide his light under a bushel basket? Nothing doing! He was a figure of international importance, a lion whom the public wanted to hear roar.

Peter shuddered. The thought of being interviewed by one of those New York super-reporters made him feel limp. Couldn't they understand he didn't want to talk? Didn't they understand that those who had really seen, those who knew, weren't doing any talking? Why,—they couldn't! As for himself, his nerves were rasped raw. Luckily, Vandervelde understood.

He asked Vandervelde a few perfunctory questions, and learned that things were very much all right. He signed certain papers presented to him. Then he asked abruptly if Mrs. Champneys had been as liberally provided for as she should have been, and learned that Mrs. Champneys had flatly refused to accept a penny more than the actual amount given her by Chadwick Champneys's will. Vandervelde added, after a moment, that he thought Mrs. Champneys intended to remarry. At that Peter looked somewhat surprised. He thought him a bold man who of his own free will ordained to marry Nancy Simms Champneys! He murmured, politely, that he hoped she would be happy, but failed to ask the name of his successor. What was Hecuba to him or he to Hecuba?

He was in Vandervelde's office, then, and the telephone began to ring. Three several times Vandervelde answered the questions where, when, how might the reporter at the other end of the wire get in touch with Mr. Peter Champneys. Had he really returned to New York? Been decorated several times, hadn't he? What was his latest picture? What were his present and future plans? Could Mr. Vandervelde give any information? In each case Mr. Vandervelde said he couldn't. He hung up the receiver and looked at the celebrity, who seemed gloomy.

The lawyer was a tower of strength. He started Emma Campbell, who didn't want to linger in New York, on her way to Riverton. Emma wanted to get home as fast as the fastest train could carry her. But Peter didn't want to go back to Riverton—yet. And then Vandervelde made a suggestion which rather pleased Peter. Why not go to a little place he knew, a quiet and very beautiful place on the Maine coast? Very few people knew of its existence. Vandervelde had stumbled upon it on a motor trip a few years before, and he was rather jealous of his discovery. The people were sturdy, independent Maine folk, the climate and scenery unsurpassed; Peter would be well looked after by the old lady to whom Vandervelde would recommend him. And to make perfectly sure that he'd be undisturbed, to drop more completely out of the world and find the rest he needed, why not call himself, say, Mr. Jones, or Mr. Smith, letting Peter Champneys the artist hide for a while behind that homely disguise? Vandervelde almost stammered in his eagerness. His eyes shone, his face flushed. He leaned across his desk, watching Peter with a curious intensity.

Peter liked the idea of the Maine coast. Sea and forest, open spaces, quietude; plain folk going about their own business, letting him go about his. Long days to loaf through, in which to reorganize his existence in accordance with his newer values. Isolation was the balm his spirit craved. Let him have that, let it help him to become his own man again, and he'd be ready to face life and work like a giant refreshed.

"You'll go?" Vandervelde's voice was studiously restrained; he had lowered his lids to hide the eagerness of his eyes.

"I think such a place as you describe is exactly what I need," said Peter.

"I'm quite sure it is. And the sooner you go, the better."

Peter got up and walked around the office. A typewriter was clacking monotonously, the telephone bell was constantly ringing. Peter turned his head restlessly.

Vandervelde had made his suggestion at precisely the right moment. Peter felt grateful to him. Very nice man, Vandervelde. Kind as he could be, too! One liked and trusted him. Clever of him to have so instantly understood just what Peter most craved!

"I quite agree with you," said Peter. "I'll start to-night."

Vandervelde leaned back in his chair. His heart thumped. He drew a deep breath, the corners of his mouth curling noticeably, and beamed at Peter Champneys through his glasses. He said aloud, cheerfully, "Well, why not?"

CHAPTER XIX

THE POWER

Grandma Baker's cottage formed the extreme right horn of the crescent that was the village. The middle of the crescent backed up against a hill, the horns dipped toward the shore-line and the water. Near Grandma Baker's front gate were currant bushes, and a path bordered with dahlias and gillyflowers led to the door, which had two stone slabs for steps, and on both sides of which were large lilac bushes,— she called them "lay-locks." Behind the house were apple-trees, and more currant bushes, as well as gooseberries and raspberries. A herb garden grew under her kitchen windows, so that her kitchen and pantry always smelled of thyme and wintergreen, and her bedrooms were fragrant with lavender.

The quiet gentleman to whom she had given an upper room that looked out upon woods and waters, a bit of pasture, a stretch of coast, and a pale blue sky full of sudsy clouds, thought that Mr. Jason Vandervelde's fervent praises hadn't done justice to this bit of untouched Eden tucked away in a bend of the Maine coast. It gave him what his heart craved— beauty, fragrance, stillness. A few weather-beaten old men, digging clams, dragging lobster-pots, or handling a boat. A few quiet women, busy with household affairs. No one to have to talk to. No one to ask him questions. There was but one other visitor in the village, Grandma Baker told him, a young widow,—"a nice common sort of a woman," who was staying up the street with Mis' Thatcher.

Mr. Johnston, as the gentleman called himself, hadn't seen the "nice common sort of a woman" yet, though he had been here a whole week, and he wasn't in the least curious about her. He didn't know that when you're a "nice common sort of a woman" to these Maine folk, you're receiving high praise from sturdy democrats. The phrase, to him, called up a good, homely creature, amiably innocuous, placidly cow-like.

Mr. Johnston slept in a four-poster, under a patchwork quilt that aroused poignant memories. At his own request he ate in a corner of the big kitchen, near the window opening upon the herb garden. Already he had struck up a firm friendship with his brisk, strong old landlady.

"Fit in the war, didn't ye?" asked the old lady, genially.

Mr. Johnston's face took on a look of weariness and obstinacy. Grandma Baker smiled cheerfully.

"Tell the truth and shame the devil," she chirped. "You fit, but you needn't be scared I'll ask you any questions about it. I mind Abner, my husband, comin' back from Virginia after he'd fit the hull dratted Civil War straight through and helped win it. And he wouldn't open his trap. Couldn't bear havin' to talk about it. Some men's like that. Ornery, o' course, but you got to humor 'em. You put me a hull lot in mind o' my Abner." And she looked with great kindliness upon the taciturn person known to her as Mr. Johnston. True to her word, she asked him no questions. She fed him, and let him alone.

He was so weary, at first, that he didn't want to do anything but lie under a tree idly for long drowsy hours, as he had lain under the trees on the edge of the River Swamp years before. This Maine landscape, so rugged and yet so tender, had a brooding and introspective calm, as of a serene and strong old man who has lived a vigorous, simple, and pure life, and to the jangled nerves and tired mind of Peter Champneys it was like the touch of a healing hand. With every day he felt his strength of mind and body returning, and the restless perturbation that had tormented him receding, fading. These green and gracious trees, bathed in a lucent light, this sweet sea-wind, and the voice of the waters, a voice monotonously soothing, helped him to find himself,—and to find himself newer, fresher, a more vital personality. This newer Peter Champneys was not going to be, perhaps, so easy-going a chap. He was more insistent, he was sterner; to the art-conscience, in itself a troublesome possession, he was adding the race-conscience, which questions, demands, and will have nothing short of the truth. He had been forced to see things as they are, things stripped of pleasant trappings and made brutally bare; and his conscience and his courage now arose to face facts. Any misery, rather than be slave to shams! Any grief to bear, any price to pay, but let him possess his own soul, let him have the truth!

He could not sit in judgment upon himself as an artist only; he had to take himself seriously as a very wealthy man in an hour when very wealthy men stood, so to speak, before the tribunal of the conscience of mankind. He could not afford to be crushed by the burden of much money. Neither could he ignore the stern question: what was he going to do with the Champneys wealth? He wished that that red-headed woman had taken half of it off his hands!

The Champneys money made him very thoughtful this morning, walking with his hands behind his back, his head bare to the wind. The water rippled in the sunlight. Out on the horizon a solitary sail glimmered. The semicircle of village houses resembled the white beads of a broken necklace, lying exactly where they'd fallen. He turned a small headland, and the village vanished.

He had a pleasant sense of being alone with this rocky coast, with its salty-sweet wind, its blue water, its limitless sky, from which poured a flood of clear, pale golden sunlight. And then, as if out of the heart of them all, came a figure immensely alive, the light focusing upon her as if she were the true meaning of the picture in which she appeared; as if this background were not accidental, but had been chosen and arranged for her with delicate and deliberate care.

He thought he had never seen any woman's body so superbly free in its movement: she had the grace of a birch stirred by a spring wind. The poise of her shoulders, the sweep of her garments blown by the sea-breeze, the joyous and vigorous grace of her whole attitude, reminded him of the winged Victory. So might that splendid vision have walked upon the glad Greek coast in the bright light of the world's morning.

The woman walked swiftly, lightly, her head held high, her long loose hair blown about her like flame. Where the rough path narrowed between two large boulders, he had paused to allow her to pass; and so they came face to face, he the taller by a head. She lifted her cool, gray-green eyes that had in them the silvery sparkle of the sea, and met his golden gaze. Her face framed in her flaming mane was warmly pale, the brow thoughtful, the mouth virginal. For a long moment they regarded each other steadily, wonderingly; and in that single moment the eternal miracle occurred by which life and the face of the world changed for them.

That long, clear, grave gaze pierced her heart like a golden poniard. He was of a thin body and visage, but the effect was of virility, not weakness,—as if the soul of him, like a blade in a scabbard, had fretted the body fine. There was a quiet stateliness in his bearing, a simple and unaffected dignity, to which the thick, blue-black hair, the foreign beard, and the aquiline features lent an added touch of distinction. One was reminded of those dangerously mild and rather sad faces of Spanish soldiers which look at one from Velasquez's canvases. This man might wear a ruff and a velvet doublet, or, better yet, a coat of mail, she reflected, instead of the well-cut but rather worn gray tweeds that clothed him.

She was not conscious of her flying hair, or the wind-blown disorder of her skirts. She was conscious, rather, that for the first time a man was looking at her as from a height, and she was filled with a beautiful astonishment, a sort of divine amazement, as if it were toward this that always, inevitably, she had been moving,—and now it was here! Her blood leaped to it, and went racing fierily through her veins, as if there had been poured into it the elixir of life. She was gloriously conscious of her youth and her womanhood. A quick and vivid rush of warm blood stained her, brow to bosom. Her every-day mind was saying, "It is the stranger who's staying at Grandma Baker's—the gentleman who's been ill." But beyond and behind her every-day mind, her heart was shouting, exultant, ecstatic, and very sure: "It is You! It is You!"

In quick sympathy with that bright flush of hers the blood showed for an instant in his pale face. He had been staring at her! An agitation new to him, an emotion to which all others he had ever experienced were childishly mild, filled him as the resistless sweep of the sea at flood tide fills the shallows of the shores. Love did not come to him gently and insidiously, but as with the overwhelming rush of great waters. This, then, must be that "nice, common sort of a woman" staying with the Widow Thatcher, at the other end of the village—this woman clothed with the sun of her red hair, and with the sea in her eyes! A smile curved his lips. His kindling glance played over her like lightning, and said to her: "I know you. I have always known you. Do you not recognize me? I am I,—and you are You!"

Had he obeyed his instincts, he would have flung himself before her and clasped her around the knees. Being a modern gentleman, he had to stand aside, bowing, and let her pass. She, too, bowed slightly. She went by with her quick and resilient tread, her cheek royally red. A wind roared in her ears, her heart beat thickly.

When she had turned the little headland she paused, and mechanically braided her hair. Her fingers shook, and she breathed as if she had been running. The incredible, the unbelievable, had pounced upon her as from a clear sky, and the world was never again to be the same. She had been so sure, so safe, with her pleasant life all mapped out before her, like the raked and swept paths of an ordered and formal garden; a life in which reason and convention and culture and wealth should rule, and from which tumultuous and tormenting passions and disorderly emotions should be rigidly excluded. In that ordered existence, she would be, if not happy, at least satisfied and proud. And now! A strange man in passing had looked into her eyes; love had come, and the gates of her formal garden had been pulled down, wild nature threatened to invade and overrun her trimmed and clipped borders and her smooth lawns.

The Widow Thatcher commented approvingly upon her fine color when she appeared at the house.

"You just stay here a leetle mite longer, Mis' Riley, and you'll be that changed you won't know yourself," said the kindly woman, heartily.

Marie Conway Oemler

"I'm sure of that!" murmured her guest.

The red-haired lady who called herself Mrs. Riley—Riley had been her mother's name—had been, up to this time, an altogether satisfying guest, simple, friendly, with a sound and healthy appetite, and well deserving that praiseful "nice, common sort of a woman" bestowed upon her. Now, mysteriously, she changed. She wasn't less friendly, but her appetite was capricious and she would fall into reveries, sudden fits of gravity, sitting beside the window, staring somberly out at the waters. She would snatch up her hat and go out, get as far as the gate, and return to the house. Mrs. Thatcher heard her pacing up and down her room, when she should have been sound asleep. She would laugh, and then sigh upon the heels of it, break into fitful singing, and fall into sudden silence in the midst of her song.

"She's gettin' religion," the widow reflected. "The Spirit's workin' on her. 'T ain't nothin' I can do except pray for her." And the simple soul got on her knees and besought Heaven that the stranger under her roof might "escape whatever trouble 't is that's threatenin' her, O Lord, an' save her soul alive!"

Although the widow didn't know it, her guest had come to the dividing of the ways. She had come to this quiet place to find peace, to rest, to escape from the world for a breathing-space. And in this quiet place that which had missed her in the great outside world had come to her, the most tremendous of all powers had seized upon her. The situation was not without a sly and ironical humor.

She wondered what Marcia would say if she should write to her: "I have fallen in love at sight, hopelessly, irremediably, head over ears, with, a strange man who passed me on the shore. He wears gray tweeds. His name, I am told, is

Johnston. That's all I know about him, except that I seem to have known him since the beginning of all things. He is as familiar to my heart as my blood is, and all he had to do to make me love him was to look at me. Yes! I love him as I could never love anybody but him. He's the one man."

She could fancy Marcia's astonishment, her shocked "Oh, but Anne, there's Berkeley Hayden!"

And indeed, there was Berkeley Hayden!

When Anne had determined to have her marriage to Peter Champneys annulled, Marcia had upheld her, though Jason hadn't liked it at all. If he hadn't exactly opposed her course, he had tried to dissuade her from it. But she had persisted, and as the case was simple and quite clear her freedom was a foregone conclusion, though there were, of course, the usual formalities, the usual wearisome delays.

She had closed the Champneys house, and gone to Marcia, who wanted her. Jason, too, had insisted that she should make her home with them for the time being. And then had come the war, and she and Marcia found themselves swept into the whirlpool of work it involved. But not even the tremendous news that filled all the newspapers had kept the Champneys romance from being featured. Her case received very much more notice than pleased her. She was weary of her own photographs, sick of the interest she aroused.

Hayden kept discreetly in the background. He behaved beautifully. But he knew that Anne was going to marry him. Jason and Marcia knew it. Anne herself knew it. Now that the war was on, a good many of his plans would have to be postponed, but when Anne had secured her freedom, and things had righted themselves, they two would take up life as he wished to live it. All the women of his family had occupied prominent social positions: *his* wife should surpass them all. She should be the acknowledged leader, the most brilliant figure of her day. Nothing less than this would satisfy him.

For all his esthetic tastes, Hayden was an immensely able and capable man of business. He had not the warmth of heart that at times obscured Jason Vandervelde's judgment, nor the touch of unworldliness that marked the behavior of the Champneys men. His intellect had a cold, clear brilliancy, diamond-bright, diamond-hard; to this he added tact, and the power of organizing and directing and of getting results. In certain crises such men are invaluable.

Hayden hated war. It was, so to speak, an uncouth and barbarous gesture, a bestial and bellowing voice. He felt constrained to offer his services, and even before America became actually involved he was able to render valuable aid. There were delicate and dangerous missions where his tact, his diplomacy, and his shrewd, cold, unimpassioned intelligence won the stakes for which he played. This in itself was good; but for the time being it took him away from Anne. He saw her only occasionally. She, like him, was immersed in work. Once or twice he was able to snatch her from the thick of things and carry her off with him to lunch or to dinner. She enjoyed these small oases in the desert of work. She liked to watch his clever, composed face, to listen to his modulated voice. The serene ease of his manner soothed her. She was tremendously proud of Hayden. She was glad he cared for her. This seemed to her an excellent foundation for their marriage. They would please and interest each other; neither would be bored! And when, leaning across the table one day at lunch, he looked at her with unwonted fire in his quiet eyes, and said in a low voice: "Just as soon as this business is finished, as soon as we've cleaned up the mess, I'm going to claim you, Anne. It's all I can do to wait!" Anne met his eyes, smiled slightly, and nodded. A faint flush rose to her cheek, and a deeper one rose to his. For a moment he touched her hand.

"You understand you are promised to me," he said. "If I dared show you what I really feel, Anne—" and he glanced around the crowded dining-room, and smiled.

She smiled in return, tranquilly. She was not stirred. His touch had no power to thrill her. She was comfortably content that things should be as they were, that was all. Yet her very lack of emotion added to her charm for him. He disliked emotional women. Excess of affection would have bored him. It smacked of crudeness, and he had an epicurean distaste for crudeness.

Busy as he was, he found time to select the ring he wished her to wear. He was fastidious and hyper-critical to a degree, and he wished her ring to suit her, to be flawless. It was really a work of art, and Anne Champneys wondered at her own coolness when she received the exquisite jewel. She understood his feeling, she appreciated the beauty of the gem, yet it left her unmoved. It gratified her woman's vanity; it did not stir her to one heart-throb. She accepted it, not indifferently, but placidly. After a while she would accept a plain gold ring from him just as placidly. This was her fate. She did not quarrel with it.

Marcia watched her pleasedly. She loved Anne Champneys, she admired Hayden exceedingly, and that they should marry each other seemed natural and inevitable. Hayden was just the man she would have chosen for Anne. Even the fact that Jason wasn't altogether happy about it couldn't dampen Marcia's delight in the affair. Jason would come around, in time. He was too fond of Anne not to.

"Well, you're free," he had told Anne, the day that the Champneys marriage was declared null and void, and both parties had received the right to remarry, as a matter of course. "You are free. I'm sure I hope you won't regret it!"

"Why should I regret it?" wondered Anne, good-humoredly. But the big man shook his head, remembering Chadwick Champneys.

Hayden had become more and more involved in war work; he was in constant demand, he was sent hither and thither to attend to this and that troublesome affair. Twice he had to go abroad. At home, Anne's work called her into the homes of soldiers; she came in close contact with the families of the men who were fighting, and what she saw she was never able to forget. She got down to bed-rock. Her own early life made her acutely understanding. Where Marcia would have been blind, Anne saw; where the woman who had never known poverty and hardship would have remained deaf, the woman who had slaved in the Baxters' kitchen, who had been an overworked, unloved child in bondage, heard, and understood to the core of her soul what she was hearing. These voices from the depths were not inarticulate to Anne!

When Berkeley came back from his second voyage abroad, he was more impatient than she had ever seen him. The end was in sight then, as he knew, and he saw no reason for further delay. He urged Anne to marry him. Why should they waste time? When he consulted Marcia, she agreed with him. Everybody, she said, was getting married. Why shouldn't he and Anne? Already the rumor of their engagement had crept out. There were hints of it in the social chatter of the papers. Why not announce it formally, and have the marriage follow immediately?

But Anne Champneys found herself in a curious mood. The

nervous strain of war work, perhaps, was accountable. She meant to marry Berkeley; but she didn't want to marry him at once. She did not object to having their engagement announced. He could shout it from the housetops if that pleased him. But in the meanwhile she wanted a little rest, a little freedom. She wished to be fetterless, free to come and go as she pleased. No work, no interviews, no photographers, no weary hours with dressmakers and tailors. No envy because Berkeley Hayden was going to marry her, no wearisome comments, idle flattery hiding spite, no gossip violating all privacies. A raging impatience against it all assailed her. It seemed to her that she had never been allowed really to think or to act for herself disinterestedly, that she had never been free. Always she had been in bondage! Oh, for just a little hour of freedom, in the open, to be just as ordinary and inconspicuous as in her heart of hearts she would have preferred to be, left to herself!

Marcia said her nerves were unstrung, and no wonder, considering how she'd worked, and what she'd seen. Jason came vigorously to her rescue. He advised her to go off somewhere and get acquainted with herself. To drop out of things for a while, and treat herself to the rest she needed. Cut and run! Scuttle for cover!

"You've been overdoing things, of course. You've been Lady Bountiful, and first-aider, and last-leaver. Like the Lord and a thumping good lie, you've been a very present help in time of trouble. But there's such a thing as being too steady on the job. You need a change of people, scene, and mind. Take it."

This conversation occurred on a morning in his office, where she had gone on some slight business, and with concern he had noticed her tired eyes. At his advice she brightened.

"Marcia thinks I should marry Berkeley, immediately, and

let him take me away, but—"

"But you aren't ready to rush into matrimony just yet?" Vandervelde growled. "I should think you wouldn't be! If Hadyen's managed to exist this long without a wife, I take it for granted he can exist unwed a little longer. You are certain you mean to marry him?"

"Oh, yes, I am certain I mean to marry him," said Anne, flatly. "But I—that is, not so soon."

"I think I understand, Anne," said the big man, kindly. "Look here, you just tell 'em all to wait! Tell 'em you're tired. Then you pick yourself up and light out for a while, by yourself. Chuck the madding throng and all that, Anne, and beat it for the open!"

"Oh, how I wish I could!" she sighed. "You don't know how I long for a chance to be just me by myself! I want to stay with people who have never heard the name of Champneys or Hayden and who wouldn't care if my name happened to be Mudd! I want plain living and plain thinking and plain people. I—I'll come back to—everything I should come back to, afterward. But first I want to be free! Just for a little while I want to be free!"

"But how could you manage it?" mused Vandervelde. "The lady who divorced Peter Champneys and is going to marry Berkeley Hayden can't pick herself up 'unbeknownst' and hope to get away with it. Not in these days of good reporting! You're copy, you understand."

"But I don't want to be Mrs. Peter Champneys! I don't want to be the woman Berkeley Hayden's going to marry! I want to be just me!" she cried. "I want to go to some place where nobody's ever heard either of those names! Some little place where there are water and trees—and not much else. Like, say,—Jason! Do you remember that place you found, in Maine, I think? You *babbled* about it. Said you were going to go there if ever you wanted to get out of the world. Said it was Eden before the serpent entered. Where's that place, Jason? Why can't I go there, just as myself—" she paused, and looked at him hopefully.

"I don't see why you can't," said he, cheerfully.

And so Anne, who didn't wish to be Mrs. Peter Champneys, or the woman whom Berkeley Hayden was to marry, or anybody but herself, came to the out-of-the-way nook on the Maine shore, and was welcomed by the Widow Thatcher.

She found the place idyllic. She liked its skies unclouded by smoke, translucent skies in which silver mountains of clouds reared themselves out of airy continents that shifted and drifted before the wind. She liked its clean, pure, untainted air. And she liked contact with these simple souls, men who labored, women who knew birth and death and were not afraid of either. It came to her that her own contacts with and concepts of life—and death—had always, been more or less artificial. Perhaps these simple and laborious folk had the substance of things of which she and her sort had but the shadow. And then she asked herself: Well, but couldn't one, anywhere, in any circumstances, make life real for oneself, meet facts unafraid? Get at the truths, somehow? That's what she had to find out!

And of a sudden she had been answered. The reality, the truth, the real meaning of life was made plain to her when a man she didn't know, and yet knew to the last fiber of her soul, had paused to look into her eyes.

For two or three days she went no further than the rambling

garden at the back of the house. She tried to read, and couldn't. From every page those eyes looked at her. There was more in that remembered glance than in any book ever written, and she was torn between the desire to meet it again and the fear of meeting it.

On the night of the third day she sat with her elbows on her windowsill, looking out at the moonlight night. A sweet wind touched her face, like the breath of love. There arose the scent of quiet places, of trees and flowers and herbs, mingled with the vast breathing of the sea. And she thought the sea called to her, an imperious and yet caressing voice in the night. She stirred restlessly. Down there on the shore-line, where she had met him, the rocks would glint with silvery reflections, the water would come fawning to one's feet, the wind would pounce upon one like a rough lover. She stirred restlessly. The small bedroom seemed to hold her like a cage. And again the sea called, a wild and compelling voice.

Her blood stirred to the magic of the night. Her eyes gleamed, her cheek reddened. She listened for a moment, intently. The Widow Thatcher slept the sleep of the good housekeeper. No one was stirring. She could have the night, the wind, the sea, to herself. Noiselessly she stole downstairs and let herself out.

Out there, with the scent of the summer night greeting her, with bushes brushing her lightly with their green fingers, her heart leaped joyously. She flung her arms over her head and went running down the path to the water, a tall white figure with flying hair. Then she turned the small headland, and the village dropped behind her. Overhead the big gold lamp of the moon lighted shore and sea. And here came the sea-wind, bracing, strong, and sweet. At the rush of it she laughed aloud, and the wind seized upon her laughter and tossed it into the night like airy bells.

She slackened her wild race when she neared the great boulders shutting in the little narrow path where she had met him, and stood flushed, panting, her shining glance uplifted, her bright hair framing the sweetness of her face. And even as she paused, he stepped out of the shadow and confronted her. As if he had been awaiting her. As if he had known she must come. He said, in a voice vibrant with fierce joy:

"It is You!"

She answered, in a shaking tone, like a child: "Yes, I had to come," and stood there looking at him, face uplifted, lips apart.

He drew nearer. "Why?" said he, in a whisper. "Why?"

She did not reply. For a long moment they regarded each other, passion-pale in the moonlight.

"Was it because—you knew I must be here!" he asked.

Her hands went to her leaping heart. She had no faintest notion of concealing the truth, for there was no coquetry in her. These two facing each other were as honest as the rocky coast, as unabashed as the wind. They had no more thought of subterfuges and conventions than the sea had. They were as real as nature itself.

He bent upon her his compelling glance, which seemed to lift her as upon golden pinions. She was thrillingly conscious of his nearness.

"You knew I would be here?" he repeated.

She drew a deep breath. "Yes!" she sighed.

And at that, inevitably, irresistibly, they rushed together. He caught her in a mighty embrace and she gave him back his kiss with a heavenly shamelessness, a glorious passion, naive and pure. It was as if she were born anew in the fire of his lips. For she was sure, with a crystal clarity. This man whose heart beat against hers was her high destiny. Body and soul, she was his. His kiss was the chrism of life. And he, fallen into the same divine lunacy, was equally sure. He had been born a man to hold this strong sweet body in his arms, to meet this spirit that complemented his own. Not in high and lonely altitudes whose cold stillness chilled the heart, but by simple paths to peace, in a simple and passionate woman's love, could he gain the purple heights!

CHAPTER XX

AND THE GLORY

He had said quietly: "You are going to marry me!"

And she had replied, as if there could be no possible doubt about it:

"Yes, I am going to marry you."

"Because you love me better than anything or anybody else in all the world, even as I love you."

"Because I love you better than anything or anybody else in all the world," she repeated.

"So far, so good. When, Beloved Lady?"

At that she hesitated for a space and fell silent. He pressed her head closer, and bending his tall head laid his cheek to hers.

"When?"

"Presently. But before that, dearest and best of men, there are so many, many things I wish to tell you, so many things I wish you to know! I wish you to know me. Everything about me! For once upon a time there was a sad, neglected child, a piteous child I must make you acquainted with. There was an ignorant and undisciplined young girl—"

"You?"

She nodded sorrowfully. His clasp tightened. He slipped a hand beneath her chin, tilted her face upward, and kissed her eyes that had suddenly filled with tears, her lips that quivered.

"Beloved Lady, I understand: for there was once upon a time a sad, neglected child, an ugly little lad, barefooted and poverty-stricken after his mother's death. There was an ignorant and undisciplined boy—"

"You?" Her arms went around him protectingly, in a mothering and tender clasp.

"Who else? And being very ignorant indeed, he sold himself into bondage for a mess of pottage, and was thrall for weary years. He got exactly what he paid for. And life was ashes upon his head and wormwood in his mouth, and his heart was empty in his breast, because he snatched at shadows. And then one day the door of his prison was opened by the keeper, and he said, 'Now I am free!' But it was his fate to go down into hell for a season. There were times when he asked himself, 'Why don't I blow out my brains and escape?' Nothing but the simple faith and heroism of common men about him saved him from despair. One day a blinded soldier said, 'See for us!' So he began to see,—but still without hope, still without happiness, until he came here and found—*you*." His voice was melted gold.

She had listened breathlessly. And after a pause she asked:

"Who was—the keeper of his prison?"

"The woman to whom he had been married."

Her arms fell from him. She tried to draw herself away, but he held her all the closer.

"Do not think unkindly of her. I don't think she really knew she was an ogress! After all, she did unlock the door and say, 'Go!' And—well, here I am, darling woman. And I'm going to marry *you*!"

"Did you *never* love her?"

"Never. I was so frightfully unhappy that the best I could do was not to hate her. I'm afraid she hated me—poor ogress! Well! That's all over and done with. Like an evil dream. I'm here, and *you*'re going to marry me." Very gently he drew her arms around him again. "Ah, hold fast to me! Hold fast! I have waited for you so long, I need you so much!" he breathed.

"I don't seem able to help myself!" she sighed. And she asked seriously: "What do the people who love you most call you when they speak to you?"

The brown and bearded faces of comrades rose before him, their voices sounded in his ears.

"Pierre."

"Pierre," said she, bravely, as if to call him by his name emboldened her, "I too have been freed from a hateful marriage. Sometime I will tell you all about it. But—oh, do not let us talk about it now! I cannot bear to think of him! I cannot bear to have his shadow, even, fall upon me now, or come near *you*!" That gangling bridegroom in his ill-fitting suit, with his wincing mouth, his eyes full of disgust and aversion, his air of a man sentenced to death—or marriage with herself—came before her, and she shivered.

Despite her words a horrible jealousy of that unknown man assailed him. He asked fiercely:

"You loved him, once?"

"Oh, no! Oh, no! Never! I—why, Pierre, until you came, I didn't even know what love meant! Once that ignorant, undisciplined girl I spoke of, thought she loved a boy. She didn't. She loved the idea of love. And once again, Pierre, because my life was so empty, and because I didn't know any better, I thought I should be willing to marry somebody else. I thought that somebody else could fill my life. But now I know that could never be. You are here."

He looked at her with infinite tenderness. There were things he, too, would have to tell her, by and by. And he was sure that the woman whose coming little Denise had seemed to foreknow, would understand. He said gravely:

"Yes, we have found each other. That is all that really matters. Nothing, nobody else, counts with you and me." And then, of a sudden, he laughed happily: "And, Beloved Lady, I do not know your name! I can't call you 'Mrs. Riley,' can I? By what name, then, shall the one who loves you most call you?"

"Anne." And she asked eagerly: "Do you like it?"

He started. Anne! Strange that the name that had been his chiefest unhappiness should now become his chiefest joy! Strange that he hadn't guessed Anne could be the most beautiful of all names for a woman! Like it? Of course he liked it! Wasn't it hers?

"Anne, you haven't yet said when you will marry me."

"Oh, but you are sure of *that*!" she parried.

"I am so sure of it that I am quite capable of taking you by the hair and dragging you off to the parson's, if you try to make me wait. Anne! Remember that ever since I was that barefooted, lonely child I have been waiting for you. My dear, I need you so greatly!"

She said passionately: "You cannot need me as I need you. You are yourself. You couldn't be anything else. You were you before you ever saw me. But I—I couldn't be my real self until you came and looked at me and kissed me."

He felt humble, and reverent, and at the same time exultant. When she said presently, "I must go now," he released her reluctantly. They walked hand in hand, pausing at the small headland beyond which the village came in sight. She took both his hands and held them against her breast.

"You are my one man. I love you so much that I am going to give my whole life into your hands, as fully and as freely as I shall some day give my spirit into the hands of God. But, Pierre, there are those who have been very, very kind to me, those to whom I owe—well, explanations. When I have made those explanations and—and settled my accounts,— then all the rest of my life is yours."

"You are very, very sure, Anne?" His voice was wistful.

"My love for you," she said proudly, "is the one great reality. I am surer of that than I have ever been of anything in this world." And she stood there looking at him with her heart in her eyes. Of a sudden, with a little cry, she pulled his head down to her, kissed him upon the mouth, pushed him from her, and fled.

When she reached her room again, she couldn't sleep, but knelt by her window and watched the skies pale and then flush like a young girl's face, and the morning-star blaze and pale, and the sun come up over a bright and beautiful world in which she herself was, she felt, new-born. Far in the background of things, unreal as a dream, hovered the unlovely figure of Nancy Simms, and nearer, but still almost as unreal, the bright, cold figure of Anne Champneys, that Anne Champneys who had wished to marry Berkeley Hayden to gratify pride and ambition. The woman kneeling by the window, watching the glory of the morning, looked back upon those two as a winged butterfly might remember its caterpillar crawlings.

All that glittering life Anne Champneys had planned for herself? Swept away as if it had been a bit of tinsel! Money? Position? She laughed low to herself. She didn't care whether her man had possessions or lacked them. All she asked was that he should be himself—and hers. All that Milly had been to Chadwick Champneys—the passionate lover, the perfect comrade, the friend nothing daunted, no wind of fortune could change—Anne could be, would be to Pierre.

There was but one shadow upon her new happiness: she hated to disappoint Marcia. Marcia had set her heart upon the Hayden marriage. It was toward that consummation, so devoutly to be hoped, that Marcia had planned. And just when that plan was nearing perfection Anne was going to have to frustrate it. She hated to hurt Hayden himself, and the thought of his angry disappointment was painful to her. She *liked* Hayden. She would always like him. But she couldn't marry him. To marry Hayden, loving Pierre, would have been to work them both an irremediable injury. A sort of horror of what she had been about to do came upon her. The bare thought of it made her recoil.

Her native shrewdness told her that Hayden's immense pride would come to his aid. The fact that she had dared to desire somebody else, to prefer another to his lordly self would be enough to prove to Hayden that she wasn't worthy of his affections. He would feel that he had been deceived in her. She couldn't help hoping that he wouldn't altogether despise her. She hoped that Marcia wouldn't be too angry to forgive her. And then her thoughts merged into a prayer: Oh dear God, help her to make Pierre happy, to grow to his stature, to be worthy of him!

* * * * *

Back there on the beach he lay with his head in his arms, humble before the power and the glory that had come to him. This, this was the face he had always sought, the beauty that had so long eluded him! Beauty, mere physical beauty, appealed to him as it always appeals to an artist, but it had never had the power to hold him for any length of time. It had palled upon him. To satisfy his demand, beauty must have upon it the ineffable imprint of the soul. This woman's face was as baffling, as inexplicable, in its way, as was Mona Lisa's. One wasn't sure that she was beautiful; one was only sure that she was unforgetable, and that after other faces had faded from the memory, hers remained to haunt the heart. And that red hair of hers, like the hair of a Norse sun-goddess!

He fell into pleasant dreams. He was going to take her down south with him; he wanted her to see that little brown house in South Carolina, to know the tide-water gurgling in the

Riverton coves, and mocking-birds singing to the moonlit night, and the voice of the whippoorwill out of the thickets. She must know the marshes, and the live-oaks hung with moss. All the haunts of his childhood she should know, and old Emma Campbell would sit and talk to her about his mother. They would stay in the little house hallowed by his mother's mild spirit. And he would show her that first sketch of the Red Admiral. And afterward they two would plan how to make the best use of the Champneys money. He was very, very sure of her sympathy and her understanding. Why, you couldn't look into her eyes without knowing how exquisite her sympathy would be!

He was so stirred, so thrilled, that the creative power that had seemed to fail him, that had left him so emptily alone these many bitter months, came to him with a rush. He got to his feet and went tramping up and down the strip of shore, his eyes clouded with visions. Before his mind's eye the picture he meant to paint took shape and form and color. And as he walked home he whistled like a happy boy.

He had brought his materials along with him as a matter of habit. With his powers at high tide, in the first glamour of a great passion, he set himself to work next morning to portray her as his heart knew her.

He worked steadily, stopping only when the light failed. He was so absorbed in his task that he forgot his body. But Grandma Baker was a wise old woman, and she came at intervals and forced food upon him. Then he slept, and awoke with the light to rush back to his work. His old rare gift of visualizing a face in its absence had grown with the years; and this was the face of all faces. There was not a shade or a line of that face he didn't know. And after a while she appeared upon his canvas, breathing, immensely alive, with the inmost spirit of her informing her gray-green eyes, her virginal mouth, her candid and thoughtful brow. There she stood, Anne as Peter Champneys knew and loved her.

He had done great work in his time. But this was painted with the blood of his heart. This was his high-water mark. It would take its place with those immortal canvases that are the slow accretions of the ages, the perfectest flowerings of genius. He was swaying on his feet when he painted in the Red Admiral. Then he flung himself upon his bed and slept like a dead man.

When he awoke, she seemed to be a living presence in his room. He gasped, and sat with his hands between his knees, staring at her almost unbelievingly. He looked at the Red Admiral above his signature, and fetched a great, sighing breath.

"We've done it at last, by God!" said he, soberly. "Fairy, we've reached the heights!"

But when he appeared at the breakfast-table Grandma Baker regarded him with deep concern.

"My land o' love!" she exclaimed. "Why, you look like you been buried and dug up!"

"Permit me," said he, politely, "to congratulate you upon your perspicacity. That is exactly what happened to me."

"Eh!" said Grandma, setting her spectacles straight on her old nose.

"And let me add: It's worth the price!" said the resurrected one, genially. "Grandma Baker, were *you* very much in love?"

Marie Conway Oemler

"Abner tried his dumdest to find that out," said Grandma Baker. "He was the plaguedest man ever was for wantin' to know things, but somehow I sort o' didn't want him changed any. You got ways put me mightily in mind o' Abner." The old eyes were very sweet, and a wintry rose crept into her withered cheek. She added: "I know what's ailin' *you*, young man! Lord knows I hope you'll be happy as Abner and me was!"

He went back to his room and communed with his picture. It was the sort that, if you stayed with it a little while, *liked* to commune with you. It would divine your mood, and the eyes followed you with an uncanny understanding, the smile said more than any words could say. You almost saw her eyelids move, her breast rise and fall to her breathing. The man trembled before his masterpiece.

His heart swelled. He exulted in his genius, a high gift to be laid at the feet of the beloved. All he had, all he could ever be, belonged to her. She had called forth his best. He said to her painted semblance:

"You are my first love-gift. I am going to send you to her, and she'll know she hasn't given her love, her beauty, her youth, to an unworthy or an obscure lover. She's given herself to me, Peter Champneys, and because she loves me I'll give her a name she can wear like a crown: I'll set her upon the purple heights!"

She was at the far end of the Thatcher garden, behind the house and hidden from it, when he arrived with the canvas, which he hadn't dared entrust to any other carrier—he was too jealously careful of it. No, he told Mrs. Thatcher, it wasn't necessary to disturb her guest. Just allow him to place the canvas in Mrs. Riley's sitting-room. She would find it there when she returned.

Mrs. Thatcher complied willingly enough. She liked the tall, black-bearded man whom shrewd old Grandma Baker couldn't praise sufficiently.

"Excuse me for not goin' up with you, on account of my hands bein' in the mixin'-bowl. It's a picture, ain't it? You just step right upstairs and set it on the mantel or anywheres you like. I'll tell her you been here."

And so he placed it on the mantel, where the north light fell full upon it, waved his hand to it, and went away. It would tell her all that was in his heart for her. It would explain himself. The Red Admiral would assure that!

Anne had been having rather a troublesome time. She had written to Marcia and to Berkeley Hayden the night before, and the letters had been posted only that morning. She had had to be very explicit, to make her position perfectly plain to them both, and the letters had not been easy to write. But when she had finally written them, she had really succeeded in explaining her true self. There was no doubt as to her entire truthfulness, or the finality of this decision of hers. When she posted those letters, she knew that a page of her life had been turned down, the word "Finis" written at the bottom of it. She had tossed aside a brilliant social career, a high position, a great fortune,—and counted it all well lost. Her one regret was to have to disappoint Marcia. She loved Marcia. And she hoped that Berkeley wouldn't despise her.

She was agitated, perturbed, and yet rapturously happy. She wished to be alone to hug that happiness to her heart, and so she had gone out under the apple-trees at the far end of the Thatcher orchard, and lay there all her long length in the good green grass. The place was full of sweet and drowsy odors. Birds called and fluted. Butterflies and bees came and went. She had never felt so close to Mother Earth as she did to-day, never so keenly sensed the joy of being alive.

After a while she arose, reluctantly, and went back to the house and her rooms. She was remembering that she hadn't yet written to Jason, and she wanted Jason to know. Inside her sitting-room door she stopped short, eyes widened, lips fallen apart. On the mantel, glowing, jewel-like in the clear, pure light, herself confronted her. Herself as a great artist saw and loved her.

She stood transfixed. The sheer power and beauty of the work, that spell which falls upon one in the presence of all great art, held her entranced. Her own eyes looked, at her as if they challenged her; her own smile baffled her; there was that in the pictured face which brought a cry to her lips. Oh, was she so fair in his eyes? Only great love, as well as great genius, could have so portrayed her!

This was herself as she might be, grown finer, and of a larger faith, a deeper and sweeter charity. A sort of awe touched her. This man who loved her, who had the power of showing her herself as she might pray to become, this wonderful lover of hers, was no mere amateur with a pretty gift. This was one of the few, one of the torch-bearers!

And then she noticed the Red Admiral in the corner. She stared at it unbelievingly. That butterfly! Why—why—She had read of one who signed with a butterfly above his name pictures that were called great. A thought that made her brain swim and her heart beat suffocatingly crashed upon her like a clap of thunder. She walked toward the mantel like one in a daze, until she stood directly before the painting.

And it was his butterfly. And under it was his name: *Peter Devereaux Champneys*.

The room bobbed up and down. But she didn't faint, she didn't scream. She caught hold of the mantel to steady herself. She wondered how she hadn't known; she had the same sense of wild amazement that must fill one who has been brought face to face with a stupendous, a quite impossible miracle. Such a thing couldn't happen: and yet it is so! And oddly enough, out of this welter of her thoughts, there came to her memory a screened bed in a hospital ward, and a dying gutter-girl looking at her with unearthly eyes and telling her in a thin whisper:

"I wanted to see if you was good enough for *him*. You ain't. But remember what I'm tellin' you—you could be."

Pierre—Peter Champneys! She slipped to her knees and hid her face in her shaking hands. Peter Champneys! As in a lightning flash she saw him as that girl Gracie had seen him. Pierre—Pierre, with his eyes of an archangel, his lips that were the chrism of life—*this* was Peter Champneys! And she had hated him, let him go, all unknowing, she had wished to put in *his* place Berkeley Hayden. The handsome, worldly figure of Hayden seemed to dwindle and shrink. Pierre stood as on a height, looking at her steadfastly. Her head went lower. Tears trickled between her fingers.

You ain't good enough for him, but you could be.

"I can be, I can be! Oh, God, I can be! Only let him love me—when he knows!"

She heard Mrs. Thatcher's voice downstairs, after a while. Then a deeper voice, a man's voice, with a note of impatience and eagerness in it.

"No, don't call her. I'll go right on up," said the voice, over the feminine apologies and protests. "I have to see her—I must see her now. No, I can't wait."

Somebody came flying up the steps. She hadn't closed her door, and his tall figure seemed to fill it. He stopped, with a gasp, at sight of the weeping woman kneeling before the picture on the mantel.

"Anne!" he cried. "Anne!" And he would have raised her, but she clung to his knees, lifting her tear-stained face, her eyes full of an adoration that would never leave them until life left them.

"Peter!" she cried. "Peter! That—that butterfly! I know now, Peter!"

Again he tried to raise her, but she clasped his knees all the closer.

"You mean you know my name is really Peter Champneys, dearest?"

But she caught his hands. "Peter, Peter, don't you under-stand?" she cried, laughing and weeping. "I—I'm the ogress! I'm Nancy Simms! I'm Anne Champneys!"

He looked from her to her portrait and back again. He gave a great ringing cry of, "My wife!" and lifted her in a mighty grip that swept her up and into his arms. "My wife!" he cried. "My wife!"

Undoubtedly the Red Admiral was a fairy!

*   *   *   *   *

On a certain morning Mr. Jason Vandervelde was sitting at his desk, disconnectedly dictating a letter to his secretary. He was finding it very difficult to fix his mind upon his correspondence. What the mischief was happening up there in Maine, anyhow? She hadn't written for some time; and he hadn't had a word from Peter Champneys. And when Marcia came home and found out he'd been meddling—well, the meddler would have to pay the fiddler, that's all!

The office boy came in with a telegram. Mr. Vandervelde paused in his dictation, tore open the envelop, and read the message. And then the horrified secretary saw an amazing and an awesome sight. Mr. Jason Vandervelde bounced to his feet as lightly as though he had been a rubber ball, and performed a solemnly joyful dance around his office. His eyeglasses jigged on his nose, a lock of his sleekly brushed hair fell upon his forehead. Meeting the fixed stare of the secretary, he winked! And with a sort of elephantine religiosity he finished his amazing measure, caught once more the glassy eye of the secretary, and panted:

"King David danced before the ark—of the Lord. For which reason—your salary is raised—from to-day."

He stopped then, snatched the telegram off his desk, and read it again:

> We have met and I have married my wife. Anne sends love. Thank you and God bless you, Vandervelde!
> PETER CHAMPNEYS.

"Put up that note-book. Take a day off. Go and enjoy yourself. Be happy!" said Vandervelde to the secretary. Then he snatched up the desk telephone.

"The florist's? Yes? How soon can you get six dozen bride roses up here, to Mr. Vandervelde's office? Yes, this is Mr. Vandervelde speaking. You can? Well, there's a thumping tip for somebody who knows how to rush! Half an hour? Thank you. I'll wait for 'em here."

He hung up the receiver and turned his beaming countenance to the stunned secretary. His eyes twinkled like little blue stars, the corners of his mouth curled more than usual.

"Anne and Peter Champneys have been and gone and married each other!" he chuckled. "I'm going to take a carful of bride roses around to the Champneys house and put 'em under old Chadwick Champneys's portrait!"

THE END

Choose from Thousands of 1stWorldLibrary Classics By

A. M. Barnard
Ada Leverson
Adolphus William Ward
Aesop
Agatha Christie
Alexander Aaronsohn
Alexander Kielland
Alexandre Dumas
Alfred Gatty
Alfred Ollivant
Alice Duer Miller
Alice Turner Curtis
Alice Dunbar
Allen Chapman
Alleyne Ireland
Ambrose Bierce
Amelia E. Barr
Amory H. Bradford
Andrew Lang
Andrew McFarland Davis
Andy Adams
Angela Brazil
Anna Alice Chapin
Anna Sewell
Annie Besant
Annie Hamilton Donnell
Annie Payson Call
Annie Roe Carr
Annonaymous
Anton Chekhov
Archibald Lee Fletcher
Arnold Bennett
Arthur C. Benson
Arthur Conan Doyle
Arthur M. Winfield
Arthur Ransome
Arthur Schnitzler
Arthur Train
Atticus
B.H. Baden-Powell
B. M. Bower
B. C. Chatterjee
Baroness Emmuska Orczy
Baroness Orczy
Basil King
Bayard Taylor
Ben Macomber
Bertha Muzzy Bower
Bjornstjerne Bjornson

Booth Tarkington
Boyd Cable
Bram Stoker
C. Collodi
C. E. Orr
C. M. Ingleby
Carolyn Wells
Catherine Parr Traill
Charles A. Eastman
Charles Amory Beach
Charles Dickens
Charles Dudley Warner
Charles Farrar Browne
Charles Ives
Charles Kingsley
Charles Klein
Charles Hanson Towne
Charles Lathrop Pack
Charles Romyn Dake
Charles Whibley
Charles Willing Beale
Charlotte M. Braeme
Charlotte M. Yonge
Charlotte Perkins Stetson
Clair W. Hayes
Clarence Day Jr.
Clarence E. Mulford
Clemence Housman
Confucius
Coningsby Dawson
Cornelis DeWitt Wilcox
Cyril Burleigh
D. H. Lawrence
Daniel Defoe
David Garnett
Dinah Craik
Don Carlos Janes
Donald Keyhoe
Dorothy Kilner
Dougan Clark
Douglas Fairbanks
E. Nesbit
E. P. Roe
E. Phillips Oppenheim
E. S. Brooks
Earl Barnes
Edgar Rice Burroughs
Edith Van Dyne
Edith Wharton

Edward Everett Hale
Edward J. O'Biren
Edward S. Ellis
Edwin L. Arnold
Eleanor Atkins
Eleanor Hallowell Abbott
Eliot Gregory
Elizabeth Gaskell
Elizabeth McCracken
Elizabeth Von Arnim
Ellem Key
Emerson Hough
Emilie F. Carlen
Emily Bronte
Emily Dickinson
Enid Bagnold
Enilor Macartney Lane
Erasmus W. Jones
Ernie Howard Pie
Ethel May Dell
Ethel Turner
Ethel Watts Mumford
Eugene Sue
Eugenie Foa
Eugene Wood
Eustace Hale Ball
Evelyn Everett-green
Everard Cotes
F. H. Cheley
F. J. Cross
F. Marion Crawford
Fannie E. Newberry
Federick Austin Ogg
Ferdinand Ossendowski
Fergus Hume
Florence A. Kilpatrick
Fremont B. Deering
Francis Bacon
Francis Darwin
Frances Hodgson Burnett
Frances Parkinson Keyes
Frank Gee Patchin
Frank Harris
Frank Jewett Mather
Frank L. Packard
Frank V. Webster
Frederic Stewart Isham
Frederick Trevor Hill
Frederick Winslow Taylor

Friedrich Kerst
Friedrich Nietzsche
Fyodor Dostoyevsky
G.A. Henty
G.K. Chesterton
Gabrielle E. Jackson
Garrett P. Serviss
Gaston Leroux
George A. Warren
George Ade
Geroge Bernard Shaw
George Cary Eggleston
George Durston
George Ebers
George Eliot
George Gissing
George MacDonald
George Meredith
George Orwell
George Sylvester Viereck
George Tucker
George W. Cable
George Wharton James
Gertrude Atherton
Gordon Casserly
Grace E. King
Grace Gallatin
Grace Greenwood
Grant Allen
Guillermo A. Sherwell
Gulielma Zollinger
Gustav Flaubert
H. A. Cody
H. B. Irving
H.C. Bailey
H. G. Wells
H. H. Munro
H. Irving Hancock
H. R. Naylor
H. Rider Haggard
H. W. C. Davis
Haldeman Julius
Hall Caine
Hamilton Wright Mabie
Hans Christian Andersen
Harold Avery
Harold McGrath
Harriet Beecher Stowe
Harry Castlemon
Harry Coghill
Harry Houidini

Hayden Carruth
Helent Hunt Jackson
Helen Nicolay
Hendrik Conscience
Hendy David Thoreau
Henri Barbusse
Henrik Ibsen
Henry Adams
Henry Ford
Henry Frost
Henry James
Henry Jones Ford
Henry Seton Merriman
Henry W Longfellow
Herbert A. Giles
Herbert Carter
Herbert N. Casson
Herman Hesse
Hildegard G. Frey
Homer
Honore De Balzac
Horace B. Day
Horace Walpole
Horatio Alger Jr.
Howard Pyle
Howard R. Garis
Hugh Lofting
Hugh Walpole
Humphry Ward
Ian Maclaren
Inez Haynes Gillmore
Irving Bacheller
Isabel Cecilia Williams
Isabel Hornibrook
Israel Abrahams
Ivan Turgenev
J.G.Austin
J. Henri Fabre
J. M. Barrie
J. M. Walsh
J. Macdonald Oxley
J. R. Miller
J. S. Fletcher
J. S. Knowles
J. Storer Clouston
J. W. Duffield
Jack London
Jacob Abbott
James Allen
James Andrews
James Baldwin

James Branch Cabell
James DeMille
James Joyce
James Lane Allen
James Lane Allen
James Oliver Curwood
James Oppenheim
James Otis
James R. Driscoll
Jane Abbott
Jane Austen
Jane L. Stewart
Janet Aldridge
Jens Peter Jacobsen
Jerome K. Jerome
Jessie Graham Flower
John Buchan
John Burroughs
John Cournos
John F. Kennedy
John Gay
John Glasworthy
John Habberton
John Joy Bell
John Kendrick Bangs
John Milton
John Philip Sousa
John Taintor Foote
Jonas Lauritz Idemil Lie
Jonathan Swift
Joseph A. Altsheler
Joseph Carey
Joseph Conrad
Joseph E. Badger Jr
Joseph Hergesheimer
Joseph Jacobs
Jules Vernes
Julian Hawthrone
Julie A Lippmann
Justin Huntly McCarthy
Kakuzo Okakura
Karle Wilson Baker
Kate Chopin
Kenneth Grahame
Kenneth McGaffey
Kate Langley Bosher
Kate Langley Bosher
Katherine Cecil Thurston
Katherine Stokes
L. A. Abbot
L. T. Meade

L. Frank Baum
Latta Griswold
Laura Dent Crane
Laura Lee Hope
Laurence Housman
Lawrence Beasley
Leo Tolstoy
Leonid Andreyev
Lewis Carroll
Lewis Sperry Chafer
Lilian Bell
Lloyd Osbourne
Louis Hughes
Louis Joseph Vance
Louis Tracy
Louisa May Alcott
Lucy Fitch Perkins
Lucy Maud Montgomery
Luther Benson
Lydia Miller Middleton
Lyndon Orr
M. Corvus
M. H. Adams
Margaret E. Sangster
Margret Howth
Margaret Vandercook
Margaret W. Hungerford
Margret Penrose
Maria Edgeworth
Maria Thompson Daviess
Mariano Azuela
Marion Polk Angellotti
Mark Overton
Mark Twain
Mary Austin
Mary Catherine Crowley
Mary Cole
Mary Hastings Bradley
Mary Roberts Rinehart
Mary Rowlandson
M. Wollstonecraft Shelley
Maud Lindsay
Max Beerbohm
Myra Kelly
Nathaniel Hawthrone
Nicolo Machiavelli
O. F. Walton
Oscar Wilde

Owen Johnson
P.G. Wodehouse
Paul and Mabel Thorne
Paul G. Tomlinson
Paul Severing
Percy Brebner
Percy Keese Fitzhugh
Peter B. Kyne
Plato
Quincy Allen
R. Derby Holmes
R. L. Stevenson
R. S. Ball
Rabindranath Tagore
Rahul Alvares
Ralph Bonehill
Ralph Henry Barbour
Ralph Victor
Ralph Waldo Emmerson
Rene Descartes
Ray Cummings
Rex Beach
Rex E. Beach
Richard Harding Davis
Richard Jefferies
Richard Le Gallienne
Robert Barr
Robert Frost
Robert Gordon Anderson
Robert L. Drake
Robert Lansing
Robert Lynd
Robert Michael Ballantyne
Robert W. Chambers
Rosa Nouchette Carey
Rudyard Kipling
Saint Augustine
Samuel B. Allison
Samuel Hopkins Adams
Sarah Bernhardt
Sarah C. Hallowell
Selma Lagerlof
Sherwood Anderson
Sigmund Freud
Standish O'Grady
Stanley Weyman
Stella Benson
Stella M. Francis

Stephen Crane
Stewart Edward White
Stijn Streuvels
Swami Abhedananda
Swami Parmananda
T. S. Ackland
T. S. Arthur
The Princess Der Ling
Thomas A. Janvier
Thomas A Kempis
Thomas Anderton
Thomas Bailey Aldrich
Thomas Bulfinch
Thomas De Quincey
Thomas Dixon
Thomas H. Huxley
Thomas Hardy
Thomas More
Thornton W. Burgess
U. S. Grant
Upton Sinclair
Valentine Williams
Various Authors
Vaughan Kester
Victor Appleton
Victor G. Durham
Victoria Cross
Virginia Woolf
Wadsworth Camp
Walter Camp
Walter Scott
Washington Irving
Wilbur Lawton
Wilkie Collins
Willa Cather
Willard F. Baker
William Dean Howells
William le Queux
W. Makepeace Thackeray
William W. Walter
William Shakespeare
Winston Churchill
Yei Theodora Ozaki
Yogi Ramacharaka
Young E. Allison
Zane Grey